Acts of Gaiety

TRIANGULATIONS
Lesbian/Gay/Queer ▲ Theater/Drama/Performance

Series Editors
Jill Dolan, Princeton University
David Román, University of Southern California

TITLES IN THE SERIES:

Tony Kushner in Conversation   edited by Robert Vorlicky

Passing Performances: Queer Readings of Leading Players in American Theater History   edited by Robert A. Schanke and Kim Marra

When Romeo Was a Woman: Charlotte Cushman and Her Circle of Female Spectators   by Lisa Merrill

Camp: Queer Aesthetics and the Performing Subject   edited by Fabio Cleto

Staging Desire: Queer Readings of American Theater History   edited by Kim Marra and Robert A. Schanke

A Problem Like Maria: Gender and Sexuality in the American Musical   by Stacy Wolf

A Queer Sort of Materialism: Recontextualizing American Theater   by David Savran

Margaret Webster: A Life in the Theater   by Milly S. Barranger

The Gay and Lesbian Theatrical Legacy: A Biographical Dictionary of Major Figures in American Stage History   edited by Billy J. Harbin, Kim Marra, and Robert A. Schanke

Cast Out: Queer Lives in Theater   edited by Robin Bernstein

Queering Mestizaje: Transculturation and Performance   by Alicia Arrizón

Bulldaggers, Pansies, and Chocolate Babies: Performance, Race, and Sexuality in the Harlem Renaissance   by James F. Wilson

Lady Dicks and Lesbian Brothers: Staging the Unimaginable at the WOW Café Theatre   by Kate Davy

A Menopausal Gentleman: The Solo Performances of Peggy Shaw   edited by Jill Dolan

Performing Queer Latinidad: Dance, Sexuality, Politics   by Ramón H. Rivera-Servera

Acts of Gaiety: LGBT Performance and the Politics of Pleasure   by Sara Warner

Butch Queens Up in Pumps: Gender, Performance, and Ballroom Culture in Detroit   by Marlon M. Bailey

Acts of Gaiety

LGBT Performance and the Politics of Pleasure

SARA WARNER

The University of Michigan Press

Ann Arbor

First paperback edition 2013
Copyright © by the University of Michigan 2012
All rights reserved

Published in the United States of America by
The University of Michigan Press
Manufactured in the United States of America
⊚ Printed on acid-free paper

2016   2015   2014   2013   5   4   3   2

A CIP catalog record for this book is available from the British Library.

Library of Congress Cataloging-in-Publication Data

Warner, Sara.
    Acts of gaiety : LGBT performance and the politics of pleasure / Sara Warner.
        p. cm.—(Triangulations: lesbian/gay/queer theater/drama/performance)
    Includes bibliographical references and index.
    ISBN 978-0-472-11853-3 (cloth : acid-free paper)—
    ISBN 978-0-472-02875-7 (e-book)
    1. Gay theater—United States.   2. Homosexuality and theater.   3. Gays and the performing arts.   I. Title.
    PN2270.G39W37   2013
    792.086'640973—dc23   2012025917

ISBN 978-0-472-03567-0 (pbk. : alk. paper)

Cover: Animal Prufrock and Susan Powter in *Hothead Paisan: Homicidal Lesbian Terrorist*, 2004. Photo by Desdemona Burgin.

To Mary Jo Watts

a continuous source of strength and guidance,
and without whose unflinching loyalty, devotion
and faith, this book could never have been written

Contents

Preface

At approximately 7:00 p.m. on May 1, 1970, just moments after Kate Millett, chairwoman of the National Organization for Women (NOW), called to order the second annual gathering of feminist groups from across the country, the lights in the auditorium at Intermediate School 70 on West Seventeenth Street in Manhattan went out, plunging the audience of three hundred activists into total darkness. One of the conference coordinators fumbled her way to the podium to ask everyone to remain calm and seated while they determined the cause of the power outage, only to discover that the microphone, too, had gone dead. A commotion erupted in the back of the room, and a group of people, some emitting rebel yells, ran down the aisle toward the stage. The lights came back on to reveal a phalanx of women, fists raised, wearing purple T-shirts with "Lavender Menace" stenciled across the front. Some held placards that read "Women's liberation is a lesbian plot," "Take a lesbian to lunch," and "We are your worst nightmare, your best fantasy." The audience, visibly shaken, denounced the demonstrators for commandeering the meeting to promote their lesbian agenda. Millett, who had been informed in advance of the protest, urged the crowd to listen to the women.

One of the insurgents, Rita Mae Brown, stepped forward and addressed the assembly. A well-known firebrand and philanderer, Brown had recently staged a public resignation from her position as the NOW newsletter editor in response to the organization's attempt to purge lesbians from its roster. Surveying the spectators as if she were cruising a Greenwich Village bar, Brown asked, "Does anyone want to join us?" This was the cue for Karla Jay, who was planted in the audience, to jump up and scream, "Yes, yes, sisters! I'm tired of being in the closet because of the women's movement."[1] As she spoke, Jay began unbuttoning her blouse, "much to the horror" of the homophobic members of the audience, who gasped and groaned with each twist of her thumb. When Jay ripped open her shirt, she revealed a Lavender Menace tee underneath. As she ran toward the front of the auditorium to join her fellow protesters, Jay was greeted with "hoots of laughter" and cheers of encouragement.[2]

Never one to be upstaged, the mercurial Brown approached the podium a second time. Grinning and flashing her best "come hither" look, she, too, began a striptease. As Brown was already wearing her protest uniform, it appeared that she actually was going to disrobe. When she peeled away the Lavender Menace T-shirt, however, she revealed another one just like it underneath. This burlesque was met with "more laughter," Jay recalls.[3] The audience, initially hostile, was now firmly on the protestors' side. When Brown asked again, this time more seductively, "Who wants to join us?" a bevy of women, none of whom had anything to do with the demonstration, rushed the stage, to thunderous applause and shouts of support from the audience. The swelling ranks of the Lavender Menace collective stood before the crowd with their "arms in solidarity around one another's shoulders" and explained how upset they were that lesbians had been excluded from the conference.[4] They called out Betty Friedan, cofounder of NOW, the sponsor of the event, for orchestrating animosity and promoting discrimination within the feminist movement. In a statement to the press, Friedan had accused lesbians of "creating a sexual red herring that would divide the movement and lead ultimately to sexual McCarthyism."[5] Friedan publicly denounced dykes as a "lavender menace" that threatened the future of women's liberation by warping the public image of feminists and alienating heterosexuals who wanted equality but also wanted to keep on loving their husbands and children.[6] When word got out that Friedan planned to deny lesbians a platform at the Congress to Unite Women, for the second year in a row, a group of activists from the Radicalesbians—a coalition of dykes from various organizations, including the Gay Liberation Front (GLF), the Daughters of Bilitis (DOB), Redstockings, and Women's International Terrorist Conspiracy from Hell (WITCH)—began plotting the Lavender Menace zap.

A zap, or zap action, as it is sometimes called, is a highly performative, nonviolent mode of social protest that uses guerrilla theater, irony, and satire to expose the ruses of power and catalyze public response to political events. First staged by anarchist hippies associated with the antiwar and free speech movements, zaps combine physical comedy, symbolic costumes, expressive gestures, and farcical timing in brief, improvised skits that are designed to shock and awe people, jolting them out of their complacency and fixed frames of reference. Zaps serve as paradigmatic examples of what I call "acts of gaiety" throughout this book. The term refers to playful methods of social activism and mirthful modes of political performance that inspire and sustain deadly serious struggles for revolutionary change.

Acts of gaiety are comical and cunning interventions that make a mockery of discrimination and the experience of social exclusion. These antics provide a creative outlet for the outrage, alienation, and sorrow that attend queer lives in the form of dramatic displays of revelry and rebellion. As the Lavender Menace action shows, sexual minorities are expert at poking fun at the physical dangers and bad feelings associated with being queer in a straight world, transforming them through jokes, humor, and parodic inversion in the service of liberatory practices. Gays and lesbians have developed an extensive repertoire of acts of gaiety, which includes but is by no means limited to zap actions, pageants, parades, spectacles, kiss-ins, camp, kitsch, and drag. These anarchic, indecorous, and amusing exploits target the contingent foundations of homophobia and the arbitrary assumptions that allow both publics and counterpublics to function in painfully constraining ways for bodies branded by the stigma of sexual transgressions.

Thanks to the daring exploits and tireless efforts of the Lavender Menace and other activists, homosexuality and same-sex desire are no longer historical impossibilities in many parts of the world. As the exigencies of the Lesbian, Gay, Bisexual, and Transgender (LGBT) movement have changed substantially in the past fifty years, sexual politics has devolved from a grassroots struggle for liberation into a conservative program of social assimilation that I term *homoliberalism*. By homoliberalism I refer to the economic, political, and social enfranchisement of certain normative-leaning, straight-acting homosexuals at the expense of other, inassimilable sexual minorities. A coercive and oppressive form of political optimism that tethers individual fortune and social progress to the workings of the nation-state, homoliberalism is indicative of what Lisa Duggan calls "the new homonormativity," a trend characterized by a "demobilized . . . constituency and a privatized, depoliticized . . . culture anchored in domesticity and consumption . . . that does not contest dominant heteronormative forms but upholds and sustains them."[7] Premised on an increasingly visible and lucrative brand of mass-mediated citizenship, homoliberalism endorses the passage of integrationist legal reforms that are profoundly undemocratic and antiegalitarian, including same-sex marriage and the right to serve in the military. These issues form the core of a consumer rights agenda that is advanced by a proliferating homosexual mainstream opposed both to conservative claims that gays pose a threat to the social, moral, and political order and to progressive calls for a more radical restructuring of society.

Homoliberalism regulates intimacy by linking it with institutions of reproduction predicated on the accumulation and transfer of wealth. It calls on gays and lesbians to invest their time and energy in the American dream—in the nuclear family, the armed forces, and a Puritan work ethic—in order to earn political capital, receive dividends of social equality, and accrue interest in the form of economic prosperity. In this redemptive narrative of progress and upward mobility, citizenship is understood as a form of volunteerism organized around private interests rather than the collective good. Banking on the promise of personal advancement, homoliberals have relinquished their struggle for revolutionary change and the emancipation of all people. Previous historical efforts to challenge state oppression, redistribute wealth, and create alternative kinship structures have given way to a normative politics of liberal inclusion exemplified by the push for state legitimacy, an unabashed embrace of global capitalism, and an uncritical celebration of traditional "family values."

Not surprisingly, homoliberals see gaiety as antithetical to their quest for legitimization. These are individuals whose pride consists in being "normal" and who desire to assimilate into existing structures and institutions, not challenge the discriminatory logic and repressive architecture of straight society. Eager to prove that they are "just like everyone else," these homosexuals refrain from any behavior that might draw attention to their differences. Since acts of gaiety involve a flamboyant and flagrant flaunting one's sexuality, those seeking accommodation within the system do just the opposite; they practice and promote acts of conformity. Believing that the faithful and earnest rehearsal of nonconfrontational displays of niceness, politeness, respectability, and dignity will confer on them the recognition and validation they crave, homosexuals have renounced gaiety in order to be taken seriously by mainstream society. This pragmatic approach to social change constitutes a hastened retreat from the pleasure principle advanced by activists in earlier decades, and it leeches the joy out of sexual politics.

The purpose of *Acts of Gaiety* is to investigate the historical emergence of homoliberalism and to reanimate gaiety as a political value for progressive social activism. I argue here that homoliberalism's precipitous rise in the United States is fueled by the increasing influence of LGBT communities' individualizing and monetizing precepts, a condition buttressed by two interlinked forces: the mainstreaming of homosexuality and queer theorists' amnesiac relation to gay history and lesbian feminist structures of feeling. This book examines alternate relations of affects and desires dissonant to neoliberal values, disciplinary regimes of the nation-state, and the circulation of capital. It asks how, and under what conditions, a renewed investment in gaiety might subtend the profound structural inequalities, economic disparities, and sobering images of sexual hegemony that accompany the normalization of lesbian and gay lives.

While this book seeks to counter the stultifying pragmatism of homoliberalism, it also serves as a rejoinder to the long-standing romance with mourning and melancholia in queer theory. Hurtful emotions, and the desire to avoid or eradicate them, play an important part in the creation of political worlds. Injury serves as a constitutive element of any disenfranchised group's identity; it is the experience of a traumatic past that gives the present meaning and provides the motivation to create a better future. This is especially true of feminism and queer theory, two utopian projects that are constituted by potent histories of violence, stigma, and suffering. One effect of sex and gender studies' focus on loss, abuse, and abjection has been the privileging of negative affects, emotions that make us feel bad (e.g., shame, despair, and alienation) but are politically efficacious, as they move disenfranchised citizens to recognize, contest, and alter the social, legal, and cultural circumstances that cause them pain. This study redirects our attention to other aspects of the history of queer life by documenting and affirming the role of pleasure, humor, fun, and frivolity in shaping the ways sexual minorities come to understand ourselves and the roles in which we have been cast.

(Un)Adulterated Glee

Once an epithet for homosexuals and a derogatory term of phobic abuse, *queer* became, in the 1990s, the name of a militant political movement and trenchant theoretical critique of the normal, the normative, and disciplinary regimes of normalization. When activists and academics reclaimed the term *queer,* they did so to distance themselves not only from identity politics but from the positive and cheerful associations of the word *gay* and the rosy rhetoric of pride that came to characterize much of post–Stonewall era LGBT activism. Not surprisingly, AIDS organizations such as ACT-UP and Queer Nation were some of the first groups to take up and resignify this insult. Eschewing the affirmative orientation of gay liberation, queer theorists advanced a politics of radical negativity. This approach has achieved its most extreme articulation among so-called antirelational theorists (e.g., Leo Bersani and Lee Edelman), who view queer sex as imbricated with the death drive rather than an exuberant life force.[8] Allergic to any kind of political teleology, including the notion that queer practices of life are, or should be, oriented toward a better tomorrow for sexual minorities, antirelational theorists are deeply suspicious of any forward-looking, hopeful, or utopian ambitions. They are skeptical of any praxis that advocates feeling better as a goal, as feeling better is too often tied to saccharine forms of sanguinity, normative notions of happiness, and capitalist models of accumulation and reproduction.

As intellectually stimulating as I find this polemical mode of scholarly inquiry—with its unsparing critique of homonormativity—I find its wholesale rejection of futurity untenable. As José Muñoz notes in *Cruising Utopia,* minoritarian subjects need the future, for it is how we stay attuned to desire.[9] He rejects the antirelational thesis on the ground that it cedes all articulations of futurity to a normative, white, reproductive sociality, and he advocates instead for a more expansive notion of futurity on behalf of those to whom it is systematically denied. This position resonates with Elizabeth Grosz's assertion that an "indeterminate future," a conceptual space created by "folding the past into the future, beyond the control or limit of the present," is essential to any transformational political project.[10] While *Acts of Gaiety* takes issue with what this author views as antirelational theorists' overinvestment in negativity, it does not deny the constitutive nature of injury to LGBT history or the intrinsic value of bad feelings to queer activism. Like Muñoz, I see "a potentiality in negative affects that can be reshaped by negation and made to work in the service of enacting a mode of critical possibility."[11]

Gaiety is a technology of endurance and agency for "arranging grief" that enables sexual minorities to accept but also to alter our painful existence.[12] What I am calling acts of gaiety are those performances and modes of performative activism that enable subaltern subjects, in the words of that fruity vixen Carmelita Tropicana, to "cry in one eye and laugh in the other."[13] While the case studies in this book all exhibit an antagonistic, menacing, or hostile reaction to oppression and are vehemently opposed to the social order as it currently exists, they all believe a better future is possible. The acts of gaiety that I survey here—Valerie Solanas's "scummy" events, anti-marriage zaps by lesbian feminist collectives, Jill Johnston's gestures of joker citizenship, Hothead Paisan's terrorist threats, and the Five Lesbian Brothers' cynical tendentious jokes—offer alternative strategies to the dominant arrangements of feelings and relationships that govern and organize national life today. Allying these examples is the actors' fierce commitment to mining the negative for pleasure and politics. Employing alternating tactics of menace and merriment, anger and affection, these acts of gaiety transform the space of negativity that shadows homosexual identity and suffuses lesbian lives with a performative force that gives rise to dreams of a better future. Arising as they do from tarrying so intensely with the negative, these dreams are as redolent with dark humor—violent imagery, homicidal fantasies of retributive justice, and psychotic breaks from reality—as they are with levity, hilarity, and (un)adulterated glee. Even the most misanthropic member of my archive, Valerie Solanas, insisted that "the female function is to explore, discover, invent, solve problems crack jokes, make music—all with love. In other words, create a magic world."[14]

Highlighting the curative, as well as the corrosive, effects of lesbian feminist cultural production, *Acts of Gaiety* responds to Eve Kosofsky Sedgwick's call for a reparative praxis, and in particular to her sense that queer theory's once productive, but now protracted, engagement with shame and suffering has contributed to a paranoid praxis so preoccupied with identifying new and ever more nefarious forms of injury and abjection, lurking in even the most hospitable places, that it has ceased to be a source of healing and sustenance. Sedgwick's turn to the happy and autotelic affects (in her last book, *Touching Feeling*) expresses her desire for an erotic and ecstatic mode of critical engagement that can balm the wounds of homophobia, not to mention other forms of discrimination, and create possibilities for a pleasurable and sustainable life.[15] My project advances a restorative hermeneutic that exposes the limits of traditional queer inquiry by conjuring, performing, and producing acts of gaiety, those embodied practices that are imbued with and generative of affective experiences of joy and jubilation, wishing and longing, felicity and good cheer.

Taking its cue from Sedgwick, *Acts of Gaiety* invites us to consider several questions. What has been sacrificed in privileging bad feelings to the exclusion of more positive affects? What has been lost in sex and gender studies by queer theory's preoccupation with abjection, abuse, and sorrow at the expense of more euphoric emotional registers? How might reclaiming gaiety enable us to create new modes of resistance, new forms of community, and new opportunities for inquiry into LGBT history and culture? What does or might gaiety do, how, when, and for whom? Do all social agents have equal access to gaiety or does it constitute a form of privilege stratified by differences of gender, class, race, ethnicity, nationality, and able-bodiedness? Do queers who are clinically depressed, incarcerated, homeless, or in the hospital have anything to be cheerful about? What do we do when situations seem so dire that we cannot muster a smile? What use is gaiety when we do not feel like laughing? What are the consequences of acting "as if" we are gay when we are not?

Grin and Bare It

Gaiety signifies a jocund and waggish response to the absurdity of the political, ideological, and environmental scenarios in which homosexuals have been cast. The Lavender Menace action showed members of the women's congress just how ridiculous homophobia is by responding to a hateful and discriminatory situation with wit and a sense of amused indignation. This zap was performative in both senses of the term: it was "staged" and consequential. Protesters created a safe and inviting space for dykes to come out of the closet and for heterosexual women to openly support their homosexual colleagues. Through their comedic performance, lesbians seduced spectators into the drama of political change by staging a scenario of what a better world might look like and inviting the audience to play along. The ludic register of the event enabled the protesters to show that the real menace to the women's movement was not the presence of lesbians but their absence. The goal of the zap was not simply to make lesbians visible or secure a place in the congress's program but to challenge NOW's integrationist logic and radically reconfigure the constitution, commitment, and priorities of the women's liberation movement.

As part of the Lavender Menace demonstration, lesbians distributed copies of "The Woman-Identified Woman" manifesto.[16] Hailed as one of the founding documents of radical feminism, "The Woman-Identified Woman" is a ten-paragraph political powder keg that defines sexuality as a political choice rather than a biological imperative. The manifesto insists that a commitment to lesbian liberation is essential to the success and fulfillment of the women's movement. The audience, won over by the demonstrators' act of gaiety and compelled by the persuasive rhetoric of the manifesto, not only listened to the collective's grievances, but they voted to make immediate and substantive alterations to the conference program, adding impromptu workshops on heterosexism and a women's dance.[17] In addition, the congress assembly voted to adopt several resolutions advanced by the Lavender Menace, including the following motions: (1) whenever the label lesbian is used against the movement collectively or against women individually, it is to be affirmed not denied; (2) in all discussions of birth control, homosexuality must be included as a legitimate method of contraception; and (3) all sex education curricula must include lesbianism as a valid, legitimate form of sexual expression and love.

The Lavender Menace's zap catalyzed real and significant change. This action empowered individuals and groups that felt marginalized by the proceedings to speak out, and it fostered solidarity among various factions at the congress. Black women expressed their anger at the lack of attention paid to cultural and ethnic differences and to the unacknowledged and seemingly intractable racism within feminist circles. Working-class women also voiced concerns about the proceedings. They railed against the elitism of the event, which, like most feminist organizations, was dominated by middle-class constituents. By the end of the zap action, workshops on multiple forms of discrimination had been added to the program.[18]

Kate Millett attributes the success of the action to the mood of gaiety it engendered. "There was fun in the Lavender Menace 'zap,'" she recalls, "impudence and humor."[19] Redstockings' Rosalyn Baxandall remembers the protest as "funny and wonderful," while Ann Snitow, a founding member of the New York Radical Feminists, commented on the "wit and vaudevillian charm" of the demonstrators.[20] "It was great theater and good fun, and defused a potentially divisive issue," remarked Anselma Dell'Olio, a founding member of New York NOW and the New Feminist Repertory Theater, which she started in 1969 with Rita Mae Brown, Jacqueline Ceballos, and Susan Vannucci. "In the end the innovators won," Dell'Olio reminds us, "and the movement was not annihilated because of it."[21] The Lavender Menace zap "completely reshaped the relationship between lesbians and feminists for years to come," and it is considered by many historians and activists to be one of the single most important actions of the feminist movement.[22] Yet, in spite of its historical import, many queers have never heard of this zap action or many of the other acts of gaiety I detail in this book. This is due, in part, to the fact that much of what was innovative, radical, and sex positive about lesbian feminism in the 1960s, 1970s, and 1980s has been ignored, obscured, or absorbed by subsequent waves of activism.

The queer canon is almost devoid of representations of lesbian sexuality, and it is sorely lacking in depictions of women laughing, joking, or camping it up. This absence reinforces the stereotype that dykes are dowdy and dogmatic, solemn and strident, and that lesbians were incapable of thinking playfully or positively about sex and politics until the 1990s when queer men showed us how. The Lavender Menace zap manifested most of the attributes of queer activism and third-wave feminism decades before the Lesbian Avengers commandeered public space with their Dyke March and Riot Grrrls hijacked the alternative music scene. This act of gaiety challenges the notion that second-wave feminists did not engage in public forms of sexual expression, experiment with hilarious and hyperbolic self-fashioning, or explore the theatricalization of identity, as many queer theorists, both male and female, have charged. The Lavender Menace transformed spoiled identities, histories of abuse, and everyday outrages into resistant political practices through humor, wit, and parody. They confronted the deadly effects of homophobia through a resignification of injurious speech—*lesbian,* like *dyke* and *queer,* is an insult, a slur—and they countered stigma by reclaiming and celebrating it with in-yer-face displays of eroticism. Through acts of gaiety, the Lavender Menace and groups like it transformed wounds into weapons, pain into pleasure. The protesters' seductive striptease made the shunned and shamed bodies of dykes visible within a symbolic order that not only devalues but pathologizes them. Lesbian sexuality was dramatized excessively as an oppositional strategy, creating an affective economy of dyke desire—a euphoric and sensuously charged atmosphere that permeated every dimension of the congress. Members of the Lavender Menace disrupted the drama of heteronormativity through the corporeal instantiation, in a public place, of a different modality of pleasure and political affiliation.

Allied Farces

In *Lady Dicks and Lesbian Brothers,* Kate Davy argues that the suppression of dyke humor was essential to the emergence of queer theory as a novel idea in the 1990s. Drawing on Joe Roach's assertion that cultural memory "is a process that depends crucially on forgetting," she writes, "Eclipsing salient features of lesbian cultural production was the necessary precondition of a process that valorized queer as an entirely new phenomenon—a phenomenon ostensibly antithetical to feminism."[23] "Such revisionist history," notes Sue-Ellen Case in "Toward a Butch-Feminist Retro Future," "promoted queer ascension through a valorization of gay male practices, arising from lesbian feminist ashes."[24] Davy and Case suggest that there is something, if not insidious then certainly opportunistic, about the elision of lesbian gaiety from the annals of queer theory. The sex radicalism and ludic play of bar dykes, working-class butches, and lesbian separatists have been obscured to make it seem as if queers were making new discoveries, engaging in innovative practices, and developing unique tactics to combat age-old problems, even as they were rehearsing and recycling critical methods and political maneuvers pioneered by lesbians and feminists decades earlier.

"Gender deconstruction and parody and everything else Judith Butler ever wrote," Jill Dolan has suggested, "were achieved with great orgasms of inventive, hilarious performance . . . at WOW Café."[25] The WOW Café Theatre is an off-off Broadway performance space and social club that has served as a laboratory of lesbian and feminist gaiety for over three decades, though it rarely appears in mainstream or avant-garde histories of queer performance. An important, though often ignored, precursor to queer theory, and to Butler's scholarship in particular, Women's One World (WOW) grew out of an international women's theater festival organized in 1980 by a group calling itself the Allied Farces. Long before *queer* reentered our critical lexicon, "the wayward girls of WOW"—Split Britches (Peggy Shaw, Lois Weaver, and Deb Margolin), Jordy Mark, Pamela Camhe, Alina Troyano (aka Carmelita Tropicana), Holly Hughes, Reno, and the Five Lesbian Brothers—were dramatizing the performative dimensions of theater and sexuality through their recognition that identities are transformed in real time by actors and spectators, in electrifyingly close proximity, who produce alternative, subversive interpretations of bodies and how they matter onstage and off.[26]

Just as gender is ineluctably linked to performance, so, too, is desire. The women of WOW, writes Dolan, "insist upon the importance of desire as history, desire as future, on our importance as bearers and shapers of different, necessary cultural meanings, through the presence of our desire."[27] These artists encourage us to indulge in and share "the pleasure we take in queer performance, because on some level, our pleasure is our resistance."[28]

At WOW, pleasure is a hot commodity, a valuable and progressive form of political currency. While scholars of the WOW Café fully acknowledge that the collective is a direct descendent of a radical lesbian feminist sensibility that emerged in the 1960s and 1970s, scant critical attention has been paid to mapping this influence, and precious little has been written about humorous and playful forms of lesbian art and activism in earlier decades. Before there were safe and welcoming spaces like WOW in which to act out lesbian plays for lesbian audiences, the figures in this study created sexual vernaculars for speaking lesbian desire in/as performance. These women understood the radical potential involved in the articulation and embodiment of lesbian desire in visible and public places.

Acts of Gaiety traces the impulses, desires, influences, and exigencies that conspired to make WOW an artistic possibility and material reality. While by no means an exhaustive or definitive history, this book brings to light lesbian performance and performative activism from the 1950s to the present that have been overlooked, occluded, and underdocumented by the amnesiac underpinnings of the queer turn and the historical selectivity of homoliberalism, both of which are characterized by an inattention to, if not a complete disregard for, satirical and subversive interventions staged by feminists and dykes in earlier epochs of sexual activism. I am not arguing for an unmediated or uninterrupted lineage from the performers in this book to the actors at the WOW Café; rather I am tracing a pattern of contagious laughter that reflects the infectious nature of a particular mode of political performance I term acts of gaiety. Through careful examination of a range of social and theatrical performances, I focus attention on several facets of lesbian gaiety (e.g., lavender menacement, ludicrousness, anarchic tendencies, practices of joker citizenship, and gallows humor) that serve as obverse values, political tactics, and aesthetic styles to those in common circulation today. Taken together, the acts of gaiety that populate this study constitute what Ann Cvetkovich calls an "archive of feeling," one that constellates and crystallizes a radical and utopic social vision that could refocus and reinvigorate LGBT performance and activism.[29]

Lavender Menacement

As we will see in the following pages, a hallmark of lesbian feminism has always been its active alliance with other progressive causes. Forty years ago union organizing, nuclear disarmament, peace, urban renewal, prison activism, immigration reform, the environment, rape, abortion, domestic violence protection, and birth control topped the list of lesbian causes. By contrast, most queers today have not made this transversal, intersectionist model a priority, and the contemporary LGBT movement remains as inattentive to issues of racial justice and as silent on the topic of white privilege as it has been since its inception. *Queer* has been defined by and reflects the experiences and worldviews of those members of our communities who are, with few exceptions, white, male identified, urban, able-bodied, and middle class, and this has not changed in any significant measure in over two decades. With the exception of a few grassroots organizations (e.g., Queers for Economic Justice, Astraea, the Audre Lorde Project, and the Sylvia Rivera Law Project), queer collectives have lost touch with issues that were once foundational to the concept of gay and lesbian liberation, namely, the redistribution of wealth and material resources and the collectivization of labor. As Kenyon Farrow, the former executive director of Queers for Economic Justice, notes, LGBT organizations devoted to an intersectional approach—and there are dozens in the United States—"have been underfunded and marginalized by the mainstream movement, in order to squelch political dissent, so that people who want to be allies to queer people assume that all of us want to get married and serve in the military."[30]

Accompanying the homoliberalization of the LGBT movement, there has been a proliferation of single-issue programs and associations at the local, national, and global levels dedicated to specific, narrowly defined platforms such as adoption and immigration for same-sex spouses. These single-issue organizations help promote visibility and raise awareness for particular causes, but they do little to promote alliances, foster coalitions, or build infrastructure. The leading national organization, the Human Rights Campaign (HRC), is a neoliberal bastion that makes NOW appear radical by comparison. As an institution, it not only fails to reflect the diverse constituencies that comprise the LGBT movement, but it is remiss in addressing the complex, intersectional forms of oppression that many homosexuals face on a daily basis. Rather than questioning or resisting homoliberalism, HRC aids and abets it by touting capitalist enterprise, individual choice, and economic self-determination as hallmarks of freedom.

Homoliberal reform tends to benefit the already privileged at the expense of underserved populations, including people of color, transgenders, sex workers, and inner city youths. As such, these initiatives alienate constituencies and weaken the movement. Equally important, they foreclose possibilities for national public debates about the imbrication of various forms of oppression and relegate conversations about importunate forms of inequality to what Lauren Berlant calls the "intimate public sphere," a sentimental space of opinion culture, normative sexuality, and privatized citizenship.[31] As recent critiques of neoliberalism have made clear, we must be mindful of the ways in which the attainment of sexual freedom, for a select few, comes at a price, and this cost is paid by "others." We must reaffirm our commitment to a holistic approach to oppression rooted in a broad-based campaign for social, sexual, and economic equality for all so that no others are left behind by neoliberal narratives of progress. Queer "rights," such as access to reproductive technologies, surrogacy, and transnational adoptions, have real material consequences for women and people of color across the globe. These "liberties" highlight the uneven effects of capitalist exploitation and social domination, and they intensify rather than mitigate racial, sexual, and economic disparities that play themselves out on local, national, and global stages. These inequities are ignored, denied, and exacerbated by the neoliberal rhetoric of individualism and exceptionalism, which codes poverty as a private failure, and indigence—no matter how systematic—as the personal choice of people who are simply unwilling to engage in the purportedly egalitarian sphere of free market capitalism.

Finding contemporary sexual politics enervating rather than energizing, I propose a counterpolitics of gaiety by indulging in instances of it and by articulating a mode of criticism that interprets ludic antics by lesbian feminists as vital strategies of resistance to homoliberalism's attempt to organize LGBT lives toward nationalist ends. The performances I chronicle here serve as antidotes to the grim and mirthless mood that characterizes contemporary sexual politics, and that have, even after all these years, the capacity to productively disrupt ossified categories of thought and calcified modes of perception. The animating force behind this book is the desire to restore to sex and gender studies a pleasurable and visceral sense of lavender menacement lest we become what performance artist Jack Smith called "pasty normals," his phrase for the colorless and soulless denizens of our planet who lack the capacity for gaiety.[32]

Acknowledgments

I am indebted to and deeply grateful for the individuals who have inspired, encouraged, and nurtured my intellectual development and for the communities that have supported the researching and writing of this book. Colleagues, mentors, students, family, and friends in a range of locales have played a role in shaping *Acts of Gaiety,* and in the process, shaping me as well.

At Rutgers University, where the seeds of this project were planted, I had the tremendous good fortune to work with Alicia Ostriker, Elin Diamond, Drucilla Cornell, Ben Sifuentes-Jáuregui, Josephine Diamond, Janet Walker, Ed Cohen, Linda Zerilli, and Carolyn Williams. This book grew roots and blossomed at Cornell University among a supportive and challenging cohort of scholars whose provocations and critical generosity have contributed to my work in a myriad of ways. For their intellectual acumen, sage advice, and spirited camaraderie I thank the faculty and staff, past and present, of the Department of Performance and Media Arts, with a special note of gratitude to Amy Villarejo, Sabine Haenni, Alison Van Dyke, Ellen Gainor, Nick Salvato, Haiping Yan, Beth Milles, Carolyn Goelzer, Byron Suber, Jim Self, Joyce Morgenroth, Marilyn Rivchin, and Debra Castillo. I include Marvin Carlson in this list as well, and I am fortunate to have had many inspired exchanges about theater and performance with him. A Mellon Fellowship on the topic of performance in 2006 helped crystallize my ideas for the book, and I appreciate the many productive conversations I had with fellow participants under the auspices of our indefatigable facilitator Andrew Galloway. A special group of intellectual companions from across the university have supplied stimulating conversations (at conferences and cocktail parties), substantive critiques of my work, and heartfelt words of wisdom about how to navigate what, for me, was a brave new world. I am thankful to Masha Raskolnikov, Jennifer Tennant, Judith Peraino, Deborah Starr, Elliot Shapiro, María Fernández, Dag Woubshet, Sherry Martin, Durba Ghosh, Shelley Feldman, Lucinda Ramberg, Hope Mandeville, and Cary Howie for their friendship and support. My students have made every class a joy to teach; I have gained much more than I have given from our experiments in learning.

This book developed in conversations and exchanges with many scholars and artists. Chief among these are the members of the Women and Theatre Program (WTP). I am extremely grateful to all of the feisty feminists who comprise this organization, and especially to Lisa Merrill and Jennifer DeVere Brody, my initiates and presidential mentors, Erica Stevens Abbitt, Natka Bianchini, Rhonda Blair, Norma Bowles, Sue-Ellen Case, Lindsay Cummings, Aileen Hendricks, Holly Hughes, Kathleen Juhl, Joan Lipkin, Ashley Lucas, Rose Malague, Deb Margolin, Jen-Scott Mobley, Domnica Radulescu, and Maya Roth. Kate Davy provided invaluable feedback on the Five Lesbian Brothers chapter. Stacy Wolf's scholarship inspired my approach to *Hothead* the musical, and Jenny Spencer published a version of this chapter in her anthology on political theater. I feel fortunate to have collaborated on a number of WTP panels and projects with Jill Dolan, whose intellectual rigor, critical insights, and utopian imaginings resonate throughout the pages of this book. I am honored by the professional and personal generosity she has bestowed on me.

Nat Hurley has read multiple iterations of this book; she is a superlative academic ally and a great friend. Nat and Susanne Luhmann's invitation to the University of Alberta proved to be a valuable lesson in the theory and practice of lesbian gaiety. Erin Hurley, no relation save for the fact that they are both brilliant, munificent, and Canadian, offered feedback on the entire manuscript and was instrumental in helping me conceptualize both the preface and introduction. Robin Bernstein's invitation to deliver an early version of the Jill Johnston chapter at Harvard University helped give this section shape and depth, as did commentary by Rebecca Schneider, who graciously served as my respondent. Anthony Lioi and his colleagues at Juilliard hosted a talk on *Hothead Paisan,* and the Center for Lesbian and Gay Studies at the City University of New York invited me to lecture on zap actions, where I benefited from the thoughtful and careful critique of Judith Milhous, Jean Graham-Jones, and David Savran, whose influence permeates this manuscript.

This book would not have been possible without the generosity of a host of artists, activists, and accidental witnesses who have shared with me their memories, both pleasurable and painful, of some of the most volatile periods in American history. These include Judith Martinez, Lisa Kron, Moe Angelos, Babs Davy, Alina Troyano, and Ingrid Nyeboe, whose wife, Jill Johnston, died while I was writing this book. One of my greatest regrets in life is that I did not have the opportunity to interview Jill for this book. This list also includes Sue Perlgut, Allan Warshawsky, Robert Patrick, Randy Wicker, Roxanne Dunbar-Ortiz, Mary Harron, Paul Krassner, Ben Morea, Donny Smith, Norman Marshall, Eddy Falconer, Jeremiah Newton, Phyllis Rafael, Larry Bob, and Morgan Ahern.

In addition to fascinating human subjects, I have had the great fortune of working with a number of collections, curators, and archivists. I thank Geri Solomon, assistant dean of Special Collections at Hofstra University; Matt Wrbican, archivist at the Warhol Museum; Bruce Kirby, manuscript reference librarian at the Library of Congress; Marvin J. Taylor, director of the Fales Library at New York University; James Maynard, assistant curator of the Poetry Collection of Buffalo (State University of New York); Blair Fornwald at the University of Regina; Gayle Cooper at the University of Virginia's Albert and Shirley Small Special Collections Library; Marisa Gorman of the Thomas J. Dodd Research Center at the University of Connecticut; James D. Folts of the New York State Archives; and Brenda Marston, curator of the Human Sexuality Collection at Cornell.

LeAnn Fields at the University of Michigan Press has nurtured this project from its infancy. There is no way for me to overstate my appreciation to her or to adequately and appropriately thank her for her enthusiasm, sound judgment, and mentorship. I commend the capable and caring staff at the press, Scott Ham, Alexa Ducsay, and Marcia LaBrenz in particular, for due diligence and meticulous attention to detail. And thanks to Daniel Gundlach for his expertise in compiling the index.

An early version of chapter five appeared as "Rage Slaves: The Commodification of Affect in the Five Lesbian Brothers' *The Secretaries*," in the *Journal of Dramatic Theory and Criticism* 23, no. 1 (Spring 2008): 21–45. Excerpts from the preface and introduction were published as "'A Terror to Gods and Men': The Furies Collective, the Theatrics of Terrorism, and the Myth of the Angry Lesbian," in *Myth and Violence in the Contemporary Female Text: New Cassandras,* eds. Julie Rajan and Sanja Bahun-Radunovic, 19–33 (London: Ashgate Press, 2011). A truncated version of chapter four,

"The Maladapted *Hothead Paisan: A Lesbian Comedy of Terrors*," serves as the concluding chapter in *Political and Protest Theatre after 9–11: Patriotic Dissent*, ed. Jenny Spencer (New York: Routledge, 2011), 219–34. Thanks to the publishers for permission to use this material in the present work. I am grateful to Diane DiMassa for allowing me to reproduce images of Hothead Paisan and to Mary Ellen Mark, Joan Marcus, and Desdemona Burgin for permission to use their photographs.

I am appreciative of the broad network of colleagues and friends who have worked directly and indirectly to support me and this work at various stages. This includes the expert editorial advice of Iris Fischer Smith, Jocelyn Buckner, V. G. Julie Rajan, and Sanja Bahun-Radunović; conversations about performance and politics with Madeleine George, Leigh Fondakowski, Roberta Sklar, Rhodessa Jones, Sean Reynolds, Bill Doan, and Kore Alexis (wherever you are); insights into riot grrrl culture and dyke humor offered by Jill Franco and Amanda Browning; the keen eye and caustic humor of Jenny Worley; the academic savvy of Sarah Chinn and the hard-working board of the Center for Lesbian and Gay Studies (CLAGS); the beautiful minds and beneficent spirits of Romana Uhlirova and Josef Benninghoff; the wry witticisms of Dana Gardner and Betsy Keller; Judy Maguire's food for thought; Kate Halliday for keeping me sane; and the many acts of gaiety I have enjoyed with Marta Pérez, Martina Gallegos, Tony Basoukeas, Alain Gourranc, Annemarie Rossi, Chris Davis, Calvin Ng, Calvin Doucet, and Michael Abbey.

My parents, Ken and Judy Warner, instilled in me the values, standards, and work ethic that have made it possible for me to travel along this tender track. My first teachers, they taught me how to fight, how to laugh, and how not to take myself, or the world, too seriously. My siblings, Shannon, Richard, and Melissa, along with their partners and children, make me proud to be part of our crazy clan. Most of all, I thank Mary Jo Watts, to whom this book is dedicated. My partner of fifteen years, MJ is my heart and soul. She provided the inspiration for many of the discoveries that I make in this book, thoughtful commentary on every chapter, and the encouragement I needed to start and finish this project. I could not and would not have written this without her.

Acts of Gaiety

Introduction

> I became a political animal in order to have a good time. . . .
> Feminism struck me as a good time, and it was. Back then, it still
> frightened the horses; it made most men foam at the mouth, and it
> got the best women horny.
>
>   —Bertha Harris

Once an sobriquet for eccentrics and a slur for sexual deviants, *queer* became, in the 1990s, a diacritical term for a wide-ranging political movement and nuanced scholarly critique of normative regimes, phobic policies,
and structural inequalities. Queer theory and activism dramatized, often
in a spectacularly theatrical fashion, the instabilities and incoherencies inherent in the purportedly stable alignment of biological sex, gender, and
sexual orientation. An aggressive, confrontational, and media-savvy mode
of engagement, *queer* stood for dissent against the oppressive mechanisms
of normativity and normalization. Very quickly, however, *queer* came to be
defined in opposition to the identity politics of earlier waves of sex and gender activism. This strategy of tactical supersession had the effect of obscur-
ing what was vital and still viable about the ideology and practices of both
second-wave feminism and the gay and lesbian liberation movement. This
methodological maneuver prompted certain foundational figures, including
Teresa de Lauretis—who is credited with coining the term *queer theory*—to
abandon the neologism on the grounds that it had "become a conceptually
vacuous creature" having more to do with marketing and branding than
social critique and political experimentation.[1]

In recent years, *queer* has continued to become increasingly disconnected from its theoretical potential and political promise. Its broad-based
critique of an array of social exclusions has devolved into an assimilationist-
oriented equal rights agenda advanced by members of an increasingly conservative mainstream whose quest for enfranchisement through liberal

reforms—such as marriage and military service—allies them more closely with heterosexuals from the "family values" faction of the Far Right than with gay and lesbian activists forged in the crucible of the New Left. Years of relentless attacks on identity politics have tended to foreclose rather than enable debates about institutionalized forms of oppression and economic disparities shaped by the material realities of gender, race, class, and ethnicity. This has resulted in the alienation of feminists, gays and lesbians of color, transgender activists, and other minority subjects from the movement, and it has given rise to what Jasbir Puar describes as the "unexpected flowering of new normativities in these queer times."[2] Commodified by the marketing and media outlets it courted decades ago, *queer* has come to signal an ever-narrowing sense of sexual identity and a depoliticized form of consumer citizenship that is complicit with rather than critical of sexual neoliberalism, or what I call homoliberalism. Homoliberalism names the quest for acceptance, legitimacy, and formal equality through a pragmatic program animated by individual economic interests, a privatized sexual politics, and a constricted notion of national-public life. A ruse of parity and inclusion, homoliberalism allows for LGBT representation without a significant or meaningful redistribution of material and cultural resources or a transformation in the structures of power.

The issue of what, if anything, remains "critically queer" about contemporary sex and gender studies, has been the subject of much debate in progressive circles in recent years.[3] In 2005, David Eng, Judith Halberstam, and José Esteban Muñoz charged sixteen scholars with the task of assessing *What's Queer about Queer Studies Now?* in a special double issue of *Social Text*. The editors called for a reassessment of "the political utility of the term queer" not only in light of the mainstreaming of the LGBT movement but also with respect to global crises that have reconfigured historical, economic, and cultural alliances among political constituencies, remapping the geopolitical terrain through armed conflict, cellular networks of terrorism, natural disasters, and the diasporic populations these phenomena produce. Two years later Janet Halley and Andrew Parker served as guest editors for a special issue of *South Atlantic Quarterly* titled *After Sex?* in which they asked contributors to discuss what constitutes queer theory other than an abiding interest in sexuality. In 2009, Heather Love hosted a conference at the University of Pennsylvania entitled "Rethinking Sex," which featured over thirty scholars debating the past, present, and future of movements for sexual freedom.[4]

The general consensus of these collections and convocations, assembling queer theorists old and new, is that we must pay greater attention to the imbrication of sexual politics with other historical forces, political dynamics, and spheres of social engagement. This was echoed in another forum on recent trends in sex and gender studies, a 2006 roundtable on the topic of queer temporalities. Here Carolyn Dinshaw suggested that "*queer* history" should acknowledge "*sex* . . . as heterogeneous and indeterminate, even as it recognizes and pursues sex's irreducible interrelatedness with other cultural phenomena," including the bodily sense of touch.[5] This position is affirmed by Ann Pellegrini, who writes, "[A]ffective relations—painful and pleasurable, enervating and energizing—are part of the process of forging alternative histories, alternative values, queer communities."[6]

Indicative of the "affective turn" in sex and gender studies (and in the humanities and social sciences more broadly), these critics have shifted the conceptual rubrics of scholarly inquiry away from epistemology (from the alleged truth of sexuality and how we can or cannot know it) and toward a consideration of phenomenology and feeling (of what motivates politics and performance).[7] The turn toward affect promises a better way of talking about the affiliations and identifications of minority subjects (better than discourses of identity and postidentity politics), and it foregrounds the emotional stakes of our scholarly projects, critical methodologies, and modes of knowledge production. This conceptual maneuver enables us to redirect our focus from locating gays, lesbians, and queers *in* previous eras (and in tracing the [in]stabilities of sexual taxonomies over time) to exploring the types of relations *with* historical figures that we hope to cultivate. Performance—which identifies, enacts, and disrupts sexual difference, not in terms of ontology or identity but through the more nuanced avenue of feelings—serves as a fertile site for exploring the affective dynamics and temporal logics that motivate sexual minorities, aligning them into constituencies and fostering networks of relationality across space and time.

While the affective turn in sex and gender studies promises new paradigms and new opportunities for the reappropriation of *queer*, it has not presented "the discursive occasion for a powerful and compelling fantasy of historical reparation" that Judith Butler cautioned, back in 1993, was necessary in order for queer to remain a viable category of critical analysis and a source of progressive political activism.[8] Far from helping *queer* "overcome its constitutive history of injury," the affective turn has had the effect of reiterating and reinscribing it.[9] This is because much of the recent scholarship on queer affects privileges bad feelings, emotions that make us feel terrible but can be politically productive as catalysts for social change (e.g., shame, loss, mourning, and melancholia), or "ugly feelings," negative affects of a minor register that produce ambivalent situations of suspended, obstructed, or thwarted agency (e.g., boredom, anxiety, paranoia, irritation, and envy).[10] *Acts of Gaiety* offers a different point of departure. It takes as its subject good feelings, positive affects that involve pleasurable sensations and foster jubilant practices of life, art, and activism. Central to my thesis, however, is the notion that affective binaries fail to adequately capture or categorize the emotional dynamics of sexual politics and that trafficking in this dichotomous logic contributes, if not directly to the rise of homoliberalism, then certainly to a sense of amnesia about LGBT history that makes it difficult, if not impossible, to combat the mainstreaming of the movement.

What is interesting to me about the affective turn in sex and gender studies is how closely the reterritorialized queer agendas it has occasioned resemble the "passionate politics" of second-wave feminism and the gay and lesbian liberation movement.[11] From the Radicalesbians' "The Woman-Identified Woman," which defines *lesbian* as "the rage of all women condensed to the point of explosion," to Audre Lorde's "The Uses of the Erotic," which promotes a euphoric mode of creation that transcends the essentialism of biological reproduction but remains firmly embedded in the corporeal, we see forceful and nuanced articulations of lesbian identifications as what Raymond Williams calls "structures of feeling."[12] Distinct from ideology or worldview, structures of feeling refers to "meanings and values as they are actively lived and felt . . . specifically affective elements of consciousness and relationships: not feeling against thought," Williams tells us, "but thought as felt and feeling as thought: practical consciousness of a present kind, in a living and inter-relating continuity."[13] Integral to the vision of second-wave feminism and gay liberation was the desire to revolutionize sexual interactions and social relationships by developing new forms of intimacy that were sensual, egalitarian, and nonmonogamous; by forging kinship arrangements that were free of sexist attitudes, gender binaries, and racist biases; and by eradicating the institutions and ordinances that perpetuate oppressive hierarchies. Groups such as WITCH, Dyketactics, the Furies, GLF, Third World Gay Liberation, and Street Transvestite Action Revolutionaries (STAR) sought to create a new world order that would bring about the affective, economic, and political liberation of all people.

Much of what transpired during this volatile time was ephemeral and/or undocumented, often by choice as the recording, preserving, and marketing of movement activities was seen by many political radicals as bourgeois. Most countercultural groups not only lacked the resources to archive their doings, but they feared, with good reason, that they were being surveilled by the government. As a result, they tended to destroy, as opposed to conserve, their histories. This was true certainly in lesbian feminist circles.[14] It is no wonder that so much of our LGBT past is lost to cultural memory or that it would be so easy for queer theorists and third-wave feminists to feel that they were creating new forms, methods, and strategies of political engagement when, in fact, these tactics had been in circulation for quite some time. The affective turn in critical theory makes me want to return to earlier waves of LGBT activism in order to identify the felt dimensions and missed opportunities of our unrealized past.

Intended as an antidote to both the sanguine sentimentality of homoliberalism and the enervating saturninity of queer theory, *Acts of Gaiety* explores the twinned and mutually informing histories of gayness as politics and gayness as *bon vivance*. This affective history of gaiety underscores the centrality of liveliness to LGBT cultures, and it shows us the folly of sober and straightlaced struggles for "full and equal rights" that sentimentalize homonormativity as a mode of political equality, sexual liberation, and domestic bliss. As other struggles for social justice make painfully clear, the best that this pragmatic approach can hope to achieve is a compromised form of citizenship. Affective histories involve ways of knowing and showing that are lived in and through moments of acute corporeal sensation. The sensate body serves as the vehicle and method for this brand of embodied and visceral consciousness. "[F]or gay people," writes Joan Nestle in *A Restricted Country*, "history is a place where the body carries its own story."[15]

Affective histories supplement our reliance on evidence and discernible fact with the sensations, impressions, and emotional connections that the remains of history can produce. As forms of knowledge production, they are less invested in recuperating the past than they are in encountering it as always already present in traces, signs, gestures, and actions. Narrating the past in a subjunctive and performative mode rather than an indicative mode, affective histories are rhizomatic rather than filiative, in Gilles Deleuze and Félix Guattari's schema, which is to say they are heterogeneous, nonhierarchical, and nonreproductive in their logic.[16] Like laughter, they are contagious, corrosive, curative, and always already open to multiple avenues of inquiry and possibilities for articulating the past, present, and future.[17] *Acts of Gaiety* moves us to confront on an emotional, physical, and intellectual register what has been unrepresented, underrepresented, and misrepresented by traditional modes of inquiry and canonical accounts of our queer past. Galvanized by a gleeful historical impulse and the desire to advance a more exuberantly progressive political program, this book reclaims gaiety as an important but neglected political affect that if revalued might revive and reorient LGBT art and activism.

Gay Play

Gaiety plays an integral part in the establishment and maintenance of LGBT public cultures. Sexual minorities can boast of a rich performance history of entertaining audiences (both straight and gay) in bars, comedy clubs, and drag shows, but historically we have been most skilled in the art of carefully crafting personas that enable us to survive the drama of compulsory heteronormativity. "All of us who are queer can loosely be described as solo performers," observes David Román, "insofar as we have had to fashion an identity around our gender and sexuality, drag being only one manifestation of this process."[18] Homosexuals learn to pass as straight to avoid insult, injury, and persecution, often before we are old enough to be conscious of what we are doing or why. Unable to express deviant desires publicly, many sexual minorities seek solace in the arts. The theater has long been a haven for queers. It is a site of yearning and fantasy, a liminal world where almost anything is possible. Desire, including same-sex eroticism, serves as a driving force in the theater, motivating characters and audiences alike. Unconventional liaisons, aberrant behaviors, lax morals, and powerful emotions are the keystones of dramaturgy. Trafficking in magic and metamorphosis, glitter and glamour, which is to say in the possibility of transformation, the theater provides both a respite and a resource for society's maligned and marginalized. Because of the crowd it attracts and the affective power it wields, playhouses are prime targets for censorship. Seen as a danger, or, like prostitution, a necessary evil, theater is often regulated and relegated to the physical margins of society.[19] Located in entertainment zones, red light districts, and bohemian enclaves where hedonism is actively encouraged, the theater is a veritable gateway into gaiety, carnal pleasures, and clandestine pursuits.

Theater is the affect machine par excellence; its most basic function is to make us feel. Whether through realist dramas, which obscure their normalizing force with claims to objectively reflect the world as it is, or through experimental forms that actively challenge received truths and thwart the normalizing function of catharsis, the theater is an engine of emotions. Performance mobilizes and marshals affects, sentiments, and sensations, giving meaning and coherence to our perceptions. In its most utopian incarnation, suggests Jill Dolan, the theater "provides a place where people come together, embodied and passionate, to share experiences of meaning making and imagination that can describe or capture fleeting intimations" of "what a better world might feel like."[20] From the halls of academia to the streets of our cities, performance has become, in recent years, the vehicle through which our concerns about affect, embodiment, identity, and sexuality are expressed, analyzed, challenged, and refashioned. Paying attention to performance, understood as the repetition of behaviors that instantiate and concretize our sense of "self" and "other," allows us to examine the simultaneous and coconstitutive frames of expression, identification, and representation that structure our possibilities for agency, sexual subjectivity, and citizenship. When we celebrate artists such as Hanifah Walidah or D.R.E.D., whose dramatized personae challenge hegemonic structures of feelings that silence and circumscribe lesbians and people of color, or when we call to task religious fanatics, such as Sarah Palin and Michelle Bachmann, who attempt to bar sexual minorities from the rites and rituals of civic participation, we concern ourselves with how bodies matter, with how they do what they do and feel what they feel, using the conceptual paradigms of performance and performativity.

Conscious of performance's role in ritual efficacy, and seeking to capitalize on ritual's role in engendering identities, Butler defines gender as a "repeated stylization of the body, a set of repeated acts, within a highly rigid regulatory frame that congeal over time to produce the appearance of substance, a natural sort of being."[21] Performance provides the occasion and opportunity to trouble gender—not to mention race, class, and ethnicity—by enabling individuals and groups to "restyle" their bodies in a variety of different contexts, conditions, and environments. Butler's articulation of gender performativity underscores how public manifestations produce private, interior identities and feelings of belonging through participation in social rites that mark one as a member of privileged or stigmatized populations. Gender performances involve complex, and often contradictory, enactments of compulsory and elective behaviors, gestures, and attributes whose truths are performatively produced through one's fidelity to prescribed social and cultural scripts. Whether on the stage or in the practice of everyday life, the successful performance of one's gender benefits the actor in question through the bestowal of recognition and rewards. Infelicitous performances, on the other hand, risk punishment and prohibition, including bodily harm and death, as the rape and murder of Brandon Teena make painfully clear. Performances that blur the boundary between legitimate and illegitimate, normal and abnormal, justice and injustice, provide a forum in which we can imagine, if not enact, alternative structures of feeling and alternative ways of being in the world.

While the theater has sheltered many homosexuals and nurtured generations of gay artists, Robin Bernstein reminds us, it has also perpetuated gross stereotypes and played a significant role in reinforcing homophobic, sexist, racist, and classist social hierarchies.[22] Plays by heterosexuals typically cast homosexuals as psychotic perverts, degenerates, and criminals, but so, too, do scripts by gay authors. Mart Crowley's landmark play *The Boys in the Band* (1968), hailed by many as the first commercially successful play to offer a sympathetic depiction of gay male sexuality, centers around a group of closeted and self-loathing upper-middle-class men who rent a hustler for their friend Harold's birthday party. Referred to only as Cowboy, this rough trade is treated as a piece of meat. Paid to be objectified, the hustler must suffer being openly mocked by the intellectually superior college graduates who contracted his services. One of the friends, Bernard, is an African American who endures "Uncle Tom" jokes by the nelliest of the group, Emory. Emory is punched in the mouth by Alan, a heterosexual friend of the host who cannot contain his disgust for effeminate men.

In *The Boys in the Band*, Crowley shows both the devastating effects of homophobia and the protagonists' indulgence in gaiety as a way to combat it. Pleasure is resistance for these queens. The men laugh and joke, drink and take drugs, sing and dance (the play calls for Michael to camp it up to Judy Garland's "Almost Like Being in Love" and for the entire group to reprise a popular Fire Island dance called "Heatwave"). These seemingly frivolous acts of gaiety are what keep these men alive. While the party ends with every one of the boys having been humiliated or abused, some to the extent that they want to kill themselves, they put on another record, mix another cocktail, and make it through another night. Unlike most plays about homosexuals prior to the gay liberation movement, these gay men are neither alone nor dead when the curtain falls. As Michael notes in the final scene, "It's not always the way it is in plays. Not all faggots bump themselves off at the end of the story!"[23]

The characters in *The Boys in the Band* may not be happy—they may not even be able to imagine themselves as happy ("[S]how me a happy homo-sexual," says Michael, "and I'll show you a gay corpse"), but they manage, somehow, to be gay.[24] Gaiety, here and throughout this book, has less to do with the expression of an inner emotion than it does with the projection, or theatricalization, of a feeling that one can inhabit, and enact so fully, that it appears "as if" it were emanating from the core of one's being. These acts of gaiety facilitate a respite from the drudgery of daily life, provide escape from untenable situations, and enable the construction of alternate realities governed by values and aspirations obverse to (and despised by) mainstream culture. At a time when contemporary sexual politics is complicit with what Sara Ahmed calls "the promise of happiness," it becomes increasingly urgent to counter coercive and pragmatic forms of political optimism with, among other things, historical accounts of the conjunctions of riot and revelry in earlier epochs of the LGBT movement.[25] Acts of gaiety do not make the world go away; they make worlds, albeit illusory and fleeting ones. The Boys create for themselves a *mundus ludibundus*. They experience life through play, as play, in play.[26] *Mundus ludibundus* is a world governed by the ludic, a world of pleasure seeking and joke telling, a world of leisure pursuits and sexual conquests. Serving as what Susan Sontag, in "Notes on 'Camp,'" calls a "gesture of self legitimization," acts of gaiety involve an awareness and appreciation of illusion, a penchant for the play of surfaces, and an understanding of appearances as distinct from reality.[27] Through parody, satire, and physical comedy, *The Boys in the Band* transforms something as ugly as homophobia into a cynical joke just as the Lavender Menace's zap creates a thing of beauty from an abject identity.

Homo Ludens :: Lesbo Ludens

Lesbians and feminists are not typically associated with gaiety. Dykes, especially those of the 1960s and 1970s, are routinely caricatured as sexless, humorless killjoys who (thankfully) lost the Culture Wars to dildo-packing, deconstruction-spouting genderqueers. Stereotypes painting dykes as strident, frigid, and frumpy abound in both mainstream and queer subcultural accounts of history. The strategies for self-definition and self-promotion successfully employed by gay men to increase their visibility, political clout, and economic capital—including camp, kitsch, and drag—have not been particularly efficacious for lesbians, not even those in the performing arts.[28]

"When lesbians make it to off-Broadway," notes butch icon Peggy Shaw, "it's the boys who are doing it."[29] Shaw is referring specifically to Charles Busch's *Vampire Lesbians of Sodom,* one of the longest-running shows in New York theater history.[30] The question of whether lesbian sexuality and dyke modes of humor can be made intelligible on the stage of national politics has preoccupied artists and activists since the 1960s.

The theater world has done comparatively little to challenge stereotypes of women and lesbians, in part because there were (and are) so few out dykes working as playwrights, directors, actors, or designers. As Roberta Sklar told the audience at a recent conference at the Center for Lesbian and Gay Studies (CLAGS) on dykes in the 1970s, "One thing you didn't do if you wanted a career in professional theater, you didn't come out. . . . [I]f you wanted to be a lesbian in the theater, you understood that it was 'Don't Ask, Don't Tell.'"[31] Many lesbian playwrights working during the era, such as María Irene Fornés, did not write lesbian plays. Why would they given that there were so few places that would stage them? Although there were many off-off-Broadway theaters where gay men could produce their work, there was no lesbian equivalent to Caffe Cino or the Play-house of the Ridiculous, not until 1976 when Medusa's Revenge, a short-lived but influential performance space founded by two Cuban exiles, Ana María Simo and Magaly Alabau, opened on Bleecker Street.[32] Peggy Shaw called Medusa's Revenge "the gayest place in town."[33]

Lesbians like Jane Chambers, who did write openly gay plays and did enjoy a modicum of commercial success, tended to work in the realist vein, which meant that her protagonists ended up dead or doomed to an equally onerous fate. Unable to break through the glass proscenium, many dykes gravitated toward agitprop or avant-garde theater collectives. Sklar, for example, joined Muriel Miguel and Megan Terry at the Open Theater, but she left the troupe when it became apparent that the group had no interest in exploring issues related to women or lesbians. Partnering with Sondra Segal and Clare Coss, Sklar cofounded the Women's Experimental Theatre (WET), which created work based on cultural feminist assumptions about innate biological differences between the sexes. Their best-known work, *The Daughter's Cycle Trilogy* (1977–80), offers a revisionist history of Greek drama from the perspective of the female characters. This work presents the mother-daughter bond as a universal condition constitutive of women's shared experience.

Many feminist collectives, such as It's All Right to Be Woman Theatre

(IARTBW, 1970–76) and At the Foot of the Mountain (ATFOTM, 1975), generated content through consciousness-raising sessions. Their productions created a public forum for what had previously been seen as private issues that women suffered with in silence, including rape, abortion, and incest. These are serious topics that most women's theater troupes felt merited serious treatment, and understandably so. While performances by WET, IARTBW, and ATFOTM were not devoid of humor, they were certainly more solemn than they were silly. Not all feminists, however, took an earnest approach to women's history or to trauma. When Miguel left the Open Theater, she started a collective with her two (heterosexual) sisters, Gloria Miguel and Lisa Mayo. Drawing on their cultural heritage as members of the Kuna and Rappahannock nations, they called their troupe Spiderwoman Theater. *Spiderwoman* refers to the goddess of weaving, and the practice of story weaving is the foundation of the collective's feminist aesthetic. Their first performance was a comedy titled *Women in Violence* (1975), and it addressed violence against women and among women, as well as self-inflected abuse. Eschewing the sober tone typically employed by other—predominantly white, middle-class—feminist collectives, these sisters used slapstick, burlesque, and bawdy humor to create powerful social satires. Spiderwoman Theater staged what many considered at the time to be politically incorrect comedies. While most feminist collectives burned out or disbanded within a few years, this troupe is still performing. Spiderwoman's gaiety is what keeps them going.

To engage in gaiety is to create a pleasurable and empowering experience out of an event or situation that is hateful or painful. Through parody, satire, and physical comedy, sexual minorities survive by replaying tragedy as farce. In so doing, they make manifest the pleasure of politics and the politics of pleasure. Before exploring further ludic forms of lesbian dramaturgy, I want to chart a longer affective history, as acts of gaiety have played an important role in LGBT world-making projects for a century, if not longer.

A Gay Old Time

> Helen Furr . . . did not find it gay living in the same place where she had always been living. She went to a place where some were cultivating something, voices and other things needing cultivating. She met Georgine Skeene who was cultivating her voice which some thought was quite a pleasant one. Helen Furr and Georgine

Skeene lived together then. . . . They were quite gay, they were quite regular, they were learning little things, gay little things, they were gay inside them the same amount they had been gay, they were gay the same length of time they had been gay every day.

—Gertrude Stein, "Miss Furr and Miss Skeene"

Although it was officially claimed as a revolutionary political identity in the late 1960s, *gay* has been used by people "in the life" to denote same-sex desire since at least the 1920s. A playfully ambiguous term, *gay* connotes good humor and indicates a positive and cheery disposition, but it also enjoys a long and storied association with passion, promiscuity, and perversion. As early as the seventeenth century, the word *gay* was associated with immorality, wantonness, lewdness, and licentious behavior. It was used to denote someone "addicted to pleasures and dissipations."[34] The Gay Nineties refers to the 1890s, the fin-de-siècle epoch when hedonists flouted Victorian social norms. By this date, *gay man* was the term one used to refer to a rakish womanizer unencumbered by the shackles of marriage, and *gay woman* was slang for a prostitute, which one procured at a *gay house,* or brothel. An 1857 *Punch* cartoon by John Leech titled "The Great Social Evil" depicts a gaily attired working girl, Fanny, in the Haymarket at midnight, posed in an open door next to a poster of *La Traviata,* Verdi's popular opera about a courtesan. She is accosted by a modestly dressed acquaintance, Bella, who, surprised at finding her friend in this situation, exclaims, "Ah! Fanny! How long have you been gay!"[35]

Gay began to take on overt political connotations in the mid-1940s, when, in the wake of World War II, sexual subcultures began to form in urban areas across the United States. Members of these enclaves began to view sexuality as an important rubric for understanding themselves as social subjects and minority citizens in relation to the dominant culture. In New York, San Francisco, and Los Angeles, they created underground networks where *gay* was used as an adjective to describe homosexual behavior, queer aesthetics, and same-sex events. A woman writing under the name Lisa Ben, an anagram for *lesbian,* wrote and self-published *Vice Versa: America's Gayest Magazine* in 1947–48 while working as a secretary at a Hollywood movie studio. She also wrote and sang what she called "gay" parodies in queer bars in Southern California, including the Flamingo, which, as Ben recalls in an interview with historian Eric Marcus, "used to have Sunday afternoon tea dances there for just the gay kids. I would go there and have

THE GREAT SOCIAL EVIL.

Time:—Midnight. A Sketch not a Hundred Miles from the Haymarket.

Bella. "Ah! Fanny! How long have you been *Gay?*"

As early as the seventeenth century, the word *gay* was associated with immorality, wantonness, lewdness, and licentious behavior. In this tableau, *gay* refers to a prostitute, which one sought at a *gay house,* or brothel. (John Leech, "The Great Social Evil," *Punch* 33 [January 10, 1857], 114.)

a gay old time."[36]

In the early 1950s, two black women, Ernestine "Tiny" Davis and her lover Ruby Lucas (née Renei Phelan), opened Tiny and Ruby's Gay Spot in Chicago. Davis, who was known as "the female Louis Armstrong," was one of the finest musicians of the swing era. She played trumpet for the all-woman band the International Sweethearts of Rhythm, an integrated ensemble that formed in 1937 and played for predominantly black audiences. Davis's fans included Count Basie, Ella Fitzgerald, and Armstrong himself, who reportedly offered her ten times her salary to tour with him. In a 1986 documentary film, Davis was asked why she did not leave the International Sweethearts of Rhythm to play for Satchmo. Grinning like a Cheshire cat, she said, "I loved them gals too much."[37] The Sweethearts broke up in 1949, after male soldiers returned from the war and made it increasingly difficult for women musicians to find work. "[W]e never got the credit we deserved,"

Davis said of the band. "But women have a hard time in anything. There's nothing you can do. Just keep on keeping on."

In 1949 Davis formed her own band, Tiny Davis and Her Hell Divers, separated from her husband and children, and moved to Chicago. Soon after, she met Lucas, a drummer, with whom she spent the next four decades. Asked to describe their relationship, Davis replied, "Ruby came over one day and never left. Hell, she stayed for forty-two years. Are we gay? Maybe we are. We have ourselves a time, I can say that."[38] For Davis, gay denotes her sexual orientation, but this has less to do with the naming of an identity than it does with indexing a pursuit of pleasure. Davis and Lucas were out when many black celebrities, such as playwright Lorraine Hansberry, were closeted. The influence of Tiny Davis and Ruby Lucas is undeniable in the Varied Voices of Black Women, a group of Bay Area poets and musicians comprised of Pat Parker, Linda Tillery, Mary Watkins, and Gwen Avery, whose US tour in the late 1970s helped many lesbians find their gay spot. Davis's legacy lives on in Ntozake Shange's choreopoems, which fuse music and sound, dance and movement, voice and the spoken word. It consonates with the eclectic, improvisational virtuosity of Sharon Bridgforth's theatrical jazz aesthetic, the subversive slam poetry of Staceyann Chin, and the haunting Haitian rhythms of Lenelle Möise's hip-hop-inflected performances.

Davis and Lucas risked a great deal in operating an openly gay club in the 1950s, as these operations were frequently the target of police raids, even if the owners paid for mob protection. Any man or woman who was not wearing at least three articles of clothing proper to their gender was taken to the precinct and booked. Groups of people assembled, even in a private home, without a balanced number of the opposite sex present were also subject to arrest. As David Carter reminds us in his book *Stonewall*, at the end of the 1960s homosexual sex was still illegal everywhere except Illinois. It was a crime punishable by castration in seven states. No laws—federal, state, or local—protected gay people from being denied jobs or housing. The fines levied against gays and lesbians for these transgressions were nothing compared to the financial hardships many homosexuals faced when they lost their jobs and/or spouses after their names and crimes were printed in the morning's newspapers. Tired of the public humiliation and social recrimination, and bolstered by bourgeoning underground networks, homosexuals began to organize themselves as a political constituency. Unfortunately, as queers began to take themselves seriously as a political entity, some individuals and groups found the gay life of Tiny Davis, Ruby Lucas, and Lisa Ben an obstacle to political enfranchisement.

In 1950 the Mattachine Society became one of the nation's first LGBT rights organizations, known as a homophile league—so named because newspapers would not print ads announcing gatherings or actions by people calling themselves homosexuals or gays, though publications such as the *Village Voice* and *Los Angeles Times* would print notices of homophile meetings and demonstrations. The Mattachine Society took its name from a secret society of masked revelers in medieval France that staged peasant revolts. Founder Harry Hay chose this moniker because he felt that "1950s gays were also a masked people, unknown and anonymous, who might become engaged in morale building and helping ourselves and others, through struggle to move toward total redress and change."[39] Gaiety was central to the founding mission of the Mattachine Society, but this would soon change. Many of the original members were communists, and they based their organization on the cellular structure of the Communist Party, complete with levels of membership and oaths of secrecy. The Red Scare and homosexual baiting of the McCarthy era precipitated a coup in which Hay and the society's leftist leaders were cast as ideological extremists and ousted, along with their ludic politics.

The Mattachine Society's turn away from gaiety resulted in a lack of imagination and creativity, as evidenced by the group's increasingly narrow political vision. The new leaders promoted integration and liberal reform rather than radical social change, focusing their energies almost exclusively on antidiscrimination legislation and the decriminalization of homosexuality. As the founders' dream of social revolution gave way to the goal of assimilation, the group's communist rhetoric and flamboyant tactics came to be seen as a hindrance to the attainment of civil rights, as they confirmed heterosexuals' fears and gave credence to stereotypical depictions of flaming faggots and angry dykes. The new focus would be on proving that same-sex desire was normal and that homosexuals were just like everyone else. By adopting a politics of respectability promoting the moral and material achievements of dignified, middle-class citizens, members hoped to demonstrate their normalcy and worthiness by distancing themselves from decadent and debauched characters like Hay.

It was the newly sober and conservative Mattachine Society that served as the model for the first lesbian rights organization, the Daughters of Bilitis, which was founded in 1955 by Del Martin and Phyllis Lyon.[40] The group published a newsletter called *The Ladder,* which filled the void left by Lisa

Ben's *Vice Versa*.[41] As the name of the periodical suggests, the emphasis was on progress and uplift, not gaiety or good times. *The Ladder's* "very establishment in the midst of witch-hunts and police harassment," notes historian Lillian Faderman, "was an act of courage, since members always had to fear that they were under attack, not because of what they did, but merely because of who they were."[42] Due to the risks publication entailed, many of the contributors used pseudonyms, including playwright Lorraine Hansberry, who signed her letters to the editor with the initials "L.H.N."[43] Not surprisingly, a shroud of secrecy permeated the meetings. Flavia Rondo, a member of GLF and Radicalesbians, recalls attending her first and only DOB meeting in New York in the late 1960s. Only three women were in attendance, and no one uttered the word *lesbian*.[44]

Shaped by complex, and at times contradictory, motives, ideologies, and objectives, homophile leagues sought to redefine the meaning of homosexuality, by disarticulating it from sexual deviance and social pathology, and to forcefully assert the role of queers in the shaping of American culture. By voicing the initial call for LGBT civil rights, homophile organizations made important contributions to sexual politics and paved the way for subsequent waves of activism. But they also set dangerous precedents by crafting policies and endorsing practices that circumscribed the movement. Believing that homosexuals would gain equality only by assimilating into mainstream society, homophile leagues required members to look and act straight. They mandated conformity to strict rules governing dress codes, social behavior, and gender norms. The DOB, for example, refused membership to "predatory butches."[45] The desire for social acceptance led homophiles to police themselves as forcefully, if not more so, than agents of the dominant culture did.

There were plenty of queers in the late 1950s and 1960s who had absolutely no desire to blend in or become part of the status quo, including: Tiny Davis; the Beat poets; the Black Mountain artists; playmakers at Caffe Cino, La MaMa E.T.C., Judson Poets' Theatre, and Play-house of the Ridiculous; Andy Warhol's Factory entourage; Jack Smith; José Sarria; Sylvia Rivera; Valerie Solanas; and Jill Johnston, to name only a few. In contrast to homophiles who pleaded for acceptance, these gender benders and nonconforming sexual outlaws staged outlandish acts of gaiety that served as potent and immensely pleasurable critiques of heteronormativity. Homophile leagues took the opposite approach, abstaining from public displays of gaiety in lieu of earnest and serious appeals for accommodation. These early activist organizations renounced gayness and gaiety as a precondition for citizenship. In casting the ludic as antithetical to the struggle for civil rights, homophile leagues inhibited impulses and legislated pleasures. Because Mattachine and DOB were so invested in assimilation, many historians cite the Stonewall uprising rather than the founding of homophile organizations as the origin of the modern gay and lesbian liberation movement.

Revelers, Rebels, and Rioters

Even the riots were a riot.
    —Jerry Hoose, GLF

Police and patrons alike were surprised during a routine raid of a mafia-run bar in Greenwich Village in the wee hours of June 28, 1969, when some of the clientele resisted arrest. In a spontaneous gesture of civil disobedience, the clients at the Stonewall Inn—which included lesbians, street hustlers, transexuals, and drag queens, a number of them queers of color—fought back against the police. Refusing to provide identification and failing to go quietly and obediently to the station to be processed, they unleashed years of pent-up rage at the injustices they had endured by attacking law enforcement officials. People smashed glasses, broke bottles, and threw chairs at the officers. Outside the Stonewall Inn, a crowd began to form. When the police exited the bar to place detainees into squad cars, they found themselves outnumbered. Surrounded by several hundred demonstrators who assailed them with coins, beer cans, and bricks from a nearby construction yard, the officers retreated and barricaded themselves inside the bar. Uprooting a parking meter, some of the demonstrators smashed through the plate glass window. As protesters seized the police, the officers drew their guns and threatened to shoot. Someone set the bar on fire, and within seconds the room was engulfed in flames. Reinforcements arrived and tried to reestablish order. The Tactical Police Force, donning full riot regalia, attempted to disperse the crowd.

In one of the greatest acts of gaiety in LGBT history, a group of queens responded to this show of force by staging an impromptu chorus line. Locking arms and kicking up their heels, they sang, "We are the Stonewall girls. We wear our hair in curls. We don't wear underwear. We show our pubic hair. We wear our dungarees above our nelly knees." Unable to counter this display of military might, homosexuals used the most effective weapon in their arsenal: gaiety. Satire and parody are disarming; they mock objects of reverence and authority, toppling them from their exalted position by rendering them absurd and ridiculous. Kicking and screaming, this chorus of queers' riotous laughter rendered the cops impotent if not pathetic. When disciplinary regimes go to such extremes—in this case tear gas and assault rifles—to show how obscene and revolting homosexuals are, often the only thing gays can do is show how ludicrous homophobia is.

The Stonewall uprising was a spontaneous but highly self-conscious performance event. Like all theatrical spectacles, acts of gaiety involve participants and observers. The spectators may be invited to join in the fun, as in the case of the Lavender Menace zap, or they may be the butt of the joke, as the police who raided the Stonewall Inn were. "For years I have heard people describe the event as angry and I suppose in a way it was," recalled the late playwright Doric Wilson.

> But that was not the main emotion I remember experiencing that night. I could never seem to find the right words. While filming the "American Experience" documentary it suddenly came clear to me. The first reaction that night was shock and then awe that we were coming out of the "twilight" and actually standing up to authority—fighting back. And what followed was a giddy and joyous glee. And somehow we knew nothing would ever be quite the same again.[46]

The rioting and revelry continued for several days and led to the formation of the Gay Liberation Front in early July. A short-lived but enormously influential umbrella organization comprised of seasoned civil rights activists, radical feminists, socialists, anarchists, and peace activists, GLF's mission statement read:

> We are a revolutionary group of men and women formed with the realization that complete sexual liberation for all people cannot come about unless existing social institutions are abolished. We reject society's attempt to impose sexual roles and definitions of our nature.[47]

The Gay Liberation Front was less interested in attaining social acceptance for homosexuals than it was in challenging the gendered and racist foundations of patriarchal society. "Gay liberation is a struggle against sexism," wrote GLF member Allen Young, against the "belief or practice that the sex or sexual orientation of human beings gives to some the right to certain privileges, powers, or roles, while denying to others their full potential. . . . The definition of sexism, as defined by women's liberation and gay liberation, presupposes a struggle against the main perpetrators of society—straight white men—and against the manifestations of sexism as they appear in all people."[48]

Part of a rainbow of identity movements that emerged in the 1960s and 1970s, GLF was the first political faction to take up the appellation "gay." Martha Shelley, a former president of the DOB's New York chapter and an active participant in the Student Homophile League (SHL), is credited with suggesting that the group add "Gay" to "Liberation Front," which members wanted to use to signal their allegiance with anti-imperialist struggles in Vietnam and Algeria.[49] Playing off the Black Panther slogan "Black is Beautiful," GLF proclaimed, "Gay is Good."[50] Countering the pathological portrait of same-sex attraction as sick and sinful, shameful and secretive, *gay* affirms homoerotic desire as healthy and happy. Some have argued that the term was attractive to activists because "*Gay* is simple and easy to say and free from the usual stigmas," which is to say that it employs "a language free from odium."[51] This line of reasoning seeks to occlude the etymology and checkered past of the word *gay* and is contradicted by the militant and oppositional politics of GLF.

The Gay Liberation Front was not for people who just happened to be gay. As Martha Shelley notes, "Other organizations were for people who wanted to join the mainstream, who thought the only thing wrong with American society is that they excluded gays." Members of GLF saw themselves as part of the counterculture, and they insisted on their difference from—not their similarity to—the rest of society. While members of the Mattachine Society wore suits and ties to demonstrations and DOB members donned dresses and heels to peacefully picket establishments, the Lavender Menace wore T-shirts and dungarees to guerrilla theater actions. These radicals staged aggressive, in-yer-face demonstrations to force public debates about homosexuality. Their media-savvy protest tactics pushed the gay agenda to the center stage of national politics.

While *gay* self-consciously connotes a positive affect, it also encodes a history of illicit and transgressive pleasure-seeking proclivities. The term acknowledges but seeks to transmute the mournful and melancholic aspects of a spoiled identity. As the antithesis of *straight, gay* carries with it a critique of bourgeois notions of decorum and respectability. To be gay is to be care-free, to be uninhibited by moral constraints, and to exhibit a disregard for conventions. The inverse of sobriety and seriousness, *gay* is frolicsome and fun-loving. Indicative of a devil-may-care attitude, *gay* worries less about the future repercussions than it does about present pleasures. It transforms what is lifeless, plain, and dull into something that is vibrant, vivacious, and festive. Animated and alive, sparkling and spirited, *gay* suggests an orienta-tion that is performative rather than static. Flashy and flamboyant, brilliant, and showy, *gay* can be as colorful as Gladys Bentley's Harlem cabaret act or as garish and gaudy as Ethyl Eichelberger's drag.

Playing as it does on and with the multiple registers of *gay*, the naming of GLF is itself an act of gaiety. To call oneself gay in 1969 was a defiant gesture and a bold expression of non-normative desires. More than a sexual identity, *gay* denoted a revolutionary attitude and a collective aspiration for a more just world. As Young wrote in *Out of the Closet: Voices of Gay Liberation* (1972), the groundbreaking anthology he edited with Radicalesbian Karla Jay, "Gay, in its most far-reaching sense, means not homosexual, but sexu-ally free."[52] Gay and lesbian liberationists argued that heterosexuality and homosexuality are artificial categories propagated by a sexist society, not fixed or immutable essences. In a more enlightened world, these radicals reasoned, the need for such nomenclature would disappear. Insisting that sexuality was much more fluid than existing structures allowed, they fought to transform the repressive sexual norms of American culture. "[I]n a free society," Young insisted, "everyone will be gay."[53]

Given the degree to which gay history has been occluded by queer stud-ies and given the degree to which *gay* has become attached to the name of certain conservative aspirations in the past two decades, with gay marriage and gays in the military dominating the gay agenda, it is easy to forget—especially for those too young to remember—that gay liberationists were vehemently opposed to such reformist measures. These activists were highly critical of the institution of matrimony and of the role US armed forces played in imperialist projects at home and abroad. The language of gay rights distorts the history of sexual politics in the twentieth century by disarticulating *gay* from its radical roots and cementing it to a series of neoliberal reforms, homonormative programs, and assimilationist aims. Members of GLF could not have imagined in 1969 that just a few decades later gays would consent, let alone volunteer, to fight an unjust war and that they would do so under the banner of equality. Nor could they have envisioned that radicals who once decried marriage as the root of patriarchal and capitalist oppression would demand their right to indentured servitude and government regulation of their intimate relationships—and that they would do so using the tenets of the 1950s homophile movement.

If GLF "hadn't exploded into existence," writes Martha Shelley in an essay titled "Our Passion Shook the World," "gays would still be pleading politely for acceptance, and the world would still be deaf to their pleas."[54] These activists "were hot and rude, joyous and angry, utopian and opinionated. 'Nuanced' wasn't part of our vocabulary," recalls Shelley. "Question authority? We didn't even recognize it!"[55] Emboldened by the feminist dictate that the personal is political, GLF activists transformed the process of coming out from a private act into a public event. They urged people to take part in the political performance of coming out and to stage it as an act of gaiety. *Come Out!* was the title of the group's newsletter, first published in November 1969. The inaugural edition of the periodical reads:

COME-OUT, A NEWSPAPER FOR THE HOMOSEXUAL COMMUNITY, dedicates itself to the joy, the humor, and the dignity of the homosexual male and female. COME-OUT has COME OUT to fight for the freedom of the homosexual and to give voice to the rapidly growing militancy within our community, and to provide a public forum for the discussions and clarification of methods and actions necessary to end our oppression. COME-OUT has COME OUT indeed for "life, liberty, and the pursuit of happiness."[56]

Liberationists saw coming out not as a panacea but as a radical act of gaiety that countered homosexual shame with gay pride. The idea was to come out and play. Ludic rites such as the Christopher Street Liberation Day March (later renamed Gay Pride) that GLF organized to commemorate the first anniversary of the Stonewall uprising served as a ribald retort to a homophobic society (it was actually a demonstration not a float-filled procession sponsored by corporate conglomerates seeking to cash in on a niche market as it is today). Gay pageants, protests, and performances served as ambient environs in which deviant subjects could fend off some of the bad feelings associated with being gay in a straight world.

From Gay Pride to Queer Shame

Chants of "Gay Power" became the battle cry for sexual liberation and coming out its paradigmatic expression. Pride has fueled the struggle for the decriminalization of homosexuality and the demand for legislation granting protection of civil liberties. It has been the impetus for the establishment of LGBT studies in universities and colleges, as well as the proliferation of gay art and cultural festivals, most of which take place during the month of June. Since 1969 the gay and lesbian movement has made incredible progress toward the goal of sexual liberation, resulting in unprecedented and, for many veteran activists, almost unimaginable political change. Despite the tremendous gains it has wrought, the concept of pride has engendered more than its fair share of discontent among sexual minorities, in part because its hard-won victories have not benefited all homosexuals equally. Reaping the greatest rewards are homoliberals, whose investment in normative social and economic structures leads them to reify rather than challenge the status quo. Seeking parity, equal access, and integration into the national fabric, homoliberals do little to problematize or expand the criteria for citizenship.

Over time the concept of pride has become disarticulated from gaiety. The desire for sexual minorities to see themselves accurately portrayed in the media and to control the means of their (self-)representation quickly turned into an imperative to put forward positive, and only positive, images of same-sex desire. This has led to the construction of constricted and confining scripts for virtually every aspect of homosexuality, from coming out to cruising, and to mandates that spokespeople for the movement be clean-cut, conventionally attractive, and respectable. In this way, pride has become complicit with social hierarchies of gender, race, class, ethnicity, and able-bodiedness in producing "proper" gay subjects at the expense of "improper" ones. Rather than offering an antidote to shame and self-loathing, the imperative of gay pride can compound these emotions by making queers feel that they are the source of their own unhappiness.

Along with the homoliberalization of sexual politics, the concept of pride has become increasingly commodified. A fatal attraction between advertisers and apolitical assimilationists has transformed the gay liberation movement into a gay free market economy. In the past forty years, the annual parade has become less a political act of gaiety and more a celebration of lifestyle and shopping habits. Whereas the Dyke March (first held in 1993 in conjunction with the March on Washington) refuses corporate sponsorship, the Pride Commission actively solicits donations and subsidies from companies seeking brand integration with a lucrative niche market. As the parade devolved into a carnival of consumption, the concept of pride came to be seen as both limited and elitist. People began to wonder: what political affects had been occluded or ignored in our fervent promotion of pride, and to what extent had the imperative to be out and proud repressed discussion of more controversial, less dignified aspects of sexuality?

A three-day international conference featuring almost fifty panelists was held at the University of Michigan in 2003 "to confront the shame that lesbians, gay men, and 'queers' of all sorts still experience in society; to explore the transformative impulses that spring from such experiences of shame; and to ask what affirmative uses can be made of these residual experiences of shame now that not all gay people are condemned to live in shame."[57] Events of various kinds commemorating gay shame have been staged across North America and Europe in subsequent years, including a series of events exploring political depression by a group of academics, activists, and artists associated with Feel Tank Chicago. On May Day, members of Feel Tank, clad in bathrobes and slippers, stand on street corners shaking Prozac bottles and holding signs that read "Depressed? It Might Be Political." The collective explores the potential for bad feelings such as shame, fear, apathy, anxiety, hopelessness, numbness, despair, and ambivalence to constitute and be constituted as forms of political resistance. These actions are a sharp contrast to the celebratory, feel-good displays of community and camaraderie that typically punctuate the month of June.

Dissatisfaction with the rhetoric of pride can be traced to the sex wars of the 1980s. Self-described "pro-sex feminists," many of whom were lesbians, reacted to the puritanical stance of antipornography feminists such as Catherine McKinnon and Andrea Dworkin by celebrating what are considered by many to be shameful sexual practices, including sadomasochism (S/M), bondage, and public sex. Susie Bright, Honey Lee Cottrell, Tee Corinne, Jewelle Gomez, Joan Nestle, and Pat Califia contributed to the inaugural issue of *On Our Backs: Entertainment for the Adventurous Lesbian* (1984), the first feminist erotica magazine and the first to feature dyke porn by and for dyke audiences. The title of the publication is a satirical jab at *off our backs* (aka, *oob*), the longest-running feminist newspaper in the United States, which served as a platform for the antipornography position. Lesbian feminists began producing adult videos, unionizing strip clubs like the Lusty Lady in San Francisco, and reclaiming the art of burlesque. The desire to counter the moralizing practices of antipornography activists prompted women in the 1980s to renew their commitment to gaiety.

The WOW Café, an off-off-Broadway performance space and social club, took root in New York's East Village in the midst of the sex wars and became a laboratory for the exploration of lesbian feminist gaiety. Opening just as Medusa's Revenge was closing shop, WOW Café produced some of the most audacious, sex-positive, feminist artists of the 1980s and 1990s, who titillated audiences with their hilarious and witty gender-bending productions.[58] Paradigmatic of the formal experimentation, political daring, and unbridled eroticism that inspired and sustains WOW to this day is the Split Britches collective, comprised of the working-class butch/femme dynamic duo of Peggy Shaw and Lois Weaver and the immensely talented writer/performer Deb Margolin, who is heterosexual. Split Britches lampoons sexual norms, social conventions, and coming-out narratives in plays such as *Upwardly Mobile Home, Little Women: The Tragedy,* and *Beauty and the Beast.* One of the group's best-known productions is the Obie Award–winning *Belle Reprieve,* a parody of Tennessee Williams's *Streetcar Named Desire,* which they created in collaboration with Bette Bourne and Paul Shaw (aka, Precious Pearl) of Bloolips, an anarchic drag troupe from London. Shaw and Bourne (who became radicalized though a cell of GLF) had worked together years earlier when both were members of the glam fab cabaret group Hot Peaches.

While on tour in Berlin in the late 1970s, Hot Peaches received a request from Spiderwoman, which was also performing there, asking to borrow some costumes, as the group's luggage had been lost in transit. When Weaver, who was part of the Spiderwoman collective, arrived to pick up the costumes, it was love at first sight for her and Shaw. Shaw left Peaches in hot pursuit of forbidden fruit. When she and Weaver returned to the States, they cohosted an international feminist theater festival in New York City. Seeking a permanent place for women's theater, the couple helped create the WOW Café, where Split Britches became a crowd favorite. It shared the stage with the likes of Alina Troyano, whose alter ego, Carmelita Tropicana, serves up Molotov cocktails of bons mots that give new meaning to *cuba libre;* Holly Hughes, an abstract painter-cum-performance artist who became notorious as one of the NEA Four; and the Five Lesbian Brothers, a collective of ballsy and brilliant women whose most recent collaboration serves as the concluding chapter in this study of gaiety.[59]

The Brothers banded together in 1989, one year before Queer Nation was formed in New York City by AIDS activists from ACT-UP. The AIDS epidemic cut short the utopian moment of gay liberation and reinforced the perception of homosexuals as degenerate and diseased. A paranoid and melancholic response to the crisis seemed much more appropriate to a threat of this magnitude than the cheery optimism inherent in the rhetoric of gay pride. As the disease spread, and the government demonstrated little more than apathy for the cause, acts of gaiety gave way to gestures of grief and mourning. This is not to suggest that gaiety was absent from or inimical to queer politics. Activists continued to stage ludic forms of protest, including zap actions, but these tended toward dark play and macabre rituals as a way to explore the complex relationships between pleasure and pain, sex and death.[60] At the same time, however, an increasingly vocal contingent of artists and activists, spearheaded by folks like Andrew Sullivan, a writer for and later editor of the *New Republic,* and ACT-UP cofounder Larry Kramer, fueled the sex panic by arguing that homosexuals were (or should be) more invested in monogamy than in having casual intercourse. Sullivan's *Virtually Normal* called for the legal recognition and social normalization of gays and lesbians, particularly through marriage. Similarly, in Kramer's deeply affecting AIDS drama *The Normal Heart,* the protagonist Ned Weeks urges gay men to "fight for the right to get married instead of the right to legitimize promiscuity."[61] Although a number of queer theorists sought to counter these critiques by outlining "the trouble with normal," the more conservative voices prevailed in redirecting the queer agenda toward a pragmatic, integrationist program of homoliberalism.[62] This is perhaps best evidenced by the fact that two recent award-winning revivals of *The Normal Heart,* one off-Broadway (at the Public Theater in 2004) and one on Broadway (at the Golden Theater in 2011) did little to foment political outrage about the persistence of AIDS or its transformation into a global phenomenon but succeeded in generating considerable amounts of money and support for same-sex marriage referendums.

Gaily Forward: Toward a Retro-Activist Future

For decades, queer theorists have prided themselves on being at the cutting edge of scholarship, and they have valorized the avant-garde in aesthetics, politics, and other forms of culture work. In retrospect, we can see how this posturing has contributed to a fetishization of evolution, advancement, and forward motion. In recent years, *queer* has become increasingly disconnected from both its critical potential and its radical aspirations. The term has come to denote a more narrowly defined sense of sexual identity, one that advances the economic interests of corporate conglomerates and the nation-state through the promotion of cultural hegemony and liberal norms of social inclusion. Today, *queer* and *nationality* no longer strike us paradoxical terms, antithetical propositions, or an ironic and parodic mode of dissent. What we thought thirty years ago was a fluid formula of antinormativity turned out to be, with a few modifications and misapplications, a recipe for the conservative and profoundly antidemocratic assimilationist project of homoliberalism.

There is no way of knowing what will be the most radical, innovative, or progressive *avant la lettre,* just as there is no way of predicting or orchestrating, with any degree of accuracy, the afterlife of sexual experiments. Oftentimes our best shot at thinking outside the box is not by privileging the vanguard but by enlisting those seemingly passé, obsolete, and useless formations deemed to be at the rear guard. *Acts of Gaiety* is organized around what many might consider a retrogressive repertoire of corporeal gestures and civic performances. My interest in seemingly outmoded acts of gaiety exemplifies what Lucas Hildebrand calls retroactivism, a form of political and affective regeneration that seeks to resuscitate the dissident dreams of the past. Valerie Solanas's man-hating manifesto, the antifamily rhetoric of WITCH protests, the separatist screeds of lesbian nationalists, and Hothead Paisan's matriarchal machinations appear to us today as "revolting," but not necessarily in the hilarious and politically offensive ways their creators originally intended. Why attempt to resurrect such cringe-worthy performances in order to reanimate a disavowed structure of feeling? The answer is that this mode of archivalism sheds light on how our construction of the past dictates political and performative possibilities in the present.

Plumbing neglected archives and seemingly antiquated practices, *Acts of Gaiety* places discarded and discredited histories of lesbian art and activism into meaningful and transformative relations with the present in order to make the conservative, hegemonic narratives of homoliberalism seem alien and unfamiliar and to elucidate different modalities for public and political life. Underwriting *Acts of Gaiety* is the notion that a Fabian strategy comprised of dilatory dyke tactics may be our best hope for countering the forces of homoliberalism. An obdurate, unyielding, and dogged attachment to outmoded ideals and aspirations is a cornerstone of lesbian feminism and of my critical methodology as well. I term this approach a degenerate diacritics, by which I mean a mode of scholarly engagement that concerns sexual deviates and reverts to an earlier stage of culture, development, or evolution in order to put the past in "touch" with the present so as to re-imagine the future.[63] In suggesting that we alter course and proceed astern, I am in no way advocating a retreat from the public sphere or calling for a return to identity politics. As Heather Love has suggested, a stubborn insistence on "backward feelings" is a feature of even the most forward-reaching lesbian feminist cultural productions.[64] While my book promotes "feeling backward" as a way to reenter a prior historical moment and circumvent the seemingly relentless forward march of homoliberalism, it resists the melancholic urge to "dwell at length on the 'dark side'" of queer life, as Love's eloquent elegy to queer history does.[65]

In its affirmation of the role of pleasure, as well as pain, in shaping the way subjects come to understand themselves and remake the circumstances in which they find themselves, *Acts of Gaiety* is sympathetic with Elizabeth Freeman's theory of temporal drag, a tantalizing neologism describing "the gravitational pull that 'lesbian,' and even more so 'lesbian feminist,' sometimes seems to exert on 'queer.'"[66] Attention to the temporal drag of dyke aesthetics reminds us that *revolution* refers to a *new* movement instigated by an insurrection but also to a circuit that is *renewed* by a force turning back on itself. Emphasizing the dual meaning of this word acknowledges the nostalgic demands of a retroactive lesbian feminism by directing our focus to the lost possibilities and unfinished business of this still potent program for social justice.

I refer to the archives that I draw on as "acts of gaiety," and each of the five chapters that follow offers an extended meditation on drama queens, jesters, guerrilla activists, and terrorists who challenge our presumptions about how much progress we have made since the lesbian and gay liberation movement began, in what directions, and at what costs. These case studies blend archival research, performance ethnographies, and close readings of texts and productions. Because the actors, objects, and events that concern me here have been so poorly documented, so systematically ignored, or so grossly misunderstood by both their peers and subsequent generations of scholars and activists, I have opted to dwell on individual acts of gaiety in specific moments of LGBT history, offering thick descriptions of a relatively small number of characters and events. This approach responds to the need for more nuanced and sustained interpretations of lesbian performance, art, and politics, and it addresses the dearth of theoretical formulations for interpreting the cultural productions and critical legacies of a pivotal period in LGBT studies.

Chapter one, "'Scummy' Acts: Valerie Solanas's Theater of the Ludicrous," offers the first documentation of the previously undiscovered publication and production history of the most provocative and profoundly seditious lesbian dramaturge in the history of pre-Stonewall American performance. Better known as the attempted assassin of Andy Warhol than as a pioneering playwright, Solanas has been denied the recognition she deserves as the preeminent lesbian feminist dramatist of the sexual revolution. Her experimental comedies bear a striking resemblance to the work of gay male playmakers and performance artists of the bourgeoning off-off-Broadway movement, but they are unique in their depiction of lesbian sexuality and nothing short of pioneering in their articulation of a feminist consciousness. Solanas's militant tone and scabrous humor were so beyond the pale that her plays scandalized theater patricians, counterculture radicals, and pornographers alike.

My focus here is on Solanas's landmark 1965 play *Up Your Ass,* an uproarious and electrifying parody of heterosexuality, gender norms, race relations, and the misogyny of queer countercultures. Gaiety functions as a structuring principle in the scummy world of queer street culture where the play is set. The multiethnic cast of *Up Your Ass,* which features a Hispanic butch dyke protagonist and black drag queen prostitutes, exposes the prerogatives and fantasies of white, middle-class liberals. When Solanas could not fight her way into the art world, she set about to make her own scene. Unable to find a home for her play, she began to create happenings, which she called "SCUMMY things." I demonstrate here that she not only intended *SCUM Manifesto* as a "SCUMMY thing," but she developed the "script" in and through performances around New York and San Francisco in 1967 and 1968. This perpetually homeless, hooker dyke self-produced, in obscure venues for a handful of people, lesbian feminist performances that for decades would be virtually unimaginable, even in the most forward-looking artistic circles.

It was in defense of Valerie Solanas, after she shot Warhol, that Ti-Grace Atkinson, president of the New York chapter of NOW, coined the term *radical feminism.* Solanas's *SCUM Manifesto* had a profound effect on Atkinson's political theory and activism, including highly theatrical antimarriage protests she conducted with The Feminists. Chapter two, "Guerrilla Acts: Marriage Protests, 1969 and 2009," juxtaposes zap actions protesting the institution of matrimony by lesbian feminists with demonstrations staged by supporters of same-sex unions after the passage of California's Proposition 8. This pairing shows how zaps, true to their name, can either incite or eviscerate debate on a given topic. More important, it sheds light on the ways in which marriagists transformed the fortieth anniversary of the Stonewall uprising, which took place just a few months after the Prop 8 vote, into a public enactment of forgetting, one that redefined gay liberation to make it consistent with a homoliberal agenda. My mission here is to reveal how LGBT historical memory is being politicized through antiludic public performances that produce amnesiac scenes of assimilation.

Chapter three, "Expatriate Acts: Jill Johnston's Joker Citizenship," looks at sapphic spectacles of anarchic civil disobedience staged by America's first shameless public lesbian. Best known for her book *Lesbian Nation: The Feminist Solution* (1973), a collection of essays credited with sparking the separatist movement, Johnston is a progenitor of what I am calling joker citizenship, a mirthful and militantly erotic mode of insurrection and communion that recasts patriotism as a desire to reterritorialize the nation as a site of pleasure. Taking seriously Johnston's insistence that the revolution should be fun or we should forget it, I argue that her unique mode of political dissent makes manifest the performative force of the ludic in lesbian nationalism and theatricalizes a structure of feeling I term national gaiety. I am most interested in how gestures of joker citizenship create an occasion and opportunity for sexual agency and how they enable subaltern subjects to imagine new forms of public and political life that counter assimilationist forms of homonormative polity.

The spirit, if not the actual practice, of lesbian nationalism, persists in a variety of forms in a number of dyke subcultures and is a guiding force behind a genre of artistic production I call the lesbian comedy of terrors. A revenge fantasy featuring vigilante heroines, scenes of graphic violence, and dark humor, the lesbian comedy of terrors exploits for humorous effect the compulsory rites and rituals of hetero- and homonormativity. Although most radical lesbians decry the use of violence to combat violence, this does not stop them from dreaming about mutiny or dramatizing fictional scenarios of sedition. Chapter four, "Terrorist Acts: The Maladapted *Hothead Paisan,* a Lesbian Comedy of Terrors," looks at a paradigmatic example of this genre, Diane DiMassa's zine *Hothead Paisan: Homicidal Lesbian Terrorist,* and a musical theater adaptation of this work by Riot Grrrl Animal Prufrock that was staged at the Michigan Womyn's Music Festival in 2004. I show that archaic structures of feeling and disavowed histories can serve as vital components of a radical agenda or, in the case of this musical, as unwitting conduits for homoliberalism. Contrasting two related but distinct enactments of lesbian gaiety, I challenge commonplace assumptions about which modes of art and activism constitute the most potent forms of resistance to gay normalization by troubling the deeply ingrained notion that culture workers who position themselves at the vanguard (as opposed to the rear guard) of social movements actually forge the more forceful and sustained interventions in national political life. This case study explores what Hothead's unique brand of retroactivism has to teach us about queers' complicity in the War on Terror.

The final chapter, "Unnatural Acts: The Tragic Consequences of Queer Homoliberalism in the Five Lesbian Brothers' *Oedipus at Palm Springs*," examines the personal and political costs of an LGBT movement that turns its back on gaiety. The Five Lesbian Brothers collectively author and stage outlandish experimental performances rooted in the parodic inversion of genres, cultural norms, and audience expectations. The troupe surprised audiences in 2005 when, after a lengthy hiatus, it returned with a work that is generically speaking a realist tragedy, but one that, I suggest, is best understood as what Freud called a cynical tendentious joke. This bourgeois, lesbian-themed *Oedipus* offers audiences a surprisingly normative worldview not to endorse the conservative political position it depicts but to challenge it. The Brothers play it "straight" with this play not because they have gone straight but because the gay and lesbian community has, and much to its own peril. This tragedy serves as a parable of the ruinous effects of homonormativity and a nuanced critique of the disastrous implications of homoliberalism. As such it constitutes a fitting conclusion to *Acts of Gaiety*, which dramatizes how in our quest for legitimization we homosexuals have come to take ourselves too seriously.

Acts of Gaiety peruses performances and protests by artists, activists, and collectives whose fiercely funny modes of social engagement pack the affective torque to counter the conservative yaw of homoliberalism. The works of these performance artists, playmakers, and political dissidents register as echoes of archaic dreams of revolution, and they make painfully clear the poverty of our current tactics and taxonomies for sexual expression. My hope is that the exploits of these backward-looking, visionary dykes can inspire us to retard the progress of the current homosexual agenda and to move instead gaily forward.

1

"Scummy" Acts
Valerie Solanas's Theater of the Ludicrous

> Humor is not a body of logical statements which can be refuted
> or proved, but is rather a quality which appeals to a sense of [the]
> ludicrous.
>
> —Valerie Solanas, *The Diamondback* (1957)

On May 10, 1965, a twenty-nine-year-old aspiring dramatist named Valerie
Jean Solanas registered an unpublished one-act play with the US Copyright
Office. Solanas called her satirical comedy *Up Your Ass*, but the official title
listed on her application is *From the Cradle to the Boat, or Up from the Slime.*
"[J]ust in case the play should ever become a Broadway smash hit," the
doggedly optimistic Solanas reasoned, "at least there would be something
acceptable to put on the theater marquee."[1] Indicative, in many ways, of
the theatrical experimentation and countercultural expressions taking root
during the mid-1960s, Solanas's script is unique in its depiction of lesbian
sexuality and nothing short of pioneering in its articulation of a feminist
consciousness. Remarkable for its explicit portrayal of female desire, sexual
subcultures, and urban street life, *Up Your Ass* chronicles the exploits of
Bongi Perez, a self-described "vivacious, dynamic, single . . . queer," who
cruises "real low-down funky broads, nasty bitchy hotshots."[2] The protagonist, like the play's author, is a wiseass butch dyke of Hispanic descent (Solanas's paternal grandparents immigrated to the United States from Spain)
who hustles for a living, panhandling and prostituting. This drama features
a multiracial cast of dueling drag queens, beatnik hipsters, hapless johns, a
feces-obsessed femme fatale, and a housewife-cum-homicidal lesbian terrorist. Homosexuality is a given rather than a problem to be addressed, and
degeneracy is redefined as a "scummy" virtue, which enables social devi-

ants and sexual minorities to escape a diseased patriarchal society. Solanas's licentious humor and risqué characters were so beyond the pale that her play scandalized avant-gardists, political radicals, and pornographers alike. Despite trying every avenue imaginable, she could find no one willing to publish or stage the script during her lifetime.

Written prior to the sexual revolution and the Stonewall rebellion, *Up Your Ass* offers a riotous and uproarious parody of heteronormativity, racial stereotypes, and gender roles. It is acknowledged here as one of the earliest, most provocative, and profoundly seditious lesbian feminist plays in the history of American drama. This work has been denied the critical attention it deserves for several reasons: the script was believed, until very recently, to have been lost; the play has been overshadowed by the author's later and better-known work, *SCUM Manifesto* (1967); and any consideration of Solanas's innovation or artistry has been eclipsed by her attempted assassination of Andy Warhol. In 2010 I discovered Solanas's copyright application (the first of three she would file in as many years to protect this and subsequent works) along with the original manuscript of *From the Cradle to the Boat*, which has languished in the Library of Congress for over four decades. My research has led to a series of startling revelations that not only recast the social drama of the 1960s but also urge us to recalibrate the models and methods we have used to construct the artistic and political legacies of this volatile period in America's past. In this, the first comprehensive critical analysis of Solanas's dramaturgy, I track the creation, "loss," and recovery of this extraordinary play, as well as its influence on a genre the author invented called a "SCUMMY thing," a guerrilla theater event that is best understood as a kind of gutter dyke "happening" or "situation." Archival evidence confirms that Solanas considered *SCUM Manifesto* to be a script for a "SCUMMY thing" and that she was in negotiations with Warhol to produce and film one at the time of the shooting. Through close readings of these performative texts and a careful charting of their social and cultural contexts, I delineate the tenets of an aesthetic of gaiety I term Solanas's Theater of the Ludicrous.

"Up from the Slime"

Much of what is written about Valerie Solanas is based on hearsay and half-truths. Like most outlaws, her identity is cloaked in myth and legend. For someone who played such a prominent part in the social drama of the 1960s, and who frequented one of the most obsessively documented sites in the twentieth century, Warhol's Factory, Solanas remains surprisingly, if not conveniently, anonymous.[3] The paucity of data and ambiguity of evidence only contribute to her lore. With so little information about her, we are free to make of this woman what we will: predator, prey, casualty, survivor, whore, man-hating menace, filthy dyke, paranoid schizophrenic, militant radical, misunderstood genius, diabolical anarchist, homicidal maniac. Some cast Solanas as the hero of an epic tragedy; others depict her life as a melodrama, painting her as the victim of oppressive social forces. My narrative tends toward farce. It explores the absurd situations in which Solanas found herself and marvels at the ingenuity, creativity, and fortitude she had to muster to play the hand she was dealt.

Solanas was nothing if not a card. Born April 9, 1936, she grew up on the Boardwalk in south Jersey, where she developed her talents as a grifter, a gabber, and a good old-fashioned working girl. Her maternal grandfather, with whom Solanas spent a great deal of time as a child, inspired her thespian proclivities with stories of working in burlesque, where he and a partner had a song, dance, and comedy routine.[4] What Solanas lacked in formal training in the theater (she had none), she made up for in raw talent, unbridled determination, and the fact that she had been performing her entire life. She cultivated her talents and developed her aesthetic sensibilities as survival skills that enabled her to make it through the 1950s and 1960s as a woman, a queer, and an aspiring artist. Long before she mastered the art of peddling conversation, hustling johns, or wheedling her way into Warhol's films, Solanas learned about the magic power of "as if." She was introduced to this technique by her father, Louis Joseph Florent Solanas, a charismatic alcoholic with a violent temper and pedophilic tendencies. Acting in the high-stakes drama of childhood sexual abuse, Solanas improvised characters with the urgency and efficiency of someone whose life depended on the part she was playing. She learned at an early age that one must, in the words of Jon McKenzie, "Perform or Else," do or die.[5]

Valerie was by all accounts a wild child, and her problems escalated after her mother, Dorothy Marie Biondo, a blonde bombshell with the visage of Lana Turner, divorced Louis, relocated the family to Maryland, and married Frank "Red" Moran. Solanas was expelled from Catholic school for hitting a nun, and by the age of twelve she was running away on a regular basis, hitchhiking all the way to her aunt's house in Baltimore. She was thought to be a lesbian by members of her extended family, though no one talked openly about Valerie's sexuality, not even when she got pregnant in high school. Solanas's younger sister Judith recalls, "I was told that Valerie had a baby, he was adopted by a 'decent' family and there was to be no more discussion about it. . . . I doubt if anyone cared about Valerie's feelings."[6] After the baby was born in 1953, Solanas and her son lived with the Blackwells, a high-ranking military family whose teenage son served in the Korean War with the sailor alleged to be the baby's father.[7] In spite of these events, she completed high school on time, with the class of 1954. The caption underneath Solanas's senior portrait in the Oxon Hill yearbook reads, "Val. Brainpower and a lot of spirit."[8] The Blackwells paid for Solanas to attend the University of Maryland, and after she went away to school, she never saw her son again.

What others saw as mistakes, moral failures, and character flaws, Solanas saw as resources. She cultivated a raw and rapacious sense of humor from the material conditions in which she lived and labored. Throughout her life, Solanas subsisted on very little, but her resourcefulness is evident in her determination to get an education and later to publish and produce her artwork. In college, she majored in psychology. She worked in an animal lab testing the conditions under which rats would learn to avoid electric shock. These clinical trials would inform Solanas's theories of biological determinism and fuel her belief that males are genetically inferior, the result of a chromosomal deficiency. When she was not in the lab, Solanas hosted a call-in radio program where she posed as a therapist offering advice. She wrote letters to the editor of the campus paper, *The Diamondback,* where her public tirades against men, marriage, and middle-class values earned her the nickname "Maryland's own little suffragette."[9] In 1958 Solanas graduated with honors (with a 4.4 grade point average) and was inducted into Psi Chi, the psychology honor society. That fall she enrolled in a PhD program at the University of Minnesota, but finding the course of study unbearably sexist, she left within the year. "The purpose of 'higher' education is not to educate," she concluded, "but to exclude as many as possible from the various professions."[10] Years before the women's liberation movement, Solanas identified the link between economic injustice and systemic misogyny.

Valerie thumbed rides from Minneapolis to San Francisco's Bay Area, where she encountered a bourgeoning counterculture, one characterized by free speech and free love, artistic experimentation, and political radicalism. It was in the Bay Area that she perfected a gay way to earn a living that satisfied her philosophical objection to capitalist exploitation and her desire to spend as much time as possible writing. In an article titled "A Young Girl's Primer on How to Attain the Leisure Class," published in *Cavalier* magazine in 1966 (as "For 2¢: Pain, the Survival Game Gets Pretty Ugly") Solanas explains her ingenious economic strategy.[11]

> Being fresh out of college I found myself in a typically feminine dilemma of carving out for myself in a male world a way of life appropriate to a young girl of taste, cultivation, and sensitivity. There must be nothing crass—like work. However, a girl must survive. So, after a cool appraisal of the social scene, I finally hit upon an excellent-paying occupation, challenging to the ingenuity, dealing on one's own terms with people and affording independence, flexible hours, great stability, and most important, a large amount of leisure time, an occupation highly appropriate to female sensibilities. I contemplate my good fortune as I begin work for the day:
> "Pardon me, Sir, do you have fifteen cents?"
> "Sure, Sweetie, here." It's my wild body—it gets them almost every time.
> "Pardon me, Sir, do you have fifteen cents?"
> "No."
> "You got a dime?" You gotta keep bugging them.
> "No."
> "Nickel?"
> "NO!"
> "Dollar bill?" Think big.
> "Here, here's a quarter."
> Adds up fast. Four-fifty an hour. Two hours and I can knock off and write.[12]

Panhandling, supplemented by the art of shoplifting, provided this budding anarchist with rent and food. Blessed with the gift of oracular spontaneity and a penchant for scatological rhetoric, Solanas specialized in selling conversation, an hour's worth for six dollars.

> "Pardon me sir, do you have fifteen cents. . . . ?"
> "What do I get for fifteen cents?"
> "How 'bout a dirty word?"
> "That's not a bad buy. Okay, here. Now give me my word."
> "Men."[13]

Occasionally these dirty words would lead to dirty deeds: a quickie in the alley, a tumble in the sheets, or a three way with her friend Mary Lou, which was a big score: up to twenty-five dollars and three days off to write.

"A Young Girl's Primer" evokes and embodies the labor of hustling, pimping, and performing in vividly material ways. Part male titillation and part pedagogical performance, this essay, rendered in the form of a dramatic monologue, educates female readers (and there were many who enjoyed erotica, even then) about the problems and pleasures of being a woman and a lesbian in a straight man's world. While not exactly the stuff of agitprop, this performative essay tempts women with the promise of a better, more fulfilling life as an out lesbian, greater opportunities for career advancement, and significantly more leisure time. If it romanticizes life on the streets and the benefits of working in the informal economy by downplaying the dangers associated with panhandling and prostitution, especially for working girls without a pimp, it also minimizes moral objections to sex work, a woman's right to self-determination, and queer forms of intimacy. Indeed, this "excellent-paying occupation" provided Solanas with ample time and resources—not to mention colorful content—with which to complete her first play script, *Up Your Ass.*

"I'm so female I'm subversive"

Solanas produced a small but revolutionary body of autobiographical work that was born out of and intimately linked to the history of her flesh. Her scripts inaugurate a critical lexicon and a performative lens through which she staged both private and public permutations of class, gender, sex, and sexuality. Solanas's plays are meditation on the ways in which socioeconomic conditions shape women's lives and how the realities of our material existence shape us as subjects. She engaged the labor of theater to embody and valorize women's work. *Up Your Ass,* like "A Young Girl's Primer," salutes the ingenuity and inventiveness of rogues, rebels, and renegades who subvert the dominant culture at every juncture, repurposing its effects to their own ends, so that others might live, love, and laugh with a greater sense of freedom than they might otherwise be allowed.

This play begins with what may be the best, and possibly the most hilarious, dedication to women's labor and creativity in American literary history. It reads:

I dedicate this play to
ME
a continuous source of strength and guidance,
and without whose unflinching loyalty, devotion
and faith, this play could never have been written.

additional acknowledgements:
Myself—for proofreading, editorial comment,
helpful hints, criticism and suggestions
and an exquisite job of typing.
I—for independent research into men, married
women and other degenerates[14]

The dedication's parodic structure, heroicomical posturing, sardonic wit, and overt feminist sensibility are key elements of Solanas's dramaturgy, and they form the cornerstones of what I am calling her Theater of the Ludicrous. Indicative of this genre is self-conscious formal experimentation; explicit eroticism that pushes the accepted boundaries of middle-class sexual norms; a pronounced anticapitalist critique; a profound engagement with European philosophy, especially existentialism, nihilism, and absurdism; the employment of a wry, irreverent, and satirical tone; and, finally, a penchant for wordplay, scatological speech, and linguistic innovation.

Up Your Ass eschews a linear plotline, and the action unfolds in a series of episodic, interrelated comic vignettes that become increasingly disturbing as the play progresses. Every scene takes place in a realistic locale, but they all involve actions and events that are so preposterous, shocking, and/or violent that they transform what are seemingly neutral or safe spaces— the steps of an apartment building, an expensive restaurant, a classroom, and a playground—into defamiliarized zones that serve as vehicles for social critique. The outrageous antics depicted in the play call for a broad acting style that defies naturalistic conventions. The humor in *Up Your Ass* alternates among corny, caustic, and campy. This play exudes the kind of scummy brilliance that radiates from glamazons of the gutter—hookers, grifters, and transvestites—who engage in battles of wit with members of the ruling class, breeders, and proponents of "great art."

The play opens with the protagonist, Bongi Perez, a cross between Beebo Brinker and Joe Orton. She is "dressed in khaki pants, a loud plaid sports jacket and tennis shoes" loitering on the steps of the apartment where she lives.[15] "Hell'o Beautiful," Bongi calls out to a woman passing by. When the broad ignores her, Bongi shouts after her, "Stuck-up bitch."[16] As is evidenced by the central character's attire and her first line of dialogue, Bongi is a dyke, and an aggressive one at that. She does not "come out"; she is openly and unapologetically queer from the word go. Bongi flirts with a second woman who wanders by, and then a third. "Give me a kiss," she tells this one, "and I'll let you pass." After yanking the broad's chain, and mocking her boyfriend to his face, Bongi declares, "[S]he's not really my type" and lets the scared straight couple go about their business.[17]

Bongi is Solanas's alter ego, and she dramatizes, in delicious detail, how the author withstood the indignities and injustices of being female and queer in Cold War America: with humor, irony, intelligence, and wit. Solanas took tremendous pleasure in exploiting the complex gendered contradictions of the 1950s and 1960s. Rather than accept received biological "truths" and cultural dictates, she rewrote the scripts about what it means to be a woman, a lesbian, and an artist. Like Bongi, Solanas presented as a butch dyke who made no effort to pass as straight. On the contrary, she costumed herself in such a way as to draw attention to her gender transgression. Her uniform, which consisted of a jaunty sailor's cap, navy peacoat, and blue jeans, served as a sartorial index of her alterity and a challenge to normative codes of comportment. Solanas performed her daily life as a gender outlaw at a time when enactments of what Judith Halberstam calls "female masculinity" were seen as not only monstrous but sufficient cause for arrest and forced hospitalization.[18] Solanas's performance as a masculine woman and an out dyke provided an arresting, if not terrifying, alternative to traditional gender norms.

Rather than rejecting her female body, as many butches at that time did, Solanas understood, validated, and harnessed its erotic power. She made her living from the art of seduction through sex work, a profession rooted in illusion and gender play. The gritty streets of Berkeley, and later New York's East Village, provided some of the only spaces in which women, not to mention lesbians, could engage in gender subversion. There was no theater scene for lesbians then, and dyke bars permitted only specific, circumscribed, and highly codified enactments of gender transgression. Solanas was known, on special occasions or at the request of a client, to sport a dress, high heels, even lipstick. Far from the idealized image of the brooding, melancholic butch that made femmes like Joan Nestle swoon, Solanas was gregarious, gay, and very public in her flagrant disregard for both hetero- and homosexual conventions. The enactment of such a complex nonconforming character is something we typically associate with the performance art of Peggy Shaw and Holly Hughes at the WOW Café in the 1980s or with drag kings like D.R.E.D. and Mo B. Dick in the 1990s, but Solanas perfected the art of gender subversion decades earlier.

As Bongi blatantly cruises chicks, two men, one black and one white, who have been watching the show from across the street join in on the action. Spade Cat tries to pick up Bongi. When she playfully rebuffs his advances, he and White Cat enter into a competition to see who can score a chick first. Undone by his tired pick-up lines and lack of finesse, White Cat exclaims, "I may as well turn in my yo-yo; all the swinging chicks're either queer or they go with spades. A white man doesn't have a chance nowadays. What're we stuck with? All the fish."[19] As White Cat exits, a well-dressed, middle-aged man walks by, discreetly eyeing Bongi. "Hey, Joe," she asks, affecting a Spanish accent, "you like to meet my seester?" The john, named Alvin Koontz, fancies himself a "connoisseur of fine living."[20] He reads all of the "zestful men's magazines—<u>Tee-Hee</u>, <u>Giggle</u>, <u>Titter</u>, <u>Lust</u>, <u>Drool</u>, <u>Slobber</u> . . . and <u>Lech</u>," which he keeps next to his revolving bed, the kind, he boasts to Bongi, that "they feature in <u>Playboy</u>."[21] Although he claims that he's so dynamite in the sack that women typically pay him for sex, Koontz tells Bongi he's willing to spend a few dollars to let her have the opportunity of seeing him in action. When he asks her the price tag for an experience that she will never forget, Bongi replies:

> Well, for fifty bucks you get five minutes with a three-quarter minute intermission. For an additional ten bucks I sneer, curse and talk dirty. Then there's my hundred dollar special, in which, clothed only in a driving helmet and storm trooper boots, I come charging in, shrieking filthy songs at the top of my lungs.[22]

When Koontz balks at the price, Bongi offers him the bargain special of twenty-five bucks and assures him that she'll do almost anything that is not repulsive, like "kiss men."[23] Bongi tricks Koontz out of dinner at the fancy restaurant next door. Over their meal, she tells salacious stories about previous tricks and performs a number of lewd dances that get her john so horny that he settles for quick hand job in the alley.

Up Your Ass explores the material reality of lives lived under particular conditions and in extreme, sometimes fantastical, situations. The play is redolent with the hunger and desperation that attends abject poverty, yet Solanas's tone is humorous and the action is interrupted, in a Brechtian sense, by song, dance, and acts of vaudevillian shtick. Over the course of this episodic drama, Bongi emerges as a picaresque hero, a charismatic rogue of low social standing and questionable ethics who chooses to live by her wits rather than "honorable" work. Picaresque literature is a highly theatrical genre, originating in Spain in the sixteenth century, in which play functions as a means of survival and empowerment that enables characters to circumvent the pathos of lives lived on the margins. An itinerate drifter, the picara wanders among people from all walks of life, exposing and ridiculing the hypocrisy and corruption of different castes, including her own. Unrestrained by prevailing moral codes, the picara lies, cheats, and steals her way in and out of situations, often barely escaping punishment. As a picaresque drama, Solanas's *Up Your Ass,* serves as an ironic and satirical comedy of manners, but it also offers audiences rich and detailed portraits of people from social, racial, and sexual subcultures rarely seen on stage, even today.

After Koontz ambles dejectedly down the street, Bongi resumes her seat on the steps of the apartment, waiting for her next adventure. "Miss Collins," she shouts to a "made-up, bitchy-looking drag queen" sashaying down the street.[24] The two greet each other warmly, sharing physical affection and complimenting each other on their looks. Their gab session is interrupted by another drag queen named Scheherazade, Miss Collins's nemesis. "Oh, Gawd. She is without a doubt, the most garish, tasteless faggot I've ever run across. I'm ashamed to be seen with her. Look at her—1965 and she's wearing wedgies."[25] Bongi and Scheherazade exchange greetings. Although she clearly likes both queens, Bongi, the consummate trickster, cannot resist the opportunity to cause some mayhem. She instigates a little drama by praising Scheherazade's physique. You've got a fine ass, she tells the belle, you've "got an ass just like a girl."[26] Jealous, Miss Collins fishes for a little flattery. When Bongi tells her, "You are very pretty, for a boy," she seethes with rage. This fuels a heated debate about whether drag queens are men or women.[27] "I AM a piece of pussy," insists Scheherazade. "That's just what I've always said," retorts Miss Collins, "you have a face like a twat. Twat Face! Twat Face." "Oooooo," fumes Scheherazade, "I despise faggots." "I despise men," Miss Collins interjects. "Oh, why do I have to be one of them? Do you know what I'd like to be? A Lesbian. Then I could be the cake and eat it too."[28] As the two queens continue reading each another, Scheherazade hits Miss Collins with her purse, which begins a game of pushing each other down the street and offstage.

The quotidian endeavors dramatized in *Up Your Ass*—trash-talking, hustling, and cruising—are more than ritualized behaviors designed to pass the time; they are acts of survival and resistance. Bongi is not simply a homeless person; she is part of the very fabric of her neighborhood, intimately connected to the stoop on which she sits, the sidewalk she paces, and the alley where she turns tricks. Bongi makes things happen—her words have an impact, and her gestures have consequences. She commandeers public space, discomforts middle-class heterosexuals, and topples sex and gender hierarchies. She lives and works on the street, which serves as the locus, indeed the heartbeat, of this queer community.

As the drag queens exit the stage, a young woman named Ginger emerges from one of the apartments. "Say, Miss, did you, by any chance, see a turd anywhere around here?"[29] Initially, Bongi thinks the woman is referring to the john she just hustled, but she quickly realizes that Ginger is searching for an actual turd. When Bongi questions this behavior, Ginger explains that she is hosting a dinner party for a man she really wants to impress and "Everybody knows that men have more respect for women who are good at lapping up shit."[30] Ginger is a "Daddy's Girl," which Solanas defines in *SCUM Manifesto* as

> passive, adaptable, respectful of, and in awe of the male. . . . Trained from early childhood in niceness, politeness, and "dignity," in pandering to the male need to disguise his animalism, she obligingly reduces her "conversation" to small talk, a bland, insipid avoidance of any topic beyond the utterly trivial—or, if educated to intellectual discussions, that is impersonal discoursing on irrelevant abstractions—the Gross National Product, the Common Market, the influence of Rimbaud on symbolist painting.[31]

Having completely internalized society's misogyny, Ginger eats what she is, a lowly, abject turd, the excremental residue of civilization.

She offers to set up Bongi on a blind date with Russell, a noted "expert on women," who is joining them for dinner. "You'll adore Russell," Ginger tells her; "he's extremely talented, absolutely brilliant mind: he writes, very unique outlook—he satirizes women; and he writes the most brilliant essays—you can't understand a word of them."[32] As they wait for their dates to arrive, the women become better acquainted. Ginger tells Bongi about her job. "I deal with really fascinating men—all neurotics. I adore Neurosis; it is so creative."[33] "Men have so much better judgment than women," Ginger asserts. To which Bongi retorts, "Yeah, they dig women."[34] "I don't like to

brag," Ginger interjects, "but I could never get along with other women;
Those mincing snots, they turn my stomach. . . . I'm completely attuned
to the gripping dynamism of the male mind."[35] We learn that Ginger is an
aspiring novelist struggling to combine marriage with a career. "What's even
trickier," Bongi tells her, is to combine no marriage with no career."[36] In the
middle of their conversation about art, philosophy, and religion, Russell ar-
rives bearing bags of gourmet goodies for the repast he is about to prepare.

Before he consents to the blind date, Russell gives Bongi a vocabulary
quiz to see if she's up to his level. Although she fails to answer all of the
questions correctly, and he is clearly not attracted to her physically, Russell
accepts Ginger's arrangement, believing it will lead to sex. "You're not too
bad looking," he tells Bongi, "or, at least you wouldn't be if you'd put a skirt
on and look like a woman."[37] "Why should I dress to give men hard ons?"
Bongi rejoins. "Let them get their own hard ons."[38] Shocked by Bongi's lack
of femininity and hostility toward him, Russell proclaims Bongi "sick" and
"unsanitary" in addition to being frigid and humorless.[39] "You women take
yourselves too seriously," he spouts. "You can't take a joke." Bongi replies,
"No, I dig jokes. I'm just waiting to get the stage so I can tell my funnies."[40]
Ginger diagnoses Bongi with penis envy and suggests that she visit a shrink.
She recommends Dr. Aba Gazavez at the Marriage and Family Institute, who
has developed a theory called creative passivity.

Bongi shares with Ginger and Russell her own theory of creative passivity: "When I'm on my knees," she quips, "I get paid."[41] The revelation that
Bongi is a prostitute both repulses and excites Russell. He inquires about the
precariousness of the profession, to which Bongi responds, "It has its ups
and downs."[42] Sensing her guest's titillation, Ginger expresses her longing
to be an "artful courtesan," a "high priestess in the temple of love, fulfilling
the time-honored role of pleasing men."[43] The noblest profession, Russell
informs her, is motherhood: "the crowning achievement, what every woman
is aching for . . . the highest honor, the supreme power."[44] Deferring to male
authority, Ginger states, "The hand that rocks the cradle rules the world."[45]
"That's a slick little maxim," Bongi interjects, for "while the hand's rocking
the cradle it won't be rocking the boat."[46] She tells Ginger that if women were
freed from the shackles of maternity, they could rule the world. Suddenly
inspired, Bongi states, "Maybe being president wouldn't be such a bad idea. I
could eliminate the money system, and let the machines do all the work."[47]

Having suffered long enough listening to Russell's drivel, Bongi launches
into a conversation about sex determinism and the elimination of the male

species. This diatribe presages Solanas's call for male genocide in *SCUM Manifesto,* which begins:

> Life in this "society" being, at best, an utter bore and no aspect of "society" being at all relevant to women, there remains to civic-minded, responsible, thrill-seeking females only to overthrow the government, eliminate the money system, institute complete automation and eliminate the male sex.[48]

Bongi explains to Russell that men are "half-assed women," or, as Solanas would soon put it, "The male is a biological accident . . . an incomplete female, a walking abortion . . . a machine, a walking dildo."[49] Russell responds by calling Bongi "a desexed monstrosity."[50] "Quite the contrary," she quips, "I'm so female I'm subversive."[51] Russell's insists that he is repulsed by Bongi and wouldn't have sex with her "for a million dollars," nor if she "were the last woman on earth."[52] Bongi demonstrates that he, like all men, is "obsessed with screwing" and will "swim a river of snot, wade nostril-deep through a mile of vomit, if he thinks there'll be a friendly pussy awaiting him. He'll screw a woman he despises, any snaggle-toothed hag, and furthermore, pay for the opportunity."[53] All Bongi has to do is unbuckle her belt, and Russell gets down on his hands and knees and begs her for sex. As the two go at it behind the bushes, Russell discover Ginger's turd, which turns into a celebration. In a ludicrous ending to a ludicrous scene, Ginger leads the cast in "Dance for Turd." Spade Cat and Bongi join in while a dejected Russell goes inside "to start soaking his squid."[54]

This musical interlude is followed by a second number, which Bongi calls "Dance of the Seven Towels," a parody of the "Dance of the Seven Veils" performed by Salome for her uncle, King Herod, in order to inflame his desire and grant her the head of John the Baptist. The "Dance of the Seven Veils" mythologizes the origin of belly dancing, and it has a long and storied association with other forms of erotic dancing, including burlesque, striptease, and, beginning with Oscar Wilde's *Salome* (1894), drag.[55] Bongi satirizes the pretensions of modern dance in her sapphic rendition of this classic form.

> [A]fter ripping off the seventh [towel], I soap myself up, work myself into a lather, then the chorus girls, all wearing shower caps, flog me offstage with wet washrags. Then there's my modernistic fan dance—I use an electrical fan. . . . For my grand finale I short-circuit myself before your very eyes.[56]

Horrified by Bongi's mockery of Isadora Duncan, Ruth St. Denis, and Loie Fuller, Ginger calls out, "Russell! These Philistines! They're trampling on ART!"[57] The scene comes to a close with Ginger hooking up with Spade Cat, while Bongi and White Cat take advantage of a free meal.

The penultimate scene takes place at Dr. Aba Gazavez's Creative Home-making Class at the Marriage and Family Institute, the purpose of which is to indoctrinate young women into compulsory heterosexuality and teach them how to be "Daddy's Girls." The course, Gazavez explains, is rooted in "the belief that marriage should be FUUNN! FUUNN! FUUNN! but, responsible fun, the fun that derives from duty and sacrifice."[58] The doctor boasts that the institute's philosophy has "kept some of the most incompatible couples together."[59] The curriculum consists of household basics: "cooking, market-ing, budgeting, dusting, childrearing and fucking," with a goal of integrating fucking into all of the other activities.[60] For example, the teacher explains, the class will work toward combining fucking with dishwashing and child care. "Wait until hubby's getting ready to take his bath; then, quick, [s]oap up the baby bottle brush, working it into a nice, foamy lather; then when hubby's all nicely naked and is leaning over to test his bath water, you come te-e-a-a-r-r-ing in . . . (Demonstrating) . . . r-a-a-m-m-ing the brush right up his asshole."[61] At this point, a group of boys enters the class for a hand's-on exercise in fucking. Assuming the (missionary) position, the girls move along to the beat of the doctor's hands. One girl, Marlene, starts deviating from the script. When the teacher catches her tweezing the anal hair of her partner, the doctor scolds her: "please confine yourself to fucking. The Mar-riage and Family Institute doesn't exist to turn out prostitutes, just simple, basic, serviceable wives."[62] Doctor Gazavez ends the lesson with a prayer: "Oh, God, Our Father, Son of the Holy Ghost, Husband of Mary, give us this day our daily cookies, but, most of all, make our marriages FUUNN! FUUNN! FUUNN! Ah-men."[63]

The final scene returns us to Bongi, who is seated on the steps cruising chicks. "Hey, Dishrag," she calls to a woman who walks by. "If you're calling me," the woman shoots back, "my name happens to be Mrs. Arthur Haz-lett." Bongi tells her that Arthur is a funny name for a woman and Dishrag is much more appropriate for a wife, which is, after all, something to wipe things up with. "What makes you so sure I won't wipe up the street with you," responds Arthur, relishing the flirtation.[64] "This could be the begin-ning of a beautiful romance," Bongi teases her; "one shared experience is all it takes."[65] Their foreplay is interrupted by Arthur's son, referred to only as Boy, who has superglued his penis and can't get it back in his pants. Exasperated, Arthur sends him back to the playground. "I'm one of society's rejects," she tells Bongi, "a wed mother."[66] Bongi asks her why she stays married if she doesn't find the relationship fulfilling. "Well, you know how women are," Arthur says, "loyal, faithful, dedicated and reliable."[67] "Yeah," replies Bongi, "and they oughta get slammed right in the teeth for it."[68] Arthur admits that she's afraid her son will grow up to be a faggot if he doesn't have a father. "That'd be just as well," Bongi tells her; "let the guys ram each other in the ass and leave the women alone."[69] Boy returns, and this time he's glued his pee hole shut, causing him to throw a tantrum. Arthur loses her temper, and the boy goes away crying.

Arthur complains to Bongi about her sex life and confesses that she'd "like to do something radical and daring."[70] Going out on a limb, she propositions Bongi. "What say you and me ball tonight? I'll bet you're a crazy lover."[71] Clearly uninterested in serving as a diversion for a frustrated housewife, she tells Arthur, "Actually, I'm a lousy lover—I'm too good a talker."[72] Pleading with Bongi, Arthur says, "Ah, come on; I'll bet you're a titillating bundle of eroticism."[73] Bongi ends the flirtation by telling Arthur that's she's just not her type. "You know what really flips me? Real low-down, funky broads, nasty bitchy hotshots, the kind that when she enters a room it's like a blinding flash, announcing her presence to the world, real brazen and public. If you ever run across any broads look like neon lights," Bongi tells her, "send 'em my way."[74] Arthur handles the rejection in stride. "Send 'em your way," she jokes. "From now on I'm in business for myself."[75] When she sees Boy coming up the street, she bellows, "Here comes that little prick again."[76] Something in Arthur snaps as she "grabs the boy by the throat and squeezes it. Snarling, her closed teeth bared and her eyes bugged, she picks him up by the neck and hurls him to the ground, squeezing hard all the while."[77] Boy tries to scream but cannot. The stage directions read, "(His face turns blue; she continues to squeeze for another fifteen seconds; she then throws him to the ground, picks up a garden shovel lying near the bush and begins to dig behind it)."[78] "Not here," yells Bongi, who has witnessed the entire scene; "it'll attract dogshit. There's enough turds rolling around here as it is."[79] Arthur chooses a spot farther back, digs furiously, tosses the boy in, and covers him with dirt. "You're a good head," Bongi congratulates her, "even if your name is Arthur."[80] In front of them passes a chick. "Hell'o, you beautiful, low-down funky doll," coos Arthur. "Hey, you like to meet my seester," offers Bongi. "Why not," responds the woman. "I have an eye for the ladies."

As Bongi and her broad move out of sight, Arthur calls out, "What's the other eye for? Whores?"[81] Their voices fade away as the play ends.

Solanas's *Up Your Ass* passes beyond the absurd, beyond the ridiculous: her lesbian feminist comedy is absolutely ludicrous.[82] What I am calling Valerie Solanas's Theatre of the Ludicrous begins in 1965 with the completion of her first play. *Up Your Ass* not only predates what is called "women's theater" by five years, if we take Its All Right to Be Woman Theatre (1970–76) as the progenitor of this movement, it was more formally innovative, politically daring, and affectively challenging than the plays created and staged by female collectives like the Women's Experimental Theatre and At the Foot of the Mountain. Trafficking in essentialist notions of gender and stereotypical depictions of feminine attributes, women's theater collectives typically performed in an earnest, didactic tone. In contrast, Solanas preferred satire and employed a highly ironic mode of storytelling that would become the hallmark of multicultural groups like Spiderwoman Theater and the Flamboyant Ladies in the mid- to late 1970s.

Thematically and stylistically, *Up Your Ass* has more in common with the work of gay male playwrights, such as Ron Tavel and Charles Ludlam, and the trashy brilliance of performance artists like Jack Smith than it does with the dramaturgy of the women's theater movement. In fact, the year Solanas copyrighted *Up Your Ass,* 1965, is the same year John Vacarro and Ron Tavel debuted their Theatre of the Ridiculous.[83] While this troupe evolved to include lesbians, such as the amazing Lola Pashalinski, it was primarily a gay male collective.[84] Although Solanas's Theater of the Ludicrous shares many traits with the Theatre of the Ridiculous, these forms were developed completely independent of one another—the former on the West Coast and the latter on the East Coast. Valerie's sister Judith confirms that Solanas wrote *Up Your Ass* before she moved to New York. She told me, "Valerie wrote the play or at least the first draft while living in Berkeley."[85]

A comparison of the inspired raunchiness of these two forms of experimental theater illuminates many of the tensions around which *Acts of Gaiety* is structured and sheds light on the misogynistic and lesbophobic underpinnings of the male-dominated queer counterculture of the 1960s. Both the Theatre of the Ridiculous and the Theater of the Ludicrous break with the dominant trends of dramatic realism by calling for a broad acting style with minimal stage settings and props, fantastical settings that reach far beyond the drawing room, and characters who exhibit neither coherent nor stable identities. Both experimental forms feature contrived scenarios, taboo subjects, and indecorous acts—nudity, graphic sex, and outrageously queer couplings—designed to shock audiences out of their conventional Cold War morality. Finally, parodic depictions of high art and campy reworkings of popular culture serve as sources of humor and vehicles for social critique. While Vaccaro and Tavel privileged improvisation over the sacredness of the scripted text (which Solanas held dear), the primary difference between these playmakers has less to do with their mode of presentation than it does with their plays' reception and success.

Spectators and critics alike loved the visually and verbally confrontational Theatre of the Ridiculous. They could not get enough of Vaccaro and Tavel's spectacles. The raunchier and grosser the better—like the performance featuring Siamese triplets joined together at the anus or *Turds in Hell,* which stars a guy whose cock (evoked by a surrealistic papier-mâché penis) is so huge that he cannot control his bowel movements. Every time he takes a step across the stage, excrement squirts out of his ass and drips down his leg. The obscene vignettes, Rabelaisian humor, and scurrilous satires of the Theatre of the Ridiculous packed houses, garnered reviews in both the underground and mainstream press, and brought Vaccaro, Tavel, and their associates (especially Charles Ludlam) at least a modicum of fame and fortune. Whereas fabulously filthy acts of gaiety by queer men evoked (then but also now) praise for being avant-garde, subversive, and revolutionary, the same acts, when committed by a gender-non-conforming dyke, elicited disgust and derision.

Although Solanas—whose path would soon cross that of the Ridiculous crowd—was working in a similar vein with analogous themes and common plot elements, her play was judged to be indecent, vile, and repulsive. *Up Your Ass's* caustic wit, unapologetically dykey sensibility, and feminist consciousness proved to be absolutely repugnant not only to producers and directors but to publishers and pornographers as well. The play, along with her subsequent work, was dismissed as the misguided musings of a maladapted, menacing lesbian. If it was ludicrous for Solanas to believe in 1965 that Americans were prepared for such a bold, brutally honest, and mordantly mirthful work of art by a female playwright, then it was equally preposterous for her to believe that she could forge an alternate world in which her talents would be valued. But this is exactly what she did—or at least tried to do—when she moved to New York City and took aim at the very heart of white, male, middle-class privilege.

Peddling her *Ass*

With *Up Your Ass* in hand, Solanas hitchhiked across the country in the spring of 1965. When she arrived in New York City, she took up residence at the Village Plaza, a seedy single-room-occupancy (SRO) hotel at 79 Washington Plaza, filed a copyright application for her script, and immediately began peddling her *Ass* all over town.[86] A supremely methodical and practical woman, Solanas systematically hawked her play to publishers, pornographers, directors, and producers. One of the first places she submitted *Up Your Ass* for consideration was a magazine called *The Realist*, a nationally distributed counterculture journal. The brainchild of future Yippie Paul Krassner, *The Realist* was popular for its sexually charged content and unflinching satirical portraits of American culture.[87] Although Krassner cannot recall exactly when Solanas shared the script with him, it seems likely, given subsequent events that I document here, that it was in the summer or early fall of 1965.[88] He does remember, however, that he declined the invitation to print the script in his magazine: "I rejected it on the grounds that I had no overwhelming desire to share Valerie's misanthropic evangelism with my friends."[89] Despite his misgivings about Solanas's man-hating rhetoric, he found *Up Your Ass* amusing and was intrigued enough to meet her in the lobby of the Chelsea Hotel. The satirists hit it off, and their conversation continued over lunch at the Automat on 42nd Street. The two became, in the words of Krassner, "deep acquaintances."[90] He invited Solanas to guest lecture in at least one class he taught at the Free University, and he most likely aided her in publishing "A Young Girl's Primer on How to Attain the Leisure Class" in *Cavalier*, a *Playboy*-style men's magazine for which he was a regular contributor.[91] Solanas's article appeared in the July 1966 issue alongside an essay on black humor by Krassner and humorous reflections by Timothy Leary, Dick Gregory, and Ray Bradbury. Ever the hustler, she tried to interest the editors of *Cavalier* in a regular column called "The Lesbian at Large," which they regrettably declined.

Undeterred by Krassner's rejection of her play, Solanas sent the script to Ralph Ginzburg, editor of *fact: a magazine* (1964–67), a satirical journal about society and politics with a muckraking bent. An author, photojournalist, and publisher of erotica, Ginzburg was convicted of violating federal obscenity laws in 1963 on the grounds that his *Eros* (1962), a hardcover "magbook" featuring writing about sexuality in history, politics, art, and literature, was pornographic. Having received the script while he was in the process of appealing his conviction all the way to the Supreme Court, Ginzburg was not only afraid to publish *Up Your Ass* but he was reluctant to return the manuscript to Solanas via the US mail lest he be charged with a second violation for trafficking in pornography.[92] He told Solanas that if she wanted her script back she would have to collect it in person.[93] Sometime after she retrieved the play from Ginzburg, Solanas sent the script to Andy Warhol.

Any number of events might have inspired Valerie to market *Up Your Ass* to Warhol in late 1965.[94] Perhaps she had seen Andy film Robert Heide's one-act play *The Bed* at Caffe Cino earlier that summer.[95] Perhaps she heard that Warhol "employed" writers like Heide and Tavel as scenarists for his films. Or perhaps she read in a newspaper that Warhol was looking for new acts to sponsor and simply cold-called him, as she had done Krassner and Ginzburg. Based on the success of the Velvet Underground, which Warhol began managing in 1965, and the popularity of his Exploding Plastic Inevitable multimedia events, the impresario had decided to solicit other interests in which to invest his capital. "We had so many people hanging around all the time now," Warhol remarked, "that I figured in order to feed them all we'd have to get other people to support them."[96] Andy ran ads seeking products, projects, and personalities to sponsor, like this one in the *Village Voice*.

> I'll endorse with my name any of the following: clothing, AC-DC, cigarettes, small tapes, sound equipment, ROCK 'N' ROLL RECORDS, anything, film, and film equipment, Food, Helium, Whips, MONEY; love and kisses Andy Warhol. EL 5-9941.[97]

However Solanas made contact with Warhol, one thing is certain: she gave him *Up Your Ass* in late fall 1965 or January 1966. On February 9, she wrote him a letter asking for the return of the script, which had been in his possession for some time.[98]

Warhol corroborates this in an interview with Gretchen Berg, conducted in the summer of 1966, in which he stated:

> [W]e have cops coming up here all the time, they think we are doing awful things we aren't. People try to trap us sometimes: a girl called up here and offered me a film script called *Up Your Ass* and I thought the title was so wonderful and I'm so friendly that I invited her to come up with it, but it was so dirty that I think she must have been a lady cop.[99]

Solanas found Warhol's suggestion that she was an undercover vice cop so amusing that she shared the story with Krassner, reenacting for him the events that transpired during that meeting. "Sure I'm a cop," Solanas told Andy, zipping down her fly to expose her vulva. "And here's my badge."[100] Warhol didn't know what to make of Solanas. "I don't know if she was genuine or not," he told Berg, "but we haven't seen her since and I'm not surprised. I guess she thought that was the perfect thing for Andy Warhol. I don't resent situations like that but I'm not interested in subjects like that, that's not what I'm pushing, here in America."[101] What Warhol was interested in pushing was male homoeroticism (e.g., *Blow Job* [1964], *Hand Job* [1964], *Taylor Mead's Ass* [1964], and *My Hustler* [1965]), the heterosexual divas and the drag queens they inspire (e.g., *13 Most Beautiful Women* [1964] and *Poor Little Rich Girl* [1965]), and female degradation (e.g., *Bitch* [1965] and *Prison* [1965]). Like Krassner and Ginzburg, Warhol had zero interest in the lesbian feminist aesthetic Solanas was promoting.

When Warhol failed to respond to her letter or return *Up Your Ass*, Solanas began phoning him on a regular basis and showing up at the Factory. By everyone's account, Warhol's "stupidstars," as Valerie liked to call his sycophantic minions, were unspeakably cruel to her, especially Viva and director Paul Morrissey. Andy, on the other hand, typically treated her with, if not civility then, bemused curiosity.[102] As time passed, he appeared—at least on the surface—to become more open to Solanas's ideas, engaging her in a number of his projects and even entertaining the possibility of producing her play. As Warhol was all artifice, a consummate performer who cultivated a reputation for being neither genuine nor sincere (except about making money), it is difficult to say whether he actually thought Valerie possessed any talent or was simply humoring her because he found her artistic pretensions and political theories amusing. He had a high tolerance for mentally unstable people, especially women, whom he enjoyed watching self-destruct. Unlike femme fatales Edie Sedgwick, Andrea Feldman, and Tinkerbelle and drag divas Holly Woodlawn and Jackie Curtis, Solanas did not attempt suicide; she attempted murder.[103]

"From the Cradle to the Boat"

Solanas enjoyed a cordial relationship with Warhol in 1966 and 1967, even after he failed to return her copy of the play, and she remained hopeful that he would help stage *Up Your Ass*. Nonetheless, she continued to pursue other production opportunities, very few of which materialized. By the mid-

1960s, there were over three hundred off-off-Broadway theaters in New York City dedicated to promoting new work, experimental dramas, and queer performances—places like Caffe Cino, La MaMa E.T.C., Judson Poets' Theatre, and the Play-house of the Ridiculous. While these venues provided an increasing number of opportunities for theater by gay male playwrights (e.g., Edward Albee, Doric Wilson, and Lanford Wilson), women (e.g., Adrienne Kennedy, María Irene Fornés, and Megan Terry), and people of color (e.g., LeRoi Jones, Larry Neal, and Ed Bullins), none of these locales was particularly receptive to plays about lesbians by lesbians. At a time in New York City when it was still illegal to stage depictions of homosexuality, no establishment was willing to risk closure to produce a sardonic, sapphic spectacle like *Up Your Ass*.

Unable to find a publisher or producer for *Up Your Ass*, Solanas decided to sell copies of the play in order to finance a production that she would direct herself. On October 13, 1966, she placed an ad in the *Village Voice*.

photo offset copies of
"UP FROM THE SLIME"
by Valerie Solanas
are now available at
$10 per copy
222 W. 23rd St. Room 606[104]

Solanas refers to the work as *Up from the Slime*, rather than *Up Your Ass* because the *Voice* did not print profanity in feature stories or advertisements. Of the various titles of the play, *Up from the Slime* most explicitly evokes a scum aesthetic, which Solanas would continue to cultivate as both a performance praxis and a political theory over the next two years. Equally important, this simple three-word title would have been cheaper to print than *From the Cradle to the Boat, or Up from the Slime*. Money was a constant problem for the author, especially after she moved to the higher-rent Chelsea Hotel (the address listed in the ad), and given the price of the script—$10.00 in 1966 is the equivalent of $66.44 in 2010—fund-raising was clearly Solanas's objective.

Within four months she had earned enough money to typeset and publish the script. On February 2, 1967, Solanas placed the first in a series of ads in the *Village Voice* book section announcing:

SCUM (Society for Cutting Up Men)
"Up From the Slime" & "A Young Girl's Primer on How to Attain the Leisure
 Class" (reprinted from Cavalier)
will be on sale starting Thurs. Feb 2 at:
8th Street Bookshop 17 W. 8th St.
Sheridan Square Paperback Corner
10 Sheridan Square
Underground Uplift Unlimited
20 St. Marks Place
Tompkins Square Book Store 97 Ave. B
East Side Book Store 17 St. Mark's Place
$1.50[105]

This ad, which lists the play at $1.50, as opposed to the original $10.00 she charged for the offset copies, offers proof that Solanas mass produced the script, thus accounting for both the lower cost and the wide availability at numerous Village book stores. Solanas placed a second, almost identical notice in the *Voice* the following week, on February 9. The next day she filed for a second copyright on the play. On February 10, 1967, Solanas registered a work titled *Up Your Ass, or From the Cradle to the Boat, or The Big Suck, or Up from the Slime* and "A Young Girl's Primer on How to Attain the Leisure Class, a Non-fictional Article Reprinted from Cavalier" under the imprimatur SCUM Book.

The text of the 1967 published version of the play is the same as the 1965 unpublished edition, with a few notable exceptions. The original manuscript, on file at the Library of Congress, is a carbon copy of a hand-typed document numbering sixty pages that is bound with two staples. It is *riddled* with typographical errors (clearly Solanas skipped secretarial classes in school!), which were corrected using white tape and blue ink in the author's hand.[106] The published version is professionally typeset (and error free). It totals twenty-nine pages (the result of a very economical mode of professional typesetting). The entire document—the play script, article, and leaves—numbers forty-three pages and is bound with a cover—yellow in the front and blue in the back held together with two machine staples down the left edge. The arresting front cover bears the title of the play, written in the author's hand, in black marker across the top. At the bottom, in the same script, is the title of the article. In between the text is a drawing of a white arm rising defiantly out of a black morass (literally "up from the slime").

Advertisement for Valerie Solanas's first SCUM Book containing the script of *Up from the Slime* (aka *Up Your Ass*) and a reprint of the article "A Young Girl's Primer on How to Attain the Leisure Class," from *Cavalier* magazine, in the *Village Voice,* February 9, 1967.

Reminiscent of the iconic "black power" fist, the hand in this image is also gesturing, but it is shooting the bird. Although the 1967 script, with its "do-it-yourself" scummy cover art, might project the appearance of a mimeographed pamphlet, the document is, in fact, a published work of literature. Many seminal texts produced in the 1960s, from chapbooks to manifestos, evidence a similar amateur aesthetic, and this is especially true of works advancing critiques of capitalism and lambasting bourgeois conceptions of art, as Solanas's play does.

It was a copy of this 1967 SCUM Book edition of the play that punk rock journalist turned cineaste Mary Harron (and her intrepid research assistant Diane Tucker) unearthed while researching the film *I Shot Andy Warhol* (1996). Harron incorporated scenes from *Up Your Ass* into the biopic's plot, treating audiences to what she thought was the world's first look at the comedy that had such tragic consequences for Warhol.[107] Harron's rich and remarkably entertaining film deserves the credit for recovering a play many people believed was lost. Her movie generated renewed scholarly interest in Solanas and led to a fully staged production of *Up Your Ass* in 2000–2001 by director George Coates.[108] Unfortunately, however, *I Shot Andy Warhol* perpetuated many fallacies about the author's personal life and artistic exploits—including the notion that the play was written in 1967, around the same time if not after *SCUM Manifesto,* and that Solanas penned it with Warhol in mind. More important, the movie reinforced misconceptions and mistaken beliefs about the role *Up Your Ass* played in the assassination at-

Cover of Valerie Solanas's first SCUM Book (1967) containing a typeset version of her play *Up Your Ass* (1965), issued with a reprint of her article "A Young Girl's Primer on How to Attain the Leisure Class," from *Cavalier* magazine (1966). (Image courtesy of Hofstra University Library Special Collections.)

tempt, namely, that Valerie shot Andy because he lost her *only copy* of the play. This theory was bolstered when a misplaced trunk belonging to Billy Name (né Linich), the photographer responsible for the Factory's silver design, yielded, buried beneath an array of old lighting equipment, the script for *Up Your Ass*. The document was nearly identical to the one Harron and Tucker found (in the collection of an erotica dealer), and both were missing both the front and back covers.[109] The obvious conclusion, everyone agreed, was that Name found *the copy* Warhol lost while Harron and Tucker had tracked down Valerie's *original* manuscript or, as they dubbed it, "The Holy Grail."[110]

Two recent treatments of Solanas by Martin Puchner and James Harding take embellished accounts of *Up Your Ass* and Valerie's relationship with Warhol from Harron's fictionalized film as historic fact. In *Poetry of the Revolution: Marx, Manifestos, and the Avant-Gardes,* Puchner cites *Up Your Ass* as exemplary of what he calls the "manifesto–performance theory nexus" of modern aesthetics. Adopting the chronology of events that Harron charts in her biopic, he concludes that *Up Your Ass* is "an enactment of the *SCUM Manifesto*," that it "was written in conjunction with the manifesto" and "takes terms and figures from the *SCUM Manifesto* and turns them into characters."[111] In actuality, the play was written two years before *SCUM*. Rather than exemplifying Puchner's theory, Solanas provides an interesting counterexample to his assertion that the manifesto is the paradigmatic genre of performance through which modern cultures have articulated their revolutionary ambitions and desires.

Whereas Puchner finds Solanas representative of dominant paradigms at play in the historical avant-garde, James Harding argues the inverse, that Valerie's "radically subversive project aimed at recalibrating the trajectory of the American avantgarde."[112] In "The Simplest Surrealist Act," he reads the shooting of Warhol as "a carefully orchestrated and radically disturbing aesthetic performance" that turned "the tropes of the avantgarde against itself."[113] Harding calls *Up Your Ass* "adolescent and contrived" and states that the script "is perhaps best understood as a provocation than a work of dramatic literature."[114] For him, the play has little merit aside from its function as "an allegorical parallel" to the assassination attempt. This theory is based on the willful misreading of *Up Your Ass* as a play "about a woman who 'is a man-hating hustler and panhandler' and who, somewhat more successfully than Solanas, actually ends up killing a man."[115] Harding cites as evidence the meme that there are two different versions of the play—one in which a woman kills a man and one in which a mother strangles her son—rather than following the plot of the actual script, which is excerpted alongside his article. *Up Your Ass* is not about a *woman* who shoots a *man* but a *mother* who commits *infanticide,* and the homicidal female in question is not Solanas's alter ego, Bongi Perez; it is Mrs. Arthur Hazlett.[116]

As I have demonstrated, there are two versions of the play, one published and one not, but their content is identical. I have also proven that Solanas did not write this play for Warhol or even with him in mind as a potential producer. The play Andy lost was the 1965 unpublished version of *Up Your Ass,* which Valerie wrote in California. This could not have been the *only* copy of the play, as Solanas sold the script on the streets and through ads in the *Village Voice.* The discovery of a copy of the 1967 version of the play in Billy Name's trunk suggests that Valerie remained on good enough terms with Warhol and his entourage to entrust someone at the Factory with at least one copy of the published edition of the play. This also proves that *Up Your Ass* was written before *SCUM Manifesto* and that the latter is based on the former, not the other way around.

This "smoking gun" was "hiding" in plain sight for forty years at the Library of Congress.[117] It never occurred to Harron and Tucker (or, in all fairness, to anyone else) to search for copies of *Up Your Ass* in libraries, not even after they recovered the script, which boasts both a publisher's imprimatur (which I discuss at length in the next section) and *multiple* copyright dates. As fate would have it, there were at least four copies of the 1967 SCUM Book edition of the play in special collections of university archives during the time Harron and Tucker were searching for *Up Your Ass.* The University of Virginia acquired the play sometime between 1964 and 1977, Hofstra obtained it in 1971, Indiana owns a copy but has no record of its acquisition date, and the University of Arizona had an edition that was lost and paid for in 2003 ("lost" by a would-be SCUM insurgent, no doubt—one I am fairly certain I could identify). I can say with absolute certainty that Solanas did not shoot Warhol because he lost her play, but whether she tried to kill him because he refused to produce it is another matter entirely.

"I dedicate this play to ME"

On February 15, 1967, less than a week after Solanas published and copyrighted the SCUM Book edition of *Up Your Ass,* she produced a multievening staged reading of the play at the Directors' Theater at 20 E. 14th Street in the East Village. This off-off-Broadway playhouse was located in the same building as the Free University of New York (FUNY), where Solanas took classes and guest lectured for Paul Krassner. Its leader was Bob Brady, who taught acting and directing at the School of Visual Arts. Brady, who is best known for his role in the cult classic B-movie *Liquid Sky* (1982), had rather unorthodox pedagogical methods, which included, among other things, recruiting homeless people from the streets to act in romantic scenes with his students.[118] This may be how Solanas first encountered Brady. According to performer and playwright Norman Marshal, who worked as a paid professional actor in Brady's directing courses, Solanas took part in at least two classes in 1967.[119]

That Solanas invested a great deal, emotionally and financially, in this staged reading is evidenced by the fact that she took out a series of ads, over a four-week period, in both the theatre and the book sections of the *Village Voice* to promote the performance and the script. The first ad for a "pre-production reading" of "UP FROM THE SLIME" appeared on February 2, 1967.[120] It was positioned just below an obituary for Joe Cino's lover Jonathan Torrey and immediately to the right of a notice for the critically acclaimed happening *Snows* by Carolee Schneemann (who would, years later, write a moving elegy for Valerie titled "Solanas in a Sea of Men").[121] A second ad, placed on February 9, appeared just above a notice for The Playhouse of the Ridiculous Repertory Club, Inc., which was showing Charles Ludlam's *Big Hotel* and two shorts by Ron Tavel, *The Life of Juanita Castro* and *Kitchenette*.[122] A third notice, printed February 16, included a cast list for the show and an announcement that Solanas would be appearing on Randy Wicker's WBAI-FM radio program.[123] The ad reads:

SCUM
(Society for Cutting Up Men)
presents
pre-production reading of
UP FROM THE SLIME
by Valerie Solanas

Beg. Wed. Feb 15. 8:30 PM
every day except Tues. & Thurs.
Directors Theater School 20 E. 14th St.

admission by contribution
Cast (in alphabetical order)
Harold Anderson,
Donald Eggena, Bonnie Greer,
Marcia Sam Ridge,
Gary Tucker, Barbara Wallace
copies of SCUM book (:)
"Up from the Slime" & "A Young
Girl's Primer on How To Attain to
the Leisure Class"
(reprinted from Cavalier 1966)
will be sold at reading for
$1.50 per copy

Listen to Valerie Solanas on
Randy Wicker's Interview Show
WBAI-FM in a few weeks
(watch Village Voice for exact date)[124]

The only names in this cast list likely to resonate with theater enthu-
siasts are Gary Tucker and Bonnie Greer. At the time of Solanas's production, Tucker was a member of The Play-house of the Ridiculous, which he
would soon leave with Ludlam to form the Ridiculous Theatrical Company.
In 1971 Tucker moved to Chicago, where, under the pseudonym Eleven, he
founded and directed the Godzilla Rainbow Troupe. A short-lived but influential collective, Godzilla, in the words of Albert Williams, "lived up to its
name. It was monstrous and beautiful; it breathed fire and gave off a glowing wet afterglow; it had a hell of an impact, and it was gone almost as soon
as it had started."[125] Carrying the torch of the theater of the ridiculous, the
troupe became notorious for its scatological content, cross-gender casting,
graphic nudity, and campy sense of humor. Their inaugural show was Bill
Vehr's *Whores of Babylon,* which was followed by *Turds in Hell* (written by
Vehr and Ludlam).[126] Bonnie Greer may or may not be the highly acclaimed
African American actress and playwright associated with the Actors Studio
and the Negro Ensemble Company who moved to London in 1986 and was
recently honored with an Order of the British Empire. I have been unable to
confirm or deny that this Bonnie Greer, who would have been nineteen in
1967, is the person in Solanas's cast list.

Advertisement in the February 16, 1967, issue of the *Village Voice* theater section announcing a pre-production reading of Valerie Solanas's play, *Up from the Slime* (aka *Up Your Ass*) at the Directors' Theater in New York City, including a cast list and press for an upcoming radio show.

The Lortell Off-Broadway Database lists a Harold Anderson in a 1964 production of *Finis for Oscar Wilde* by one Reverend Edward A. Molloy at the Blackfriar's Guild Theatre. Neither Anderson nor Donald Eggena enjoyed a very distinguished acting career, but the latter was clearly a skilled entertainer. In 1971 he opened Lend-a-Hand Personnel Service, which offered a variety of services—from dog walking to gourmet catering—to luminaries such as Lauren Bacall and Tony Bennett. Staffed by unemployed actors, Eggena's operation featured a crew of livelier, better-looking temps than other agencies, which gave Lend-a-Hand a competitive edge, not to mention a number of nods in high-profile places such as *New York* magazine. For whatever reason, this esteemed publication tracked many of Eggena's entrepreneurial activities, including his purchase of eighty-five pairs of Joan Crawford's false eyelashes for $325, which he sold for $30 a pop.[127] The only female member of the cast that I have positively identified is Marcia Sam Ridge, who at the time of the production worked at Paul Krassner's *The Realist* as an administrative assistant or, as she titled her position, "the Shit-On."[128] Ridge described her job as the lowest on the totem pole, lower even than a secretary, or "scapegoat," as *The Realist*'s Sheila Campion dubbed her office.[129] Did Marcia play one of the two "shit-on" women in the play, Ginger or Mrs. Arthur Hazlett? Or did she strut her stuff as Bongi Perez? How I would love to know.

The quantity, quality, and content of these ads show how dedicated Solanas was to this play, how hard she worked peddling her *Ass* all over New York, and how confident she was about its future. The designation of this show at the Directors' Theater as a "pre-production reading of UP FROM THE SLIME" suggests that the February run was a prelude to a larger event. Archival research indicates that she discussed with Warhol the possibility of producing the play at Grove Press's Evergreen Theatre in 1967. At the time Warhol made this alleged pact with Solanas, he was engaged in contract negotiations with Grove over *a: A Novel,* which it published in 1968. The press's Evergreen Theatre, named after its literary journal *Evergreen Review,* showed both theatrical productions and movies, including the Factory film in which Solanas starred, *I, a Man*.[130] A letter in the Warhol Museum archives states that Andy was ready to mount a two-part dramatic production of Solanas's work, the first being a staged version of her panhandling article, the second being the play itself.[131] The letter goes so far as to detail the fact that *Up Your Ass* was too short for a full production, so "A Young Girl's Primer," in dramatic form, was to be used as a lead-in. According to this document, Warhol, after learning that Solanas had signed a book contract with Olympia Press, changed his mind, became vague, and did nothing more about the production despite his former enthusiasm.

On or around August 15, 1967, Solanas received a five-hundred-dollar advance from Maurice Girodias at Olympia Press to write two novels. Girodias, a publisher of modernist literature and erotica, including Vladimir Nabokov's *Lolita,* William S. Burroughs's *Naked Lunch,* Pauline Réage's *Story of O,* and Samuel Beckett's trilogy (*Molloy, Malone Dies,* and *The Unnamable*), was intrigued by Solanas. He recalls:

> Her manner was friendly, lively, and she had a sense of humor—which somewhat took the edge off the anti-masculine doctrine she proceeded to preach to me. The title of her play, *Up Your Ass,* was sufficiently indicative of her iconoclastic disposition. . . . The play was rather clever, and I found it amusingly wild.[132]

Unable to or uninterested in fulfilling the contract for Girodias, Solanas granted him permission, in the spring of 1968, to publish *SCUM Manifesto,* which Olympia Press put into production only after the shooting in order to capitalize on the publicity it generated.[133]

Sensing that Warhol's interest in *Up Your Ass* was waning, Solanas pitched the play to other producers. She terrified the Roundabout Theatre's Gene Feist (a classmate of Warhol's at Carnegie Tech) when she barged into his office unannounced, introduced herself, and threw a copy of her script onto his desk. "The lady was a lunatic," Feist recalls.

> People who are either severely ill or have been institutionalized get this kind of sexless, dumb look, an oxen look. That's what she had. I was getting more and more alarmed—here I was a natural born coward, and it was obvious she was insane. "I'm sorry we only do the classics," I said. She took her script and left. I locked the door and breathed a sigh of relief, and as soon as I calmed down, you know the first thing I thought? I should have told her to go see Andy. She had a threatening presence. But Andy felt crazy people were gifted. Anyway, that was that.[134]

Feist's memory of how menacing Solanas was may be accurate, but the fact that he recalls the play being titled *Up Your Ass with a Meathook* and the fact that he interjects Warhol into the story lead me to believe that his recollection of this encounter may be embellished, or perhaps influenced by the violence Valerie would soon perpetrate against Andy.

What this account makes perfectly clear, however, is that Solanas tried to apply the same rules of engagement she used in panhandling—namely, aggressively and sarcastically harassing passersby until they gave in to her demands—to the art of contract negotiations. While the adoption of a menacing posture may have scared many people into donating a dime, a quarter, or even a dollar to her tip jar, this tactic, not surprisingly, failed to attract patrons willing to pony up hundreds of dollars to produce her work. While I admire Solanas because she was a politically astute, artistically daring dramatist who refused to compromise or acquiesce to make herself more acceptable to mainstream society, I have to wonder how her life (and, by extension, history) might have played out differently had she mastered the art of subtlety, which is a necessary skill for anyone who wants to attract a producer, not to mention an audience.

Solanas came very close to securing a fully realized production of her play in the fall of 1967. "The Cino might have been the fountainhead of feminist theatre if not for my prudery," laments Robert Patrick. "Charles Stanley begged me to direct a play by a fetid, somehow fetal woman who wandered in. But I found its coprophagic theme disgusting, so Valerie Solanis [sic] took *Up Your Ass* elsewhere, to Andy Warhol, whom she shot for not producing it."[135] This agonizing admission lies buried under the heading "Issues: Uncategorized" on Patrick's extensive Internet archive documenting the birthplace of off-off-Broadway. Patrick has expressed deep remorse over his refusal to stage the play: "I . . . regret not directing it, not only because of its importance, but because I have the grandiose idea that if I had, I might have saved Mister Warhol's life."[136] Patrick does not remember when or under what circumstances he first met Valerie. "I only remember coming into the Cino one afternoon and seeing her standing there looking just like Ms. [Lili] Taylor [who played Solanas in Mary Harron's *I Shot Andy Warhol*]. Mister Stanley introduced us and gave me the play. Ms. Solanis [sic] left. I am sure she said something, but nothing that I remember."[137] Patrick may be a southern gentleman, but he is no prude; while his revulsion over Solanas may have prevented him from seeing the merit in what he correctly intimates is a landmark feminist play, his rejection of *Up Your Ass* had little bearing on, and certainly no causal relationship to, Valerie's attempted assassination of Warhol the following June.[138]

Caffe Cino was not a place for lesbians. Despite its reputation as a queer utopia, the Caffe promoted theater that was, for the most part, by and for gay men, most of whom had little time or interest in dykes like Solanas. The queens of Cornelia Street may have fawned over conventionally attractive females like Bernadette Peters and Mary Woronov, but they had little patience with (or stomach for) gender nonconforming women with a radical feminist agenda. There were some lesbians at Cino, including playwright Claris Nelson (née Erickson) and director Roberta Sklar, but they did not write or stage work that was as brazen as *Up Your Ass*. Only two people at Cino exhibited any degree of tolerance for or interest in Solanas: Charles Stanley and Magie Dominic. "I can't remember how I met Valerie," recalled Dominic. "She was like the Caffe. One day she was suddenly there."[139] In her memoir *The Queen of Peace Room,* she writes, "Joe Cino and Valerie Solanas were alike in some ways. People saw what they needed. A Rorschach test."[140] Dominic certainly saw something in Solanas, for they had a brief affair. "Valerie and I slept together on two occasions," she notes in her memoir. "At her room in the Chelsea Hotel. Valerie was the only woman I slept with in the '60s. We never called it forbidden love. We just called it sleeping together. And we did. In each other's arms like two old tired women."[141] Dominic recalls a particularly intimate and loving exchange with Valerie. "Someone should write a play about you," she told Magie, "and call it *Cleopatra.*"[142]

This remembrance is one of the few records I have found of an affectionate encounter between Valerie and another human being. Dominic is the rare witness to Solanas's tenderness and vulnerability, but she was also acutely aware of the playwright's volatile temperament and propensity for violence. "I think if people had tried to harm me while I was with Valerie," Dominic writes in her autobiography, "she would have killed them with her bare hands."[143] Solanas asked Magie if they could become roommates (something Valerie asked almost everyone—those she slept with and those she did not). "She was having trouble at her hotel and wanted to stay with me at my hotel room," Dominic remembers. "I said a difficult no. [After Joe Cino's death] I didn't know how to cope with anyone anymore."[144] Solanas told Magie she was having some sort of dispute with the Factory. "She was afraid Warhol was going to steal her idea," Dominic writes, "It was during this time that Valerie kept phoning the Caffe wanting Charles to produce her play."[145]

Charles Stanley, a dancer, writer, and actor best remembered for his exploration of genderfuck in H. M. Koutoukas's *Medea or Maybe the Stars May Understand or Veiled Stranger (a ritualistic camp),* was perhaps Solanas's greatest champion.[146] Patrick recalls, "when I refused to do the play, I remember only him literally thrashing about in anger, repeating over and over that it was an important play. I never understood why he did not direct it himself."[147] By all reports Stanley was so overwhelmed by the administrative demands of the Caffe, in the wake of Joe Cino's amphetamine-fueled suicide (which coincided with an influx of hopped-up Factory habitués at the Caffe), that he was too busy to take an active role in staging productions.[148] What he lacked in administrative skills, Stanley made up for in artistic vision and political daring. During his brief tenure as Caffe Cino manager, he pushed the envelope at the already cutting edge venue. Stanley was less interested in work that promoted dignified portraits of gays or presented positive images of homosexuality than he was in exploring deviant desires, sexual fetishes, and internalized homophobia. Had he remained at the helm, Stanley might have produced Solanas's *Up Your Ass*. In December of 1967, however, he was relieved of his duties, and the Caffe closed for several weeks as a new administrative team took over.

A "SCUMMY Thing"

The *Village Voice* ads tell us a great deal about Solanas's plans for *Up Your Ass*, but they also provide insight into SCUM (Society for Cutting Up Men). Indicative of Valerie's audacity and mentality agility is her transformation of *scum*, a slur hurled at her repeatedly from the time she was a girl, from an insult into an aesthetic. Solanas resignified this four-letter word, changing it from an epithet into a badge of courage that she donned with defiance, determination, and pride. The promotional materials for the "pre-production reading" of the play begin, "SCUM (Society for Cutting Up Men) presents," and the announcements for the sale of the script (published separately in the same issues of the *Voice*) read, "SCUM (Society for Cutting Up Men) Book." These ads indicate that Solanas conceived of SCUM as a "literary trope" under whose imprimatur she published and promoted her creative work long before she envisioned it as an activist organization or the title of a political tract.[149] In February of 1967, when Solanas published *Up Your Ass* as a SCUM Book, she had neither written nor conceived of *SCUM Manifesto*. The creation of this notorious document was something of an afterthought.

When Solanas realized that she could not beg, borrow, or steal her way into the male-dominated art world, she set about to create her own scene. Unable to find an audience for her play, she attempted to create one by placing ads in the *Village Voice* that she hoped would attract like-minded people. In the March 30 edition of the weekly newspaper, she printed the following announcement in the public notice section.

SCUM (Society for Cutting Up Men) is being formed to eliminate through sabotage all aspects of society that are not relevant to women (everything), to dispose of the garbage pail that men have made of the world*** to effect a complete female take-over, to end the production of males (It's now technically possible to reproduce without the aid of males and to produce only females) and to begin to create a swinging, groovy, out-of-sight female world. SCUM has a men's auxiliary to accommodate those men who wish to perform a public service and hasten their inevitable demise. If you'd like to work to help end this hard, grim, static, boring male world & wipe the ugly, leering male face off the map, send your name and address to Valerie Solanas, Box Office 47, NY 14.

***war, money, marriage, and prostitution, work, prevention of automation, niceness, politeness, clean language, "dignity," censorship, trivial "entertainment," secrecy, suppression of knowledge & ideas, ignorance, fatherhood & mental illness (fear, cowardice, timidity, humility, insecurity, passivity), authority, government, boredom, monotony, "Great Art," "Culture," philosophy, religion, morality based on sex, competition, prestige, status, formal education, prejudice (racial, ethnic, religious, etc.), social, economic classes, domesticity, motherhood, materialism, sexuality, ugliness, destruction of cities, poisoning of air, hate, contempt, distrust, prevention of conversation, friendship & love, isolation, suburbs, violence, disease & death.

With this ad, Solanas attempted to create a mailing list of militant, fun-loving, radical feminist guerrillas and their male allies whom she might persuade to produce, attend, or purchase *Up Your Ass* or other work.

One month later Solanas ran an ad in the *Village Voice* announcing a gathering of the Society for Cutting Up Men.

Valerie Solanas
SCUM
Fri., April 28. 8:30 PM/Farband House 575 6th Avenue (at 16th) Men 2.50, women $1.00[150]

The fact that Solanas is charging admission suggests to me that this event was some kind of performance. This is supported by a transcribed conversation between her and Warhol in which Solanas tries to recruit Andy for the men's auxiliary. In this exchange, she describes SCUM "as some sort of forum— except it wouldn't be exactly a forum—there's no word for this, I mean, it

VALERIE SOLANAS will conduct SCUM Forum, explaining how and why SCUM (Society for Cutting Up Men) will eliminate male sex, on Tues., May 23, 8:30 P.M. at 20 E. 14 (men $2.50; women $1.00). For copy of "SCUM Manifesto" send $1.00 to Valerie Solanas, 222 W. 23.   (1)

Announcement in the *Village Voice* on May 18, 1967, for a SCUM Forum conducted by Valerie Solanas at the Directors' Theater. This is the first known advertisement for the sale of *SCUM Manifesto*, which, in this iteration, consisted of a single-page flier.

doesn't fall into any place or occasion. I don't know what to call it. Just a SCUMMY thing. You know, sort of—not really a lecture—except that there'd be a lot of interaction with the audience.[151] Solanas harnessed the power of performance to create a novel and, as we shall see, utterly ingenious social, political, and aesthetic form she called a "SCUMMY thing."

On May 23, 1967, one month after the Farband House gathering, Solanas staged a "SCUMMY thing" at the Directors' Theater, where she had held the "pre-production" reading of *Up Your Ass*. Solanas billed this event as a "SCUM Forum, explaining how and why SCUM (Society for Cutting Up Men) will eliminate [the] male sex."[152] The price of admission is the same as the previous SCUM event, $2.50 for men and $1.00 for women. This notice includes what I believe to be the first ad for *SCUM Manifesto*, listed as $1.00. This first edition of the manifesto consisted of a single page flier with the text of the March 30th *Village Voice* ad and the drawing of the bird-flipping hand coming "up from the slime" that graces the cover of the SCUM Book edition of *Up Your Ass*. That Solanas refers to this version of the manifesto as a "recruiting poster" in conversations with Warhol, offers further evidence that her primary motivation was to generate an audience for her performances.[153]

I believe the motivation to create *SCUM Manifesto* had less to do with an attempt to earn a few extra bucks or the desire to articulate a revolutionary political theory than it did with the fallout from a disastrous appearance on a popular television program. On the bottom of this first edition of the manifesto, which was clearly created to promote the "SCUMMY thing" at the Directors' Theater on May 23, Solanas includes the following statement.

> Valerie Solanas, because she was kicked off the Alan Burke Show (to be shown Sat., May 20) for "talking dirty" after only fifteen minutes on and prevented from fully explaining to the public how and why SCUM will eliminate the male sex, will conduct a SCUM Forum.

It is immediately after being humiliated by Burke that Solanas decides to create a manifesto, and even so, her aim is the generation of an audience for her live event, not the elaboration of a political tract. Valerie came to this project the way she lived her life, impulsively, reacting viscerally and violently to life's indignities and people's intolerance.

Solanas continued to develop the manifesto, in and through performances of her "SCUMMY things," over the course of the next few months. In a letter to Warhol dated August 1, 1967 (written between the filming of *I, a Man* and its premier), Solanas states that she is almost finished with *SCUM Manifesto* and that she intends to sell it on the street within days. She asks Andy if he would like to film some of the SCUM Forums and outdoor rallies that she is planning in conjunction with the *Manifesto*'s launch. The world will be corroded with SCUM, Solanas promises him, noting that she has already had a large and positive response to the draft of the *Manifesto* she published in the *Village Voice* and that the majority of respondents were male.[154] Later that fall, she brings up the issue again. She tells Andy that her SCUMMY things are very successful, and by successful she means that they are popular; they aren't well known, she tells Warhol, but they are popular.[155]

A brilliant, caustic, and satirical analysis of the cesspool men have made of the world, the *Manifesto* is more than a performative genre advancing a SCUM aesthetic. Like SCUM Book, which consists of a play and a dramatic monologue, *SCUM Manifesto* is a script for a production. Solanas's sister told me Valerie's "intent, at the time was to have various people read from the manifesto."[156] This is confirmed by the fact that Solanas submitted her manifesto to a variety of off-off-Broadway venues, including the Directors' Theater and Judson Poets' Theatre, as a play.[157] Undeterred by rejection from these two locations, Solanas tried alternative venues, including Café Bizarre, an edgy Village coffeehouse on West Third that Bob Dylan made famous. A former coach house, Bizarre was "seedy, loud, a haven for hitter-chicks, the kind who'd take you home for the night without asking you your name and number, tolerant of rock-n-roll, off-beat, and off-limits to the tourist."[158] Another site Solanas considered was the Electric Circus, a popular East Village dance club and pleasure dome that featured a variety of entertainment from experimental theater and circus performers to light shows and cinematic projections.

As she had since 1965, Solanas continued to hustle Warhol, hoping that he would finance one of her productions for a cut of the profits. A transcript in the Warhol Museum archives documents negotiations between the artists in the fall of 1967. From the casualness of the conversation, the number of jokes the two trade, and the range of topics they discuss, it is clear that Solanas and Warhol were on friendly terms and had been for quite some time. It is also clear that Valerie harbored no delusions of—or any desire to be—one of his superstars. After lighthearted banter and being interrupted by a number of people waltzing in and out of the Factory, the conversation takes a serious turn about their work.

Solanas tells Andy she's been selling SCUM Manifesto and working on a couple of new projects, including a novel and a nonfiction book. She asks him if he's been promoting SCUM during his college lecture tour, as he promised he would. Warhol insists he has. Valerie then tells Andy of her conversation with the owner of Café Bizarre about staging a "SCUMMY thing" there and of her plans to talk with the owner of the Electric Circus, where she knows she could negotiate a percentage of the cover charge. She says the problem she's having is a lack of funds; she does not have the money to advertise or promote the show. Solanas asks Warhol if he'd finance a production, adding that naturally he would get a cut of the proceeds. Rather than dismissing Valerie or changing the subject, Warhol engages her in a conversation about specifics, including the kind of financial investment she has in mind and the logistics of the event: where it would take place, when, how frequently, and what his investment would be. Solanas tells Andy that he should partner with her because he would not only make money off the deal but would garner great publicity for I, a Man. She adds that she's been telling everybody she talks to, including Randy Wicker at WBAI, that he's going to produce and direct Up Your Ass. Warhol's next statement suggests that he not only takes Solanas seriously but he is familiar enough with her work to believe that it might serve as a suitable project for his newest "It" girl. You know Candy Cane, Andy asks Valerie.[159] Yes, she replies. He's the drag queen one who looks like Joan Bennett. Well, we'll talk to Paul Morrissey about it Warhol says.[160]

"The Big Suck"

Somehow, some way, negotiations between Solanas and Warhol and Solanas and Girodias went terribly awry, and in her mind they were not only related but part of a vast conspiracy by powerful men to steal her work and cheat her out of money and fame. On June 3, 1968, Valerie entered the Factory on Union Square armed with two pistols and shot Andy at point-blank range, along with two of his associates, Mario Amaya and Fred Hughes (who dodged a bullet when Valerie's gun jammed).[161] Girodias is believed by many to have been the target that day. An analysis of the "long involved story" that led Solanas to shoot that saintly satanic prince of pop lies beyond the scope of this inquiry.[162] Whatever the shootings reflect—a desperate bid for fame, a desire for revenge, a paranoid schizophrenic breakdown, the demented logic of psychosis—they most certainly do not exemplify the deconstructive logic of parody embodied in Solanas's performance texts. In other words, while the assassination attempt may have been a carefully plotted (though ultimately botched) production, it was *not* a "SCUMMY thing" acting out the tenets of her manifesto, as Harding and others have suggested.

As far as Girodias was concerned, Solanas was crazy or paranoid or both. "Obviously," he wrote, "the pixies were moving in, pretty fast." No other explanation made "any sense since she had nothing that anyone would want to steal."[163] Was Solanas insane to think that the most famous artist of the twentieth century would want to stage her plays? Was it delirium that made her feel her scripts were valuable enough not only to publish, copyright, and produce but also to steal? Was it crazy for this intelligent, acerbic, fiercely ambitious, ass-peddling, penniless dyke to consider herself an artist? Was it madness that engendered Solanas's profane political imaginary, her audacious alter ego Bongi Perez, and her scatological sense of humor? Was it lunacy? Perhaps. But it was certainly ludicrous. What is even more ludicrous than this dyke's ballsy gestures is the fact that had she not shot Warhol there might not have been a radical feminist movement.

Roxanne Dunbar-Ortiz, an American socialist who was in Mexico City on her way to Cuba, glimpsed, out of the corner of her eye, a newspaper headline proclaiming, "Super-Woman Power Advocate Shoots Andy Warhol." "[T]hrilled" by the idea that "a woman shot a man because he was using her," Dunbar-Ortiz believed this was a sign that "finally women were rising up."[164] Hopping the first plane back to the States, she "planned to form— or find and join—a female liberation movement" with "warrior women" and to "find Valerie Solanas and defend her."[165] By the time Dunbar-Ortiz landed in Manhattan in August, two rogue members of NOW, veteran civil rights activist Florynce Kennedy and New York chapter president Ti-Grace Atkinson, had already installed themselves as Solanas's counsel. The former dubbed Valerie "one of the most important spokeswomen for the feminist movement," while the latter proclaimed, "She has dragged feminism kicking and screaming into the 20th Century, in a very dramatic way."[166]

In a press release delivered on June 13, just hours after her initial meeting with Solanas, Atkinson made the "first public use of the concept of 'radical feminist'" in describing her client's political program.[167] Incensed by these events, Betty Friedan fired off this telegram to Atkinson and Kennedy.

DESIST IMMEDIATELY FROM LINKING NOW IN ANY WAY WITH VALERIE SOLANAS MISS SOLANAS MOTIVES IN WARHOL CASE ENTIRELY IRRELEVANT TO NOW'S GOALS OF FULL EQUALITY FOR WOMEN IN TRULY EQUAL PARTNERSHIP WITH MEN.[168]

Ignoring Friedan's order that they drop the Solanas case, Ti-Grace and Flo continued to advocate for Valerie. The issue caused a major rift in the ranks of NOW, as a mass exodus of feminists, including Atkinson and Kennedy, fled in the liberal wing of the women's movement in search of more militant organizations advancing the kind of revolutionary agenda they understood Solanas to be advocating.

Solanas had endured painful ostracism from aesthetic and political movements until she shot Warhol and was hailed as a hero by a handful of extremists. Although she desperately desired the attention, admiration, and camaraderie, Solanas's longing for recognition and community were overshadowed by her fear (however irrational) that any attention she received would only benefit Warhol and publicize Olympia Press's version of her *Manifesto,* which it rushed into production in the fall of 1968 to capitalize on the shooting. Valerie maintained, to her death, that Girodias's edition was a crass and opportunistic bastardization of her art. Solanas grew increasingly ambivalent about the political changes her actions inspired, in part because she felt her ideas were being misunderstood and misrepresented by both her detractors and her supporters. In fact, she came to see the embrace of *SCUM* by radical feminists as disingenuous and predatory. After she was released from jail, she engaged in vicious and protracted battles with leaders of the women's liberation movement (in *Majority Report* and other print publications) over feminists' use, and in her eyes abuse, of her manifesto.

What Solanas wanted to talk about was not *SCUM* but *Up Your Ass.* This surprised Dunbar-Ortiz, who prior to meeting Solanas imagined her as "a martyr for all women everywhere."[169] After spending three hours with her in jail in August 1968, Dunbar-Ortiz came to see Valerie in a different light. In a letter to a friend, she wrote:

What a mind Valerie has. I can guarantee she is not a violent person, nor is she anti-male. She is angry and she is Anti-Man. . . . I think of her more as Rimbaud than Ché, and I don't think she will ever be a revolutionary in the left political sense. Perhaps destroyers like her can never transform their energy, but only inspire others.[170]

Years later Dunbar-Ortiz would recall that Solanas spent the majority of their meeting talking about her play. In what was likely the final performance of the Theater of the Ludicrous, Solanas acted out *Up Your Ass* for Dunbar-Ortiz and her comrade Dana Densmore in the visitors' room at the Matteawan State Hospital for the criminally insane in Beacon, New York. Not only did Valerie "reconstruct the whole play from memory," but she gave distinct voices to each of the different characters.[171]

By the time Solanas was released from prison in 1971 (she was charged with assault, sentenced to three years for the shootings, and given credit for time served), the movement had moved on, and she was no longer a central player in the drama of women's liberation. Solanas tried to stage a comeback by republishing (an authorized edition of) *SCUM Manifesto* in 1977, but the "treatment" she received from the "correctional" system, made her worse instead of better. Mentally unstable and in poor physical health, Solanas died in 1988 at the Hotel Bristol, a welfare residence in San Francisco's Tenderloin District, a neighborhood that bears a striking resemblance to (and may very well be) the scummy setting of *Up Your Ass*. It is not surprising that Valerie drifted back into a state of abject obscurity from whence she once rose "up from the slime," nor is it surprising that this play remained hidden, or should I say repressed, for so long, tearing as it does at the conceptual fabric of American society and the contingent foundations of patriarchal culture. Scandalous even today in its insolence and seditiousness, Solanas' picaresque political aesthetic makes the contemporary LGBT agenda seem ludicrous by comparison.

2

Guerrilla Acts
Marriage Protests, 1969 and 2009

Florynce Kennedy and Ti-Grace Atkinson's defense of Valerie Solanas, against the express wishes of Betty Friedan, incited rancor within the ranks of NOW. Citing "irreconcilable ideological conflicts," Atkinson resigned as president of the New York chapter of NOW and founded the October 17th Movement, named after the day of her stormy departure in 1968. Shortly after its inception, members of this militant faction rebranded themselves The Feminists.[1] Claiming credit as "the first radical feminist group" in the United States, this small but influential collective worked toward the goal of annihilating sex roles.[2] Influenced by and seeking to enact the ideas dramatized in *SCUM Manifesto,* The Feminists took as axiomatic the notion that sexual orientation is elective and fluid, not innate or fixed, and they promoted political lesbianism as a positive path to women's liberation. Feminism is the theory, Atkinson proclaimed, and lesbianism is the practice, by which she meant, "It is the commitment, by choice, full time, of one woman to others of her class, that is called lesbianism."[3]

In stark contrast to Friedan's position that dykes constituted a "lavender menace" that threatened the women's liberation movement, The Feminists insisted on "the political and tactical significance of lesbianism to feminism," going so far as to argue: "any feminist should fight to the death for lesbianism because of its strategic importance" in combating patriarchy, which the group defined as a coercive social contract, a discriminatory cultural institution, and a scripted set of ambitions and behaviors.[4] Political lesbianism was less a prescribed identity for members of the collective than it was a glorious aspiration. In an effort to achieve "consistency" between The Feminists' political beliefs and their actions, the group limited the number of committed heterosexuals who could join their ranks.[5] The Feminists valorized lesbianism (not necessarily lesbians) as an idealized model of egalitarian relationships. Rooted in an androgynous, desexualized notion of woman-identified women's bonding, the collective ultimately reinforced, rather than challenged, the heteronormative view that dykes are emotional rather than erotic beings. Because The Feminists regrettably saw women's liberation and sexual liberation as mutually exclusive, the group's contribution to the development of radical feminism is often disavowed or downplayed by subsequent generations of scholars and activists.

The majority of The Feminists' time was dedicated to consciousness-raising and the development of theoretical tracts, but these Aretmesian warriors possessed a flair for the dramatic and engaged in a number of high-profile political performances that serve as paradigmatic examples of acts of gaiety. On September 23, 1969, The Feminists staged a guerrilla theater action at the New York City Marriage Licensing Bureau. Atkinson, a former artist and model-cum-doctoral student in philosophy, led her entourage—fiercely coiffed and dressed to the nines in miniskirts and chic sunglasses—into the waiting room where they foisted on future wives, or "hostages" as The Feminists liked to call them, pamphlets peppered with incendiary prose.[6] "Do you know that you are your husband's prisoner?" the fliers asked the brides-to-be. "Do you know that rape is legal in marriage?"[7] Arguing that heterosexual love is a pathological condition, the internalization of a coercive fantasy, and the contingent foundation of patriarchal oppression, The Feminists sought to abolish the institution they claimed legalized rape and profited from women's unpaid physical and emotional labor. "All the discriminatory practices against women are patterned and rationalized by this slavery-like practice," the group's leaflets pronounced. "We can't destroy the inequities between men and women until we destroy marriage. We must free ourselves. And marriage is the place to begin."[8]

The Feminists may have harbored strident views on sex, but no one could accuse these dissidents of being dowdy dykes or frumpy feminists. These Amazons possessed charisma, intelligence, and a penchant for haute couture, making them the object of everyone's gaze. The media followed their every move. A photograph of the Marriage Licensing Bureau zap in *Life* magazine captures five of The Feminists posing for the camera beside what appears to be the mother of a bride, who has turned her back on the protesters to shelter the happy couple to her left. The beaming bride, in full wedding regalia, is oblivious to everything except her fiancé, a balding,

The Feminists' zap action at the New York City Marriage Licensing Bureau on September 23, 1969. Pictured are Ti-Grace Atkinson, Linda Feldman, Pam Kearon, Sheila Cronan, Barbara Mehrhof, and members of an unidentified wedding party. Note the mother of bride attempting to keep the activists at bay and the groom twiddling his thumbs. This image first appeared in *Life,* May 18, 1970. (Photo by Mary Ellen Mark.)

middle-aged man slumped in the chair next to her who, because of nervousness or boredom or both, is literally twiddling his thumbs.[9]

As part of their zap action, The Feminists issued a declaration charging "the city of New York and all those offices and agents aiding and abetting the institution of marriage, such as the Marriage Licensing Bureau, of fraud with malicious intent against the women of this city."[10] Zap participant Sheila Cronan penned an influential essay titled "Marriage" that further explicates the guiding principle inspiring this act of gaiety. "Since marriage constitutes slavery for women," she writes, "it is clear that the women's movement must concentrate on attacking this institution. Freedom for women cannot be won without the abolition of marriage."[11] The Feminists were not alone in their full-frontal assault on this venerable institution. Throughout the 1960s, 1970s, and into the 1980s, activists of various sexual proclivities and political persuasions staged spectacle after outlandish spectacle to protest the *sine qua non* of what Adrienne Rich called "compulsory heterosexuality": matrimony.[12] This position, put forth in Solanas's *Up Your Ass* and *SCUM Manifesto* (1965, 1967), is echoed in the Radicalesbians' "The Woman-Identified Woman" (1970), Roxanne Dunbar's "Female Liberation as the Basis for Social Revolution" (1970), Kate Millett's *Sexual Politics* (1970), Shulamith Firestone's *The Dialectic of Sex* (1970), Jill Johnston's *Lesbian Nation* (1973), Atkinson's *Amazon Odyssey* (1974), and the Dyketactics "Declaration" (1975), to name only a few. These tracts call for replacing marriage and the nuclear family with communal households predicated on nongendered divisions of labor and for using advances in reproductive technology to free women from the biological imposition to bear children.

While lesbians of color were often as adverse to marriage as white dykes, many black and Latina activists contextualized their critiques of the nuclear family in an understanding that this structure, however problematic, provided a safe haven in a racist society. Still others were reluctant to enter into the discussion at all, for, as Barbara Smith notes in the preface to *Home Girls: A Black Feminist Anthology:*

> Raising issues of oppression within already oppressed communities is as likely to be met with attacks and ostracism as with comprehension and readiness to change. To this day most Black women are unwilling to jeopardize their racial credibility (as defined by Black men) to address the reality of sexism. Even fewer are willing to bring up homophobia and heterosexism, which are of course inextricably linked to gender oppression.[13]

One of the first black lesbians to risk ostracism was the spoken-word poet and activist Pat Parker, who before she came out in 1969 was married twice, the first time to the Black Panther Party's minister of culture, the playwright Ed Bullins. Parker claimed, "As long as women are bound by the nuclear family structure we cannot effectively move toward revolution. . . . [T]he nuclear family is the basic unit of capitalism and in order for us to move to revolution it has to be destroyed. . . . [W]e must make a commitment to change it; not reform it—revolutionize it."[14] Another vocal critic of matrimony was Barbara Smith's twin sister Beverly, who claims in "The Wedding" (1975) that "celebrating marriage is like celebrating being sold into slavery."[15] Whereas slavery served as a powerful conceptual analogy for Atkinson, Cronan, and other white women, it indexes for Smith and lesbians of color the lived experience of a brutal colonialist legacy. As Gloria Anzaldúa observes in *Borderlands/La Frontera,* "The dark-skinned woman has been silenced, caged, gagged, bound into servitude with marriage, bludgeoned for 300 years, sterilized and castrated in the twentieth century. For 300 years she has been a slave, a source of cheap labor, colonized by the Spaniard, the Anglo, by her own people."[16]

Identifying marriage as the keystone in a tower of interlocking oppressions, lesbian and feminist critiques of heterosexism served as the foundation for a broad-based liberationist agenda aimed at radically transforming society. This approach could not be more antithetical to the contemporary LGBT movement, which is dominated by pragmatists who consider the right to wed the litmus test of freedom. Same-sex marriage is touted, even by members of the Left, as a progressive cause, when, in fact, it is a heavily freighted issue that has as much to do with conformity and propriety as it does with basic human rights. For many gays and lesbians, formal marriage equality is an important civil liberty, one that should be an option for any citizen who wishes to enter into this kind of relationship. Others, myself included, want no part of what the poet Marianne Moore called "[t]his model of petrine fidelity" promoted by "savages" obsessed with "the silly task of making people noble."[17]

My objective here is not to disparage queers (or straights) who wish to wed but to contribute to conversations about the contested role of formal marriage equality in the LGBT movement by bringing back to the table a marginalized perspective: lesbian feminism. Many scholars and activists, from Lisa Duggan to Urvashi Vaid, have argued that marriage reform exemplifies the neoliberalization of sexual politics insofar as it represents a narrow, formal, nonredistributive mode of social and political equality, one that is predicated on prejudicial forms of economic advancement and social respectability. Surprisingly scant attention has been paid, however, to marriage critiques by second-wave feminists and gay liberationists who opposed the institution of matrimony, challenged sexual hegemony, and created a number of viable alternatives for organizing and living out their lives in ways that facilitated the reallocation of power, public space, cultural capital, political liberties, and sexual pleasures for everyone.

In this chapter, I look at zap actions from 1969 and 2009, comparing ludic, anarchic, antimarriage demonstrations by lesbians and feminists to dramatic displays by outraged liberals in support of same-sex unions after the passage of Proposition 8 in California. Juxtaposing zaps from two different time periods characterized by opposing views on matrimony offers a unique way of charting the diachronic status of marriage and its imbricated relationship with the rise of homoliberalism. This approach reverberates with what Carolyn Dinshaw calls "a queer historical impulse," an orientation "toward making connections across time between, on the one hand, lives, texts, and other cultural phenomena left out of sexual categories back then and, on the other, those left out of current sexual categories now."[18] When different historical moments "touch"—even ones that are just decades apart—sparks fly and tempers flare as signifiers brush against one another, unsettling naturalized categories and normative structures.

A complex historiographical inquiry into the practice of zaps offers a particularly generative approach to the topic of same-sex marriage. It enables us to take critical stock of a divisive issue, provides a broad basis for understanding the current political landscape in the context of a longer trajectory of social and political activism, and sheds light on the models and methods being deployed to construct and evaluate LGBT history. A spectacularly theatrical mode of performative protest designed to jolt the public into consciousness, zaps provide an electric charge that energizes and enlightens constituencies, but they can also effect the inverse, annihilating opposing viewpoints, eradicating debate, and anesthetizing critical faculties. My aim in undertaking this study is to show how the push for marriage equality zaps history, occluding lesbian and feminist opposition to matrimony in order to make the past consistent with today's conservative, integrationist mission. This chapter culminates in an exploration of the fortieth anniversary of the Stonewall uprising in June 2009, which took place just a few months after the Proposition 8 vote. Manipulating cultural memory through carefully scripted performances, homoliberals turned this event commemorating movement veterans and four decades of political struggle into a public enactment of forgetting, eliding early activists' resolutely antimarriage stance. Transforming Stonewall 40/Pride 2009 into an amnesiac site of assimilation, marriagists used this event to zap dissenting opinions about marriage reform within LGBT communities and rewrite the historical record.

Altared States 1969: WITCH's Bridal Affair

At 11:00 a.m. on Saturday, February 15, 1969, a coven of radical feminists known as the Women's International Terrorist Conspiracy from Hell (WITCH) disrupted the first annual Bridal Fair at Madison Square Garden in New York City.[19] Thousands of fliers calling all feminists to "Confront the Whore-makers," a play on the anti-Vietnam slogan "Confront the War-makers," had been plastered in subway stations, bathrooms, and bookstores across the city. "Bring posters, brooms, costumes, consciousness, anger, witches' brew, love, bridal gowns, tambourines, hexes, laughter, solidarity, and alternatives," the fliers announced, to protest the packaging of women into "'loving' commodities on the marriage market."[20] Approximately 150 women took part in the "Bridle Un-Fair" demonstration. Donning black veils and trains of Monopoly money, demonstrators sang "Here comes the slave / Off to her grave" to the tune of the wedding march while picketing the convention center. They brandished placards that read, "Always a Bride, Never a Person," "Ask not for Whom the Wedding Bell Tolls," and "Here Comes the Bribe." Agitators distributed leaflets proclaiming that "marriage is a dehumanizing institution—legal whoredom for women" along with complimentary "shop-lifting bags," which they hoped would call attention to the "consumptive hegemony" of the bridal industrial complex.[21]

In one of the many mock rituals conducted that day, WITCHes staged a mass "unwedding ceremony" in which they took a "pledge of disallegiance" and "gathered together . . . in the spirit of . . . passion to affirm [their] love and initiate [their] freedom from the unholy state of American patriarchal oppression."[22] The dissidents took a vow

> to love, cherish, and groove on each other and on all living things. We prom-
> ise to smash the alienated family unit. We promise not to obey. We promise
> this through highs and bummers, in recognition that riches and objects are
> totally available through socialism or theft (but also that possessing is irrel-
> evant to love) . . . [and] in the name of Revolution, we pronounce ourselves
> Free Human Beings.[23]

The Bridal Fair demonstration culminated with a small group of wom-en taking the protest from the street inside Madison Square Garden, using passes procured by WITCH Judith Duffet who infiltrated *Bride* magazine. Dressed in ladylike drag to avoid suspicion, these insurgents made their way to the showroom floor where they proceeded to hex the vendors, those manufacturers and marketers of fantasy dream weddings and bridezillas. They cast spells on three of the event's sponsors: International Coffee, which engaged in slave-labor practices in South America; J. P. Stevens, a fabric company with lucrative defense contracts to supply the armed forces with uniforms and shrouds; and Chase Manhattan Bank, which hoped to cash in by financing not only wedding gowns and ceremonies but honeymoon packages, mortgages, and loans for furniture and appliances. Just as the activists were about to be escorted out of the convention center, they released cages of white mice onto the showroom floor.

The Bridal Fair protest and The Feminists' occupation of the New York Marriage Licensing Bureau are what counterculture radicals in the 1960s called zaps, humorous, highly theatrical, nonviolent acts of civil disobedience involving skits, costumes, and props. Infusing social protest with guerrilla theater, zaps are parodic, satirical, and symbolic actions designed to wow spectators and attract media attention. A zap, as the name suggests, is a jolt or charge, a sudden infusion of energy, one that typically takes the form of a strike or attack. According to the *Oxford English Dictionary*, the first recorded usage of the term was in 1929, as a linguistic representation of the sound of a bullet, ray gun, or laser.[24] By the 1940s, the term had become synonymous with murder, with the rubbing out of an individual or the extermination of entire populations. This linguistic transformation was the result, no doubt, of two world wars, the Holocaust, and the looming threat of nuclear annihilation.[25] In the 1950s and 1960s, *zap* (along with *bam, splat, pow, wham,* and other sonorous, onomatopoeic, terms) was used to punch up comic books, from commercial publications such as *Batman* to the underground zine *Zap* featuring the work of R. Crumb. The term was also used to punctuate a new form of painting called pop art (e.g., Andy Warhol and Roy Lichtenstein) that drew inspiration from comics, advertising, and popular culture. *Zap's* bellicose associations returned during the Vietnam War, where it was deployed to describe American soldiers' mission to eviscerate the Vietcong and the United States' desire to extinguish the communist threat. During this time, the word also referred to states of intoxication and numbness. *Zapped* was how revelers described how they felt after imbibing too much alcohol or taking too many mushrooms. According to *The Routledge Dictionary of Modern American Slang and Unconventional English,* soldiers used the term to describe the trauma of war and the lack of sensation they felt after battle, while homosexuals employed it to describe the experience of electroshock treatments, a common form of aversion therapy.[26]

Since the word *zap* was first introduced, artists and activists have played on the antithetical meanings of the term in an effort to smash antiquated ideologies and create new aesthetic and political models. In the 1960s dissidents saw zap actions as a way to shock a comatose public into consciousness, revitalize a moribund leftist labor movement, and conscript a complacent and complicit citizenry in the fight against capitalist exploitation and imperialism. Answering the call for a "participatory democracy," these actions enabled the direct involvement of individuals in "social decisions determining the quality and direction" of their lives.[27] Political activists saw in zaps a way to combat the suffocating apathy engineered by architects of the Cold War and to remediate the global crisis in civil rights it left in its wake by conspiring with radical contingents all over the world to "replace power rooted in possession, privilege, or circumstance by power and uniqueness rooted in love, reflectiveness, reason, and creativity."[28]

The purpose of zaps was to ensure that the revolution would be televised. Agitators used guerrilla theater tactics to create a media circus, drawing attention to underrepresented causes and unpopular viewpoints, to stories and perspectives that were not likely to be covered by journalists at mainstream presses or television studios. Through spectacular, highly publicized zap actions, activists introduced America to the New Left, the second-wave feminist, and the new homosexual. These actions showed the masses that flower power was a potent weapon, that women were a force to be reckoned with, and that gays constituted a legitimate but unrecognized political minority. Early lesbian and gay zaps mimicked surprise police raids on bars and nightclubs, which persisted long after the Stonewall riots, offering straights a taste of their own medicine. Activists of all stripes used this mode of protest to force politicians to take a stand on controversial issues such as civil rights, abortion, and AIDS, or have their unwillingness to do so be aired for all to see.

Zap actions were first staged by the Yippies (aka, the Youth International Party), a group of radicalized hippies associated with the antiwar and free speech movements who combined the Situationists' theories of mass media with the utopian aspirations and direct actions of the anarcho-theater collective the Diggers.[29] The Yippies, as Charlotte Canning has observed, "spectacularized politics using the media to point up the representational nature of public action. Theater was almost inevitable because everyday life on the Left picked up on two of the important components of performance for most experimental theaters: the creation of work out of a collaborative community and the focus on representation and spectacle."[30] Founded on December 31, 1967, by Abbie Hoffman, Anita Kushner, Jerry Rubin, Nancy Kurshan, and Paul Krassner, the Yippies were a band of merry pranksters whose penchant for outrageous antics earned them the name the Groucho-

Marxists. Cells soon sprang across the country, attracting the attention of flower power gurus Allen Ginsberg and Timothy O'Leary, as well as the support of militant radicals such as Eldridge Cleaver and Tom Hayden.

The Yippies' mission was to make the revolution fun by any means necessary, and their promotion of "a politics of ecstasy" aroused the ire and condemnation of "serious" leftists.[31] In *Revolution for the Hell of It,* Hoffman explains the group's moniker: "What does Yippie! mean? Energy—fun—fierceness—exclamation point!"[32] The Yippies' name evokes joy and exhilaration, and their zaps were acts of gaiety designed to foster pleasurable communion through daring displays of ribald humor and acerbic wit. The Yippies' most famous acts of gaiety included applying for a permit to levitate the Pentagon, addressing the House Un-American Activities Committee dressed in the garb of revolutionary soldiers while dispensing copies of the Declaration of Independence, closing the New York Stock Exchange by dropping hundreds of dollar bills from the visitor's gallery onto the trading floor, and nominating Pigasus the Immortal, a swine, for president of the United States at the Festival of Life, which they cohosted during the Democratic National Convention in Chicago in 1968.

Robin Morgan, a cofounder of WITCH, was a Yippie who employed the performative and participatory art of zaps in the service of radical feminism, as a way to put theory into practice.[33] As a writer, editor, and former child actress—she played Dagmar in the television series *I Remember Mama* with Dick Van Patten in the 1950s and hosted a weekly radio program, *The Little Robin Morgan Show,* in the 1940s—this Yippie knew firsthand the power of the media in shaping a public image. She drew on her acting skills to stage the Bridal Fair zap and used her extensive television and journalism contacts to publicize the demonstration, just as she had done a few months prior for the now legendary Miss America protest in Atlantic City (September 1968), the event credited with making second-wave feminism headline news.[34]

Taking their cue from the Yippies, WITCH eschewed formal membership and organizational hierarchy, which meant there was little or no contact between autonomous cells across the country. Jo Freeman, a member of the Chicago chapter, describes WITCH as "more of an idea-in-action than an organization." According to Morgan, it was a commitment to gaiety that connected the disparate cells, "A certain common style, insouciance, theatricality, humor, and activism unite the Covens, which are otherwise totally autonomous and unhierarchical to the point of anarchy."[35] The group's commitment to gaiety is reflected in the New York coven's manifesto, coauthored by Morgan, which reads:

> WITCH is an all-woman Everything. It's theater, revolution, magic, terror, joy, garlic, flowers, spells. It's an awareness that witches and gypsies were the original guerrillas and resistance fighters against oppression. . . . Witches were . . . the first birth-control practitioners and abortionists, the first alchemists. . . . WITCH lives and laughs in every woman. She is the free part of each of us, beneath the shy smiles, the acquiescence to absurd male domination . . . [so] if you are a woman and dare to look within yourself, you are a witch . . . you are free and beautiful. . . . Whatever is repressive, solely male-oriented, greedy, puritanical, authoritarian-those are your targets . . . [and] you are pledged to free our brothers from oppression and stereotyped sexual roles as well as ourselves.[36]

Committed to dramatic acts of political dissent, this collective imagined itself as "the striking arm of the Women's Liberation Movement, aiming mainly at financial and corporate America, at those institutions that have the power to control and define human life."[37] The first annual Bridal Fair was an obvious target for a WITCH zap, for it combined "racism, militarism, capitalism—all packaged into one 'ideal' symbol, a woman."[38]

In an interview with the *New York Times* reporter dispatched to cover the exhibit, Judy Klemesrud, Morgan explained that WITCH was on hand to protest "the commerciality of the Bridal Fair and the institution of marriage as it exists in this culture to dehumanize both parties—but especially women."[39] Klemesrud, clearly amused by what she describes as the day's "unofficial" entertainment, was perplexed by WITCH, and in particular "Miss Morgan," whom the reporter notes "prefers to use her maiden name, is married and expects her first child in July."[40] An advocate of flexible, antiheterosexist, politicized sexuality, Morgan had recently come out as a lesbian and was involved in an open marriage with fellow Yippie Kenneth Pitchford, an out gay poet ten years her senior.[41]

WITCH attracted creative rebels who, in Morgan's words, were "generally bored by marching and would prefer to demolish things—by magic, of course."[42] Tired of "comatose tactics" and "dull, overlong speeches," these activists could not imagine anything more tedious than petitions, anything more stultifying than sit-ins.[43] These dissidents wanted to get to the root of oppression not by talking but by dramatizing the problem. As Morgan recalls, "[W]e were . . . newly aroused and angry about our oppression as women—and we wanted to *move*. It seemed intolerable that we should sit around 'just talking' when there was so much to be done. So we went and did it."[44] The problem, according to many women's liberationists, was that WITCH was moving in the wrong direction. Its popular but often poorly planned demonstrations were a source of consternation for many activists, who feared that these amateur antics would make a mockery of feminism and detract from the seriousness of the cause.

Liberal feminists felt that the group was extremist, that its denunciation of the institution of marriage alienated heterosexual women and its indiscriminate attack on men estranged potential allies. Such hyperbolic posturing, reformists feared, would encourage the general public to dismiss feminist claims as frivolous acts by hysterical women and angry lesbians. Feminists at the other end of the political spectrum felt WITCH was not radical enough. Redstockings admonished the collective for its antiwoman stance—in likening wives to slaves and prostitutes—and its uncritical adoption of confrontational tactics of the male Left.[45] These radical feminists took WITCH to task for denouncing consciousness-raising, which, they argued, the coven needed more rather than less of. As Canning has observed, feminists "felt that this kind of protest was not appropriate because it attacked the women participating in the contest instead of simply attacking the power structure behind the contest."[46] Liberal and radical feminists were united in their fear that WITCH would impede the progress of the women's liberation movement. They disagreed, however, in their definition of progress and on which policies, programs, and political actions would best advance their cause.

A look back at lesbian and feminist zaps from 1969 shows how complicated it can be to lobby a critique of marriage (or any other liberal reform) without offending the people who take part in this ritual. Equally illuminating, it sheds light on the ways in which members of minority groups can squelch dissent among their own ranks. Succumbing to the molar logic of second-wave feminism, Morgan came to see the Bridal Fair action as "a self-indulgent insult to the very women [WITCH] claimed [it] wanted to reach."[47] The protest, she would write upon reflection, "was aimed at the institution of marriage itself, at the structure of the bourgeois family, which oppresses everyone, and particularly women," but the tactics the group employed made attendees feel as if they were the target of the protest.[48] Morgan attributed the action's failure to the fact that zaps, as a mode of protest, are rooted in techniques developed by the Yippies and the "counterfeit male-dominated Left."[49] She not only recanted the action, but she renounced the practice of zaps as a patriarchal tool that could never be used to dismantle the master's house.

The Bridal Fair backlash convinced Morgan that the "revolution must be led by, *made* by, those who have been most oppressed: black, brown, and white women—with men relating to that the best they can."[50] Members of WITCH took a hiatus from direction action, during which time Morgan immersed herself in feminist theory and published one of the most influential and widely circulated anthologies of the women's liberation movement, *Sisterhood Is Powerful*. She also helped orchestrate the feminist takeover of *RAT: Subterranean News*, a New Left periodical. In the first women's liberation issue of *RAT* (published in January 1970), Morgan issued a feminist declaration of independence from the male Left in which she repudiates both the confrontational, "ejaculatory tactics" of macho revolutionaries and the "clownish proto-anarchism of groups such as the Yippies."[51] In "Goodbye to All That," she writes:

> To hell with the simplistic notion that automatic freedom for women—or nonwhite peoples—will come about ZAP! with the advent of a socialist revolution. Bullshit. Two evils pre-date capitalism and clearly have been able to survive and post-date socialism: sexism and racism. . . . How much further we will have to go to create those profound changes that would give birth to a genderless society.[52]

In this essay, Morgan encouraged feminists to be "*the women that men have warned us about*" and to create acts of gaiety in which they "Let it all hang out. Let it seem bitchy, catty, dykey, Solanasesque, frustrated, crazy, nutty, frigid, ridiculous, bitter, embarrassing, man-hating, libelous, pure, unfair, envious, intuitive, low-down, stupid, petty, liberating."[53]

Feminists bullied WITCH members into thinking the Madison Square Garden zap was an utter failure and pressured them into adopting a position of gender essentialism, just as queers today are pressed into supporting a conservative, antiliberationist agenda. While WITCH may not have raised the consciousness of every woman on the scene that day, the event inspired covens across the country to engage in similar (and sometimes more enlightened) protests at bridal fairs in 1969, and for many years after. In addition, this demonstration prompted other activist organizations, such as The

Feminists, and artistic collectives, such as Caravan Theatre in Cambridge, Massachusetts, to stage agitprop spectacles dramatizing the horrors of matrimony.

Caravan Theatre's *How to Make a Woman* (1969) opens with two women (played by Aili Singer and Barbara Fleischman) shopping for dresses.[54] The pair is seduced by male proprietors into trying on a variety of outlandish garments that restrict their movement, contort their figures, and objectify their breasts, hips, and vagina. Through a series of flashbacks and dream sequences, the women rehearse the rites of passage that prepared them for womanhood: walking in heels, learning how to type, being raped, getting married, having children, and so on. The choreography of their movements, inspired by the Open Theater's transformations and the Living Theatre's abstract acting style, heighten the sense of ritual and suggest that women's oppression is a carefully crafted social drama.

How to Make a Woman enacts Simone de Beauvoir's now commonplace assertion in *The Second Sex,* "One is not born, but rather becomes, a woman."[55] This declaration is typically read as evidence for the social construction of Woman, a maxim of second-wave feminism. What is often forgotten, however, is that a critique of marriage lies at the heart of de Beauvoir's philosophy: a critique that is enacted frequently in feminist performance and protest of the 1960s and 1970s. De Beauvoir, who never married, details the specific ways in which religious, political, and scientific traditions create a mystified image of Woman characterized by impossible and contradictory ideals of femininity. The social construction of Woman as Other supports the fallacy of women's inherent or "natural" inferiority to men and provides justification for the patriarchal exploitation of sexual difference. De Beauvoir's claim that existence precedes essence and her phenomenological insight that it is only as embodied beings that we experience and engage the world laid the groundwork for feminist theory and the practice of consciousness-raising.

Consciousness-raising and zap actions informed the praxis of Caravan and other theater collectives. The immediacy of live theater proved to be a particularly fecund site for exploring the corporeal contingencies and lived experiences of sexism, misogyny, homophobia, and racism. Feminist collectives created performances based on their personal experiences of discrimination. The development of this new content necessitated the invention of new theatrical forms and new modes of production—including a nonhierarchical division of labor, the use of nontraditional venues, and the insistence on there being no separation between audiences and actors. Like zaps, these feminist productions blurred the line between performance and protest, and events often ended with women taking to the streets. Feminist theater collectives shared several ideological and formal aspects with direct action groups such as WITCH and The Feminists. They used performance to put politics into action, employed theatricality to foreground gender as constructed, and engaged in role-playing to rehearse new ways of being in the world.

Antimarriage protests in 1969 inspired countless women to join the feminist and gay liberation movements and to think about ways other than marriage and maternity to make, mark, and measure their lives. These acts of gaiety underwrote vast socioeconomic changes in America, engendering revolutionary chronologies that promoted alternative ways of advancing history. Eschewing teleological notions of progress, lesbian and feminist zaps endowed leftist politics with a distinctly dykey chronometry, one that was enjoyable rather than industrious, collective rather than individual, and ludic rather than linear. Marrying pleasure with political activism, these spectacular public protests promoted a visionary praxis that was redolent of ecstasy. Theatrical zaps served an important function in the dramaturgy of radical feminism, and they were an integral element of the gay rights movement. The Gay Activist Alliance (GAA), a splinter group of the Gay Liberation Front that formed in December 1969, became so skilled at the art of zaps that many histories of the LGBT movement, queer theory, and AIDS activism mistakenly credit GAA as the progenitor of this form of political protest, ignoring not only lesbian and feminist guerrilla actions but the Yippies' spectacles as well.[56] The Gay Activist Alliance is of particular importance to this study because it is the progenitor of today's single-issue, reform-oriented, corporate-structured LGBT movement, and because it staged the first pro-marriage zap. The emergence and success of GAA plays a large part in the zapping of lesbian and feminist opposition to marriage from the historical record, and it marks the moment at which gay rights became synonymous with gay marriage.

A Husbandly Approach: GAA and the First Pro-marriage Zap

The Gay Activist Alliance began when a cohort of disaffected GLF members left the group over ideological, procedural, and financial issues, including

GLF's decision to donate five hundred dollars to the Black Panther Party and fund women's dances.[57] Unhappy with GLF's broad-based political agenda, activists conceived of GAA as a single-issue, politically neutral organization whose goal was to secure basic human rights, dignity, and freedom for all gay people.[58] A central tenet of the GAA was that the organization would devote its resources solely and specifically to gay and lesbian causes, though most members remained active in other movement work. A moderate and, over time, increasingly conservative alternative to GLF, GAA worked within the system for political reform. The group sought to abolish discriminatory sex laws, promote civil rights, and challenge politicians to publicly state their views on gay issues.

Though reformist-oriented, GAA engaged in militant, confrontation politics, publicly exposing and aggressively challenging the homophobic rhetoric and deeds of government officials, corporate conglomerates, and media entities, often through zap actions. They protested negative portraits of homosexuality on television shows (e.g., *Marcus Welby, M.D, Police Woman, the Dick Cavett Show, the Mike Douglas Show,* and broadcasts by Walter Cronkite), in films (e.g., *Cruising*), and in newspapers (e.g., *the Village Voice,* where GAA member Arthur Bell was a columnist). New York mayor John Lindsay was a frequent GAA target, with activists commandeering his press conferences and even hounding him at the opera. Zaps were used by GAA as "political theater for educating the gay masses" and awakening the consciousness of straight America.[59] The group became so famous for its protests that simply threatening to zap a person of authority often resulted in a victory for the organization. Through bold, political actions, it achieved a number of important reforms and assisted in many more, including the declassification of homosexuality as a psychopathology in the Diagnostic and Statistic Manual of Mental Disorders (DSM).[60]

These zaps provided a way for lesbians and gays to come out in support of a cause. In fostering a collective identity, these actions made it safer— and indeed more pleasurable—for others to do the same. As a reporter for *Life* magazine observed, zaps "offer [homosexuals] the best therapy for the humiliations inflected by an anti-homosexual society. 'One good zap,' they say, 'is worth months on a psychiatrist's couch.'"[61] Arthur Evans, a founding member of GAA, speaks to the potential of zap actions as a recruiting tool.

Gays who have as yet no sense of pride see a zap on television or read about it in the press. First they are vaguely disturbed at the demonstrators for "rocking the boat"; eventually, when they see how the straight establishment responds, they feel anger. This anger gradually focuses on heterosexual oppressors, and the gays develop a sense of class-consciousness. And the no-longer-closeted gays realize that assimilation into the heterosexual mainstream is no answer: gays must unite amongst themselves, organize their common resources for collective action, and resist.[62]

Although many in GAA worked to create an organization that reflected the diversity of the LGBT community, the collective suffered from a lack of gender and racial parity. Membership consisted primarily, though not exclusively, of white, middle-class men, and GAA's tactics and targets reflected the needs and desires of this constituency. The aim of GAA, according to Evans, "was to reach . . . *gay men* who were not interested in politics" and "who did not connect their sexuality with political issue[s]."[63] Women's issues were something of an afterthought, if they were addressed at all.

Seeking to attract more dykes to GAA, a group of women formed the Lesbian Liberation Committee (LLC) in the fall of 1971. Although its activities were primarily social, consisting of film screenings, panel discussions on topics like coming out and lesbian motherhood, and women's dances at the Firehouse, the men of GAA were less than thrilled about this development. "We had arguments every single day," recalls Jean O'Leary, chair of LLC. "We had debates on the floor. The men were listening, but they just weren't hearing what we had to say, and they held on to their stereotyped views of women. They would also make a point of crashing our women-only events."[64] Tensions escalated, and in the spring of 1972 a group of women, O'Leary included, broke with GAA to establish Lesbian Feminist Liberation (LFL), a hierarchical, reform-oriented organization that focused on lesbian issues but cultivated alliances with both gay and feminist groups.

The lack of gender parity and the timing of the lesbian split from GAA are important because they coincided with the group's pro-marriage zap— the first of its kind for the LGBT movement—on June 4, 1971. Not a single lesbian took part in this event, a fact that is rarely, if ever, reported in histories of this action. The absence of women is glaringly obvious in video footage of the protest, however.[65] Just as The Feminists had done two years earlier, GAA staged a guerrilla theater action at the New York Marriage Licensing Bureau. Whereas the former had protested the coerced participation of women in this institution, the latter decried gay men's exclusion from it. The zap was precipitated by a story in the *New York Post* about Father

Robert Clement of the Church of the Beloved Disciple, who performed ceremonies of "Holy Union" for gay couples.[66] When City Clerk Herman Katz
threatened Clement with legal action, the pastor, whose congregation was
primarily homosexual men, fought back. He told a reporter for the *Post* that
his church was not in the business of performing "marriages," and thus the
rites he conducted were neither illegal nor of any concern to the City Clerk's
Office. GAA plotted to zap Katz at his office and demand that he apologize
to Clement and all gay Americans for disparaging and defaming them.

Demonstrators decided to stage the zap as an "engagement party" for
two male couples—John Basso and John C. Bond and Steve Krotz and Vito
Russo.[67] In a beautifully choreographed event, thirty members of GAA
descended on the Marriage Licensing Bureau bearing invitations, musical
instruments, coffee, cups, cutlery, even a folding table on which to place
everything. Activists serenaded employees and couples applying for their
marriage licenses with chants of "gay power" before serving them wedding
cake, an elaborate multitiered confection decorated with one male couple
and one female couple, a ludicrous gesture given that this protest reflected
a decidedly husbandly perspective on marriage. The figurines were joined
by a large lambda, a Greek letter used as GAA's symbol for gay unity, which
is ironic since lesbians either boycotted or were not invited to the event. On
the side of the cake, written in a large heart, was "gay power to gay love."
While cake was being served, Evans commandeered the phone lines. He
told callers that the office could only grant licenses to same-sex couples and
invited them to come down and join GAA's celebration. Katz, who was duly
chastised by these firebrands, phoned the police, who arrived on the scene
within the hour to break up the party.

This highly entertaining and effective protest led by white gay men gives
credence to David Eng's assertion that the legalized nuclear family to which
pro-same-sex-marriage activists aspire is a racially privileged form of intimacy that offers the greatest benefits to those individuals who are cisgendered,
male, Caucasian, and middle-class.[68] As such, it sheds light on the multiple
and contradictory functions of zap actions: they simultaneously energize
debate and abate or silence dissent. While the GAA marriage bureau zap
enlightened straight spectators about the heterosexist nature of matrimony,
it not only obscured the misogynist underpinnings of this hallowed institution but it made it seem—through the token gesture of the cake topping—as
if gay men and women were in solidarity on the subject of same-sex unions,
which, at the time of this demonstration, they were not. I am not suggesting

that all dykes in the 1960s and 1970s opposed marriage. What I am suggesting is that there was something missing in GAA's pro-marriage zap, namely, a lesbian feminist optic that might have encouraged the male protestors and their captive audience to think in broader terms about the institution of marriage and to go beyond the simple, binary logic and reductive reasoning animating this protest. The zap reflects a fundamental difference between lesbian feminists and gay men over the issue of marriage at a key moment in LGBT history. It has received scant critical attention despite the fact that it has exerted a profound influence on contemporary politics and activism.

Sensational, confrontational zaps, such at the Marriage Licensing Bureau action, helped make GAA one of the most effective and longest-lasting political entities to form in the wake of the Stonewall uprising. As time went on, however, some members of the group began to question the efficacy of these shock tactics. Believing that the promotion of positive, less aggressive, and more domesticated images of homosexuality would appeal to a wider audience—beyond major metropolitan cities and into the heartland of middle-class America—thereby garnering LGBT citizens more allies and greater political influence, a small but increasingly vocal contingent of assimilationist-oriented GAA activists called for the collective to tone down its militant rhetoric and dispense with zap actions. This conservative faction suggested that the long-haired hippies and fairies—like Arthur Evans, who led many of the high-profile actions and served as the public face of GAA—be replaced with clean-cut, conventionally attractive, straight-acting spokespersons. Disagreements over the future of the collective prompted many members to leave the organization, including former GAA president Bruce Voeller, who went on to found the National Gay Task Force (1973), an influential lobbying group for gay rights, and Michael Lavery, who started Lambda Legal (1973).[69] These two national rights organizations have played a key role in the enormous gains that LGBT citizens have gained over the past four decades. Dedicated primarily to juridical reform, these entities have been instrumental in the mainstreaming of the movement and in making marriage equality the galvanizing issue that it is today.

Altared States 2009: California's Proposition 8

Prior to 1973, there was no statute prohibiting same-sex unions in any US state, but according to common law, or precedent, this was a heterosexual contract; gay marriage simply did not exist. Around the time of the GAA marriage bureau zap, a gay male couple from Minnesota, Jack Baker and Michael McConnell, who had been denied a marriage license, appealed their case (*Baker v. Nelson*) all the way to the Supreme Court, which refused to hear the matter. It was in direct response to the growing gay rights movement, and to lawsuits such as *Baker v. Nelson,* that states began to enact legislation defining marriage as a union between a man and a woman. Maryland was the first state to do so, followed by Arizona, Colorado, and Virginia. By 1980, twenty-five out of fifty states had passed similar bills into law, and by 1994 the number had risen to forty-five. Two years later President Bill Clinton signed the Defense of Marriage Act (DOMA), which defines marriage for purposes of federal law as an opposite-sex relationship and mandates that no state may be required to recognize as a marriage a same-sex relationship considered a marriage in another state. While some LGBT activists would have fought for the right to marry irrespective of these legislative acts, the fact that our government went to such lengths to institutionalize discrimination ensured that marriage equality would become a primary target of activist energies, even for gays and lesbians with no personal investment in the institution, who are ambivalent about it, and who otherwise oppose this normalizing institution.

Performance artist Holly Hughes speaks to the conflicted position in which many contemporary lesbian feminists find themselves when it comes to the issue of same-sex marriage. In 2010 she created with Megan Carney (of Chicago's About Face Theatre) and Moe Angelos (of the Five Lesbian Brothers) *Let Them Eat Cake,* a performance advertised as "a gay marriage in one act with confections." Based on the enormously popular *Tony and Tina's Wedding, Let Them Eat Cake* asks the audience ("guests") to salvage a gay wedding gone wrong by interrogating what it means to be married, single, gay, straight, commitment phobic, a joiner, included, or jeering from the outskirts. In an interview with Diana Cage, Hughes admitted:

> I didn't really want to get married. I thought that was one of the perks of being gay. I mean, a lot of people have said that . . . you didn't have to get married, you couldn't be in the military, you didn't have to have kids. But then, I did want to get married when I was told I couldn't. . . . My desire to get married was uncovered by the religious Right.[70]

Another lesbian artist whose support of same-sex marriage was sparked by opposition to it is Joan Lipkin, whose That Uppity Theatre Company in St. Louis staged *The State of Marriage* in 2010. This show tells the story of gay and lesbian couples who board the Show Me Marriage Equality Bus, crossing state lines from Missouri, where same-sex marriage is prohibited, to Iowa, where it has been legal since 2009, in order to get hitched. Like Hughes's *Let Them Eat Cake,* Lipkin's pro-marriage performance piece was inspired, in large part, by the passage of Proposition 8 in California.[71]

In May 2008, California became the second state, after Massachusetts, to legalize same-sex unions when the State Supreme Court found the ban unconstitutional (*In re Marriage Cases*).[72] Factions on the religious Right, opposed to what they considered activist judges' ruling in the case, drafted an initiative, Proposition 8, to amend the state Constitution to limit marriage to opposite-sex couples. This referendum was placed on the November 2008 ballot, and it passed, by a slim margin (less than 5 percent), overturning the Supreme Court decision. Proposition 8 did not affect domestic partnerships in California, nor did it invalidate same-sex marriages granted during the brief six-month window (from May to November) in which they were legal.

Many liberals were stunned by the results. In the same election in which Americans selected Barack Obama as the nation's first African-American president, Californians delivered a severe blow to LGBT civil rights. Early exit poll data showed that voters were divided along religious, political, and racial lines, with whites opposing the measure, Latinos divided, and blacks in support, by 70 percent according to cable and Internet news sites. These statistics led many gays and lesbians to blame racial minorities for the outcome.[73] Columnist Dan Savage, for example, posted the following message, which he titled "Black Homophobia" on his blog on the morning of November 5.

> I'm done pretending that the handful of racist gay white men out there—and they're out there, and I think they're scum—are a bigger problem for African Americans, gay and straight, than the huge numbers of homophobic African Americans are for gay Americans, whatever their color.[74]

Savage's knee-jerk reaction belies the fact that the majority of people who supported Proposition 8 were white homophobes: 63 percent of the electorate in 2008 was white, compared to 10 percent African-American, and 49 percent of Caucasians supported the referendum.[75] Blaming black homophobia, as Savage and others did, occludes the real problem: a predominantly white LGBT community took for granted the support of people of color. As we have seen time and time again over the past four decades, when the movement ignores the issue of race and fails to make coalition building a priority, the consequences are devastating. While the queer nation benefits from having many black, Asian, and Latino members, not to mention advocates, it consistently fails to promote people of color to positions of leadership. As Urvashi Vaid notes, ethnic minorities constitute 25 percent of the LGBT population, but this is not reflected in the institutional hierarchy of most agencies, as racial equality is not considered a priority by the white, middle-class men, or the handful of similarly positioned women, who set the contemporary gay agenda.[76] While the Left was busy ignoring the issue of race, the antigay Right (spearheaded by the Mormon church) actively courted the ethnic vote in the 2008 election. Its coalition was better funded (having raised an estimated twenty-five million dollars), better organized, and did a superior job of grassroots outreach, developing strong ties with racial conservatives.

The passage of Proposition 8 and the legal limbo in which it put many people created both anger and confusion among LGBT communities and their allies. Almost immediately citizens began to mobilize, plotting an appeal to the Supreme Court and staging protests to generate a media blitz. As the tenor and purpose of LGBT activism had shifted considerably in recent decades, so, too, had the types of organizations and the modes of civil disobedience they favored. None of the entities that staged marriage protests in and around 1969 were still active in 2009. Most of them had dissolved within a year or two of forming, save GAA, which functioned until 1981 and had a profound impact on the militant tactics of AIDS activists in groups such as ACT-UP and Queer Nation. As was the case in the 1960s and 1970s, the most prominent and powerful collectives in the 1980s and 1990s were comprised primarily, though by no means exclusively, of white, middle-class gay men, a significant number of whom became champions of the cause of same-sex marriage. Denied visitation rights and locked into costly battles with the biological families of their dead and dying lovers over health care directives, inheritance, shared property, and child custody, many gay men came to see marriage as the best and most expedient way to secure the benefits, not to mention the social legitimacy, that the government bestows on straight couples. These activists made marriage the cornerstone of the queer agenda, ignoring, just as the men of GAA had done decades earlier, lesbian and feminist objections to this discriminatory institution.[77]

The direct action group Lesbian Avengers tried to reanimate this critique through wonderfully wicked acts of gaiety, to no avail. Founded in 1992 by a coalition of theater artists and activists fed up with the marginalization of women in the queer movement, the Avengers focused on issues vital to lesbian survival and visibility.[78] They are remembered for their smart, saucy, and satirical ads featuring the group's logo, an ignited bomb; for their spectacular sapphic hijinks (e.g., unleashing plagues of crickets on ungodly ministries, eating fire, and marching topless with duct-taped nipples); and for establishing the tradition of the Dyke March on Pink Saturday before the Gay Pride Parade. Opposed to conservative gays' attempt to legitimize same-sex marriage, the Avengers staged a series of demonstrations surrounding Andrew Sullivan's 1995 speaking tour for his book *Virtually Normal*. Playing, as they often did, on the conflation of lesbians and terrorists (a topic I take up in chapter four), demonstrators positioned themselves outside of bookstores where Sullivan was holding autograph sessions. They carried signs bearing an enormous picture of the author's face over which they placed bulls-eyes and crosshairs, as if to say—in no uncertain terms—marriagists are misogynists, regardless of their sexual orientation, and thus the target of radical lesbian feminists' ire.[79]

By the time of the Proposition 8 vote, ACT-UP, Queer Nation, and the Lesbian Avengers were, for all intents and purposes, defunct. Like GLF, these anarchist collectives burned out as quickly as they burst on the scene while more conservative, mainstream organizations, including the National Gay and Lesbian Task Force (NGLTF, formerly NGTF) and the Human Rights Campaign (HRC), founded in 1980, gained traction. These centrist-leaning, reformist-oriented institutions actively reject confrontational modes of protest, including zap actions. Seeking to integrate into existing social structures, not challenge the tenets of the status quo, NGLTF and HRC eschew aggressive, in-yer-face actions by militant activists in favor of more polite tactics of persuasion such as letter-writing campaigns and political lobbying. This is evident in the names of the organizations. Unlike the Gay Liberation Front, The Feminists, and WITCH, whose titles announce themselves as radical, if not extremist, both NGLTF and HRC are devoid of revolutionary references. Even their acronyms signal serious business, with nary a hint of playfulness. More corporate than democratic in their structure, these agencies are comprised not of political dissidents but of "insiders" who are out. Governed by paid officials and boards of directors, as opposed to members of the rank and file who donate their time, these agencies choose leaders based on their credibility, respectability, and financial clout, not their political acumen, zealousness, or fervor. With unprecedented access to the halls of power and well-endowed coffers, NGLTF and the HRC reflect the extent to which "the dominant national lesbian and gay civil rights organizations have become," according to Lisa Duggan, "lobbying, legal, and public relations firms for an increasingly narrow gay, monied elite."[80] These agencies represent the co-option of a radical social movement by homoliberal conglomerates that fight for the special interests of a few rather than the emancipation of all people.

As zaps are antithetical to the mission of the organizations with the greatest interest in marriage reform, most of the performative protests staged in the wake of Proposition 8 were conducted either by individuals or by new, single-issue groups that sprang up after the election such as Join the Impact (JTI) and NOH8 (which stands for "no hate"). By their own admission, many of the people involved with these initiatives had little or no history of activism (LGBT or other), scant interest in broader issues of social justice, and a lack of familiarity with social, economic, and political theory. Who needs Marx, the Situationists, or the Yippies when we have the Internet, vast media repositories such as YouTube, and social networking platforms such as Facebook and Twitter. Media-minded political activism has changed considerably over the past several decades. A flash mob of hundreds or even thousands can be organized in a matter of minutes, and with a simple text message or tweet. Protestors no longer need to court reporters to publicize their events; they can do it themselves with relatively inexpensive digital technology and the push of a button. A picture or video that goes viral can be seen by millions of people around the globe in a single day, far more than read print journalism or watch network and cable news. In fact, traditional news sources not only report on but increasingly take their headlines from items initially broadcast in the blogosphere.

Almost all of the zaps responding to Proposition 8 utilized Internet technology in some way. Many actions were staged in virtual space, including *Prop 8—the Musical,* a star-studded, three-minute video released on December 3, 2008, that was designed to galvanize public support for the appeals process. Created and written by Marc Shaiman, a Tony Award–winning composer, lyricist, and arranger (best known for his work on *Hairspray, South Park,* and *Saturday Night Live*) and choreographed by Adam Shankman (director of *Hairspray* the movie), this web video depicts a student production of *Prop 8—The Musical* at a fictitious Sacramento Community College. The location is a reference to the California Musical Theater in Sacramento

(CMT), the largest nonprofit arts organization in the state. The theater's artistic director, Scott Eckern, became the target of Shaiman's outrage when it was revealed that Eckern—a Mormon with a lesbian sister—had donated money to a Yes on Prop 8 campaign (California law requires that all contributions of a thousand dollars or more be made public, and donor rolls were widely circulated after the election). Shaiman called his colleague to say he was boycotting CMT to ensure that no profits earned from his labor were being "used to put discrimination in the Constitution."[81] Next Shaiman sent an impassioned e-mail about Eckern's donation to over a thousand people in his address book. Adam McKay, actor Will Ferrell's collaborator, wrote back inviting him to record a protest song on their website funnyordie.com. On reading McKay's reply, Shaiman recalls having a "slapping-my-head moment. Oh yeah, why didn't I think of that? Or why didn't I do that in the first place?"[82] So "six weeks too late" to impact the election, Shaiman became a marriage activist. In less than seventy-two hours, he wrote *Prop 8—The Musical,* recorded it with a few dozen of his Hollywood friends, and posted it online. The video received 1.2 million hits its first day.

Like the archival footage of the nation's first pro-marriage zap staged by GAA forty years before, Shaiman's video is curiously (though not surprisingly) devoid of a lesbian presence. While *Prop 8—The Musical* features many self-identified queer women, such as Margaret Cho (a bisexual who is in an open marriage with a man), it does not include any out dykes (one closeted one, perhaps, in Allison Janney, but no proudly visible ones). This protest was created and staged almost exclusively by gay men and their heterosexual allies.[83] The setting is a school auditorium, which is decorated with a beach scene. Enter a festively attired ensemble, "California Gays and The People That Love Them," featuring Cho, Andy Richter, and Maya Rudolph.[84] Elated by the results of the presidential election, the group dances and sings: "It's a brand new bright Obama day. What a time to be black, a girl, or gay. No, nothing could go wrong. So, join us in this song." The "Gays" are so busy celebrating the end of the Bush administration and preparing for the inauguration of Obama that they fail to take seriously the threat posed by "Proposition 8'ers and The People That Follow Them," a caustic coalition of bigots, homophobes, and religious conservatives plotting to "spread some hate and put it in the constitution."

As the Proposition 8 leader (played by John C. Reilly), his first wife (Allison Janney), and his second wife (Kathy Najimy) rally the troops, Jesus Christ (Jack Black) intervenes, challenging the groups' tactics, and in particular their selective interpretation of the Good Book.[85] The Bible "says a lot of things," notes Jesus, including "shellfish is an abomination" and "you can, stone your wife or sell your daughter into slavery!" Rather than "pick and choose" particular Bible verses to justify homophobia, Jesus counsels them, "choose love instead of hate. Besides," he reminds them, "your nation, was built on separation, of church and state." The word of god does little to convince these haters to love thy neighbor, but where Jesus fails theatrical conceit prevails. Enter the deus ex machina, A Very Smart Fellow (Neil Patrick Harris), who offers a different way "to wrap things up," one that eschews religion in favor of economics. Why spend time and money condemning homosexuals, he asks "Proposition 8'ers and The People That Follow Them," when the Right could profit from them instead. The Smart Fellow sings:

Oh, every time a gay or lesbian finds love at the parade
There's money to be made.
Each time two grooms say, paint the wedding hall and lavender's the shade
There's money to be made.
Think of all the carriages and four white horses.
There's millions lost from all of your disapproving.
Think of all the lawyers for the gay divorces. . . .

Persuaded by Smart Fellow's argument, the "Proposition 8'ers" join forces with the "California Gays and the People That Love Them." Together they sing, "I can see. America's calling me. Gay marriages will save the economy!" The screen fades to black with a link to jointheimpact.com, "a grassroots and netroots organization geared toward gaining full equality for the LGBTQI community through outreach, education, and demonstration," which started just days after the Proposition 8 vote. The founders of JTI, like Shaiman, had no activist experience prior to getting on the marriage equality bandwagon.

Based on the genre of musical comedy, Shaiman's *Prop 8* stays true to the form by depicting two opposing forces—the older/conservative/religious Right and the younger/liberal/Hollywood Left—locked in an antagonistic situation. The warring factions are comprised of stock characters whose predictability of behavior makes it difficult, if not impossible, for them to resolve the conflict. The seemingly inextricable problem of homosexuality is suddenly and abruptly ameliorated with the contrived intervention of a new character, in this case a messenger spreading the gospel of the greenback. A Very Smart Fellow convinces the older/conservative/religious side that homosexuality is a minor transgression, one that, if embraced, will not only reinforce the status quo but church and state coffers as well. A happy ending results when the two opposing factions reach a consensus on the economics (as opposed to the ethics) of same-sex marriage. Shaiman's micro–musical comedy ends with the promise of lucrative gay weddings (not to mention divorces!) and consumer citizenship for all.

One of the most popular justifications for marriage equality is that it will boost state and federal coffers. A report by the Williams Institute at the UCLA School of Law (2008) predicted that same-sex marriages would contribute nearly seven hundred million dollars to California's wedding industrial complex, generate approximately sixty-five million in revenue in the first three years alone, and create twenty-one thousand new jobs.[86] A study by the Congressional Budget Office (2004) estimated that same-sex unions would generate over a billion dollars annually. Similar studies suggest this number could be as high as sixteen billion.[87] As the country was in the midst of deep recession in 2009, one that has showed few signs of reversing course in the near future, many conservatives who previously opposed same-sex unions began to reconsider their positions on the issue. One of the most vocal supporters of same-sex marriage during the Proposition 8 debacle was the Republican governor of cash-strapped California, Arnold Schwarzenegger.

Zapped by a Right Hook

While a solid base of the Republican Party clings to the notion that marriage is a sacred bond between a man and a woman, a number of prominent members of the GOP have come out in support of same-sex unions, including Dick Cheney, whose daughter Mary is an out lesbian, former first lady Laura Bush, and the mother-daughter duo Cindy and Meghan McCain. This change of heart on the issue of gay rights reflects a larger political trend. In recent years the Republican Party has distanced itself from the extremist groups that helped solidify its power base over the past forty years—namely, the homophobes, religious moralists, and white supremacists who have allied under the banner of the Tea Party—and it has courted instead conservative factions of various identity constituencies—homosexuals, blacks, and

Latinos—seducing these minorities into networks of neoliberal alliances with calculated acts of accommodation. This strategy appears to be working, as one-quarter of all lesbian and gay voters list their political affiliation as Republican, and this number is growing. In the 2008 presidential election, 27 percent of LGBT voters supported the McCain/Palin ticket, despite this duo's public objection to gay marriage and military service.[88] If this trend continues, Lisa Duggan warns, we may be facing a seismic shift in political alliances akin to the Southern Strategy of the 1970s when white Dixie Democrats, opposed to forced racial integration and other civil rights legislation, flocked to the GOP.

The McCain family cleverly straddles both sides of the fence. John McCain's support of the military's ban on gay soldiers and his objection to same-sex marriage appeal to older and more socially conservative members of the GOP, while Cindy and Meghan McCain's vocal support of these issues speaks to both younger members of the party, who are less homophobic than previous generations, and Log Cabin Republicans. The McCain women took part in a slick media campaign called NOH8, a silent photo protest turned nonprofit organization that plays on the advertising aesthetics of Gran Fury and the Silence = Death Project. Cofounded by fashion and celebrity photographer Adam Bouska and his partner, Jeff Parshley, NOH8 began as a photo spread featuring "everyday Californians who support Marriage Equality."[89] In these portraits, subjects wearing white shirts are shot against a white backdrop.[90] Their mouths are bound with huge pieces of shiny silver tape, and on their cheeks "NO/H8" is written in bold black letters, save for the 8, which is in red. Bouska and Parshley advertised for volunteers on Facebook and Twitter. Within one year, they had taken thousands of photographs, which they posted on their website. By this time their campaign had blossomed into a conglomerate, and the number of models had expanded to included celebrities and politicians, including the McCains.

Meghan McCain was the first to join, in January 2009, followed by her mother several months later, when Cindy accompanied her daughter to a photo shoot for Meghan's book, *Dirty, Sexy, Politics.* The photographer was none other than the artist turned activist Bouska. During the session the group talked about the status of the NOH8 campaign, and Cindy made a spontaneous decision to join the effort. The team rounded up a white T-shirt from the fashion closet and Bouska shot her on the spot. In the photograph, Cindy McCain looks directly at the camera, her torso turned slightly to her left to accentuate her right hand, which is placed over her heart in a pledge of allegiance to America and the family values for which it stands. She has writing on her right cheek, whereas the more liberal Meghan has the words on her left. Meghan was photographed in profile, with her arms raised to her neck and her palms stretched open. In her hands, she holds a gray elephant, the symbol of the Republican Party—its tusks wrapped in silver tape. Meghan's fingernails are painted red to match the 8 on her cheek.[91] Few people blinked twice when Meghan McCain, a self-described renegade Republican, defied her father's official (public) views on gay marriage by participating in the NOH8 campaign, but when the former would-be first lady's photograph was released, the media went wild with speculations that John McCain would soon announce a change in his views, that the Republic Party was deeply divided on the issue, and that the conservative movement was in turmoil.

Republican support for same-sex marriage is not only gaining momentum; it is bankrolling the issue.[92] One of the most ardent supporters of marriage equality is former solicitor general Theodore Olson, a staunch conservative and veteran of both the Reagan and (George W.) Bush administrations. Olson joined his adversary in the Supreme Court case *Bush v. Gore,* David Boies, in filing *Perry v. Schwarzenegger,* the federal court case seeking to invalidate Proposition 8.[93] In a *Newsweek* article defending his position, "The Conservative Case for Gay Marriage: Why Same Sex Marriage Is An American Value," Olson writes:

> Same-sex unions promote the values conservatives prize. Marriage is one of the basic building blocks of our neighborhoods and our nation . . . We encourage couples to marry because the commitments they make to one another provide benefits not only to themselves but also to their families and communities. Marriage requires thinking beyond one's own needs. It transforms two individuals into a union based on shared aspirations, and in doing so establishes a formal investment in the well-being of society. The fact that individuals who happen to be gay want to share in this vital social institution is evidence that conservative ideals enjoy widespread acceptance.[94]

Gay marriage serves the Republican Party's plan to privatize dependency through the rhetoric of personal responsibility. It facilitates neoliberal economic policies by enabling the government and private sector to abdicate their responsibility for ensuring social welfare. Marriage transfers the burden of care from corporations (which, between government subsidies and

offshore bank accounts, are paying very few taxes) to families, where wom-
en, members of the working-class, and people of color are expected to perform the lion's share of the physical and affective labor.

In his *Newsweek* article, Olson claims that nothing short of the right to
marry will end the "discrimination against decent, hardworking members
of our society."[95] The story features a number of photographs to illustrate
his point, images of well-heeled gay couples on their wedding day. Decency
has a predictable color, normative whiteness. All of the subjects appear to
be Anglo. Decency is unsurprising in other ways too. The images depict
people who are conventionally attractive and staged in traditional poses that
are intimate but not sexual. Many of the couples are locked in embraces,
for example, but none are kissing. The grooms are wearing suits and the
brides dresses (come on!), with all, save one, donning the customary white.
One photograph features a pair of women whose heads are cropped out of
the picture (were they not pretty enough?) in coordinating silk dresses and
pearl bracelets; they are holding matching bridal bouquets, posed in such
a way as to show off their wedding rings. There are no captions under any
of the photographs, and the subjects are not named in the editorial, as if to
suggest that the issue is not about individuals but "the people," not about
specific homosexuals but all Americans. Through the performative force of
word and image, Olson and his exemplars exhibit same-sex marriage for
what it is: a deeply conservative social ritual that reinforces rather than challenges normative notions of sexuality.

Zapping History

The passage of Proposition 8 and the Dream Team of Olson and Boies inspired a wave of activism that many dubbed Stonewall 2.0, as these events
coincided with the fortieth anniversary of the uprising. Global celebrations
from San Francisco to Sydney commemorating the birth of the gay and lesbian liberation movement became occasions for promarriage rallies. The pride
parades, civic celebrations, exhibitions, and panels staged that summer had
less to do with paying tribute to the memory of veteran activists than they
did with promoting marriage and military equality, two goals that could not
have been more antithetical to the desires of Stonewall activists. Lesbian and
gay liberationists in the 1960s and 1970s decried marriage for its exclusive
and propertied attitude toward desire, for its constriction of people's future

growth and development, and for its mimicry of heterosexual social roles. "A Gay Manifesto," written in December 1969, captures the essence of early activists' position on the issue.

> Traditional marriage is a rotten oppressive institution. . . . [M]arriage is a contract which smothers both people, denies needs, and places impossible demands on both people. . . . Gay people must stop gauging their self-respect by how well they mimic straight marriages. Gay marriages will have the same problems as straight ones except in burlesque. . . . To accept that happiness comes through finding a groovy spouse and settling down, showing the world that "we're just the same as you" is avoiding the real issues, and is an expression of self-hatred.[96]

The manifesto goes on to state: "[L]iberation for gay people is defining for ourselves how and with whom we live, instead of measuring our relationship in comparison to straight ones, with straight values."[97]

Alas, no one at NYC Pride 2009 recited "A Gay Manifesto," conducted a dramatic reading of Sheila Cronan's "Marriage," or cast WITCH hexes on any of the corporate sponsors. Activists were preoccupied with fund-raising for HRC, distributing temporary "NOH8" tattoos, and collecting coupons for wedding packages from the many vendors on site. The thoroughly commodified spectacles surrounding the celebration of Stonewall 40 had less to do with marking the history of the LGBT movement than they did with creating a public act of forgetting, one that enabled homoliberals to rewrite the past in order to conform to present aspirations.

Securing the right to marry does not guarantee the end of prejudice, nor does it substantively transform society or its institutions. If the civil rights movement and the women's movement are any indication, the attainment of formal equality does little to ameliorate deeply engrained cultural biases and institutionalized forms of discrimination. The disparity of incarceration rates among African-Americans and the persistence of the glass ceiling are indicators that juridical reform does little to challenge bigotry, biases, or social hierarchies. For the past three decades, the LGBT agenda has been propelled in large part by the misplaced faith that legal victories and symbolic acts of recognition, such as the right to marry, are radical achievements that will guarantee equality for sexual minorities. We have invested our political capital in what Duggan calls "the false promise of 'equality' on offer through liberal reform," a conception of "'equality' disarticulated from material life and class politics."[98] In return, LGBT subjects have been granted what Urvashi Vaid terms "virtual equality," a conditional and partial simulation of freedom that is contingent on adherence to the status quo.[99] In the mid-1990s, Vaid warned us that a single-issue LGBT movement—one that ignores the broader dynamics of gender inequity, racism, economic disparity, and cultural freedoms—would have no significant impact on the socioeconomic structures that oppress, denigrate, and marginalize minority subjects. A myopic focus on marriage reform diminishes the LGBT movement by foreclosing debate about the intersectionality of various forms of oppression.

While many gays and lesbians have fought for marriage equality, others have struggled equally hard to establish and promote alternatives to matrimony, including civil unions and domestic partnerships.[100] For some of us, myself included, these are not inferior arrangements to be engaged in while biding our time waiting to legally marry. On the contrary, these relationships have enabled us to organize our lives in ways that afford us far greater freedoms than are granted to LGBT citizens by the hegemonic institution of marriage. Some of us choose not to forget that until very recently gays and lesbians were criminals in the eyes of the law and could be jailed or institutionalized against our will for engaging in same-sex acts. The thought of the state sanctioning and regulating our intimate affairs is tantamount to adding insult to historical injury. Happily alienated from the prospect of marriage, we have created erotic and nurturing forms of attachment and care that not only exceed but improve on the limited and confining definition of matrimony. I, for one, am not inclined to abandon my extramarital ways of living and loving simply because some LGBT couples want this option.

Formal marriage equality is an important right, but it should be one of many possibilities available to people. As Nancy Polikoff argues in *Beyond (Straight and Gay) Marriage,* our aim should be to recognize and protect a wide variety of kinship arrangements not to gain access to increasingly insular forms of marriage and ever narrowing definitions of families. We need to acknowledge that there are many ways to create meaningful, sustainable, committed bonds outside the confines of traditional marriage. Not all gays and lesbians want to be treated just like heterosexual couples, and we should not be forced into marriage to have our lovers recognized and our families validated, or to keep the rights we have labored tirelessly to earn. All too often, however, winning the right to wed entails the loss of existing rights, disenfranchising many gays and lesbians as public and private employers in states that pass same-sex marriage laws often rescind domestic partnerships protection, forcing couples to marry in order to keep their status and benefits. If marriage equality zaps existing rights, what use is it? Individuals, be they gay or straight, who have no personal or political interest in marriage should not be coerced into it, nor should they be thrust into the role of "compulsory witness" to an institution they feel is oppressive and discriminatory.[101]

In this comparative study of zaps from 1969 and 2009, I have tried to show that when homosexuals walk down the aisle to the tune of the wedding march (a straight tempo if there ever was one), we place ourselves, intentionally or not, into all sorts of compromising positions. Same-sex marriage puts queers in the honeymoon suite with the likes of Cindy and Meghan McCain. It aligns us with facinorous figures such as Dick Cheney and Ted Olson. Many lesbians and gays fighting for marriage rights are all too pleased to have conservative support, even from constituencies on the far right, and rarely do we consider the consequences of our political congress. Such forms of communion enmesh us into complicities of power and privilege with reprobate right wing zealots. Attention to lesbian feminist zaps sheds light on the ways in which cultural memory is actively and egregiously manipulated by homoliberals. More importantly, it enables us to consciously embody history in ways foreclosed by the stultifying heterogeneity of the mainstream LGBT movement. (Re)inhabiting these performative and participatory actions of our recent past, we can conjure, create, and enact other possibilities for sexual life in the present and the future.

3

Expatriate Acts
Jill Johnston's Joker Citizenship

> Suddenly I became someone who did not know her place, and
> having no *knowledge* of my place, I became an instant anarchist.
> Only those whose sense of place has been internalized out of habit
> and programming can move safely into such a dangerous position.
> Strictly speaking, an anarchist has no (political) objective; loosely
> speaking, anarchy is a catchword for a stance that veils political
> ambitions.
>
> —Jill Johnston

> I was a luxury that the women's movement could not yet afford and
> I didn't know how true it was and still is apparently even among
> lesbians[.]
>
> —Jill Johnston

On August 9, 1970, Ethel "Spike" Scull and her husband Bob, a taxi mogul
who at one time owned the largest collection of pop art in the world, held a
benefit for Women's Strike for Equality at their house in East Hampton.[1] The
organizers of the fund-raiser were Betty Friedan, cofounder of NOW, Gloria
Steinem, author Edith de Rham, and fashionista Gloria Vanderbilt. Among
the select group of female journalists invited to cover the event was *Village
Voice* columnist Jill Johnston. Just one month prior, Johnston had done what
was "hitherto socially unthinkable and suicidal."[2] In a "spirit of marvelous
megalomania," she came out as a lesbian in her column, making official the
open secret this gadfly had been whispering for years.[3] This formal admission made Johnston "the paper's, and arguably the country's, first shameless
public lesbian."[4]

An ill-fated attempt to engage Friedan in a conversation about lesbian feminism, on the heels of the Lavender Menace zap, sent the presi-

dent of NOW into a tizzy. As Johnston, a proponent of new journalism and experimental—what she called extreme—writing, observed in the *Voice:*

> What went wrong between Betty Friedan and me was a lapse of sexual interest. I liked her below the chin and was ready to talk at that level but she got super huffy when I arsked if there shouldn't be a pub(l)ic conjunction between Women's Liberation and the Gay Liberation Front. Here eyes went big 'n bulgy and her lipstick leered crimson and she said crisply enunciating each word that "it" was not an issue . . . *And,* there's no relationship between the movements.[5]

Friedan's flippant dismissal would not go unchecked. "In a flash," Johnston recalls, she "turned into a One Eyed One Horned Flying Purple People Eater. . . . It was time," she told herself. "Something had to happen."[6]

When Friedan approached the microphone, which had been set up at one end of the swimming pool, Johnston stripped to her denim shirt and black panties and dove into the water, screaming "Tarzana from the trees at cocktails."[7] Showing off her athletic prowess, she swam a ten-point Australian crawl. When people played it cool, pretending not to notice Johnston's water ballet, she raised the stakes by removing her shirt and swimming three more laps, this time opting for "a little exhibition breast stroke."[8] Friedan tried in vain to divert everyone's attention by leading a group of women in the song "Liberation Now," but Johnston climbed out the pool in the middle of the musical interlude and dripped her way past the chorus. As if by osmosis or some perverse form of contagion, Friedan experienced a wardrobe malfunction. While she was singing, her right breast popped out of her polka-dot party frock. To her credit, Friedan did not leave the stage until her song was finished. A former actress, she soldiered on, knowing that come hell or high water the show must go on. After she thanked everyone for attending, Friedan muttered something about Johnston being "the biggest enemy of the movement" and excused herself, ostensibly to go in search of a safety pin.[9] Mrs. Scull, not sure how to respond, allegedly shook her head and chortled, "I always say if you have a pool, you have a pool."[10]

Within minutes of emerging from her swim, Johnston was accosted by the paparazzi: "Why did you do this?" "Are you a radical lesbian?" "Are you part of a Redstocking plot to sabotage the event?" Feigning ignorance, Johnston claimed that she did not dive "into the pool to protest the discrimination against lesbians by feminists. . . . I wasn't nearly so organized." She told reporters, "I was hot and drunk and I like empty swimming pools and I'm a very good swimmer so I like to show off my skills."[11] She pretended to be put out by the suggestion that an innocent attempt to cool off on a scorching summer day was being "hailed as a disruption," and of such an austere and important occasion.[12] Johnston used the Women Strike for Equality fund-raiser to practice what she called "the improbable art of being a public nuisance and a maverick or a martyr at the service of the principle of chaos and corruption."[13] She not only disrupted the benefit; she co-opted the press coverage. Charlotte Curtis, reporting for the *New York Times,* detailed Johnston's antics, under the subheading "Enemy within Surfaces," and her article featured a lead photograph of Johnston, clad only in her skivvies, accepting a towel from a bemused Bob Scull. Below this image, the paper ran a much smaller photograph of Friedan, who is shot from the waist up. The right sleeve of her frilly summer dress has fallen off her shoulder revealing a hint of skin, which Friedan has tried to contain by crossing her arms. This gesture of modesty, one might even say prudishness, stands in sharp contrast to the central image and Johnston's shameless public nudity.

I call Johnston's performance at the Sculls' home an act of joker citizenship, an anarchic and antiassimilationist gesture of civil disobedience that provides an opportunity and occasion for subaltern agency. This mirthful and euphoric form of political dissent stands in stark contrast to the serious, no-nonsense mode of civic engagement favored by NOW. A spirited, seditious, and militantly erotic mode of insurrection that challenges audiences to question, if not transform, the criteria for social belonging, acts of joker citizenship occur when individuals who are typically the object of scorn, ridicule, and derision steal the spotlight, creating a public spectacle of their private shame in order to expose the operations of power and oppression in society. Seducing spectators with their daring displays, jokers manipulate and redirect our gaze, distorting our clouded perceptions and disrupting our preconceived notions.

Disarming the opposition with a punch of humor, the joker pushes the boundaries of acceptable behavior and makes a mockery of the arbitrary institutions and authorities, precepts and protocols that govern our worlds. Interactive and dynamic acts of joker citizenship show the absurdity of injustice and make discrimination, along with anyone who supports it, appear silly. They create scenarios for public life that have nothing to do with integrating into the mainstream or becoming the newest member of the status quo. On the contrary, these eruptions create a position from which to speak and act where none is permitted in the established social drama. Calling attention to the disciplinary regimes and normalizing forces that create docile bodies, domesticate desire, and stifle creativity, what I term expatriate acts of gaiety thwart attempts—by both majority and minority cultures—to organize sexuality in accordance with a statist agenda. Staking out spaces for fugitive identities and outlawed socialities, the joker shifts the terrain of the political landscape, remapping the erogenous zones of the body politic and reterritorializing the nation into sites of pleasure.

This study of joker citizenship contributes to conversations in feminist and queer theory about public sentiments, national affects, and the role performance plays in both. Performance is the key to making political claims in the public sphere, to rehearsing alternative social formations, and to challenging people's feelings about controversial issues. A consummate performer, the joker is a jester, a player, an actor (which the ancient Greeks called a hypocrite), and her talents include feigning, forging, imitation, impersonation, deception, duplicity, manipulation, and magic. When faced with impediments, insurmountable obstacles, or social barriers, she does what any trickster would do: she cheats, defying or exploiting the rules of the game in order to get what she wants. The tactics jokers deploy show us the gap between reality and representation, and they urge us to consider the virtues associated with being bent, twisted, and crooked, which is to say queer. Wags, wisecrackers, and wits such as Valerie Solanas's Bongi Perez, Rita Mae Brown's Molly Bolt from *Rubyfruit Jungle,* and Diane DiMassa's *Hothead Paisan* (the subject of chapter four) remind us that the joker is an important, if overlooked, aspect of lesbian feminist dramaturgy.

I argue here that Johnston's spectacular enactments of joker citizenship stage a vital, yet neglected, intervention into the workings of national sentimentality. By "national sentimentality," I refer to what Lauren Berlant terms the peculiar form of "patriotic intensity" that "makes citizenship into a category of feeling."[14] Rooted in the false promise that a nation can be built across fields of social, economic, and cultural difference through "channels of affective identification and empathy," national sentimentality abjures politics by reducing complex, historically specific forms of structural inequalities into questions of feelings.[15] Pain, which is taken to be a transparent and objective form of knowledge, serves as the index of injustice. National sentimentality is dramatized in and through affecting melodramatic spectacles—such as *Uncle Tom's Cabin, The Burning Bed,* and ACT-UP die-ins—wherein disenfranchised populations portray themselves as suffering victims in order to elicit the sympathies of their entitled peers. Claims to subjectivity are based not on one's capacity to think or work but on one's ability to feel pain and endure acute physical and psychic violence. Berlant calls sentimental politics "a terribly flawed vehicle" for achieving a more equitable democracy because it confuses feeling better with the attainment of justice and obfuscates the need to address institutionalized forms of violence and abuse.[16] The reduction of politics to a program of protection, rescue, and reparation from pain impoverishes the definition of freedom, and it obscures the ongoing social antagonism inherent in democratic struggles.

National sentimentality operates through anguished scenarios that dramatize the pain of denied citizenship so vividly that it burns into the conscience of enfranchised subjects, enabling them to feel the pain of the other as their pain, but without having to experience the conditions that create and sustain the injury. Jokers like Johnston take an alternate tack; they traffic in gaiety, which incites critical reflection through a differently embodied affect: the tickle of laughter. The convulsive contractions of laughter resemble the shudder of catharsis, but they produce a different experience of embodiment and a very different field of vision. Whereas the tragic tenor of national sentimentality purges and liberates, the infectious humor of comedy contaminates and implicates. While generative of pleasurable sensations, including empathetic identification, acts of joker citizenship do not jettison or abjure bad feelings through purgation, nor do they necessarily make actors or spectators feel better. Laughter makes us uncomfortable, both physically—think of the heart palpitations and shortness of breath that accompany a good chortling—and ethically, insofar as it incites us to confront, if not reposition, our bodies, boundaries, and moral principles. "Laughter," writes Suzan-Lori Parks in "Elements of Style," "is very powerful—it's not a way of escaping anything but a way of arriving on the scene. Think about laughter and what happens to your body—it's almost the same thing that happens to you when you throw up."[17] When we laugh really hard, it can feel as if we are dying.

While the laughter an act of joker citizenship elicits aligns constituencies—by revealing previously undisclosed resemblances, bridging ideological divisions, and inspiring collective action—it simultaneously isolates and alienates certain factions, inverting the established social order by making the familiar appear strange and the strange familiar. Thus, while jokers build and bolster communities, they also dismantle hierarchies and institutionalized power structures. Humor may be inherently social, but it achieves this by inveigling subjects of various persuasions and opinions into volatile propinquity, transforming the political arena into a speculative territory, a place of incongruity and instability, a locus of opposition and contestation. "[L]aughter resides," according to Boal practitioner Mady Schutzman, "in the place of conjugality with those we don't necessarily agree with." As such, "laughter might be understood as a place where ethics—notions of relational decency, social laws that must address wide differences—are born, and where 'new cartographies of social space' might be drawn."[18] For many lesbians in the 1970s and 1980s, including Jill Johnston, that place was the lesbian nation.

The lesbian nation, at least as Johnston imagined it, was more of an endeavor than an actual entity, and it was constituted by expatriate acts of joker citizenship. A return to that much maligned and, in some ways, grossly mischaracterized utopian project gives rise to a daring diacritics, one that confounds the dynamics of national sentimentality. The feats of joker citizenship I explore here make manifest the performative force of the ludic in lesbian nationalism, and they show the inherent poverty of any liberation movement that is organized around spectacles of wounded subjectivity. Dramatizing different ways in which sexual minorities might produce themselves as subjects, Johnston's expatriate acts of joker citizenship theatricalize an insouciant mode of political insurgency I call national gaiety.

"Slouching toward Consciousness"

An aesthetic and political provocateur whose book *Lesbian Nation: The Feminist Solution* (1973) is credited with sparking the separatist movement, Johnston played a central role in the artistic and social revolutions of the twentieth century. A dancer by training and a writer by trade, this British-born and American-bred rapscallion rejected models of passive spectatorship, championed postmodernism, and created a new, personalized language for criticism.[19] Her reviews of dance, theater, music, art installations, environments, and happenings provide, in some cases, the only documentation of seminal art events in the 1950s and 1960s that would have disappeared from our collective memory were it not for her visionary impulses. Johnston's style is perhaps best described as a kind of discursive decoupage. The structures and strategies she employed as a critic correspond with those of the art and politics she wrote about: her free associational prose correlates to assemblage and collage in Robert Rauschenberg's paintings and Trisha Brown's improvisations in dance; her use of found text parallels the found sounds in John Cage's sonicscapes and the found movements in Yvonne Rainer's dance compositions. Johnston celebrated intermedial connections in art, and she created her own as well, using visual metaphors to describe choreographed movement and spatial imagery to analyze sculpture and painting.

Johnston's defection from literary tradition and journalistic protocol in the 1950s paralleled her rejection of compulsory heterosexuality and bourgeois rules of decorum. Her mission "was to mongrelize the language, deform and debase every convention, create a freak of culture, engender a misbegotten blot on the authorial landscape."[20] Johnston wrote for a number of publications (including *Dance Observer* and *Art News*), but it was at the *Village Voice* (1959 to 1981) that her fractured, Steinian-inflected, stream of consciousness prose and electrifying libidinal impulses were given free rein.[21] Exemplary of her highly sexualized staccato rhythm is this excerpt from a review of Lotte Goslar and Company's performance at the Delacorte Theatre in 1968: "A queen is a queen is a boy is a girl is a ballerina is a boy is a dyke is a fag is a butch is a boy is a girl is just a kinky son of a gun like the rest of us. Hello all you sexes. We're too good to be true."[22]

In *Cruising Utopia,* José Muñoz celebrates Johnston for her contributions to a pre-Stonewall queer avant-garde, and so he should, but he comes perilously close to romanticizing her views on the postwar period and what he calls the utopian aspects of preidentitarian subjectivity. To quote Johnston, "The fifties just sucked. . . . For me the sixties was the great opportunity. The fifties was hopeless everybody knows that"; it "was the bleakest decade of all."[23] Lesbianism was considered both an illness and a form of criminal intimacy. "I never said I was a dyke even to a dyke," recalls Johnston, "because there wasn't a dyke in the land who thought she should be a dyke or even that she was a dyke so how could we talk about it."[24] "Dykedom was not a reality for the world," she notes, "nor was it real for any of us who were actually doing it."[25] Unmarked sexuality may have been extremely beneficial to some queer men in the 1950s, insofar as it enabled them to retain their male privilege, social status, and economic prospects, but this state of ambiguity was much less expedient for women, who had few options for creating and sustaining a life aside from yoking themselves to a husband.[26]

Dykedom was, of course, a reality for some women in the 1950s, but even if Johnston had been interested in building clandestine communities with homophiles, which she was not, her anarchic sensibility and penchant for making a spectacle of herself made her unsuited for membership in the integrationist-oriented Daughters of Bilitis. Johnston was equally ill equipped for participation in the lesbian bar community, where writers such as Patricia Highsmith, Marijane Meaker, and Joan Nestle found drama, sexual intrigue, and intellectual sustenance. She could not abide by the shadowy locales, far removed from the spotlight, or the scripted behaviors of butch-femme sexuality. While Johnston relished being an outlaw, she hated the real and persistent danger associated with being a sexual deviant. Wise enough to play the fool, Johnston knew she was "better off trying to get it on with a repulsive man," so she "turned in the proper direction of social neurotic womanhood and eventually became one of those dykes who gave up" and took a husband.[27] Opting for the "desperate expedient" she called "the grave of marriage and the hell of motherhood," Johnston waited "until the revolution began and concrete external social support was at last at hand."[28] Marriage, that "melodramatic genealogical solution" to the problem of lesbian desire, was not without consequences or collateral damage.[29] Johnston's relationship with Richard Lanham, which she describes as "an exercise in violence interrupted by short periods of violence," lasted six years (1958–64) and produced two children.[30] She survived the dark ages of her submission by going mad.

Johnston liked to call herself "a culture star from the bowery and Bellevue."[31] The Bowery is the bohemian neighborhood she frequented for art events, and Bellevue is "new york's infamous depot for revelatory casualties," the asylum where she was institutionalized when her rarified world of libertines and luminaries failed to protect her from the insane realities of homophobia, misogyny, and the drudgery of her domestic life.[32] These psychotic breaks were expatriate acts that exposed the limits of reality and the confines of Cold War America. Jokers are often associated with madness, which can take the form of lunacy, divine inspiration, or both. As a visionary artist, Johnston was attuned to the invisible, the unseen, and the irrational forces of the universe that gesture toward utopian possibilities lying just beyond the horizon of objective reality. Jokers like her remind us that transformational aesthetics and utopian civic projects are guided not only by rational thought, discursive logic, and empirical truths but also by intuition, improvisation, and embodied forms of knowledge. Lewis Hyde calls the joker's labor joint work because it takes place betwixt and between bodies (us and them), temporalities (past, present, and future), and things (truth and illusion).[33] The success of their endeavors depends, Schutzman reminds us, on the joker's "ability to survive, even evolve, in ruptured land-scapes and negative spaces (the nought)—that liminal space where stable positions unravel."[34] Johnston experienced her last nervous breakdown some time around 1969, just before she came out.

The 1960s ushered in a brave new world of possibilities. This was a time of melodious rhythms and mystical communions, of political upheaval and social unrest. Recreational drugs and casual sex offered brief respites from social constraints, and a pervasive spirit of progressive idealism permeated the culture. Johnston gamboled into the 1960s with what Nietzsche in *The Gay Science* calls "the saturnalia of a spirit who has patiently resisted a ter-rible, long pressure—patiently, severely, coldly, without submitting, but also without hope—and who is now all at once attacked by hope, the hope for health, and the intoxication of convalescence."[35] As the postwar period of "privation and powerlessness" gave way to "a sudden sense and anticipa-tion of a future," Johnston indulged in "a bit of merry-making" and "more than a little foolishness," breaking aesthetic boundaries and breaching social taboos.[36]

Johnston was drawn to the gay liberation movement long before she felt compelled to explore feminism. So preoccupied was the artist with sexual shame—with that fact that what she "liked and wanted was sick or sinful or illegal or criminal"—that she did not realize the extent to which her gender dictated her biological destiny, career prospects, personal happiness, and mental health.[37] For Johnston, the stigma of sexual deviancy was so heavy that she had never thought about the stigma of being a woman. In the 1950s, she writes, "Most of us didn't know yet that it was wrong to be a woman but we did know it was wrong to be lesbian . . . and in this way some of us were acquiring the rudimentary emotions of a gay consciousness."[38] Whereas most lesbians came to the cause having participated in other liber-ation struggles, including the homophile movement, the civil rights move-ment, and the New Left, Johnston had no history of involvement in progres-sive politics. The kind of organized insurrection favored by politicos was incompatible with what Johnston referred to as her "east west flower child beat hip psychedelic paradise now love peace do your own thing approach to the revolution."[39]

Her sense of creativity and radical nonconformity was cultivated through close communion with the Beats, the Black Mountain artists, and the degen-erate denizens of Warhol's Factory. These innovators were more interested in how countercultural ideas and practices played out in the art world than they were in movement politics per se. In these queer enclaves, Johnston felt empowered to experiment with altered states of consciousness and to engage in alternative forms of intimacy. She became deeply invested in replacing the practice of criticism with the art of engagement and in breaking down hierarchical power structures by abolishing the division between spectator and performer. She challenged elitist conceptions of what qualifies as an aesthetic event by highlighting the performance of everyday life, dissolving arbitrary distinctions between aesthetic categories, and mixing new media with live and visual arts.

Not content simply to cover the New York art scene, Johnston fashioned herself into one of its luminaries. She performed alongside her friends, appearing, for example, in John Cage's *Music Walk*, which he adapted especially for her, as *Music Walk with Dancer* (1962), and in Karlheinz Stockhausen's *Inside Originale* (1964).[40] Andy Warhol made her the star of one of his films, *Jill Johnston Dancing* (1964). Johnston's most accomplished feats were her own acts of gaiety: scandalous scenes of lesbian theatrics that she staged whenever and wherever possible. She treated her coming out as an artistic event and wrote about her sexual exploits in the *Village Voice,* reviewing them alongside performances by Merce Cunningham and Paul Taylor. By the late 1960s, Johnston's writing had become positively "picaresque," with her peccadilloes being given as much, if not more, space in her reviews than critiques of aesthetic productions.[41] Johnston's editorializing of her own acting out—her alcohol- and drug-induced escapades, lesbian liaisons, and evolving political consciousness—eventually eclipsed her coverage of everything else: "Gradually life became the theater became the column. The life being everything of course included everything." An avid interpreter of her own process, Johnston noted, "An art form of pure novelty and invention might naturally be expected from someone undergoing the birth of an historically unprecedented identity."[42]

The decision to take herself as an "object of complex and difficult elaboration" and her "aesthetic" commitment to making her very existence into a work of art resonate with Foucault's charge that we perform a "critical ontology of ourselves" as a practice of freedom.[43] This process of self-care and strategic self-styling has less to do with creating "a permanent body of knowledge," according to Foucault, than it does with fostering "an attitude, an ethos, a philosophical life in which the critique of what we are is at one and the same time the historical analysis of the limits imposed on us and an experiment with the possibility of going beyond them."[44] Johnston's performance reviews of her own hedonistic pursuits did more than *epater le bour-geoisie;* they contributed to the birth of the gay liberation movement and to the sanctioning and structuring of an inchoate lesbian identity.

Using the *Village Voice* as both a mouthpiece and a marketing device, Johnston became one of the most visible and vibrant spokespersons for radical feminism and gay rights, much to the vexation of more serious activists, who viewed her as a rogue whose antics were frivolous, flippant, and self-serving. Allergic to ideology and averse to dogma, Johnston eschewed mass movement activities in favor of personal acts of rebellion. "I dislike meetings for purposes other than parties," she famously quipped, indicating her preference for cocktails over consciousness-raising.[45] Claiming, "Politics cramped my style," Johnston resisted Marxist doctrine and leftist dictates.[46] Finding movement politics "insufficiently lighthearted," she "lugged dada forward with [her] into the lesbian feminist arena," staging scenes of subversion and propagating acts of gaiety.[47] As Melissa Deem has observed, Johnston "disrupted established politics" through "an adroit politics of mobility, which not only evaded certain majoritarian logics, but also cut across the molar logics of feminism and the gay liberation front."[48] For this she was castigated as a counterrevolutionary and a disgrace to the cause. Ostracized by many of her peers, Johnston's contributions to the artistic and political history of the era have been obscured. If she is mentioned in studies of the 1960s, it is usually in a footnote.[49]

In the same way that Johnston drew Dada into lesbian feminism, I want to pull this joker into contemporary LGBT politics. In an act of "temporal drag," Elizabeth Freeman's term for "a crossing of time, less in the mode of postmodern pastiche than in the mode of stubborn identification with a set of social coordinates that exceed our own historical moment," I want to tarry with this controversial figure in lesbian herstory who resisted the siren song of integration and defied pressure—from factions on both the left and the right—to assimilate.[50] In taking seriously Johnston's insistence that the "revolution should be fun or we should forget it," we can see how acts of joker citizenship produce possibilities for national public life.[51] Her simultaneous assertion of gayness as sexual politics and gayness as *joie de vivre* underscores the centrality of liveliness to the LGBT movement, and it rehearses dramatically different ways in which sexual minorities might produce themselves as subjects above and beyond enactments of national sentimentality.

"Better latent than never"

Johnston's latent feminism, what she would call her "ponderously slow real-ization of the political truth" of women's oppression, aroused the incredulity and ire of many lesbian activists in the early days of the sexual revolution.[52] Her first real movement encounter took place in November 1969 when she was recruited by the Gay Liberation Front's Lois Hart (a former nun turned house painter) and her lover Suzanne Bevier (a graphic artist) to contrib-ute to GLF's newsletter *Come Out!* Although Johnston toyed with the idea of writing for *Come Out!,* she elected to make her official print debut as a lesbian in her own column, in a review called "Of This Pure but Irregular Passion"—a title borrowed from a line in Colette's "The Pure and the Im-pure" ("Ces Plaisirs").[53] What shocked and angered the women of GLF was not that Johnston chose the *Voice* for her grand declaration but that she came off as someone who was not "politically enlightened at all."[54]

Although she stressed "the positive identity of the homosexual" and the need for gays to "celebrate [their] sexuality," Johnston exhibited more shame and ambivalence about her sexual orientation than she did pride. Calling herself "sexually confused," she wrote, "In my best moments I feel tran-sexual and relate to the classical and ancient myths of the sacred char-acter of the androgynous creature, which is rooted in our primordial bio-logical origins."[55] Rather than promote the cause of lesbian feminism, John-ston seemed to renounce it. "[S]ince my personal campaign to 'come out,'" she opined, "I have never liked men better and wish they would like me as well."[56] What many read as evidence of internalized homophobia might be understood as an expatriate act of joker citizenship, which, while admit-tedly naive and undertheorized, was designed to thwart the dynamics of national sentimentality. Johnston went to great lengths in this essay to not portray herself as a victim or as someone in need of rescue, a position she saw as antithetical to her artistic aspirations. "[F]or me it's a downer and a bummer to dwell on the oppression of women," writes Johnston. "I can't dwell on our oppression and remain a relatively liberated fugitive artist."[57]

In this coming-out column, she actively distances herself from women who were more interested in waging a battle of the sexes than they were in sexual liberation. What starts out as a daring polemic devolves into a per-sonal attack on political lesbian Ti-Grace Atkinson, who Johnston dismisses as a hysterical woman who simply needs a good lay.

I can't accept any program for resisting or attacking the "enemy" such as feminist Ti-Grace Atkinson advocates in the struggle for the liberation of women. Ti-Grace spoke at the Daughter's [*sic*] of Bilitis during gay week. She says that men are the enemy and she speaks of spokes and armor and militant tactics and ideological pitfalls and the murder of feminist revolutionaries in Russia in 1919 and the vaginal orgasm as a mass hysterical survival response and frightening things like that. I like Ti-Grace and I'd be happy to help her by going to bed with her but I think she needs intensive bio-energetic Reichian therapy by a male chauvinist pig who wouldn't rape or redeem her but who would be kind to her.[58]

In response to this very public piece in the *Village Voice,* and in particular her ad hominem attack on Atkinson, Johnston experienced a swift and immediate backlash by the lesbians of GLF. Within two weeks of its publication, she was denounced at a meeting (on July 14), and shortly thereafter (on July 22), she had a final heated argument with Hart, who told Johnston, "[Y]our politics are not sympathetic to the aims and aspirations of [GLF]."[59]

In *Lesbian Nation,* published three years later, Johnston concedes that her coming-out column lacked "any kind of feminist consciousness," that it was a toxic combination of "bravado and bucolic innocence. all gay but not much woman."[60] She called the article "embarrassing" and refused to reproduce it in any of her compilations, omitting it even in her chronicles of the gay liberation years.[61] The fallout from this experience jolted Johnston into a feminist consciousness. She began reading foundational texts in women's liberation, starting with Simone de Beauvoir's *The Second Sex* and *Notes from the Second Year,* published by Shulamith Firestone and Anne Koedt of the New York Radical Women. This was followed by feminist interpretations of Marx, position papers such as the Radicalesbians' "Woman-Identified Woman," and Valerie Solanas's *SCUM Manifesto.* "Gay liberation," she came to realize, "cannot be considered apart from women's liberation."[62] Although she continued to disagree, rather vehemently, with the antisex platform of groups like The Feminists, Johnston became convinced that Atkinson was right about one thing: lesbianism was the ultimate goal of feminism.

Like most people who are born again, Johnston became something of a zealot. She compensated for her latent feminism by developing an ardor and urgency for the cause, and with a missionary fervor she set about trying to convince every female in America to become a "lesberated woman."[63]

As Sally Banes has observed, after Johnston came out in the *Village Voice*, her column "became a soapbox for her evolving political ideology."[64] In 1971, the title of her *Voice* column was changed from "Dance Journal" to "Jill Johnston," a reflection of her popularity and prominence as a critic but also an acknowledgment of the fact that she was the subject, as well as the author, of her writing. Banes laments this shift, categorizing it as evidence of the critic's slow but steady slide into narcissistic navel gazing and self-indulgent grandstanding. Others, however, viewed this transformation as nothing short of heroic. "Have you read anything like this?" asked a contributor to *The Ladder*; "The dance this lady discusses is of vital importance to all of us."[65] As the novelist Bertha Harris recalls, by publicly and repeatedly declaring her sexuality in the *Voice*, Johnston "began an extraordinary dance of her personality, an illuminating revelation that established her as one of the bravest and strongest writers of her generation. Jill made it possible for me and others to breathe by her artistry and her personality."[66]

Unlike most zealots, Johnston never lost her sense of humor, her penchant for playing the merry prankster, or her interest in having a gay old time. In developing a lesbian feminist consciousness, however, she did move from engaging in random, impulsive acts designed primarily to shock audiences to more carefully choreographed performances of political propaganda. Taken together, these acts of gaiety reflect what we might call "the evolution of an art form" of joker citizenship.[67]

Town Bloody Hall

One of Johnston's greatest acts of joker citizenship took place on April 30, 1971, at a roundtable discussion on the topic of women's liberation at New York's Town Hall. The event was sponsored by Shirley Broughton's ongoing series, "Theater for Ideas," a forum for "culture stars with fancy credentials."[68] Participants included Jacqueline Ceballos, president of the New York chapter of NOW; literary critic Diana Trilling; Professor Germaine Greer, whose *Female Eunuch* (1970) was an international best seller; and Jill Johnston, the token lesbian. The moderator was Pulitzer Prize–winning author Norman Mailer, who had recently published "The Prisoner of Sex" (March 1971 in *Harpers*) as a rebuttal to Kate Millett's *Sexual Politics* (1970), in which she depicts him as a perpetrator of sexual violence and "a prisoner of the virility cult" that is patriarchal society.[69]

Johnston claims that no one on the panel harbored any "illusions that the event [Broughton] was arranging was in the interests of women's liberation—rather it was to be a farce . . . a vehicle for Mailer to star and to make box office [in]."[70] The "Prisoner of Sex," she writes, "provided the foreplay for the orgasm of our appearance at town hall."[71] As far as Johnston was concerned, the event was less about women's liberation than it was about fomenting an "official male backlash" to the movement.[72] She characterized the debate as the "first shot like fort sumter of the male retaliation to the new wave of feminism."[73] The purpose of the Town Hall affair was the "instant conversion of a movement for revolutionary social change into an expensive gladiatorial performance."[74]

Everyone loves a good fight, and everyone who was anyone was at Town Hall that night, with the exception, that is, of the leaders of the radical feminist movement, who boycotted the event. To participate in the forum, even as a member of the audience, was to concur in the absurd premise of the occasion, which was that women's liberation was a debatable issue.[75] It was also to acknowledge that Mailer, a man who had stabbed his second wife, was a suitable and appropriate moderator for a dialogue about feminism. Kate Millett, Ti-Grace Atkinson, Susan Brownmiller, and Gloria Steinem had all declined Broughton's invitation to serve on the panel.[76] Robin Morgan consented to appear on the condition that she could bring a gun and pop a cap into Mailer.[77]

Convinced that she could accomplish more by attending the event than boycotting it, Johnston decided to accept the invitation. As Solanas, whom Johnston considered "very advanced," wrote in *SCUM Manifesto*:

> Dropping out is not the answer; fucking-up is. Most women are already dropped out; they were never in. Dropping out gives control to those few who don't drop out; dropping out is exactly what the establishment leaders want; it plays into the hands of the enemy; it strengthens the system instead of undermining it, as it's based entirely on the non-participation, passivity, apathy and non-involvement of the mass of women.[78]

Like Solanas, Johnston was neither loyal nor faithful to the feminist cause. As a joker, her allegiance was to herself and her own creativity and desires. "[T]hat the event occurred at all," Johnston reasoned, "it was a disaster for women. As a social event," however, it was sure to be "the victory of the season."[79] "I was a performer and an opportunist," she rationalized, "and I couldn't think of anything more drastic and wonderful than to appear before thousands of people who lived above 14th street to tell them that all women were lesbians."[80] Driven by artistic impulses rather than political dictates, Johnston was less interested in promoting consensus or achieving a harmonious resolution than she was in advancing a vision of community that thrives on conflict and contestation. Besides, Johnston relished the opportunity to upstage Mailer, who, in addition to being a highly acclaimed novelist, was also her boss, the cofounder of the *Village Voice*.[81]

As far as Johnston was concerned, Town Hall was not a debate; it was an opportunity to play court jester to the king of the counterculture in the court of public opinion. A jester is a talented entertainer, a gifted storyteller, and a foolish clown. Imbued with the power to mock and revile, to criticize and dispense frank observations, the joker is entrusted with the onerous task of announcing bad news that others are afraid to deliver (in this case: "the lesbians are coming, the lesbians are coming!"). The joker is a subaltern who not only speaks but speaks truth to power. While her status is one of privilege, this position comes with considerable danger and risk. This kind of clowning involves what Clifford Geertz, drawing on Jeremy Bentham, called "deep play," and it exacts a considerable toll on both the performer and her audience. If the jester manages to play with fire without getting burned, she gets the last laugh; if not, the joke is on her.[82]

To get into character, Johnston spent the afternoon of the debate having martinis with friends at the Algonquin Hotel bar. She arrived at Town Hall late and inebriated. With flask in hand, she was whisked onstage so the delayed proceeding could begin. Johnston had put a great deal of energy into her costume, which she acknowledged as a form of "butch fatale"drag.[83] Opting for patchwork dungarees with a matching denim jacket, work boots, and an enormous woman's symbol necklace, she looked the fool in comparison to her well-heeled colleagues, all of whom wore dresses, save for Mailer, of course, who had donned a coat and tie. On being seated, Johnston immediately began to agitate, refusing to speak in the order that had been established. She successfully jockeyed for a higher position in the ranking of guests, taking the podium after Greer, who was billed as the event's main attraction.[84]

When it was her turn, Johnston failed to deliver the requested ten-minute speech on why feminism matters, launching instead into a thirty-minute poem titled "New Approach." "All women are lesbians," Johnston began, "except those that don't know it naturally they are but don't know it yet. I am a woman who is a lesbian."[85] Initially, she had to raise her voice to speak above the titters, gasps, and groans emanating from the audience. In no time, however, Johnston had the crowd squealing and squirming, hooting and hollering with a series of cunning linguistic puns. Her playful demeanor countered any semblance of dogma her manifesto might imply. She delighted the crowd with a ribald exegesis of the biblical begats, supplanting the "ecce homo-ness" of history with a gynocentric countercreation narrative.[86] In this poem Johnston addresses the glaring absence of women in the historical record and confronts the homophobic stereotype of the solitary and lonely lesbian. She charts a literary lineage of Amazons, Sapphists, and bulldaggers from remote geographical regions and different historical eras. This act of joker citizenship confers identity while at the same time calling attention to the shifting, volatile, and labile process of identity formation. Johnston's gay genealogy offers a hopeful analogy of lesbian desire, one redolent with a gleeful historical impulse and the yearning for more ecstatic modes of erotic and political congress.

As the audience was enjoying the show, Mailer was content to let Johnston prattle on past her allotted time. As a literary titan, he was game for a little fun in the form of intellectual jousting and witty repartee. When Johnston's clowning began to overshadow her host, however, Mailer's patience started to wane, and when her jokes came at his expense, his temper flared. His willingness to play with Johnston was contingent on her adhering to the script and deferring to his authority. When Mailer attempted to restore order and put Johnston in her place, he was met with resistance. The audience booed and heckled him. Worse yet, they questioned his power as master of ceremonies, suggesting that he had no right to order Johnston to sit down. After several polite entreaties that she cede the rostrum, Mailer bellowed, "You've written your letter, Jill, now mail it."[87]

Unbeknownst to the host, who was engaged in a screaming match with audience members demanding that Johnston be allowed to finish her poem, the joker picked a woman out of the front row of the audience, pulled her onto the stage, and started making out. Mailer realized something was going on when the crowd went nuts. "What about me?" yelled another female from the audience, as she jumped up to join them in a ménage à trois on the floor.[88] Some spectators covered their mouths and averted their eyes; others careened their necks to get a better look. "It's great that you paid $25 to see three dirty pairs of overalls on the floor," Mailer yelled into the microphone, "when you could see lots of cocks and cunts just down the street for $4."

Jill Johnston (*left*) and an unidentified spectator making out on the stage at the Theatre for Ideas Town Hall debate on women's liberation, April 30, 1971. (Photograph by Fred W. McDarrah.)

"What's the matter Norman," a woman shouted from the auditorium, "can't handle women who won't let you fuck them?"

Johnston untangled herself from her the limbs of the two women to return to the podium. She asked Mailer if she could forgo taking questions in order to finish her poem, to which the moderator replied, "Either play with the team or pick up your marbles and get lost. There's a lot we want to talk about, and I want to talk to you about lesbianism, goddamn it. I'm interested in what you have to say. Now, you can play these games, but they're silly." To quell the pandemonium brewing in the Town Hall, Mailer called for a vote. Deeming the results a tie, he cast the deciding ballot and bade Johnston sit down. Bested by his jester and in danger of losing his crown, Mailer called out in desperation, "Come on, Jill, be a lady." This was about the most ridiculous thing he could have said at this point, and it sent the crowd into hysterics. The trio left the stage to cheers and thunderous applause.

The king of the counterculture was brought low through Johnston's bit of Rabelaisian ribaldry. Such burlesquing of sacred events through profane displays and parodic mockery is the stuff of the carnivalesque, but Johnston's acts of gaiety pushed beyond the riot and revelry of carnival in two important ways. First, her transgression was not part of a structured ritual sanctioned by the powers that be and staged as a diversion to relieve tension and renew the existing order. It was a rogue gesture, a liminoid act, that deliberately distorted the rites of privilege and the sacraments of social hierarchy in order to provoke an unprecedented response.[89] Second, Johnston intended her live performance to be the first act in what she knew would be a much larger social drama. Her gesture of joker citizenship, though staged at Town Hall, was a spectacle made for the media. Not only were the city's most prominent journalists on hand to cover the event, but filmmaker D. A. Pennebaker was shooting the debate for a documentary, titled *Town Bloody Hall*. Johnston played her scenes directly to the camera lens, which amplified her cunning wit and erotic audacity, transmitting and reproducing the story of her mock-heroic exploits across generations and geopolitical borders.

Johnston's performance at Town Hall made quite an impact. First, it called into question the reliability of truth claims and the apparatus of belief systems. Shattering the stereotype that same-sex desire is a tragedy, her comedic turn as court jester recast homophobia as a heterosexual farce. Second, in besting Mailer, whom most people hailed as a literary genius and a counterculture crusader, Johnston revealed him to be little more than a liberal martinet who wielded his heterosexual male privilege in a despotic manner. By outplaying the master, this joker showed lesbian feminism to be a potent political force that was not to be mocked by likes of Mailer. Her spoken-word poem offered both an alternative history of the world and a utopian vision of the future in which women would be relieved of the tyranny of patriarchal preeminence. Third, in simulating intercourse onstage, Johnston exemplified the radical lesbian position that 'the sexual satisfaction of the woman independently of the man is the *sine qua non* of the feminist revolution."[90] This sapphic spectacle underscored the fact that lesbianism is not a private sexual identity but an enactment of public intimacy. Intimacy is not the result of two distinct selves coming together in a dyadic union sanctioned by law but of polyamorous pairings guided only by the pleasure principle.

Johnston said that her only regret was that the debate continued after she left, as her goal had been to bring the entire proceeding to a halt. She lamented the fact that her "schemes for theatrical stunts and sideshow in the tradition of dada the absurd and the happenings" fell "discouragingly sort of any masterful plan to tear that place apart."[91] Johnston may have felt differently had she been a fly on the wall for the remainder of the proceedings. After Trilling delivered the fourth and final feminist position, Mailer, still somewhat frazzled, took the rostrum to offer a response and field questions. In the midst of his unscripted, rambling remarks, in which he cast feminism as a form of leftist totalitarianism, he suggested that there might be "a profound reservoir of cowardice in women that made them welcome this slavish life" then made a number of homophobic remarks about men and women. He said, "Something about women's liberation terrifies me because it is humorless." The irony of this statement, in the wake of Johnston's performance, must have registered somewhere in Mailer's unconscious, because a few moments later he blurted out, in the middle of a riff on liberty, "If you wish for me to be a clown, I'll take out my modest little Jewish dick and put it on the table. You can spit at it and laugh at it, and then I'll walk away and you'll find it was just a dildo I left there. I hadn't shown you the real one." Unfortunately, Johnston did not have the satisfaction of seeing Mailer worried about his jester running off with his scepter. The joker had left the building.

Johnston's "career as an impromptu clown is studded with glorious exploits," but Town Hall remains one of her greatest performances.[92] In her review of the debate in the *Village Voice*—which she titled "On a Clear Day

You Can See Your Mother"—Johnston applauded her performance: "I gave a fine speech. I made everybody laugh. I got a lot of women excited. I made a lot of men furious. I gave them a floor show. I provided some good copy. I enjoyed myself. I felt victorious."[93] The event, which received extensive press coverage, helped seal Johnston's status as a spokesperson for women's liberation.[94] The media attention she garnered would be hailed by many gays and lesbians today as a victory in the struggle for visibility, but in the 1970s the publicity elicited charges that she was colluding with the enemy, that she was an ego-driven artist who craved power and prestige more than political transformation, and that she was more interested in personal and financial rewards than she was in fomenting a revolution. Radical lesbian feminists viewed with suspicion anyone who assumed the position of movement star. They believed the star system was a plot by the rich, white, male-run media to destroy women's liberation by misdirecting women's attention away from social activism and toward behaviors that keep them oppressed.[95]

"Movement Schmoovement"

Johnston was, in many ways, an unlikely candidate for movement stardom. She was a scraggly hippie dyke who lacked Steinem's visage, Atkinson's wardrobe, and Greer's legs. She did, however, have a certain *je ne sais quoi,* the "it factor," which Joe Roach defines as "the easily perceived but hard-to-define quality possessed by abnormally interesting people."[96] Johnston's position as a movement star was cemented with the publication of *Lesbian Nation: The Feminist Solution* in 1973. The title is a reference to Ti-Grace Atkinson's dictum: feminism is the theory; lesbianism is the practice. Although Johnston criticized Atkinson's militant ideological stance in 1970, in her coming-out article, the author came to endorse this position herself. While feminism may have been "the complaint that got the movement going," writes Johnston, it can offer no solution. "When the Feminists have a solution they'll be Gay/Feminists."[97]

In *Lesbian Nation,* Johnston argues that any woman who remains male identified, diverting her emotional and sexual energies toward men and male institutions, cannot become an emancipated subject or an autonomous human being. In the book she calls for "all gay people, those who know and accept it, to stand up and speak for themselves," insisting that coming out is the "only way" to ignite a revolution.[98] The dedication reads, "for my mother, who should have been a lesbian and for my daughter in hopes she will be." With its galvanizing rhetoric, its insistence that "the lesbian is *the* revolutionary feminist" and its call for "the creation of a legitimate state defined by women," *Lesbian Nation* is often cited as a paradigmatic example of the trappings of essentialism and the pitfalls of identity politics that plagued second-wave feminism.[99]

Many feminist and queer scholars erroneously equate *Lesbian Nation* with the practice of separatism, with the retreat of radical dykes from the public sphere into safe spaces free of the male gaze. In an essay titled "Queer Nationalism," Lauren Berlant and Elizabeth Freeman's assertion, "The blinking question mark beside the word 'nation' in Jill Johnston's separatist *Lesbian Nation* . . . reveal[s] an evacuation of nationality as we know it," represents a common misinterpretation of the artist and her work.[100] Judging the book by its cover, or more specifically its title, Berlant and Freeman ignore the content, which has less to do with mapping out a separatist society than it does with troubling the codes and conventions that confer identity, govern expressivity, and establish the categories of intelligibility through which citizenship is defined, regulated, and protected by law. Regrettably, these queer theorists reinforce numerous misconceptions about lesbian nationalism: that it was identical to or coterminous with separatism; that dykes sought to escape from rather than engage with the public sphere; and that women were incapable of mounting humorous, playful, and erotic spectacles on the stage of national politics until gay men showed us how.

Johnston's vision of a lesbian nation had little to do with the formation of an actual geopolitical entity and everything to do with fostering emotional states of rapture and joy. The felicity of the performative utterance "I am Gay," as far as this joker was concerned, had as much to do with coming out as a homosexual as it did with "coming into that abnormal condition known as elation."[101] While Johnston's *Lesbian Nation* came to serve as a blueprint for the formation of separatist communities—one collective in Toronto even referred to itself as "the house that Jill built"—this was never the author's intention.[102] This legacy is, perhaps, Johnston's most outrageous, and most durable, act of joker citizenship. The author never lived in a women's commune, nor was she closely aligned, personally or politically, with separatist collectives that existed in various parts of the country at the time.[103] Johnston was not an active member of any lesbian or feminist political organization. Her brief flirtation with GLF went terribly awry, and her only other attempt to participate in a feminist collective was in the summer of

1971 when she attended three consciousness-raising sessions with some up-town women artists, including Gloria Steinem, Kate Millett, and Yoko Ono (who brought John).[104] Johnston recalls, "I couldn't sustain their straight-ness and they couldn't tolerate my challenges."[105] By November of that year, she claimed she was through with organized feminism. "[M]y final impression of movement politics," she writes, is "Movement Schmoovement . . . if you're having fun you're not having a movement and I like to have fun so I've decided to refuse myself the dubious political pleasure" of collective action.[106] Reaffirming her commitment to personal acts of rebellion, Johnston decided, "I constitute a movement totally myself complete period."[107] Her decision to fly solo was made a full two years before the publication of *Lesbian Nation.* To crown Johnston queen of the lesbian separatists or install her as a leader of the feminist movement, then, is oxymoronic, as jokers have no fixed place in the social hierarchy. Fundamentally opposed to authority, structure, and categorization, her mission was to disrupt balance, order, and the status quo.

This legacy has less to do with Johnston's vision for a separatist revolution than it does with the marketing of *Lesbian Nation* by Johnston's publisher. The text was issued by a mainstream press, Simon and Schuster, which meant it enjoyed much wider circulation than most of the feminist literature produced during the women's movement.[108] When Johnston signed the contract for this, her second book, back in 1969, she was recovering from her third (and final) schizophrenic breakdown. As a result of this "awakening," Johnston notes, "I became motivated to write about myself instead of others."[109] She wanted her next endeavor to reflect this shift, so she signed a contract for a book to be titled *Autobiography.* Johnston envisioned this project as an experiment in "creating the 'universality' of the 'minority point of view,'" much like Monique Wittig's *Lesbian Body* and *Les Guérillères,* where lesbian feminism dovetails with textual innovations in the creation of "a personal and political tract but not a unified text."[110] By 1972, when the book went into production, feminism had become a hot commodity, a lucrative niche market, with Kate Millett's *Sexual Politics,* Robin Morgan's *Sisterhood Is Powerful,* and other texts selling tens, sometimes hundreds of thousands of copies in multiple printings to mainstream audiences.[111] Seeking to capitalize on this trend, Simon and Schuster proposed to Johnston that it pitch the book not as a critical memoir but as a feminist manifesto.

In a 2006 interview Johnston acknowledged, "*Lesbian Nation* was bought by a male editor, titled by him, and produced and publicized by his male-owned corporation."[112] She admitted to being not only complicit with the publisher's agenda but also "agreeable, sometimes enthusiastic" about the deal, especially when she walked past Brentano's on Fifth Avenue in Manhattan and saw that her book took up the entire window display of the store. Johnston rationalized her actions by claiming that the entire feminist revolution, such as it was, "was male-supported, -defined, and -perpetuated right down to the barricades." She claims that she was always acutely aware of the fact that the movement "was a gift of the male-owned media," as was her own fifteen minutes of fame. "It was probably the singular definition of myself as sexual that gave me the franchise I had for several years, at a man's newspaper, to run on at great length about myself and women, once I'd said who or what I was. I mean the curiosity, the prurience of the man was there."[113]

It was Johnston's editor at Simon and Schuster who gave the book a "consensus and identity" that the experimental writing itself actively refuses. Lesbian Nation, like Johnston's first book, Marmalade Me, is comprised primarily of selected columns from the Village Voice (1969 to 1972). This collection of diatribes and dalliances chronicles dyke life, queer art, and the author's complicated and circuitous path to gay feminist consciousness. The preface of the book instructs readers that the text should be read as "an interlocking web of personal experience and history and events of the world forming a picture of an evolving political revolutionary consciousness of one who was female who emerged from straight middle unconscious postwar amerika."[114]

A polemically pleasurable text, Lesbian Nation is a mesmerizing mélange of political theory, incisive social critique, and painful personal reflection peppered with humorous anecdotes, wry witticisms, and salacious gossip.[115] Anyone familiar with the critic's work would immediately recognize that Lesbian Nation is much too literal, serious, and straightforward a title for Johnston to have chosen it. The chapter headings are much more indicative of the author's style and sensibility: "The Making of a Lesbian Chauvinist," "The Second Sucks and the Feminine Mystake," and "Amazons and Archedykes." Despite the editor's best intentions to create an easily digestible, coherent narrative, the experimental prose is pitched at such "a high level of difficulty and complexity" that it is "hardly the stuff of political pamphleteering."[116]

As far as manifestos go, Lesbian Nation is severely lacking in prescriptive dogma. Johnston's vision of a gyno-utopia is inchoate at best. She calls her dream "a cosmic plan," as if to suggest it is more fantasy than an attainable reality, and she admits to having no "real strategy" as to how to go about it.[117] The goal, as she articulates it, is "to somehow buy up a lot of space and establish a chain of lesbos on the mainland and invite the lesbian population and introduce the rest to the mysteries and just forget about the men, leaving them to their own devices destroying themselves with their machines and frozen foods."[118] True to her joker nature, Johnston does not dictate a course of action; rather she leaves the exact nature of any subsequent action to the reader.

Although she calls for the creation of a legitimate state by and for women, the author had no interest in women separating from men, as this would have meant, among other things, giving up her position as a prominent art critic; instead, she wanted to inspire her sisters to dedicate their emotional energies to other women. While Johnston may have trafficked in an essentialized notion of "woman," she clearly understands "lesbian" to be a social construction, and a fluid one at that. "[L]esbian is a label," she notes in her Town Hall poem, "invented by anybody to throw at any woman who dares to be a man's equal and lesbian is a good name it means nothing of course or everything so we don't mind using the name in fact we like it for we can be proud to claim allusion to the island made famous by Sappho . . ."[119] More than a static identity, "the lesbian" was a character Johnston performed in her expatriate acts of gaiety. She had an entire repertoire of selves, in fact, but the lesbian, being her most famous, came to symbolize, if not to stand in for, her person. Although it was a dramatic effect, Johnston's lesbian persona came to resemble, through repeated performances, an essence. As the sociologist Erving Goffman wrote in 1959, the year Johnston began contributing to the *Village Voice:*

> In our society the character one performs and one's self are somewhat equated. . . . A correctly staged and performed scene leads the audience to impute a self to a performed character, but this imputation—this self—is a product of a scene that comes off, and is not a cause of it. The self, then, as a performed character, is not an organic thing that has a specific location, whose fundamental fate is to be born, to mature, and to die; it is a dramatic effect arising diffusely from a scene that is presented, and the characteristic issue, the crucial concern, is whether it will be credited or discredited.[120]

Johnston's image as a lesbian separatist was credited, in Goffman's sense of the term, by a cadre of women, by dykes who wanted and needed to believe in a coherent and legitimate sexual identity, and by radical feminists who saw women loving women and women loving themselves as revolutionary acts.

Lesbian Nation captured and rehearsed Johnston's gesture of joker citizenship in performative prose for a broad public audience, one that extended far afield of New York City, carrying the practice of consciousness-raising and the idea of lesbian feminism beyond the urban enclave of her *Village Voice* readership. The author's sexual self-definition and her affirmation of a deviant desire expanded the artistic and performative possibilities of lesbianism through the articulation and enactment of alternative modes of thought, feeling, and existence. Johnston's tome allegorized a "national" lesbian culture, one that is hailed by print media but also, as I have shown, by live performance. Like the paperback pulp fiction of the 1950s, by Ann Bannon and others, *Lesbian Nation* helped foster an "imagined community," in Benedict Anderson's sense, of gay feminists.

Nationalism, as Anderson has suggested, is performatively enacted. It does not involve the awakening of a nation to self-consciousness. Rather, "it *invents* nations where they do not exist."[121] This is especially true for nations without a state, according to Erin Hurley, as these entities rely on theatrical and cultural performances to vouch for their legitimacy. Her adroit analysis of Quebec's national mimesis "opens the door to thinking through how people may produce themselves as national in conditions that militate against it . . . and how one may identify *with* the nation (its values, types, etc.) without identifying *as* national."[122] For lesbians of Johnston's generation, whether they identified as separatists or not, the nation served as a powerful metaphor for the visible and tangible existence of a subculture previously consigned to a marginal existence predicated on shame and debilitating secrecy.[123] It was an emotional cartography forged by a conscious sense of identification rooted in sexual identity and a shared sense of history, culture, and affective experiences of the world. Influenced by the radical insurgency of groups such as the Black Panthers and the National Liberation Front in Vietnam, lesbians did not renounce or reject the idea of nation. Instead, they inverted the dominant paradigm by challenging static, heteronormative notions of citizenship, kinship, and governance.

The conceptual force of the nation's performativity is evidenced in the myriad ways lesbians signaled their sense of collective agency to one another across expansive physical spaces, multiple historical eras, and vast ideological differences. The lesbian nation was propagated through shared rituals, such as consciousness-raising groups, and collective spectacles, including protest marches, pride parades, and music festivals. It was reinforced through the creation and transmission of images, icons, and metaphors, such as the labrys and the figure of Sappho, and through collective practices of commodity consumption, including everything from flannel shirts to rainbow flags. The lesbian nation had a constitution (The Radicalesbians' "Woman-Identified Woman" manifesto), a national anthem (Maxine Feldman's "Amazon [Woman Rise]"), a state seal (the woman's symbol), a national economy (a network of women-owned businesses and laborers), a system of defense (an army of lovers), and a declaration of independence (Johnston's *Lesbian Nation*).

The lesbian nation, as Johnston imagined it, lies somewhere between the virtual and the actual. Exemplary of what José Muñoz in *Cruising Utopia* calls a "spatio-temporal (im)possibility," it is an idea that exists primarily in its affective potential. Radiating the "anticipatory illumination" of a utopian dream, Johnston's lesbian nation exhibits a profound yearning for a way of life that does not yet exist but is desirable and thus worth working toward.[124] In gesturing toward a territory of futurity, a chrono- and geopolitical coming to be, the lesbian nation reflects the world-making efforts of both radical feminism and the gay liberation movement.

"A Truly Dated Idea"

In 1993, Johnston took part in a performance that surprised many people: the woman who vowed she would never be the "victim of lesbian monogamy" entered into a civil union with her longtime partner, Ingrid Nyeboe, in her lover's native Denmark.[125] The timing of this event seemed particularly significant, and more than a bit ironic, as 1993 marked the twentieth anniversary of the publication of *Lesbian Nation* and the year it went out of print.[126] Johnston's decision to settle down may seem antithetical to the expatriate acts of gaiety for which she was notorious; however, we must consider that gestures of joker citizenship are not designed to stand the test of time but to respond to its vicissitudes. The bent of these anarchic antics is toward transience, not permanence. Johnston's predilection, as a peripatetic, was to remain fluid, mobile, and nomadic and to resist the pressure to commit herself to a singular identity, a specific cause, or a fixed ideological camp. From the 1950s until her death in 2010, this joker traversed to and fro, circled forward and back, zigzagged left and center, defying any and all attempts to arrest her motion or pin her down.

Johnston is one of many lesbians whose views on matrimony, monogamy, and motherhood have changed dramatically as they have faced the realities of growing older in a country that is not only homophobic but ageist as well. The circumstances of Johnston's nuptials and the ceremony commemorating them offer ways for us to consider how same-sex unions might be something other than conformist or indicative of homoliberalism. By way of conclusion, I will show how this couple's civil union serves as a gesture of joker citizenship that complicates and questions the homonormative strivings and homonational aspirations that typify the conservative case for gay marriage I outline in chapter two.[127]

Johnston and Nyeboe's ceremony was staged as a Fluxus performance by artist Geoffrey Hendricks in conjunction with a retrospective of his work titled "Day into Night."[128] The festivities began with a traditional civil union conducted at the Town Hall in Odense, a city on the island of Fyn, where same-sex couples have been legally joined since 1989 when Denmark became the first country in the world to grant registered partnerships to homosexuals. The rather perfunctory bureaucratic proceedings were made less mundane by a most unconventional procession through the city streets to the Kunsthallen Brandts Klaedefabrik (art school and museum). Part pageant and part political demonstration, the Fluxprocession's dramatis personae included a canine, a Great Dane, which led the merry band of marauders and a host of revelers in various costumes and states of undress. Fluxus artist Ben Patterson, who designed the musical accompaniment, pulled a cart carrying two portable radios, which played simultaneously. One blasted the overture to Wagner's *Lohengrin* and the other a version of Bambi in Danish. A band of local art students distributed white chrysanthemums to passersby who paused to take in the spectacle. Next came Hendricks, whose nude-to-the-waist body was painted sky blue and adorned with twigs and branches, so that he looked "like an aging Pan."[129] Johnston and Nyeboe, dressed in white pants, white shirts, and white shoes, marched in front of an enormous, thirty-person, blue bridal gown designed by Eric Andersen. Friends and family trailed behind the dress, and strangers who were swept into the festivities served as the rear guard of this retroactivist ensemble. "It's a crazy wedding," exclaimed one impromptu member of the Fluxprocession.[130]

Once the party arrived at the museum, the group climbed several flights of stairs to the gallery where Hendricks's exhibit was being held. As Johnston recalls, "it seemed we were literally part of his show."[131] Hendricks, as Fluxminister, conducted the service. He offered the couple sanctified libations, which consisted of champagne poured into glasses the artist had blown especially for the occasion. Johnston and Nyeboe exchanged rings, for the second time that day, and climbed into one of Hendricks's installations, *Sky Car,* a 1979 Volkswagen Bug painted to look like the heavens. Guests stood behind the car, jingling tin cans that had been tied to the bumper below a sign proclaiming "Just Married." The brides tossed their bouquets from the windows as the assembled crowd cheered. The gay old time continued over erotically shaped food and drinks prepared by the Kunsthallen art students. The delicacies, arranged in intricate patterns and arresting sculptural forms, included what Johnston describes as possibly the most unusual wedding confectionary ever created, "a pyramidal jumble of cake chunks topped by two marzipan brides."[132]

The museum portion of the ceremony was actually an inverted restaging of Hendricks's 1971 *Fluxdivorce,* an event that featured the artist and his then wife Bici, who dissolved their marriage as part of the couple's joint coming-out ceremony. Using scissors, knives, axes, and chainsaws, the pair literally divided their assets. *Fluxdivorce* was, coincidentally, one of the first Fluxus events Johnston attended.[133] While the civil union constituted part of Hendricks's retrospective, the event was, in many ways, an archival exhibition of Johnston's Fluxus activities as well. Intimately associated with Fluxus since the 1960s, as both a critic championing the artwork and a participant engaged in actions and events, Johnston helped popularize and preserve this neo-Dada aesthetic sensibility.[134] I say sensibility because Fluxus is neither an aesthetic movement nor a style, but an attitude and spirit. The term, derived from the Latin word meaning "to flow," was coined by George Maciunas, who organized the first Fluxus event in 1961, at the AG Gallery in New York City, and the first Fluxus festival in Europe the following year.

Like Dada, the historical Fluxus was not an ideology or a school of thought but a constellation around which artists and activists briefly coalesced, providing a means of alignment for various networks of geographically dispersed individuals, collectives, and cultures. Estera Milman describes Fluxus as a "conceptual community, a country whose geography was a figment of communal imagination, whose citizenry was transient and, by definition, cosmopolitan."[135] Johnston's participation in the conceptual country of Fluxus clearly influenced her own gestures of joker citizenship, including the Scull pool incident and the Town Hall intervention. It also shaped her evolving vision of a lesbian nation as an expatriate act. Fluxus' emphasis on assemblage rather than assimilation and interdisciplinarity rather than integration explains, perhaps, the substantial number of women, queers, and people of color who were attracted by and integral to this particular revolution in aesthetics.[136]

To be in flux is to be in a constant state of change. Johnston and Nyeboe's ceremony exemplifies what is known in the domain of Fluxus as an intermedial chance composition. Chance, contingency, and chaos are fundamental aspects of Fluxus art. Modeled, in part, on John Cage's experiments with indeterminacy and sound in the 1950s, chance compositions consist of an event score, a basic set of notes, instructions, or conditions describing who and what should be assembled. Intermedial chance compositions are similar to happenings but differ in both duration and degree of complexity. Emphasizing simplicity, the scale of Fluxus art tends to be small, the texts short, and the enactments brief. Simplicity maximizes the degree of chance in a given composition, and it allows anyone to initiate or restage a Fluxus action.

Hendricks did not script Johnston and Nyeboe's ceremony; rather, he structured the event so that action would flow from the score. Unlike traditional weddings, which are plotted (typically by the bride) down to the minutest detail to avoid mistakes, Hendricks's choreographed performance invited accidents and established itself so as to be subject to any and all contingencies that might arise during the course of its unfolding. "Most everything that happened was a surprise," recalls Johnston, "some of it to Hendricks himself, who assembled all the elements but wasn't always sure when and in what order they were to take place, or even what some of the particulars were."[137] The couple played almost no role in the preparation of the event score. All they were required to do was show up, "look happy, and follow instructions."[138]

The celebration of change and chance in Fluxus projects, according to Mary T. Conway, "helps resituate the art practice as an element of time rather than space, and shifts the emphasis away from being toward becoming, and representation toward presentation."[139] By staging a Fluxus union, in other words, Johnston and Nyeboe are demonstrating that they are less interested in *being* married or entering into a (fixed) *state* of matrimony than they are in *becoming* engaged, with each other and with their communities, which consists of and blurs the lines between families of origin, choice, artists, and strangers. Their ceremony shows the potential of civil unions to disrupt and divert the temporal trajectory of traditional weddings. Whereas weddings typically mark the beginning of a life together, same-sex civil unions often occur in the middle or, depending on the age of the couple, at the end of a very long, fugitive relationship, as in the case of Del Martin and Phyllis Lyon. Having been together for well over a decade, but without official status, Johnston and Nyeboe's service was as much about the future as it was the past, as much about envisioning a life together as it was a retrospective of the many years they shared before civil unions became a possibility in Denmark in 1989 (or gay marriage became legal in New York in 2011).

As chance compositions, Fluxus actions are noncommodifiable events that have little or no exchange value. Opposed to the notion that art has anything to do with utility, purpose, or efficacy, Fluxus is an antiart form of art that opposes tradition. Johnston and Nyeboe's Fluxus union can be seen as an antimarriage marriage, one that counters normative conceptions of love, kinship, and forms of social belonging that are tied to property, capital, and the state. George Brecht describes a Fluxus event score as "the smallest unit of a situation."[140] In contrast to most couples, who view their wedding as the biggest, most important day in their lives, Johnston and Nyeboe's Fluxus ceremony suggests that their civil union is actually the smallest unit of their relationship. By minimizing both the importance and the seriousness of their "big day," the women follow the Fluxus tradition of critiquing the commercial and consumerist aspects of society. Their service actively resists the capitalist trappings of the marriage industry and works against one of the most popular arguments in favor of same-sex unions: that they boost the economy.

Following the Fluxus tradition of lampooning the seriousness of art and culture, Johnston and Nyeboe satirize the gravity accorded to the institution of marriage. The ceremony also mocks the solemn and sanctimonious tone that characterizes homoliberal appeals for gay marriage. That legal recognition of same-sex unions is nonexistent in most places in the world was as absurd to Johnston and Nyeboe as it is to many people. Fluxus artists respond to absurdity with absurdity. Even the most serious Fluxus events, such as Carolee Schneemann's *Viet-Flakes* (1965), and the most dangerous actions, such as Yoko Ono's *Cut Piece* (1964), respond to social injustice with highly theatricalized performative interventions that privilege aesthetic play and the subversive power of humor. Humor, along with chance, is a key component of Fluxus art. As Kristine Stiles notes:

> At its best, the humor in Fluxus performance is of an entirely different order than either the self-satisfied satire, irony, and parody characteristic of modernism or the self-aggrandizing superiority and cynical pastiche claimed for

postmodernism. Filled with the marvel of a sense of discovery and release, Fluxus humor escorts freedoms: the freedom to play and goof-off, the freedom to value that play as an aesthetic habit . . . the freedom to abandon reason and aesthetics and to just be.[141]

The emphasis on gaiety in Johnston and Nyeboe's ceremony reflects the couple's sense of humor, but it also registers their ambivalence about the institution of matrimony and what it means for lesbian feminists to enter into it.

Johnston and Nyeboe serve as paradigmatic examples of antiestablishment radicals who, compelled by a potent economic impetus, embrace a pragmatic course of action. Johnston was sixty-four when she wed Nyeboe. Facing retirement without a steady source of income or a secure benefits package, she married not because she wanted to assimilate into the mainstream but because she simply could not afford to be queerer. In a performance review of her ceremony published in *Art in America,* Johnston describes being asked by a friend if the service would change things. "I said I didn't know. I did know that as a Danish spouse I would qualify for advantages unheard of in America—access to all of the benefits provided by a high-level social welfare system."[142] That Johnston did not see gay marriage as a radical political gesture is evident by her response to a young man who ran up to her and Nyeboe during the ceremony "to enthuse over the event, saying, 'It was the wedding of the future,' meaning, [Johnston] supposed, the form of it, not (necessarily) the political aspect."[143] In "Deep Tapioca," a second performance review she wrote about the ceremony—this one for a progressive women's periodical—Johnston likens getting hitched to putting a rope around her neck. The conflicted critic recalls that she almost called the whole thing off the night before the ceremony but was persuaded to go through with the service for two reasons. First, people had gathered from far and wide to celebrate with her, and she did not want to disappoint her friends and family. Second, the economic exigencies drove her to it. "I'm married now," she writes after the fact, "and if I get sick I can fly over for medical services."

In the introduction to *Admission Accomplished: The Lesbian Nation Years,* published five years after her ceremony, Johnston attributes her change of heart about same-sex unions to transformations in the culture wrought by the feminist and LGBT movements. Johnston admits that she could not imagine living the life she did in the 1960s and 1970s had she not been a disenfranchised mother free from the demands of child rearing and family life. Like many lesbians, she was cast into a role for which she was terribly unsuited at the time, not motherhood per se but motherhood at a moment in history when having a career and a family seemed mutually exclusive. Johnston says the "anti-family, anti-monogamy leitmotif" of the counter-culture ceased to interest her "by at least 1980," and she longed for the opportunity to become a belated mother to her children.[144] "With the nu-clear family model breaking down, and a postmodern pluralism growing up alongside it," she notes, "many of us saw an opportunity to create or recreate family."[145] Johnston and Nyeboe's Fluxus ceremony works toward creating and re-creating kinship structures by actively deconstructing the model of the insular, nuclear family weddings are designed to solidify.

What makes Johnston and Nyeboe's civil union gay is not the fact that they were two women but that they self-consciously conducted their cer-emony as an expatriate act. Staged as part of a Fluxus retrospective, their service is best understood as a counterculture costume drama enacted in the present. Their event reflects the iconoclasm of Fluxus art, which not only is indebted to Cage and Dada but, as Robert Pincus-Witten notes, is "inflected by an idealistic anarchy that evokes a political history reaching back to the Wobblies, the Patterson Strike, and the Feminist model of Emma Goldman."[146] This Fluxwedding did more than drag the past into the pres-ent, however. Hendricks conducted the ceremony in such a way that it will be "complete" only when it can be seen in retrospect. The procession and the conditions of its occurrence—its participants, foreign locale, and con-nection with a retrospective art exhibit—draw our attention to the fact that civil unions are, at this moment in time, still a novel act, a contemporary event that eventually will become, like Fluxus, canonical and traditional. In the future, when gay marriage is legal in the United States and civil unions are disallowed and/or stripped of their significance as an alternative to the homoliberal institution of matrimony, we will look back at this ceremony as a period piece. Enacting a temporal drag, Johnston and Nyeboe's Fluxwed-ding plays itself out according to a gay chronometry, one that pulls the past into the present from the vantage point of the future.

At a time when we are inundated with romanticized images of queer nuclear families and idealized portraits of LGBT patriots, it becomes in-creasingly urgent to counter such sentimental displays with, among other things, accounts of riot and revelry in earlier epochs of gay and lesbian his-tory. This study of Jill Johnston's expatriate acts invites us to rethink the possibilities for sexual agency and social belonging by expanding the conceptual contours of citizenship for LGBT subjects through a retroactivist orientation toward other political cartographies in a remote space and time. This backward glance disrupts and denaturalizes the uncritical conflation of assimilation with political progress by bringing to light forgotten, discredited, and disavowed practices of communion and collectivity that register as sites of contestation and dissent. In addition to providing a particular perspective on the mainstreaming of the LGBT movement, this gesture enables us to move beyond the geopolitical borders of the nation-state, which insists on the homogenization of sexual alterity in exchange for social inclusivity. Johnston's acts of joker citizenship remind us that we are actors in a social drama: we are a composite of conflicting personae, motivations, and feelings—about ourselves, the roles we play, and the worlds we inhabit. Without the joker's anarchic interventions, we run the risk of forgetting that the only thing constant is change, our identities are not essences, and sometimes the best way to challenge injustice is not to take the threat so seriously.

4

Terrorist Acts
The Maladapted Hothead Paisan,
a Lesbian Comedy of Terrors

> Gay is not enough anymore. It's a really good start but we have
> to get our humor back. . . . We could even be gay terrorists with
> humor.
>
> —John Waters

Jill Johnston's *Lesbian Nation* helped spawn many separatist endeavors,
from communes to co-ops. Arguably the most enduring and self-sustaining
experiment in sex-segregation has been the women's music scene, which
includes a host of entertainers, engineers, producers, labels, and a lively
concert circuit. Out of this separatist sphere of cultural production came
the first songs written, recorded, pressed, and distributed by lesbians and
feminists for themselves, including Maxine Feldman's single "Angry Atthis"
(May 1969, recorded in 1972)—the title is an allusion to Sappho's lover—
and the album *Lavender Jane Loves Women* (1974) by vocalist and songwriter
Alix Dobkin, flautist Kay Gardner, and bassist Patches Attom. Many of these
pioneering artists were women of color; Gwen Avery, Linda Tillery, Mary
Watkins, Pat Parker, Judith Casselberry, Jaque Duprée, and June Millington
regularly toured and sometimes recorded with Holly Near, Cris Williamson,
Meg Christian, and Teresa Trull. Several of these performers appear on the
hilarious and satirical album, *Lesbian Concentrate: A Lesbianthology of Songs
and Poems* (1977) issued by Olivia Records in response to Anita Bryant's
virulent anti-gay campaign, Save Our Children. This complication of music and spoken word poems features tracks with tantalizing titles, such as
"Leaping Lesbians," "Sugar Mama," "Ode to a Gym Teacher," and "For The
Straight Folks Who Don't Mind Gays But Wish They Weren't So Blatant."

Women's music was sold through mail order, at lesbian feminist bookstores, coffeehouses, and festivals, the largest of which is the Michigan Womyn's Music Festival (Michfest), founded in 1976.

On August 13, 2004, Animal Prufrock, of the dyke punk band Bitch and Animal, staged the world premier of *Hothead Paisan: Homicidal Lesbian Terrorist* on the famed Friday Night Stage at the twenty-ninth annual Michigan Womyn's Music Festival. This musical theater extravaganza featured a star-studded cast of lesbian feminist icons, including Ani DiFranco, founder of Righteous Babe Records; Toshi Reagon of Sweet Honey in the Rock and BIGLovely; television personality Susan Powter; and Alyson Palmer of *BETTY RULES!* and *L Word* fame, to name only a few. Animal wrote the music and lyrics in addition to playing the title role. *Hothead Paisan* is based on Diane DiMassa's underground comic zine (a cheaply produced, self-published graphic novella) of the same name. A cult phenomenon beloved by Michfest veterans, DiMassa's zine chronicles the exploits of a "mood-disordered, developmentally arrested," hypercaffeinated, ball-busting dyke with "scary hair and an even scarier fetish for guns, grenades" and justice.[1] Equal parts Joan of Arc, Bongi Perez, and Aileen Wuornos, Hothead's mission is to make the world safe for women and queers by eradicating evil, one man at a time.

Hothead the musical was hailed by critics and fans alike as the highlight of Michfest, and this despite the fact that what audiences saw was a work-in-progress, a prelude to what Animal joked would be a full-fledged production she planned to take all the way to Broadway. Not surprisingly, *Hothead* never made it to the Great White Way. It did not even make it to New York City. There are obvious reasons why a musical by a relatively unknown artist about a homicidal lesbian terrorist in the wake of 9/11 might fail to generate mass appeal. This has less to do with Americans' desire to avoid plays about terrorism during a war—Steven Sondheim's *Assassins* made its Broadway debut in April 2004 and won five Tony Awards—than it does with the lack of support for any kind of theater (mainstream or avant-garde, musical or straight) by, for, or about lesbians. What interests me here, however, is not what the impossibility of bringing *Hothead* to Broadway may or may not have to do with theater's persistent and relentless lesbophobia, but what the performance's success at Michfest reveals about feminist and queer responses to the War on Terror.

DiMassa's *Hothead Paisan* exploits the deep historical convergences between sexual minorities and political terrorists. Cast as degenerate outlaws whose perverse desires threaten to destroy the nuclear family, the nation, and, by extension, civilization itself, lesbians and gays have been condemned as duplicitous traitors, communist defectors, and criminal conspirators who imperil the forward movement of human and historical progress. Blamed for the spread of physical, psychic, and moral diseases, we have been treated as cankerous elements plaguing an otherwise healthy society. In response to the alleged dangers lesbians pose to the world, medical, juridical, and religious authorities have sought to terrorize us into submission. We have been incarcerated and institutionalized against our will, subjected to torturous "cures" such as shock therapy and lobotomies, disowned by family members and friends, denied housing and health care, relieved of our jobs and children, and brutalized by passersby and police alike. The LGBT movement has made incredible gains toward decriminalizing and depathologizing homosexuality. Over the past fifty years, activists have won hard-fought battles for the legalization of sodomy, domestic partner benefits, same-sex unions, hate crime protections, and the end of the military's ban on openly gay troops. Juridical reform has been accompanied by greater representation in the mainstream media, enhanced political visibility, and increased market capital.

Not all sexual minorities have benefited from these seismic shifts in the social order, however. As we celebrate the slow but steady enfranchisement of gays and lesbians, we would do well to consider the consequences of our assimilation into the national fabric. Who gets incorporated and at what cost? To what extent does the folding of "proper" homosexual subjects (those who want to marry, reproduce, and die for their country) into the nation-state occur at the expense of "improper" or profligate queers who cannot be accommodated because they exceed or fail to achieve the narrow terms of acceptability? People whose identities, politics, and sexual practices fall beyond the boundaries of what is considered appropriate behavior are ostracized, excluded, and left behind. These individuals often experience increased discrimination from heterosexuals, but also from homosexuals who feel their personal progress is impeded by the presence of such nonconforming queer kin.

In *Terrorist Assemblages,* Jasbir Puar argues that the neoliberalization of the LGBT movement—with its investment in pragmatic goals, commodity ownership, and state-sanctioned sexual relationships—engenders "homonationalism," a normalizing rhetoric of patriotism and citizenship. The dual dynamics of homonationalism, in which queers embrace a statist agenda and the state, in turn, embraces queers, transforms homosexuality's association with terror, disease, and death into symbols of life, virility, and productivity.[2] This rebranding of the homosexual—from terrorist to citizen—applies only to those exemplary gays and lesbians who promote "family values" (e.g., marriage, monogamy, and procreation) and who perform their patriotic duty by advancing free market capitalism as the American way of life. This transformation aligns gays and lesbians, however unwittingly, with the violent structures of nationalism and the bellicose rhetoric of exceptionalism that sanction American imperialism. Homonationalism has been instrumental in perpetuating the War on Terror and the racist remapping of terrorist identities onto Muslim corporealities. The tactics and strategies of our current war machine rely on and benefit from the proliferation of queerness to produce both the (white, neoliberal) homonational and its (colored, fanatical) counterpart, the Islamic terrorist of elsewhere, a figure imbued with colonial fantasies of sexual perversion, gender dysphoria, and racial stereotypes. Insisting that resistance to homonationalism will require increasingly queerer forms of art and activism, Puar allies queerness with extremism not to stake out an oppositional political stance but rather to reanimate the "*convivial* relations" between queerness and terrorism in order to unsettle and destabilize both terms, realigning them into new ontological and affective assemblages.[3]

There is perhaps no better figure, real or imagined, to speak to the imbricated and potentially transformative relationship between sexuality and terrorism than Hothead Paisan. The two modalities in which Hothead appears—zine and musical—produced at two different historical moments—before and after 9/11—by two different artists—DiMassa and Animal—provide a unique vantage point from which to consider the complex and shifting dynamics of homonationalism. I explore here what a maladapted dyke like Hothead has to teach us about the affective economy of terrorism, the theatrics of revolutionary violence, and the efficacy of militant forms of LGBT protest. This lesbian comedy of terrors challenges commonplace assumptions about which modes of art and activism constitute "queerer" forms of resistance by troubling the deeply ingrained notion that culture workers who position themselves at the vanguard (as opposed to the rear guard) of social movements actually forge the most radical interventions into national-political life. Given that homonationalism seizes on and distorts feminism and the LGBT movement's investment in advancement, evolution, and forward motion, it can be advantageous to attend to the regressive rhythms of anachronistic and recalcitrant forms of retroactivism, like *Hothead Paisan,* which aim to reanimate the dissident dreams of the past. Archaic structures of feeling and disavowed histories can serve as vital components of political progress. This affective etymology of terrorism seeks to restore a differently queered body and a defiantly gay agenda to sex and gender studies.

Stages of Revolt

Animal Prufrock was a sophomore theater major in Chicago in the 1990s when she first discovered *Hothead Paisan.* A gender nonconformist, this budding artist was actively discriminated against at school, especially when it came to casting. "The faculty," she was told, "is just having a hard time imagining you as a woman."[4] Animal refers to her undergraduate theater training as "one of [her] biggest heartbreaks."[5] Browsing a bookstore one day, she came across DiMassa's zine. Her identification with the comic's protagonist was immediate and overwhelming. "I SAW ME," Animal recalls, and "I immediately said, 'I'm gonna make a fucking musical out of this.'" She envisioned a production that would serve as "revenge to the theatre school, to all that bullshit."[6]

Revenge fantasies featuring homicidal lesbian terrorists play an important role in the dramaturgy of radical feminism. They were especially ubiquitous in the art, theory, and activism of the early years of the women's liberation movement, from the late 1960s to the mid-1970s when civil rights struggles, anti–Vietnam War protests, and militant forms of ethnic nationalism (e.g., the Black Panthers, the Young Lords, and the American Indian Movement [AIM]) prompted some revolutionary organizations (e.g., the Weather Underground and the Symbionese Liberation Army) to engage in terrorist acts against the government. Most feminists decried the use of violence to combat violence, but this did not stop them from dreaming about the forceful elimination of oppressive regimes or dramatizing hypothetical scenarios of armed insurrection.

DiMassa's *Hothead Paisan* is the animated progeny of Valerie Solanas's *SCUM Manifesto,* the Radicalesbians' "Woman-Identified Woman," and Monique Wittig's *Les Guérillères.*[7] These lesbian revenge fantasies are deadly serious satires featuring vigilante feminist heroines, graphic scenes of retaliation and retribution, cunning linguistic puns, and black humor. Lesbian comedies of terrors exploit for humorous effect the compulsory rites and rituals of heteronormativity. Their plots revolve around the frustrations and unrepressed rage of the disenfranchised and dispossessed. Episodic in nature, they depict highly theatrical spectacles, dark play, blood sports, and war games. Like comedies of manners, these sardonic texts feature stock characters that are rewarded rather than punished for sexual deviance. Marginalized by the ceremonies and sacraments that govern human behavior, sexual minorities are in an optimal position to observe the excesses and hypocrisies of straight society, the artificiality of gender roles, and the disciplinary regimes that govern erotic desires. Parodying normative codes of conduct, comedies of terrors correct gross forms of injustice and reverse conventional moral judgments. Their humor stems from the protagonist's skillful manipulation of ludicrous situations and her virtuosic display of anarchic wit. Cutting up, verbally and physically, is the heroine's primary defense against the tyranny of sexism and homophobia.

Comedies of terrors are caricatures, inked in acid, of the white, middle-class, American male and the political, environmental, and economic cesspool he has made of the world. Constitutive of this genre is the transformation of a terrorized sexual minority into a terrorist, which occurs when the protagonist realizes that compulsory heterosexuality is little more than a thinly disguised plot designed to keep women subordinate. Male genocide is depicted as an ethical gesture and an act of mercy, one that will put a death-driven species out of its misery and save the planet from destruction. Some revenge fantasies are premised on the notion that the "real" terrorists are not deadly dykes but what transgender performance artist Kate Bornstein calls "Gender Defenders," the people, institutions, and sociopolitical structures that terrorize gender outlaws and sexual deviants with the punitive forces of heteronormativity. In *Gender Outlaw*, Bornstein writes:

> I thought that it would be fun to call what I do in life gender terrorism. Seemed right at first—I and so many folks like me were terrorizing the structure of gender itself. But I've come to see it a bit differently now—gender terrorists are not the drag queens, the butch dykes, the men on roller skates dressed up as nuns. . . . Gender terrorists are those who . . . use gender to terrorize the rest of us. These are the real terrorists: the Gender Defenders.[8]

Most lesbian revenge fantasies, however, embrace and exploit the conflation of dykes and terrorists. These works are predicated on an ironic resignification of what Lynda Hart calls "fatal women," the predatory and sadistic phallic female of patriarchy's paranoid delusions come true. By putting "the historical displacement of violence onto lesbians into lesbians' own hands and keeping their guns loaded," these comedies of terrors offer the most pointed and potent challenge to forms of hetero- and homonormativity.[9]

A resurgence of lesbian revenge fantasies took place in the late 1980s. These comedies of terrors emerged as a response to the AIDS epidemic, Reaganomics, the feminist backlash precipitated by the Culture Wars, the rising tide of the religious right, and the misogynist underpinnings of certain strands of queer theory, which was in its nascent stage of development. Lizzie Borden's futuristic mockumentary *Born in Flames,* the fire-eating direct-action group Lesbian Avengers, Split Britches' *Lesbians Who Kill,* the Five Lesbian Brothers' *The Secretaries,* Queen Latifah's butch bank robber in the film *Set it Off,* and Staceyann Chin's "Dykepoem," which begins with the line "I killed a man today," represent some of the more brazen members of this new generation of deadly dykes.[10] The most important and influential revenge fantasy penned during this period is DiMassa's *Hothead Paisan: Homicidal Lesbian Terrorist.*

Hothead: The Zine

"Tell us," asks an unidentified interlocutor in the inaugural issue of DiMassa's zine, "how does one become a homicidal lesbian terrorist?" To which the character replies, "How does one not, you asshole?!"[11] Similar to traditional comics, *Hothead* begins with a creation myth, but it is immediately apparent that this protagonist—a tattooed, mullet-sporting rogue—bears no resemblance to the anatomically exaggerated, bikini-clad mistresses of the Marvel and D.C. pantheons. DiMassa's zine recounts how a relatively well-adjusted lesbian snaps one day while watching television. Annoyed by images of graphic violence against women, degrading racist caricatures, and homophobic stereotypes, she switches from channel to channel, from sitcoms to the news to commercials, but the messages are the same. She begins to succumb to the propaganda blasting from the boob tube and is on the verge of complete indoctrination when, just in the nick of time, a shadowy figure emerges from her psyche. Personality #2 urges the young woman to resist the "constant onslaught of white heterosexism," which she does by grabbing an ax and smashing the television.[12] Convinced by her psychic

Hothead Paisan: Homicidal Lesbian Terrorist. (Image courtesy of Diane DiMassa.)

projection that she must eliminate not only "the machine" but "the man" as well, Hothead ventures maniacally into the world hell-bent on vengeance, packing a small arsenal and an enormously overinflated ego. Like the Incredible Hulk, her actions are swift, her decisions are final, and her judgment is impaired by a rage of epic proportions.

Hothead's "terrorist drag" consists of Doc Martins and a leather jacket, which enables her to hide in plain sight as she looks just like every other punk dyke in any major metropolitan area.[13] She has a faithful sidekick, Chicken the Cat; a sage mentor, Roz Goldhart; and a signature weapon, the labrys, which she wears around her neck and wields without remorse, glee-

Hothead Paisan reading to her friend Roz from Valerie Solanas's *SCUM Manifesto*. (Image courtesy of Diane DiMassa.)

fully castrating offending members of the opposite sex.[14] Hothead's pals try to keep her from going over the edge, but their efforts are futile. Chicken the Cat practices yoga, deep meditation, and other healing rituals. She has been known to hide Hothead's coffee, to turn off the television before she blitzes out, and to hightail it before things really get out of hand. Roz is a recovering hothead, a former radical lesbian separatist, whose physical blindness serves as a metaphor for the emotional blindness caused by the unchecked rage of her youth.[15] She tries unsuccessfully to persuade Hothead that change is best achieved through nonviolent resistance and a commitment to institutional and social reform, not by trying to resurrect the matriarchy through a program of male genocide. Roz's liberal humanism stands in stark contrast to Hothead's militant feminism, and the zine offers a nuanced deliberation on the ethical and philosophical differences between these modes of political activism. Hothead is constitutionally incapable of engaging in peaceful forms of protest. When she marches, it is straight over someone's face; when she strikes, it is in the dark with a six-inch blade. Taking her cue from So-lanas's *SCUM Manifesto*—in one issue of the zine DiMassa depicts Hothead reading to Roz from it—this lesbian terrorist is out to destroy the system, not attain certain rights within it. Like Valerie, she prefers anarchy and crim-inal antics to polite displays of civil disobedience.

Hothead pushes the envelope, even for a subcultural mode of expression like zines, the medium of choice for disaffected do-it-yourselfers. Stephen Duncombe describes zinesters as "everyday oddballs . . . speaking plain-ly about themselves and our society with an honest sincerity, a revealing intimacy, and a healthy 'fuck you' to sanctioned authority" who write not for fame or recognition but to communicate their views to "an audience of like-minded misfits."[16] Produced largely by and for members of the white middle class—by people who are not without certain privileges but who feel at odds with mainstream society—zines are often dedicated to topics that are ignored or mocked by the arbiters of culture. In the 1930s science fiction fans created zines to share their love of a genre deemed low-brow by literature aficionados. In the 1970s punks produced zines to celebrate an underground music scene ignored by the rock 'n' roll establishment. In the 1980s and 1990s, zine production grew by leaps and bounds, especially among riot grrrls and punk dykes like DiMassa and Animal.

Zines are characterized by handwritten text and graphics on found or "borrowed" paper haphazardly assembled and cheaply reproduced. Authors often make no attempt to number pages or correct spelling and grammar mistakes—as little attention is paid to bourgeois concerns such as order, etiquette, and "proper" form. Like the performative textual productions of the dadaists, surrealists, and futurists, zines typically juxtapose text and im-ages in ways that are meant to be arresting, if not shocking, to the uniniti-ated. Punk dyke and riot grrrl zines draw on these sources but they also find inspiration in feminist and gay periodicals such as *The Ladder* (1956–70), *The Furies* (1972–73), *On Our Backs* (1984–2006), and *Lesbian News* (1974–present). These zinelike publications feature art, creative writing, personal reflections, erotica, and critical theory. Riot grrrl zines combine music reviews, artist profiles, interviews with bands, and graphic art along-side articles on sexual harassment, rape, abortion rights, body image, eating disorders, and relationships. They offer critiques of normative beauty stan-dards and challenge acceptable modes of female behavior.

Zinesters tend to be employed in what Duncombe calls "the grim new economy of service, temporary and 'flexible' work."[17] A "protest against the drudgery of working for another's profit," zines produce and circulate within "a culture whose value isn't calculated as profit and loss on ruled ledger papers, but is assembled in the margins."[18] DiMassa was unemployed and in rehab for alcohol and drug addiction when she created Hothead. She began drawing the character, at her therapist's suggestion, as a way to channel her anger. DiMassa's then partner, Stacey Sheehan, encouraged her to produce a zine from the material she was generating in recovery. Together they published *Hothead Paisan: Homicidal Lesbian Terrorist* quarterly and sold it for three dollars an issue at a handful of independent feminist and gay bookstores across the country. They called their outfit Giant Ass Publishing. From 1991 to 1996 *Hothead* grew in circulation and consistently sold out in the United States, Canada, England, and Australia. Despite *Hothead*'s popularity, DiMassa and Sheehan have profited very little from the zine. Not exactly suited for syndication due to its graphic violence and post-politically-correct satirical tone, *Hothead* has not achieved the success or longevity of Alison Bechdel's *Dykes to Watch Out For,* a rare example of a lesbian subcultural success story.[19] *Hothead* was, however, anthologized by Cleis Press, which "publishes provocative, intelligent books in the areas of sexuality, gay and lesbian studies, erotica . . . and human rights," in three different volumes, thus making the lesbian terrorist readily available not only to urban guerrilla gals but also rural dykes and budding suburban riot grrrls at some mainstream bookstores and, of course, on the Internet.[20]

Due to its explicit content, DiMassa's zine has generated a fair amount of controversy among both straights and queers who fail to appreciate its irony and dark humor. She has received hate mail from members of the religious right and has had bricks thrown through her windows by "feminists chanting anti-violence slogans."[21] One issue in particular (number 8) led to charges of obscenity and censorship by Canadian customs.[22] In this episode a woman, Roberta, is gang-raped by three men. Despite overwhelming evidence, the judge dismisses the case and fines Roberta five hundred dollars for being a temptress. Infuriated by the decision, Hothead takes it upon herself to settle the score. In an act of retributive justice, she kidnaps the perpetrators, takes them to a deserted warehouse she dubs "The Misogynists' Hall of Fame," and tortures them. Hothead performs a "reverse rape" on two of the men, and the third she castrates using a guillotine.

The guillotine is a reference to the French Revolution, where terrorism

had, at least at the outset "a decidedly *positive* connotation."[23] This anachronistic trope calls to mind disavowed political projects and obsolete structures of feeling. DiMassa's zine cites the past to incite the present, indexing
failed programs for social change from the 1970s but also from the 1790s.
In her defense of Roberta, Hothead assumes the role of the Robespierre of
lesbian feminism (if she had a battle cry, it would be "off with their [little]
heads").[24] By making the avenger an avatar of both the French Revolution
and second-wave lesbian feminism, DiMassa urges us to confront on an intellectual and emotional register what has been forgotten, obscured, abandoned, and erased in dominant historical accounts of liberation movements.
Hothead's attachment to discredited and outmoded ideals exemplifies her
commitment to an affective and dissident potentiality that the past cannot
contain. The lost possibilities of unfinished and incomplete revolutions
serve as touchstones, as ways for Hothead to think beyond the pragmatic
present and to imagine different structures of being and belonging. They
also serve as reminders that Hothead is the successor to spirited radicals
whose democratic and egalitarian desires devolved into despotism.[25]

DiMassa's zine embodies both a celebration of the revolutionary impulses that gave rise to the French Revolution and an astute critique of terrorism
as a means of effecting social change. It dramatizes the danger Hothead faces, namely, that the struggle for justice will consume her, just as it did Robespierre, and it reminds us that similar fates have befallen other homicidal
lesbian terrorists, including Solanas, whose image and influence pepper the
pages of this zine. In this way, DiMassa underscores the fact that there is
no simple or universally agreed upon definition of terrorism. Nor can there
be, according to Walter Laqueur, as "there is not one terrorism, but a variety of terrorisms and what is true of one does not necessarily apply to the
others."[26] Terrorism has been practiced by liberal and conservative political
organizations, religious affiliations and nationalistic groups, and resistance
movements and state institutions. Though difficult to define, there are two
generally agreed upon aspects of terrorism. The first is that it involves the
systematic use of violence and/or the threat of violence to induce a state of
fear in a population in order to achieve a particular political objective. The
second is that it is inherently theatrical.

Political violence has become increasingly theatricalized since the advent of television, rising to new heights during 9/11. Terrorist acts are media
events. Intensely dramatic, and oftentimes tragic, the bombings, hijackings,
kidnappings, and assassinations that constitute terrorist acts transform un-

wary publics into hostages of bloody spectacles. While seemingly random, terrorist attacks are carefully plotted, meticulously executed, and designed to deliver the greatest shock value. In order to attract and maintain the widest possible audience, terrorists must generate publicity and sustain media interest, which results in increasingly violent, high-profile antics. Many postmodern theorists have gone past the level of analogy, conceptually conflating modern media-dependent terrorism with theater. Herb Blau has suggested that terrorism *is* theater, as has Jean Baudrillard, who calls these spectacles "our theatre of Cruelty."[27] Not only is this polemical posturing wrong, it is irresponsible, amounting to what Jean-François Lyotard called theoretical terror.[28] As Anthony Kubiak notes, "[T]errorism may be *designed* as theatre . . . it may be simulation, a hyperreality," but "it is not theatre."[29] Maintaining the distinction is important if we are to have any hope of creating and sustaining a response to political violence.

Hothead Paisan engages in the theatrics of lesbian terrorism. What distinguishes her fictional rampages from real violence, according to DiMassa, is that she "acts out the fantasies that we would never really carry out ourselves, even though we're thinking them."[30] Similar to the terrorist spectacles in Western theater, Hothead's violence offers a cathartic release for its spectators, a way for lesbians to purge their outrage and sadness at social injustice in a productive and salutary way, "without getting injured."[31] As a comedy of terrors, *Hothead* enables us to laugh at oppression, but it does not spare the protagonist (or audiences) from the suffering political change entails. Nor does it liberate us from the ethical quandaries implicit in these imaginings. DiMassa captures the joy Hothead experiences each time she saves a woman from danger, as well as the pain and alienation her life as a terrorist entails. The zine highlights the affective dialectic between hope and despair that animates all social activists. Hope compels disaffected radicals to act out against individuals and institutions, and desperation incites them to disrupt and destroy corrupt systems and the humans who profit from them. Hothead underscores the fact that terrorists, however we feel about them, are, in the words of John Orr and Dragan Klaić, the "*ultimate* utopians," the "last believers in dreams no one wants to take seriously any longer."[32] A walking anachronism, Hothead wants to be a revolutionary in a country that no longer believes in revolution. She has lost faith not in feminism or gay liberation but in these movements' ability to effect social change.

What is radical about the zine is not its advocacy of political extremism but its acknowledgment of Hothead's complicity in the affective economy of terror. By recognizing her participation in the normalization of violence, DiMassa disrupts the dichotomous logic that produces troubling binaries: revolutionary/terrorist, patriot/traitor, radical/conservative, regress/progress. DiMassa's active connivance of a convivial and productive relationship between queerness and terrorism is what makes the zine a potentially powerful and effective antidote to homonationalism.

Re-enlisting Hothead Paisan

DiMassa retired *Hothead Paisan* in 1996, but the zine's eponymous paladin would not rest for very long. In 2001 the United States suffered a devastating series of attacks at home and abroad, which prompted then president George W. Bush to declare a War on Terror, perhaps the most egregious of his many malapropisms—as if we were battling not the forces of fear but fear itself.[33] In the period leading up to and during the war, a series of forces (including carefully choreographed strikes by cellular networks of suicide bombers, a resurgence of religious fanaticism, and neoliberal socioeconomic policies) worked to align terrorism with Islamic jihad and Muslim extremists. Bush claimed that people were either with America or against it in the fight for freedom. Criticizing or questioning the war was cast as sympathizing with the mujahideen, which Bush suggested was itself a terrorist act. These geopolitical events and rhetorical maneuvers effectively disarticulated terrorism from its grounding in the revolutionary struggle for liberation that it had come to epitomize not only for lesbian feminists like DiMassa but for generations of political radicals.

The experience of 9/11 scared many queers straight and engendered a period of fervent homonationalism from which we have yet to recover. A number of gays and lesbians lost their lives and loved ones in the attacks and subsequent counterinsurgency. President Bush's polarizing rhetoric of "us versus them" allied American victims, irrespective of their sexuality, and his insistence on forging a united front made dissenting from this form of "binary terror" nigh impossible.[34] Government officials, including conservative Republicans, publicly acknowledged "gay heroes" who died in service to their country, such as New York fire chaplain Father Mychal Judge, who was inside the World Trade Center, and United Airlines passenger Mark Bingham, who helped divert one of the hijacked planes before it could reach its target. Bush, Dick Cheney, and Donald Rumsfeld justified the War on Terror, in part, by citing a moral obligation to liberate women and gays oppressed by Islamic rule. These extenuating circumstances have contributed to the lack of LGBT opposition to the War on Terror. This silence has been compounded by the fact that national organizations such as NGLTF and HRC have elected not to articulate an official position on the war. Instead, they worked to take advantage of the shortage of qualified service personnel to staff the fronts in Iraq and Afghanistan as grounds for the repeal of DADT.

Given the post-9/11 political climate, it did not take much to coax Hothead out of retirement. Shortly after her return, an interviewer for *Bitch* magazine asked DiMassa, "[W]hat happens to the terrorist part of Hothead's name, now that terrorism has acquired such an emotional payload?" "It was mine first!" the defiant artist proclaimed, "I'm not changing it."[35] DiMassa's nostalgic insistence on an outmoded form of radical feminist terrorism encourages us to see the term as a complex and highly contested construction with a long and complicated history. This stance troubles the rigid distinction the Bush administration sought to naturalize between war (legitimate violence committed by sovereign states) and terrorism (acts of aggression enacted by illegitimate entities). In redirecting our attention to the past, DiMassa reminds us that the modern origins of terrorism are imbricated with revolutionary impulses and democratic ideals while simultaneously privileging the role of lesbians in any survey of terrorist taxonomies.

In "'68 or Something," Lauren Berlant asks, "[H]ow do we secure the importance of transformational, radical openness and departures from the past for our languages and practices and politics in a time when revolutionary projects are so widely and effectively dismissed?"[36] How do we counter attempts, by forces on both the left and the right, to frame liberation struggles as historical, as finished, over, and done? How do we work against narratives that frame "that 'revolution' with a black edge, an edge that has become a bar" to reanimating progressive thought and action?[37] Berlant suggests that the Left is hamstrung by fear, fear "of repeating the definitional exclusions, violences, and imaginative lapses" of liberation movements since 1968, and in particular the fear of rehearsing their "imperialist, racist, heterosexist, class-based, culture bound, and overly optimistic parochialism."[38] It is not simply the fear of failure that paralyzes us, however; it is also the threat of shame, the shame of being rearward or nostalgic, of being caught in the act of feeling and doing things whose time, allegedly, has passed. Hope and the belief in revolution are naive attachments we postmodernists have supposedly outgrown. Berlant alludes to this when she insists upon "the necessity of preserving, *against all shame,* a demanding question of revolution itself, a question about utopia that keeps pushing its way through a field of failed aspirations, like a student at the back of the room who gets suddenly, violently, tired of being invisible."[39] A transformational political practice requires a willingness to risk embarrassment. It demands both courage and a certain degree of shameless.

DiMassa's Hothead Paisan is a dissident subject who shamelessly refuses to learn the lessons of history, to relinquish utopian longings, or to cede faith in revolutionary ideals. Her impassioned defense of lesbian terrorism in the wake of 9/11 made it seem as if she were reenlisting Hothead as a rejoinder to both Bush's imperialist warmongering and the homoliberal queers who sought to capitalize on the crisis. As the War on Terror escalated, it became clear that we needed Hothead more than ever. A self-professed defender of the stigmatized, marginalized, and dispossessed, Hothead is a radical lesbian feminist whose revolutionary aspirations are born out of a long history of antiracist and anti-imperialist struggles. As a white dyke, she dislodges terrorism from its contemporary, racist, patriarchal, and orientalist associations. Adopting a downwardly mobile punk aesthetic, Hothead rejects "middle-class tactics of polite persuasion in favour of in-yer-face proletarianism."[40] Her last name is Paisan, which is Italian-American for "compatriot," a greeting used among members of the Italian immigrant working class. This appellation signals Hothead's affiliation with a working-class ethnic subculture, just as her first name identifies her as a militant lesbian feminist. While the time was ripe for the zine's return, DiMassa, much to the dismay of her fans, did not resume publication. Instead, she granted another artist the right to adapt *Hothead Paisan* as a musical. The creative and political force behind the project was riot grrrl Animal Prufrock.[41]

The riot grrrl movement is a subcultural phenomenon that began in the early 1990s amid accusations that feminism was dead, Anita Hill was a liar, and all Gen Xers were apathetic slackers. While many sites played a role in the development of this genre, the origin of the term is typically traced to an exchange between members of the band Bratmobile—Jen Smith and Allison Wolfe—after the Mount Pleasant riots in 1991 in Washington, DC. In response to the turmoil, Smith suggested that the two friends ought to start a girl riot. Shortly thereafter Wolfe and Bratmobile's Molly Neuman, together with Kathleen Hanna and Toby Vail of *Bikini Kill* (a zine and later a band), collaborated on a zine called *Riot Grrrl.* The term *grrrl* first appeared, however, in the pages of Vail's fanzine *Jigsaw* (1988–) when she called for a "Revolution Grrrl Style Now."

Grrrl features a triple *r* to give *girl* a growling, guttural force and reclaim a diminutive and derogatory term for females. Equally interesting is the use of *riot* as both a compound noun and an adjective. Like riot gear and riot police, these riot grrrls are prepared for battle. The term also encodes other, more archaic meanings of *riot,* specifically a flamboyant or theatrical display (as in a riot of color in the participants' clothes and hair), an unbridled outbreak of emotion (as in a riot of laughter that erupts unexpectedly), a moment of uproarious hilarity, and a mood of unrestrained revelry. To riot is to disturb the peace. Like the lesbian feminist zaps examined earlier in this book, riot grrrl actions blur the distinction between politics and play, rebellion and recreation. Creating disturbances through dalliances, ones that are as redolent of fury as they are of frivolity, rioting is an act of gaiety by another name.

An important and highly visible front of third-wave feminism, riot grrrls rejected women's marginalized status in the alternative music scene by forming their own garage bands and fanzines to promote them. Animal Prufrock, whose desire to study musical theater in college was thwarted by her department's misogyny and homophobia, teamed up with a classmate to form the duo Bitch and Animal (1995–2004).[42] This group, along with Tribe 8, Sleater-Kinney, Le Tigre, and the Butchies, constitute the most radical element of the riot grrrl movement. As Judith Halberstam has noted, this "new wave of dyke subcultures" draws on two radically divergent strands of 1970s music, British punk and women's folk.[43] Punk is an anarchic, aggressive, and highly stylized mode of revolt, and queer punk, or queercore, as it is often called, delivers a potent critique of hetero- and homonormativity. Women's folk music, though typically associated with acoustic guitars and ballads, includes a hard-edged fringe comprised of angry dykes shouting confrontational lyrics over their electric guitars. Infusing the rogue aesthetics of punk with a feminist consciousness, bands like Bitch and Animal oppose the hegemony of the music industry and the mainstreaming of gay and lesbian culture.

Bitch and Animal see themselves as heirs to the tradition of cultural feminism that paved the way for riot grrrls, and like their predecessors, they have tried (sometimes succeeding, though often failing) to ameliorate the classism and racial exclusivity that haunt the women's music scene. The duo's "Pussy Manifesto," a secret track on their self-published debut album,

What's That Smell?, and their collaboration with June Millington of Fanny, a pathbreaking women's rock band in the 1970s, on their third album, *Sour Juice and Rhyme* (2003), exemplify the lesbian feminist ethic of generational continuity that rejects "the Oedipal imperative to overthrow the old and bring on the new."[44] This ethic is reflected in Animal's direction of a multigenerational, multicultural cast for the show. Animal played Hothead opposite her then lover Susan Powter (Personality #2). Ani Difranco starred as Chicken the Cat; Rhiannon, known for her jazz inflected, body-based vocal improvisations, as well as her work in the theater, took on the role of Roz; Kate Wolf appeared as Daphne, Hothead's ambiguously gendered love interest; Suhir Blackeagle played the protagonist's friend and former lover Sharquee, a prostitute and witch; and Edie Klecka performed the role of Hothead's inner light, Lampy. The musical also featured a chorus, or, as Animal dubbed it, a "Whorechestra," with Toshi Reagon, Alyson Palmer, Julie Wolf (twin sister of Kate), Jami Sieber (a vocalist who plays a mean electric cello), and Debi Buzil (a yoga teacher and chanter).[45]

Riot grrrls' amateur aesthetic is reflected in the fact that Animal had never written or directed a musical when she set about adapting *Hothead Paisan*. Musical theater, while typically seen as a cultural haven for gay men, has long served as a source of pleasure and power for lesbian spectators, according to Stacy Wolf, because it "features women as neither passive objects of desire nor subjects of vilification."[46] Whereas most musical theater, notes David Savran, is decidedly middle-brow, indulges in blatant consumerism and is both financially and aesthetically unavailable to members of the working class, *Hothead* the musical is unabashedly "no-brow."[47] Animal's riot grrrl adaptation of *Hothead* combined the lesbian revenge fantasy structure of a comedy of terrors and the musical mettle of John Cameron Mitchell's *Hedwig and the Angry Inch* (1998), a rock opera about a botched sex reassignment surgery that was developed at Squeezebox, a (now defunct) punk drag club in New York. Created by and for disenfranchised dykes, Animal's *Hothead* rejects the commercial values of a neoliberal consumer culture. Produced by and for dispossessed queers on a shoestring budget with only four days of rehearsal, the musical was not intended as a slick production or designed to reap exorbitant profits. The premier was a rough-and-tumble debut plagued by missed cues, technical glitches, and a shoddy sound system, none of which bothered a Michfest audience accustomed to do-it-yourself (DIY) production values.

The Michigan Womyn's Music Festival serves as a textbook example of the industrious spirit of cultural feminism and the DIY ethic that has always been an integral part of its activist aesthetic. For four decades feminist folk singers, spoken-word artists, dancers, drummers, and punk dykes have played "The Land," a 650-acre compound in Hart, Michigan, that is transformed each August into a gyno-utopia built, staffed, and run collectively by more than five thousand women.[48] When Animal pitched the musical to Michfest producer Lisa Vogel in the fall of 2003, the project was in its infancy. She had a basic concept, a few songs, and an eager cast of friends. Although Vogel had included plays in previous festivals, including the Five Lesbian Brothers' *Brides of the Moon,* she had never commissioned a musical. The time seemed right for Animal's adaptation. "I think 2004 needs Hothead," Vogel told the *Advocate.* "Hothead's fearless commentary and relentless 'fehmuhnist' underpinning are smart, feminist, and fun. Michigan will love it."[49]

Vogel gave this interview in July, four weeks prior to the premier and just a few months after the War on Terror took a grotesque turn with the revelation of torture at the Abu Ghraib prison. Disturbing images of American soldiers abusing the bodies and defiling the corpses of Iraqi nationals were revealed to the American public by the television program *60 Minutes* on April 28, 2004, and by the *New Yorker* on April 30. Coverage of Abu Ghraib dominated the news throughout the summer, and it included chilling details about the role women and lesbians played in the maltreatment of detainees. The picture of reservist Megan Ambuhl watching Private Lynndie England drag a nearly nude man from his cell on a dog leash challenges conventional wisdom about women, violence, and victimization, as do the photographs of England forcing nude male detainees into suggestive sexual positions. Many of these scenarios involve the simulation of homosexual acts, which American soldiers believed would shame detainees into cooperating with the United States. Specialist Sabrina Harman took most of the pictures. Like England, she posed triumphantly with the bruised and lifeless bodies, flashing a smile and giving a thumbs-up. The hundreds of photographs Harman took of the rape, torture, and murder of prisoners provided damning evidence in the prosecution and conviction of eleven American soldiers, as did letters she wrote describing in detail the abuse—letters addressed to the woman she calls her wife.[50]

Although the events of Abu Ghraib coincided with the development and production of Animal's adaptation of *Hothead Paisan,* neither they nor the War on Terror feature in the Michfest premier. When I look at these photo-

graphs, I can't help but think of Hothead Paisan in her "Misogynists' Hall
of Fame." The context is different, absolutely, as are the motivations and
intended audience, but many of the violent tableaux staged in Abu Ghraib
are eerily similar to the fictional scenes of torture animating the Roberta
episode. While Animal, who is one of third-wave feminism's most outspo-
ken and controversial artists, is under no obligation to respond to the racist,
homophobic, and inhumane treatment of enemy combatants in a musical
theater piece, the notion that this riot grrrl would completely ignore these
events in a show about a homicidal lesbian terrorist is nothing if not curious. Even more vexing is the fact that Animal envisioned this project as the
spark that would reenergize the feminist movement. In a fund-raising DVD
about the making of the musical, Animal states that her goal was "to ignite
something that is dead in this comatose land" and to "get women out of the
coma, back to shouting."[51]

In her call to unleash the Furies and rile the Maenads of Michfest into
an ecastic man-killing frenzy, Animal displays her homicidal lesbian terrorist leanings. While this riot grrrl is motivated by the same admirable, yet
naïve and self-aggrandizing goal—the eradication of the patriarchy—as the
fictional Hothead Paisan, her rant lacks the crucial element of self-parody
integral to DiMassa's zine. As such, the artist risks collusion with the staid,
self-serving agendas of homoliberalism and American exceptionalism. The
greatest political gesture, notes Judith Butler, "is not a grandiose act, it's
not a narcissistic act," in which one is "responsible for the entirety of the
world," for one "cannot take responsibility alone. It is something taken with
others." In order to forge modes of participation, communication, and deliberation that allow for a culturally diverse, democratic culture to exist in
all its contradictions and complexities, Butler asserts, we must "work to
foster understanding, without mandating unity," and in order to do this, we
must position ourselves "in a vividly decentered way in a world with others,
who are their own centers."[52] In other words, we should not assume, as that
well-meaning rogue Hothead Paisan mistakenly does, that our struggles are
the same struggles, that our pain is the same pain, or that our hopes for the
future are for the same hopes, or even for the same futures.

The zine mocks the ways in which Hothead is so self-righteous, so sure
of herself and the validity of her mission, that she ignores Chicken and
Roz when they implore her to consider the collateral damage wrought by
her investments in a program of male genocide. Hothead fails to ask questions of the future or to pose the future as a question, with all of the care
and humility that such a question entails. Animal, like the comic crusader

she brings to life, appears to be acting on behalf of the women in the world without consulting those women about whether they agree with or support her activities. In her desire to foment a revolution and get the women back to shouting (at what she does not specify), she advances an overly simplified political program for revivifying lesbian feminism that she assumes others embrace. As such, the musical serves as a cautionary tale about the trappings of solidarity and how activism can morph from a desire for a particular outcome into a disposition and a predetermined future. This slide into certitude restages the follies of second-wave feminism, and it risks complicity with neoliberal assumptions about power, namely that one can will into being a particular outcome or effect. In purporting to speak on behalf of the entire Lesbian Nation, but not to the theater of war playing out just beyond its borders, the musical dramatizes how exceptionalist discourses of queer sexuality can conspire with political fervor and zealotry in the service of empire.

Animal chose Michigan for the premier because the festival serves, in her words, as a "cocoon in which women can be truthful about their rage."[53] Since the 1970s, Michfest has provided an occasion and outlet for women's anger. Like the labrys-sporting, Solanas-citing, separatist-leaning Hothead Paisan, Michfest keeps alive many of the archaic myths and symbols around which lesbian feminist subcultures have constructed sexual identities, political affiliations, and counterpublics. Its geographic isolation and insular environment provide a safe haven in which women can express themselves. Designed to shelter females from the violence of the outside world, Michfest takes place in a remote and idyllic landscape far removed from both Hothead's gruesome theater of war and the grim realities of Abu Ghraib.

Whereas DiMassa's zine acknowledges and explores the ways in which feminist fury participates in an affective economy of terror, Animal's adaptation disavows it. Encouraging audiences to root for a fictional lesbian terrorist without acknowledging the fact that real dykes are torturing real Iraqi men in the name of freedom makes *Hothead* the musical party to troubling forms of homonationalism. The Michfest production exemplifies how terror can arise from the very institutions and practices designed to insulate individuals from it. The festival's admission policy prohibits anyone who is not a "womyn-born womyn" from entering, which contributes, however unintentionally, to the terrorizing of transgender subjects. Michfest's policy underscores the ways in which violence, and in particular liberal violence, is perpetuated by those who deny culpability because they see themselves as innocent victims outside the circuits of institutionalized power. In recent years the women-born women rule has been the subject of much controversy, and a protest site, Camp Trans, has been created nearby. Animal, who describes herself as a "cosmic tranny," a transidentified person who eschews surgery and hormones, not only supports the women-only rule, but she applauds Michfest as the only festival in the world "that's filled with cunts. You have to have a cunt to be there, it's cunt energy. Yes, that is real. That is beautiful. That needs to be honored. We need that in the world."[54] DiMassa, too, defends Michfest's homogendered, separatist policy. To view Michigan as antitrans is to miss the point, she writes. It "is a gathering for 'women who have grown up female in our patriarchal society.' . . . It is for women who have been at the ass-end of life here on The Planet of the Apes their whole life. This usually does not apply to MTF's."[55]

While DiMassa publicly supports Michigan's women-born women policy, her zine advocates a more inclusive model of collectivity. One of the central characters in the comic is Daphne, Hothead's ambiguously gendered love interest. Despite repeated and persistent requests from fans, DiMassa refused to disclose the sexual identity of Daphne. As a lesbian terrorist, Hothead harbors many undertheorized, essentialist, and deeply problematic ideas about gender and sexuality, but even she recognizes the tyranny of gender binaries. Despite her mission to rid the world of men, Hothead's vision of utopia is surprisingly inconsistent with a separatist ideology. In an issue of the zine entitled "The World of Her Dreams," DiMassa depicts a planet populated by hermaphrodites and intersex folks, by "people with willies and breasts oh my!" This model of citizenship, Hothead notes, represent an "infinitely more excellent form than a mere gender takeover."[56]

The women-born women rule made Michfest an imprudent location for *Hothead* the musical, as it meant that no males could take part in the production. Without men to stalk, torture, and annihilate, Hothead is cut off from her primary identification as a homicidal lesbian terrorist. As much as she hates men, without them she is nothing. Animal could have circumvented this limitation by casting women in male roles (risking the cliché that lesbians are a bad copy of men) or she could have used dolls, puppets, and effigies in place of male bodies. The latter would have enabled her to perform much more graphic displays of violence than if she had used human actors. Rather than portraying or heightening the sense of horror and hilarity in DiMassa's comedy of terrors, Animal opted to downplay the violence altogether, focusing instead on Hothead's sexual escapades, Roz's crone consciousness, and the cute and cuddly antics of Chicken the Cat. In an interview promoting the Michfest production, Powter notes:

The musical is astoundingly made for the stage. It is romantic, and beautiful, and wild, and crazy, and touching, and truthful. It fucking works. The "Chicken" song that Animal wrote, sung with Ani . . . there isn't a lesbian on earth that isn't going to love that song, because it's a love song to their cats! When Animal does Hothead, the audience is going to come out and want more information about the truth of patriarchy.[57]

Disconnected from the forces that inspire lesbian revenge fantasies, namely, men and the media, *Hothead* the musical is domesticated and defanged. In the zine Hothead's relationship with Chicken humanizes this terrorist and complicates our understanding of her bloody killing sprees, but in the musical, the prominence given to the love songs between them, in some ways an inevitable result of casting Ani DiFranco, the undeniable star of the show, as the frisky feline, overshadows DiMassa's principled exploration of violence, torture, and social justice. While the zine makes sexuality central to an antiracist and anti-imperialist project, the musical, or at least the first act of it, does not; it opts instead for a more parochial approach to dyke life. Like George Coates's production of Solanas's *Up Your Ass,* Animal used music to defuse her source text's revolutionary message rather than capitalizing on it. Instead of recruiting DiMassa's zine to intervene in the War on Terror, the production succumbs to the climate of disavowal and denial sweeping the country, conscripting Hothead to the cause of homonationalism.

Some colleagues have asked me why I bother writing about a production that I found disappointing when there are so many more provocative and compelling acts of gaiety that I could have included in this book. Why expend emotional and theoretical labor criticizing a production that was poorly conceived and poorly executed by an artist whose work I admire? The answer is that we must compose our histories of LGBT art and activism not simply to archive the exploits of heroes and saints, icons and idols, but also to record acts of insult and injury, carelessness, complicity and cowardice, exclusion and injustice, acts that are embarrassing and shameful, apolitical and racist, and that collude with state power, war machines, and the devastating effects of globalization.

As Puar notes in *Terrorist Assemblages,* it is quite easy to point our fingers at conservative queers and blame them for the sad state of LGBT politics, but it is more difficult, not to mention more painful, to acknowledge that everyone, even the most radical among us, are accomplices in violent and oppressive forms of homonationalism. While the trope of the homicidal lesbian terrorist offers a provocative and compelling model for thinking about the convivial relations between terror and queerness, it is not enough to simply reenlist *Hothead Paisan* in the service of feminist or gay political projects. In transforming DiMassa's revenge fantasy into a sentimental comedy, Animal commits character assassination. Her maladapted *Hothead Paisan* calls into question the mantra that theater constitutes "the queerest art" and musical theater the queerest of the queer.[58] This riot grrrl production repackages lesbian terrorism into a subcultural style, and it underscores how easy it is for radical politics to devolve into a sartorial pursuit. *Hothead* the musical shows that conservative queers are not the only proponents of homonationalism; artists and activists in the cultural vanguard are equally responsible for the remapping of terrorist identities and the evacuation of history that this entails.

In completing only the first act of the musical and staging this work-in-progress at Michfest, Animal was destined to fail, and fail spectacularly she did. "Failing," as Judith Halberstam argues in her recent book, "is something queers do and have always done exceptionally well."[59] As I have shown in every chapter of *Acts of Gaiety*, failure is for lesbians not simply an expectation but an aesthetic and a way of life. Animal's failure could have been a source of embarrassment and humiliation, and perhaps it was as she politely declined my repeated requests for an interview, but it also leads to a kind of euphoric exposure of the contradictions of the Lesbian Nation and American imperialism. By implication, it also reveals the precarity of queer aspirations for citizenship and national belonging.

There are advantages to failing, observes Halberstam, and this is true for both artists and audiences. Relieved of the pressures, limitations, and lesbophobia of commercial theater, playmakers are free to create raw, renegade, hilarious, and poignant productions that they would never be possible in the terms established by mainstream theater and that are so much more liberating than those afforded by the trite scenarios of success to which it is conscripted. By conventional standards, most dyke dramas are doomed to fail, and happily so. The failure of queer theater to reproduce normative production values, plot structures, and moral standards is perhaps the clearest indication of its continued vitality. Spectators (and critics too) can use the experience of failure to escape the exacting norms that discipline desires and micromanage affective responses in the service of producing proper homonormative subjects. In addition, scenes of failure enable us to confront the consolidation of inequalities and the reinscription of social stratifications that reify rather than challenge the forces of homoliberalism.

5

Unnatural Acts

The Tragic Consequences of Homoliberalism in the Five Lesbian Brothers' Oedipus at Palm Springs

One of the fiercest and funniest comedies of terrors, *The Secretaries*, was penned by the Five Lesbian Brothers, an irreverent troupe of sapphic satirists who have made audiences squeal and squirm with polymorphously perverse, politically incorrect, ribald sex comedies since 1989. Delighting spectators with their gallantry and gallows humor, this theatrical troupe—which consists of Maureen Angelos, Babs Davy, Dominique Dibbell, Peg Healey, and Lisa Kron—wields a rapier wit and a mordant sensibility. These thespians stage outlandish, shamelessly licentious performances rooted in the parodic inversion of genres, cultural norms, and audience expectations. The collective honed its talent and temerity at the WOW Café in New York City's East Village, a site that has served as an incubator for the production of progressive lesbian communities and radical artistic experimentation for over thirty years. The Brothers' choice of a fraternal moniker signals their interest in fugitive forms of sociality that run roughshod over essentialist categories. Like their WOW compatriots Split Britches, Holly Hughes, and Carmelita Tropicana, the Brothers offers living proof that dykes do, in fact, have a funny bone and feminist theater is much more than art for the "terminally earnest."[1]

The troupe's raison d'être "is to explore such dark themes as homophobia and sexism with devastating humor and the occasional musical number."[2] Their plays delve deep into prurient interests, pathologized identities, and stigmatized forms of erotic desire. As Brother Dibbell explains:

> Lesbian feminism of the 1970s and the 1980s had placed a heavy emphasis
> on "positive images of lesbians." But by the late eighties the emphasis had

become a mandate. No good art can come of a mandate, so we incorrigibly did the opposite of what we were told: we instinctively returned to the image of the lesbian as pervert.[3]

Like Valerie Solanas's Bongi Perez, the Brothers' dramatis personae revel in debauchery, degeneracy, and criminal intimacies, and they extol the virtue of seeking pleasure for pleasure's sake, with little regard for conventional morality, familial piety, or juridical authority. By creating worlds where fantasies and fetishes, no matter how bizarre, are given free rein, the troupe grants audiences license to indulge in the offensive, indecent, and unmentionable aspects of lesbian sexuality. Their performances—episodically structured, preposterously plotted farces with no concern for logic, laws of probability, or coherent characterization—feature profligate protagonists in ludicrous situations involving complex erotic entanglements, murder, mayhem, cross-dressing, and flagrant nudity.

Known for their uproarious and seditious comedies, the Five Lesbian Brothers shocked fans and critics alike when they returned from a seven-year hiatus in 2005 with a finely tuned tragedy, and not just any tragedy—the *mother* of all tragedies, Sophocles' *Oedipus Rex*. The adaptation stunned *Variety*'s Mark Blankenship, who could not believe that the group that had set "the gold standard for campy queer satire" had produced "what is almost a conventional play." He hailed the premier of *Oedipus at Palm Springs* as a "breathtaking" drama situated at "that intersection of mythic symbolism and realistic detail that . . . stabs at the heart."[4] The *New York Times*' Charles Isherwood echoed Blankenship's incredulity ("surprising/ly" appears three times in his review). The Brothers' "serious inquiry into the unforeseen extremities of despair," he marveled, "is a far cry from the loopy exercises in scalpel-sharp satire they once favored." Isherwood applauded the troupe's decision to "forgo another romp in the familiar pastures of zany comedy to aim at something more complex," something "brave, funny and quite lovable."[5]

Not everyone greeted the highly anticipated return of this beloved collective with such accolades, however. The play struck a sour chord with audiences who viewed the Brothers' *Oedipus* as a tragic fall, a calculated sacrifice of their aesthetic and political ideals in an effort to attract mainstream audiences and garner greater commercial success. Jill Dolan, one of the Brothers' most ardent supporters, found the production "heavy-handed and full of perplexing bathos."[6] The troupe's "desire to gain widespread recognition forced" it, in Dolan's estimation, to make a number of disagreeable compromises and unsavory concessions, including pandering to stereotypical depictions of tortured homosexuals, capitulating to sexual taboos, and indulging in the theatrical conceit most deadly to lesbians, dramatic realism. Another avid enthusiast, Hilton Als, dubbed *Oedipus at Palm Springs* "disappointing" for similar reasons.[7] In the *New Yorker,* he wrote, "It's as if the Brothers, in their bid to be taken seriously by the mainstream, had forgotten that life's lessons can be addressed comedically, too—which doesn't necessarily mean lightly."[8] Whereas Blankensmith and Isherwood lauded the troupe's tragic turn as a sign of maturation and progress, Dolan and Als saw it as selling out. "With 'Oedipus at Palm Springs,' the latter lamented, the Brothers have gone straight."[9]

While the group's adaptation of Sophocles' tragedy features out lesbian actors playing out lesbian characters, it is indeed a "straight" play—if by this term we mean a well-made, realist, nonmusical production intended for a broad audience.[10] Although this drama is technically speaking a "straight" play, it is neither as narrow nor as normative as Dolan and Als would have us believe. The Brothers may have been angling for a hit with *Oedipus at Palm Springs,* but to suggest that this production succumbs to market pressures, accedes to discriminatory social and artistic conventions, or perpetuates homophobic caricatures solely, or even primarily, for financial gain constitutes an act of *hamartia,* a missing of the mark. The players haven't "gone straight," I argue here, but they are "playing it straight" in order to turn their critical eye not on the oppressive forces of heteronormativity, as their earlier work does, but on the more urgent problem of homonormativity.

In this drama, the troupe sets its sights on contemporary LGBT culture, delivering a caustic critique of the mainstreaming of the movement, one that makes visible the emotional and political blind spots produced by a privatized, depoliticized, and narrowly defined notion of gay life. *Oedipus at Palm Springs* serves as a parable of the tragic consequences of homoliberalism. The plot of this broodingly luminous play hinges on what Freud called a cynical tendentious joke. If this dark comedy fails to deliver the chortles and sidesplitting cackles audiences have come to expect from Brothers' productions, this is because it traffics in what Samuel Beckett termed mirthless laughter—laughter that laughs at that which is unhappy. There is nothing unhappier, and thus riper for absurdist parody, *Oedipus* suggests, than lesbians who have solemnly sworn to uphold the strictures of heteroized society.

The Brothers' Pre-oedipal Phase

Given the date of the Brothers' emergence on the American theater scene, it is tempting to group them under the umbrella of queer performance, as many critics have done. While this troupe's rise to prominence may have coincided with the queer turn, and while it may have benefited from this cultural shift, these players have insisted on "dragging" their lesbian feminist sensibility along with them. Their artistry, collaborative method of play creation, and participatory forms of spectatorial engagement reflect their indebtedness to the tradition of "women's theater" of the 1970s and 1980s and to the gender-bending playmakers of troupes such as the Ridiculous Theatrical Company and Hot Peaches, which mixed high art with pop culture, worked in a camp aesthetic, and explored homoerotic themes and characters.

The influence of both early feminist and gay performance practices is evident in the Five Lesbian Brothers' inaugural production, *Voyage to Lesbos* (1989). This show features four midwestern gals who try in vain to "cure" their friend with benefits, Bonnie (Healey), of her homosexual tendencies before she takes her wedding vows. It is set in the fictional town of Lesbos, Illinois, in the early 1960s, in what Brother Kron calls "that vaguely defined pre-Stonewall, post-Freudian period of American culture."[11] Inspired by pop psychology and distorted media representations of lesbian desire, the play explores, in the words of Brother Dibbell, "the warping effects of internalized homophobia."[12] In *Voyage to Lesbos,* the characters labor, unsuccessfully, to convince themselves, and each other, that marriage is every girl's dream. As one of the women, Mimi (Kron), sings, "Today is Bonnie's wedding day. But no one looks happy to me. Today is Bonnie's wedding day, but it looks more like a funeral to me."[13]

Mimi's words prove prophetic when the maid of honor, Evelyn (Davy), who is infatuated with Bonnie, murders the groom, Bradley, just before he is to walk down the aisle. In a parodic inversion of ritual protocol, it is the groom, described at various moments in the play as "a good guy. Steady . . . sweet . . . [with] a huge peter," "a man who will suffice," "a bastard," and "a rapist," who becomes the sacrificial victim in an exchange between women.[14] In the Western dramatic tradition, weddings typically serve as the resolution to comedies. Marriage marks both an end—a conclusion to the narrated chaos through the restoration of order—and a beginning—the start of a new life and the promise of future generations that will be begat on and after the honeymoon. *Voyage to Lesbos* exposes marriage as a theatrical and sociocultural plot designed to domesticate desire, regulate intimacy, and enforce normative social relations. The play asks us, in the words of Peggy Phelan, "[H]ow can we change the world without first changing the (marriage) plot? If 'all the world's a stage,' how can we restage the world to include the dramas of lesbian lives"?[15]

Similar themes run through *The Secretaries* (1993–94).[16] Heterosexuality is depicted as a fatal attraction and marriage as a death sentence in the troupe's retelling of Euripides' *Bacchae*. Set in a clerical pool of a lumber company in the 1980s, this maenadic masterpiece chronicles the transformation of a mild-mannered clerk, Patty (Dibbell), into a chainsaw-wielding serial killer. Patty's coworkers (Kron, Angelos, and Davy), Slimfast-swilling sadists, coerce her into joining their secret cabal, a group whose sole purpose is to ritually slaughter a male coworker at the mill once a month. The sacrificial victim is a lumberjack who has made the mistake of falling in love with one of the secretaries. The pitiful fool is given the ax (literally) on the day when the secretaries get their periods, which the department manager, Susan (Healey), has manipulated to be in synch, to maximize the killing rage of her administrative minions.

This play offers an interesting spin on the lesbian comedy of terrors by exploring the ways in which females are conditioned by society to be the enforcers of sexism. Men may run the company and make the rules, but it is Susan who subjects her employees to dehumanizing office policies that govern their sexuality, physical appearance, and food intake. This work investigates the forces that motivate women to participate in their own subordination. While *The Secretaries* acknowledges patriarchal oppression, it is more interested in internalized misogyny, in the ways women abuse other women. "We are equitable in our parody," notes Brother Kron, "skewering homosexuals and feminism with the same vigor we apply to mainstream culture."[17] "The genius of their work," according to Alisa Solomon, "is that the Brothers don't use comedy to make a feminist, anti-homophobic point go down easy. The comedy *is* the point—and so is the anxiety and terror."[18] No one is safe from the troupe's stinging satires, least of all members of the lesbian establishment.

Like *The Secretaries, Brave Smiles . . . Another Lesbian Tragedy* (1992–93) investigates the fraught world of female relationships in a homosocial milieu, in this case a girl's boarding school. A parodic pastiche, this play mines the storehouse of sapphic stereotypes from the theater (e.g., *The Chil-*

dren's Hour), movies (e.g., *Mädchen in Uniform*), and literature (e.g., *The Well of Loneliness*), exploiting tired tropes deployed in mainstream representations of dyke life, including closeted schoolmarms, menacing butches, and mythic, mannish lesbians, to name only a few. The action spans several decades and multiple continents. Act I begins in the 1920s at the Tilue-Pussenheimer German academy for orphan girls where Miss Philips, the pupils' favorite teacher, hangs herself. This tragedy precipitates the closure of the school and the scattering of the wayward girls.

Act II takes place in a French cabaret just after World War II. Two of the orphans, reunited after many years apart, confess their love for one another. Immediately after their confession, one of them is struck by a truck and killed. The survivor becomes an alcoholic and moves to New York's Bowery district where she encounters another classmate from the academy. In the midst of their reunion, the two women are accosted by an aggressive panhandler, and in self-defense they stab him to death. The alcoholic hits the bottle even harder after her friend is sentenced to the electric chair for murder. She finally sobers up when she meets her last remaining schoolmate, with whom she falls madly in love. On the verge of living happily ever after, she is diagnosed with a brain tumor and dies. Such misfortune is the price one pays, society tells us, for succumbing to the love that dare not speak its name. "If," explains Brother Healey, "the story of the lesbian is that she was always doomed to suffer an unhappy life and then die a tragic death, then we really wanted to pile it on" in *Brave Smiles*.[19] The cumulative effect of so much carnage, and in such absurd situations, is that it inspires audiences "to crave some other outcome, not only in the play, but in life, too."[20] *Brave Smiles* represents, in the words of the collective "what we love about being Brothers and what we love about being lesbians: the tragedy of it all which can be so bitingly and relentlessly funny sometimes."[21]

The troupe's fourth full-length play, *Brides of the Moon* (1996–97), disrupts the assumption that the heterosexual marriage plot is a prerequisite for theatrical comedy by staging sex far outside the boundaries of conventional arrangements, proper positions, and prescribed locales. The drama's sexual scenarios are completely adrift from normative kinship arrangements and the imperative to reproduce. A futuristic, intergalactic, interspecies farce, *Brides of the Moon* depicts a group of female astronauts handpicked by the government for a covert operation. The team's leader is Mrs. Steve Powers (Healey), a sixty-something housewife savant who, in the 1950s, was forced by misogynistic social structures to conceal her scientific genius. Progress has enabled Mrs. Powers to come out of the closet with her intelligence, and she is chosen to lead a quirky quartet to boldly go where no woman has gone before, or at least that is what she's made to believe by the space agency. Mrs. Powers and her crew are dismayed to learn, sometime after blastoff, that their top-secret task is to provide conjugal recreation for male comrades stationed on the moon and to populate the new colony with earthlings. Angry about being duped, the women abort the mission. They rebel by having sex with each other, and they indulge in all sorts of queer couplings, including bonking the space chimp riding with them in the rocket.

Brides of the Moon, like *Brave Smiles* and *The Secretaries* before it, debuted at WOW Café then moved to the New York Theater Workshop (NYTW), an off-Broadway establishment that has nurtured many lesbian and gay artists, including Tony Kushner, Jonathan Larson, and Doug Wright. While the majority of WOW artists have positioned themselves, consciously and strategically, in opposition to mainstream theater—avoiding anything (including certain grants) that might impinge on their creative freedom and political ideals—the Brothers have actively courted not only a broader audience base but the kinds of financial and emotional rewards crossover success can bring.[22] The troupe's tagline reads "commercially viable yet enchantingly homosexual."[23] Although WOW and NYTW are located on the same street in the Village, the two theaters are worlds apart. When the Brothers perform at WOW, it is like preaching to the converted (not to mention the perverted, as Holly Hughes reminds us).[24] The crowds consist primarily (though not exclusively) of lesbians and feminists, many of whom are fellow artists and friends; audiences, in other words, who speak the Brothers' native tongue and get the inside joke. The spectacular acts of gaiety performed by lesbians for lesbians about lesbians at WOW serve as what Diana Taylor calls "vital acts of transfer," carnal conduits for the embodied transmission of knowledge, memory, and a shared sense of identity.[25] Staging work at NYTW exposes the group to a broader, more diverse audience, one comprised of a loyal subscription base of fairly conventional white, middle-class New Yorkers and an erudite coterie of avant-garde aficionados whose political opinions and aesthetic sensibilities are more progressive than they are radical. Productions at NYTW are infinitely more likely to be reviewed by critics, be nominated for awards, and make the transition to Broadway. As is the case in any journey involving foreign travel, crossing the border, even when that boundary is just a few blocks away, involves a certain degree of translation.

Brave Smiles and *The Secretaries* moved from WOW to NYTW with only minimal changes to the script and the troupe's poor aesthetic, but the theater went to great lengths to explain to its audience that the plays were satires and intended to be funny. The artistic and administrative staff of NYTW went so far as to state this explicitly in advertising material and the program notes. The pedagogical component of the playbill seemed designed to foil reactions that might upset heterosexual patrons or provoke unsuspecting and unprepared clientele to storm down the aisles, demand their money back, or worse, cancel their subscriptions. As Jill Dolan has observed, packaging the Brothers in this way is a "form of discrimination—why the need to teach people about parody when it was being wielded, finally, by lesbians?"[26] Kate Davy feels these caveats were, in some way, necessary because "lesbian desire played out excessively as an oppositional strategy [is] lost outside the context of WOW."[27]

The Secretaries' successful run at NYTW coupled with a glowing *New York Times* review by Ben Brantley led to a special citation Obie Award. Hoping for an even bigger critical and commercial hit with *Brides of the Moon,* the Brothers consented to having the production "facelifted" (their term) prior to the transfer to NYTW.[28] Like Mickey Rourke and Jessica Lange, *Brides of the Moon* underwent a few too many nips and tucks and was essentially unrecognizable after the procedure. Alterations included upgrading the sets, softening the satire, and replacing director Kate Stafford with Molly D. Smith, the founder of Perseverance Theatre in Alaska, who had helped launch Paula Vogel's career.[29] In his *New York Times* review of the enhanced production at NYTW, Peter Marks described *Brides of the Moon* as a

> two-hour-plus production, directed laboriously . . . [and] loaded down with the type of jokey ballast that spoofmeisters as shameless as Mel Brooks would have jettisoned. The painfully, at times irritatingly unfunny comedy is of the sort that depends on tired double-entendres: there are multiple jokes, for instance, at the expense of the planet Uranus.[30]

The facelift was, for all intents and purposes, a disaster. Discouraged by their negative reviews and disillusioned by their failure to break through the glass proscenium, yet again, the troupe decided to call it quits, at least for a while. Like many talented lesbian playwrights, they are angry, bitter, and more than a little resentful about their lack of success, especially compared to that of gay male artists working in a similar aesthetic who have achieved far greater recognition by both the mainstream and queer establishments.

During their seven-year hiatus, some members of the collective worked on solo performances and collaborative theater projects with other artists while others tried their hand at film and television.[31] Lisa Kron reached new heights with two works she created: an exquisite monologue titled *2.5 Minute Ride* and a remarkable full-length play, *Well*. The former juxtaposes a trip the artist took to Auschwitz with her father, a Holocaust survivor, and her family's annual vacation at an amusement park in Sandusky, Ohio. *2.5 Minute Ride* takes spectators on an emotional roller coaster that careens so rapidly between horror and humor that the two become almost indistinguishable. Kron premiered this piece at the Public Theater, where it received much critical acclaim, and a special citation Obie Award, and then embarked on a regional theater tour. *Well* continues the author's autobiographical odyssey, this time mining the maternal for content. This play, which Kron dubs a "solo performance with other people in it," explores chronic pain (stemming from physical illness but also social diseases such as racism, misogyny, and homophobia) in an effort to understand why some bodies, histories, and injuries heal while others do not.[32]

When The Brothers reunited for a fifth full-length collaboration, the players did not yet know that Kron's *Well* would make the transition from the Public Theater in 2004 to Broadway (two years later).[33] At the time, they were still searching for a winning formula, so they looked to gay male writers they admired for inspiration on how to best craft their play, which would debut at NYTW rather than WOW Café. The promotional materials for their production begin with the line "Love! Valour! Lesbians!"—an obvious reference to Terrence McNally's *Love! Valor! Compassion!* (1994), a play that made the leap from off-Broadway to Broadway, won Tony Awards for best play and best featured actor, and was made into a Hollywood film.[34]

The Brothers' Oedipal Phase

Oedipus at Palm Springs is precisely the kind of moralizing tragedy that the Brothers typically satirize, and this is initially what the troupe set out to do to Sophocles' torturous tale of woe. This was in the early to mid-1990s, at what would turn out to be the apex of the queer theater movement (Kushner won the Pulitzer for *Angels in America* in 1993) and the zenith of a revitalized struggle for sexual liberation, both of which were integrally related to the AIDS epidemic. The original title for the play was *Oedipussy,* and it was set in a Greek diner called the House of Pan Kakés. This idea for a farce never fully jelled, so the script was shelved. When the Brothers decided to resurrect it a decade later, the artist and political landscape looked vastly different. Responding to changes in the zeitgeist and seeking to avoid another *Brides of the Moon,* the group gave *Oedipussy* a complete overhaul. They enlisted Leigh Silverman, the rising star who directed *Well,* and set off for Palm Springs to make some magic.[35] When their retreat was over, they emerged with what was essentially a brand new play. The result was a comedy of anguish so dark that it would leave audiences not only shaken but stirred.

Geography played an important role in the revised script. Palm Springs, aka the L-Spot, is a vacation mecca for lesbians, especially well-to-do white ones. For five days in April, during Dinah Shore Week (so named for the Ladies Professional Golf Association tournament she helped establish), this resort community is home to one of the largest women's circuit parties in the country, if not the world. Soon after arriving in Palm Springs, the Brothers decided that an exclusive lesbian oasis seemed a much more appropriate locale than a greasy spoon for their adaptation. As Brother Healy explains, "*Oedipus* deals with royalty, so we chose lesbians who make money" and "move in the mainstream."[36] The idea of this was intriguing to the collective, adds Brother Dibbell, because "bourgeois lesbians" were "almost like a foreign species to us."[37] They approached the topic from an ethnographic standpoint: "I don't understand you, and I want to. You're in my tribe but you're so different from me."[38] The protagonists of *Oedipus at Palm Springs* are members of the lesbian elite, and these chic sophisticates, with their Saabs, six-figure salaries, and private world of monied exclusion, bear little resemblance to the orphans, alcoholics, and disaffected housewives who populate the Brothers' pre-hiatus farces.

Oedipus at Palm Springs takes place at a posh women-only resort in Southern California. The play opens with a hotel manager, Joni (Davy), pushing a cleaning cart. When this middle-aged female with close-cropped gray hair steps from behind a stack of towels, she is completely naked, except for sunglasses, a cell phone strapped around her waist, and a single braid that extends to her butt and is tied with feathers. She jingles a large set of keys as she moves from bungalow to bungalow dropping off welcome baskets. A buzzer rings, interrupting her work flow. "Mother! Fuck!" she exclaims, as she crosses the stage to an intercom. For the first time, we see that the manager is blind.[39]

The buzzer announces the arrival of the first couple—Con (Kron) and

Fran (Angelos)—who come, the stage directions tell us, "with tons of baggage."[40] They are struggling to rekindle their romance, which has suffered since their birth of their son, Basil, almost four years ago. The problem is biomom Fran, who does not feel amorous because she is *still* nursing. "It's like my breasts aren't for sex," she explains, "They're for food."[41] Con, on the other hand, is horny as a satyr, and she refuses to let lesbian bed death be the death of her any longer. She issues Fran an ultimatum: sex by sundown on Sunday, or else. The majority of the play's comedic moments stem from Con's frustration and attempts at release, including a memorable scene involving hot tub jets. Commitment, not passion, is the problem for the second couple, ardent intergenerational lovers who have very different views on cohabitation. The elder partner Prin (Dibbell), an old-school butch with a long history of jumping ship when relationships get too intimate, has grown soft with her new lover Terri (Healey), a sensitive and needy graduate student who is mourning the death of her adoptive mother. Prin has planned the desert outing to celebrate Terri's birthday, and the surprise part of this party is that she plans to pop the question. Although the two couples are old friends, they rarely see each other. Fran's too embarrassed to tell her dear buddy Prin that she's celibate, and Prin hasn't spoken to Fran about her plans to tie the knot. The mystical Joni foresees the inevitable tragedy that befalls the four upper-middle-class white women when she performs a key reading for Terri, who wants to know if she will ever find her birth mother.

The events are set into motion when Con and Fran present Terri with her birthday gift during dinner at the Shame on the Moon restaurant. It is a report from a private investigator disclosing the identity of Terri's birth mother, Laura Campbell, who turns out to be none other than her lover Prin (aka, Princess, her childhood nickname). The pregnancy was the result of a one-night stand, the butch's first and only sexual experience with a man (she was in love with the guy's girlfriend, of course). Prin, who opens the envelope for the nervous Terri, initially tries to keep this horrifying revelation to herself by pushing her paramour away and into the arms of another woman at the dance club they attend after the meal. Terri takes the bait, or so she makes everyone believe, which results in a nasty altercation back at the resort ending with an intoxicated and distraught Prin punching Terri in the mouth instead of popping the question.

Wounded and writhing in pain, Terri runs away, but not before she rouses Con and Fran, whose long-overdue sexual reunion is interrupted by the commotion. The couple mistakenly interprets their old friend's mood swing

The blind resort manager, Joni (Babs Davy), in the Five Lesbian Brothers' *Oedipus at Palm Springs* (New York Theatre Workshop, 2005) performs a key reading for Terri (Peg Healey) as Prin (Dominique Dibbell), Fran (Maureen Angelos), and Con (Lisa Kron) watch with a mixture of skepticism and amazement. (Photograph by Joan Marcus.)

as a case of cold feet, and they try to salvage the relationship by telling Terri about the planned proposal. While the others are gone, Prin attempts to drown her sorrows, first with alcohol and then by throwing herself into the swimming pool. The pool, which has served during the entire play as a metaphor for the maternal womb, provides neither harbor nor haven for this wretch. Rescued by Joni, as she makes her morning cleaning rounds, Prin is denied a watery tomb.

Terri returns later that morning. News of the aborted engagement triggers her abandonment issues, and she begs Prin to take her back. When Prin tells her that they can never see each other again, Terri has a breakdown. "No. No. . . . Nobody wants me. Nobody ever wanted me. Nobody ever will," she cries.[42] The pain of Terri thinking the breakup is her fault because she is unlovable is more than Prin can handle. She confesses to being Laura Campbell and, in high melodramatic fashion, collapses on the ground, prostrating herself at the feet of Terri and pleading for forgiveness. The disclosure causes Terri to recoil in horror. Fran and Con, who have witnessed the entire spectacle, are equally revolted. They rush to Terri's side to take her away. She refuses to leave, however, until Prin tells the story of her birth. "I would've kept you if I could," she assures Terri. "You were better off without me."[43] The disgust and shame Terri feels at this moment is complicated by the tremendous relief she experiences at having found her birth mother and by the comfort she takes in knowing, beyond a shadow of a doubt, that Prin loves her, wants her, and would do anything in her power to keep her. Please stay, Prin entreats Terri, while grabbing her hand. "I can't live without you."[44] This time it is Terri who gives Prin away. "I can't be your baby. Not any more," she tells her mother/lover. Finding solace in the arms of Con and Fran, Terri leaves the stage, deserting Prin at the desert resort.

The sight of Prin reduced to such a state, ostracized and alienated by her friends and family, disturbed many fans, who could not fathom why the Brothers, who had spent the better part of their twenty-year career together lampooning limitations on sexual freedom, would place such stock in the incest taboo and punish this character for transgressing a boundary she did not even know she was breaching. The choice to depict Prin's relationship with Terri as erotically charged, mutually satisfying, and emotionally sustaining only to end it in shame and sorrow simply because Prin turns out to be Terri's biological mother is what prompted some critics to charge the troupe with having "gone straight." "Under the Brother's old logic," notes Jill Dolan, "this would be a minor detail. Here, it's not only a deal breaker, but it's horrible, sinful, enough to leave Prin alone, degraded and exiled from her lesbian community, a state to which the Brothers bring no irony and no comment."[45] I would agree with Dolan if the play ended with this scene, but, crucially, it does not. An analysis of the final episode shows that the troupe does bring irony to the situation and it does so as a way of commenting on the homoliberal dynamics that necessitate Prin's humiliation and banishment.

Since their inception, the Brothers have refused to treat tragic situations tragically, and they do not waver from this position here. Exemplifying Samuel Beckett's dictate that "Nothing is funnier than unhappiness," the collective mines Prin's horror for humor.[46] The degradation and abandonment of the protagonist takes place in the penultimate scene of the play, not the finale. The performance continues, if only briefly. The stage directions read, "The wind starts to blow. Joni enters and closes the doors."[47] She sits beside Prin, motionless and silent. After a moment, Joni turns to face her. "Didn't see it coming, did you," she asks Prin, who shakes her head as the

Prin (Dominique Dibbell) confesses to her lover Terri (Peg Healey) that she is her birth mother, Laura Campbell, in the Five Lesbian Brothers' *Oedipus at Palm Springs*. (Photograph by Joan Marcus.)

lights fade to black.[48] The play ends with a joke, which brings irony to and undermines the situation that precedes it. In fact, the punch line operates on multiple registers of irony. This sarcastic comment is an example of verbal irony, drawing attention to the fact that Prin could not see that Terri was her child but Joni, who is blind, could see this clearly. It also highlights the situational irony: Prin said she would help Terri find her birth mother, and she does, though not in the way she intended.

Joni's joke addresses the spectator as well, highlighting the dramatic irony that undergirds the play. That one of the characters in this oedipal drama will turn out to be Terri's mother is a given, though most (straight) audiences are shocked to learn that it is Prin. "A lot of people don't figure out which character is the mother until very late in the action," notes Brother Kron, "because lesbian sexuality isn't enculturated. It's not read."[49] Heterosexual spectators rule out Prin, Kron reasons, because she is so butch she "gets read as a man," and men cannot be mothers.[50] Last, but certainly not least, the final scene speaks directly to lesbian and gay audiences, who are shocked, not by the revelation that Prin is Terri's mother—for this is obvious enough—but by the consequences of this disclosure, namely, that Prin's friends and family would find her actions not only "unnatural" but so inexcusable that they would make her a pariah and an outcast. The irony of this situation is that sexual transgression dooms Prin to a life of alienation and sorrow but saves her from an even worse fate: marrying Terri and turning into Con and Fran. This paradox gets to the heart of the play's last line, which serves as what Freud calls a cynical tendentious joke.

"Mad Vow Disease"

Struck by the curious presence of jokes in our dreams, Freud deduced that these phenomena are the products of our unconscious, whose involuntary processes work to discharge repressed energies. Jokes express wishes blocked by the psyche's censoring mechanisms, replacing something that scares, saddens, or frustrates us with something that makes us laugh. The pleasure they produce has less to do with the content of the joke, according to Freud, than it does with the economy of psychic expenditure. He distinguished between two types of jokes: the nontendentious and the tendentious. The former consist of relatively innocuous puns and plays on words. The childlike pleasure of these experiences comes from the delight we take in the chance analogies highlighted by their linguistic constructions. In contrast to nontendentious jokes, which have no hidden agenda and are ends in themselves, tendentious jokes satisfy sexual and aggressive impulses, giving playful expression to repressed urges and inhibited emotions in socially acceptable forms. The energy one would normally spend on self-restraint is discharged in laughter, which generates additional pleasure.

Freud identified two types of tendentious jokes: obscene and hostile. The first exposes hidden, secret, and shameful thoughts whereas the second reveals antagonistic or defensive feelings. Sometimes the intended target of a tendentious joke is the person telling the story, in which case these constitute a subgroup of hostile jokes that Freud termed cynical tendentious jokes. A particularly favorable occasion for this type of humor "is presented when the intended rebellious criticism is directed against the subject himself, or, to put it more cautiously, against someone in whom the subject has a share—a collective person, that is (the subject's own nation, for instance)."[51] Freud offers examples of cynical tendentious jokes told by Jews about Jewish characteristics, which serve, among other things, the function of inoculating this persecuted group from the slurs, insults, and stereotypes levied on them by outsiders. Oppressed minorities are well versed in this type of humor, and the Brothers' plays abound with lesbian characters playfully mocking lesbian culture.

Cynical tendentious jokes assail, through their victims, the modes of affiliation and rituals of induction that bind individuals to society. As such, they are frequently directed against institutions of morality and respectability. Among the institutions these jokes are in the habit of attacking, none is more foundational to society—and hence more rigorously subjected to moral regulations—than marriage. While matrimony authorizes carnal pleasures, it also installs many obstacles to sexual fulfillment, not the least of which is the competing presence of children. Marriage is not, as Freud noted, an arrangement calculated to gratify partners sexually. The reason there are so many cynical tendentious jokes about marriage is because it makes people so very unhappy. "What these jokes whisper," wrote Freud, "may be said aloud: that the wishes and desires of men have a right to make themselves acceptable alongside of exacting and ruthless morality."[52]

While many gays and lesbians revel in their exclusion from marriage, as Prin has done for years, increasing numbers are demanding to be subjected to the same "exacting and ruthless morality" as heterosexuals are. Con, Fran, and Terri are three such examples. By adopting the same rituals, protocols, and sacraments of straight society, these characters are bound to the structures and strictures that govern them, including the incest taboo. *Oedipus at Palm Springs* features lesbians who act just like heterosexuals, not to endorse same-sex marriage or promote assimilation but to make visible, through a series of cynical tendentious jokes, the emotional tunnel vision and political blind spots produced by this blinkered vision of equality. Just as *The Secretaries* investigates the furthest extremes of femininity, *Oedipus* examines acute forms of homonormativity. This play does not condone the abjection of Prin by her prudish, family-values-spouting friends any more than *The Secretaries* sanctions the killing of male coworkers by PMS-raging clerks. By giving Joni and Prin the last laugh, the Brothers gives voice to a host of hostile feelings about the adoption of heterosexual paradigms, the regulation of intimacy this entails, and the fracturing of lesbian communities that results when "normal" gays distance themselves from "abnormal" monsters like Prin, who fail, for whatever reason, to conform to increasingly constrained forms of affective and sexual expression.

Throughout *Acts of Gaiety,* I have described these dynamics as hallmarks of homoliberalism, which is best understood as a complex and shifting set of alliances promoting the economic, political, and social enfranchisement of certain, normative-leaning gays at the expense of other, unassimilable sexual minorities. Through the vehicle of a cynical tendentious joke, the Brothers' *Oedipus at Palm Springs* dramatizes the tragic consequences of homoliberalism, which, in this play, includes a privatized and depoliticized lesbian culture rooted in domesticity and consumption, an uncritical celebration of the nuclear family, a romantic idealization of biological reproduction, and the enforcement of rigidly gendered sexual relationships.

The Five Lesbian Brothers have a long history of parodying hetero- and homonormative institutions, but *Oedipus* is the troupe's first foray into the world of same-sex marriage and gay parenting. When the troupe went on hiatus in 1997, gay marriage was not legal in any state, and only a handful of municipalities and private institutions offered civil unions or domestic partnership benefits. As I discussed in chapter two, it was passage of the Defense of Marriage Act (DOMA) in 1996 that made marriage into the litmus test for sexual freedom. The institutionalization of discrimination by the federal government is primarily responsible for the outbreak of what comedian Kate Clinton calls "mad vow disease." This condition, which had previously been "limited to wholesome, unimpeachable gay couples earnestly seeking to take on the rights and responsibilities of marriage . . . jumped the pen and crossed into the general population."[53] Mad vow disease is highly communicable, warns Clinton, and the symptoms—"frothing apocalypticism, fractured reasoning, knee-jerking, and involuntary eye rolling"—can change a progressive into a conservative faster than a bride can say "I do."[54] When the Five Lesbian Brothers reunited to write *Oedipus,* same-sex marriage had just become legal in Massachusetts (the first state to sanction it, in 2004). This landmark legislation unleashed a love bug that infested all but the most remote outposts of the lesbian nation. Given the political climate in which the women were writing, not to mention the geographic locale, it is not surprising that their protagonists contracted a particularly virulent and normalizing strand of mad vow disease.

Wedded to Normalcy

Con and Fran, both in their forties, have been together seventeen years when the play opens, and it is clear that they love each other and their son very much. They have both sacrificed a great deal for their relationship and family. Fran gave up a lucrative business partnership with Prin to take a desk job working nine-to-five so she could spend more time with her wife and kid. When Con could not conceive a child, Fran reluctantly agreed to have their baby. In sharp contrast to dykes and feminists in the 1970s, like Valerie Solanas, who hailed reproductive technologies as a means of liberating women from traditional female roles, Fran and Con use recent medical advances to create their own lesbian nuclear family. The problem is that when butch Fran became a biomom it short-circuited her sexual motherboard and transformed her into something of a femme. Having lost her swagger, Fran does not feel amorous toward Con; she feels resentful. She channels all of her sexual desire into motherly love for her son, which leaves Con feeling both unattractive and abandoned. Neither couples counseling nor sex therapy has helped one bit.

Con is jealous of her lover for giving birth, of baby Basil for getting all of Fran's attention, and of that magical bond she believes only reproductive mothers and their children share. "They have this mystical connection," Con says, envious of Fran and Basil, "their special thing."[55] She reverts to essentialist notions of maternity to make herself feel better. "It's biology," Con tells herself. "You can't get around it."[56] Fran does little to dispel her partner's sense of disconnection; in fact, when she's angry at Con for making her sacrifice her career, her body, and her butch bravado, she plays up the alleged "mystical connection" with Basil. "I feel like he's—me," Fran says of the boy. "It's like his shit is my shit. When he pukes it's the same as my puke."[57] In retaliation, Con further emasculates Fran by objectifying her breasts, which have become quite voluptuous since giving birth. When Con really wants to humiliate Fran, she not only comments on her partner's rack in public, she goes into great detail about lactation, thereby drawing attention to her very curvaceous and feminine figure.

When Con launches into this routine in front of Prin, Fran is mortified, but this tactic backfires on Con when Prin, bored by all of the talk about Fran's breast milk, pops a nipple into her mouth to see for herself what all the fuss is about. Fran not only lets Prin suckle her in the hot tub, but she gets incredibly turned on (for the first time in years) by the experience of being topped by her butch buddy in this way. This scene enrages Con, who lays into Fran later that night when they are alone in their room. "Shut the fuck up about my tits," Fran finally snaps.

You don't love my tits. You never even talked about my tits until we had Basil and after that . . . that's all I am to you. . . . Your tit obsession has nothing to do with loving me or wanting me. It has everything to do with the fact that you couldn't get pregnant and can't nurse Basil and you feel left out! You hate my tits, you're mad at my tits and you're mad at me for having a baby—which I did for you because I love you—and I'm tired of it. I'm sick of being blamed for everything.[58]

Fran confesses to Con, "I never liked having tits. If I had my way I'd cut them off to improve my golf swing."[59] "That's sick," a devastated Con responds. "That's not true. That's not the least bit true. You're just saying those things so you have an excuse not to fuck me."[60] Fran tells Con to go fuck herself, which is what she has been doing for the last four years. This couple's lack of intimacy represents the sexual barrenness of homonormativity, a barrenness Terri reproduces when she rejects Prin at the end of the play.

Con and Fran have kept their sexual dysfunction a secret from Prin and Terri by putting on the mask of a happy couple, in part because they are so jealous of their friends' passionate and public sex life. Hearing about Fran's mystical connection to Basil, and nothing about the pain this has caused her or Con, makes Terri even more determined to find her birth mother. Despite the fact that Terri had, in her own words, "a wonderful mother," Betty, who reared her with love, she has "this hole in [her] that nothing can fill," nothing, she believes, except finding the woman who birthed her. "I need my mom. I need a mom who wanted me. I am lost," she tells Prin. "I'm lost and I'm all alone." Caught up in the fantasy of the family romance, Terri is obsessed with Con and Fran's baby and what she believes is their picture perfect life.

When Fran spills the beans about her marital troubles, after a few margaritas, Prin is nonplussed. "I told you that kid was gonna fuck everything up."[61] She tells her friends they need a little "phantom penis. . . . some butch/femme sustaining energy. . . . a little testosterone in the relationship."[62] "It's not the dick," Prin explains, "it's the attitude."[63] Con tells Prin she refuses "to take relationship advice from someone who thinks a lap dance is intimacy," adding that she does not see "the point of being a lesbian if you're just aping some heterosexual paradigm."[64] What Con fails to see, because she is in such a deep state of denial, is that butch/femme couples do not, in the words of Sue-Ellen Case, "impale themselves on the poles of sexual difference"; rather they "constantly seduce the sign system, through flirtation and inconstancy into the light fondle of artifice."[65] Prin understands that the subversive potential of the highly theatrical and deliberately self-conscious artifice of butch/femme role-playing is its insistence on roles as roles. This playful expression of an excess of genderedness unmasks the performative nature of roles, which have their origin in social constructions rather than nature, and fosters, through camp and irony, other options for sex and gender identification. Fran and Con fail to see the role of biological mother as a role, choosing instead to idealize it as some kind of natural, essential function that cannot be replicated, copied, or shared. It is not the butch/femme lovers Prin and Terri who are aping heterosexual paradigms, in other words; it is Fran and Con. They are the unhappily married couple trapped in a sexually unsatisfying monogamous relationship that they continue for the sake of their child.

Basil is both a blessing and a curse (insofar as he has contributed to a serious case of lesbian bed death), but neither of his mothers is capable of saying this aloud, though clearly they both think it. In fact, the couple goes to great lengths to deny that Basil is anything other than a gift. "Yeah, me and Con we don't fuck all the time like you guys," Fran tells Prin. "But there's more to love than sex. Con, Basil, they make my life all worth it. I'm not going to apologize for that."[66] Fran need not apologize for her lifestyle choices, but she is clearly envious of and excited by Prin's undomesticated eroticism, which threatens her charade of conjugal bliss to its core. This is why Fran goes to such great lengths to try to salvage Prin's proposal. It is the same reason why married people, even the ones who are utterly unhappy (or especially the ones who are unhappy?), constantly harangue their single friends into taking the plunge. This also explains why Fran is the cruelest and least forgiving of Prin once the incest is revealed. The fact that Prin had inappropriate sexual contact with another woman is not what bothers Fran. What horrifies and repulses her is Prin's lack of "proper" and "natural" maternal instincts, namely, that she gave up her baby for adoption, and, even more troubling, that she did not recognize her long-lost child when Terri came into her life. For Prin to be this kind of parent, one of two things must be true. Either "motherhood is overrated," as Prin has always claimed, and there is nothing inherently mystical or magical about it, or Prin is defective, deficient, immoral, a monster. Having invested so much stock in the former, Fran tells herself that it must be the latter. "A mother knows," Fran chastises Prin when the secret is revealed, "A mother always knows."[67]

Fran must excise Prin from the communal fold lest the fantasy world of domestic bliss she has constructed with Con and Basil unravel before her eyes. This gesture constitutes an act of percepticide, Diana Taylor's term for the (voluntary or involuntary) self-blinding effect trauma can have on individuals and communities. Although Taylor is speaking specifically about military atrocities and spectacles of state violence, this provocative concept can be applied to personal crises that render individuals "silent, deaf, and blind."[68] "To see without being able to do, disempowers absolutely," notes Taylor. "But seeing, without admitting that one is seeing, further turns the violence on oneself. Percepticide blinds, mains, kills through the senses."[69] Fran, Con, and Terri turn away from Prin rather than defy the normalizing force of the incest taboo because they cannot or will not bear witness to the events unfolding in front of them, as they call into question the contingent foundation on which they have constructed their relationships. Rather than face the truth—namely, that the lives they've been living and values they've been spouting are rooted in a fiction, the protagonists look away. This gesture may insulate them from the horror and chaos of their immediate surroundings, but it also undoes their sense of personal and communal cohesion. Fran, Con, and Terri don't simply turn away from Prin; they turn away from the possibility of political and social alternatives.

The cynical tendentious joke at the end of *Oedipus at Palm Springs*— "Didn't see it coming, did you?"—draws attention to the act of percepticide. We might say it is the antithesis of percepticide because the punch line focuses our attention on the act rather than away from it. In so doing it invites us to imagine a different response to the dramatic events than the one Fran, Con, and Terri exhibit. Jokes, and the category of the ludic to which they correspond, defamiliarize the familiar, demystify the exotic, and invert the "natural" order of things so as to show us the arbitrariness of social mores and the contingency of power structures. By enabling us to see the constructedness of the prohibition that dooms Prin, Joni's joke invites us to challenge the rules, regulations, and taboos that govern erotic desire and sexual conduct and to imagine alternative customs, traditions, and systems in their place. Through this and other jokes, the Brothers identify opportunities for transformative and substantive change, even in the face of seemingly insurmountable obstacles and calcified modes of thinking.

As the surrealist André Breton observed, "There is nothing . . . that intelligent humor cannot resolve in gales of laughter, not even the void."[70] The cynical tendentious joke that concludes the Brothers' *Oedipus* is not particularly funny, and it certainly does not elicit gales of laughter. As Louise Kennedy of the *Boston Globe* said of the play, "It may be the saddest comedy you'll ever see."[71] Rather than provoking unbridled hilarity, as their earlier satires do, this play injects a grave situation with a dose of what Breton, drawing on Freud's theorization of jokes, called "black humor," a term he coined in 1939. If humor is "the revenge of the pleasure principle (attached to the superego) over the reality principle (attached to the ego)," Breton wrote, then black humor is "a superior revolt of the mind."[72] Ironic, macabre, and absurd, dark comedy represents "the mortal enemy of sentimentality," and the laughter it generates constitutes "one of humanity's most sumptuous extravagances."[73]

Samuel Beckett, the modernist master of black humor, suggests that the more tendentious a joke is the less likely it is to induce laughter and the more likely it is to provoke ululations, howling sounds, or shrill and wordless laments. Beckett distinguishes between three types of ululations: bitter, hollow, and mirthless. This taxonomy appears in *Watt,* the author's fourth novel, written during World War II and published in 1953 by Maurice Girodias of Olympia Press (who would issue Solanas's *SCUM Manifesto,* a cynical tendentious joke if there ever was one, fifteen years later). In *Watt* the oracular servant Arsene—to whom Joni bears more than a passing resemblance—exclaims that

> of all the laughs that strictly speaking are not laughs, but modes of ululation, only three I think need detain us. . . . The bitter laugh laughs at that which is not good, it is the ethical laugh. The hollow laugh laughs at that which is not true, it is the intellectual laugh. Not good! Not true! Well well. But the mirthless laugh is the dianoetic laugh, down the snout—Haw!—so. It is the laugh of laughs, the *risus purus,* the laugh laughing at the laugh, the beholding, the saluting of the highest joke, in a word the laugh that laughs—silence please—at that which is unhappy.[74]

Arsene's nomenclature helps us to understand Prin's response to Joni's cynical joke. Her wordless rejoinder ("she shakes her head") is a mirthless ululation. According to this prophetic custodian of men and minds, only mirthless laughter is dianoetic, indicative of decisive insight. In the *Poetics,* Aristotle includes *dianoia* as a central component of drama, following only plot and character in terms of significance. A protagonist's *dianoia* determines whether or not she will be able to discern the truth, and if so, how she will react in the face of it.[75]

In Sophocles' play, both Jocasta and Oedipus discern the truth, but only the latter faces the void without flinching. Jocasta is actually the first to piece together the incest plot, and she seems willing to continue with the taboo relationship as long as it remains a secret (or perhaps in order to keep it a secret). When it becomes apparent that neither she nor Tiresias can dissuade Oedipus from seeking this knowledge, thereby ensuring that the story will be made public, Jocasta hangs herself. Oedipus, upon discovering Jocasta's body, stabs his eyes out with her brooch, then asks Creon to send him into exile. In the Brothers' adaptation, Prin is the only character (aside from Joni, the Tiresias figure) to discern the truth—the other characters learn when she tells them her secret. Prin moves from avoidance of the truth (pushing Terri into another's arms) to denial (insisting that she did not know), and, finally, to acceptance. "That's my daughter!" she cries, as "she lets out a yowl."[76] Prin's *dianoia* enables her to bear witness to the truth while the other characters look away in horror, in a gesture of percepticide.

When Freud says, "humour has in it a *liberating* element," as well as "*something fine and elevating*," what he means is that laughter can be therapeutic—reparative, healing, cathartic—insofar as it enables us to recover from delusory happiness (in this case of homonormativity) and enter into the lucidity of beholding things for what they are.[77] Through a cynical tendentious joke, the Brothers make a dark comedy out of a perfectly hopeless situation, transforming this tragedy into an absurdist farce and the spectacle of Prin's suffering and misfortune from a devastatingly negative experience into something ridiculously sublime. When Prin sees her reality for the absurd actuality it is, she laughs the mirthless laugh. This ululation is an act of gaiety, an acknowledgment of the folly that is the world and an embodiment of the courage that is required to persevere in spite of it. Prin could not have accomplished this alone, as humor is an inherently social phenomenon.

The Joke's on Us

The fact that *Oedipus at Palm Springs* ends with a cynical tendentious joke enacts the belief that these characters' lives could be organized differently, and it offers of a glimpse of what one alternative might look like. While Prin has been abandoned by Con, Fran, and Terri, she is neither alone nor friendless at the end of the play, as Dolan suggests; she has Joni. While Joni may not be the company Prin desires, she is company nonetheless. Joni neither rejects nor judges Prin, as the other women do. It is she who takes Prin in after the others have cast her out. Joni saves Prin's life, fishing her out of the pool into which she has thrown herself to drown her sorrows. By saving, I do not mean in the existential sense, as in Joni giving Prin a reason to live, for she does not; she rescues her from death. Joni exhibits little that qualifies as comfort at Prin's darkest hour, though she is physically present and emotionally open to the protagonist. This is important because Joni—the oldest character in the play and the mother of a now deceased child—actively eschews any kind of maternal role in her dealings with Prin. She's less an earth goddess, in other words, than a wizened old crone.

The reason Joni can foresee the tragic events that will transpire (while the others cannot) is because she has a special kind of prescience that we might call retro-foresight. A relic from the 1970s, a more communal, less commercial moment in lesbian history, Joni is the only character in the play who has not embraced a neoliberal lifestyle, sacrificed her political ideals for the personal benefits homonormativity affords, or ensconced herself in a privatized sphere of domesticity divorced from material life and class politics. As such Joni offers insight into how we might move beyond the stultifying pragmatism of queer hegemony. The shared intimacy between Prin and Joni stands in sharp relief to the nuclear, biological model of kinship championed by the other characters.

These two social outcasts—Prin for knowing too little and Joni for knowing too much—constitute a model of community formation that is well known to sexual and social deviants, a family of choice. What we can say about this arrangement is that it is not based on identity politics or any kind of common experience, real or imagined, that the two share simply because they are women, lesbians, or mothers. Aside from exile, the two have little in common. Prin is a swaggering lothario and a clannish urban capitalist. Joni is of indeterminate sexuality, reclusive, and an artist. Together they represent an intentional community, one centered on kinship systems of choice, on adoptive forms of relationality. The play does not proffer a utopian vision of a new lesbian nation, a gynocentric paradise in which these two outliers settle in together, start a pottery collective, and live happily ever after. Prin's and Joni's prospects for survival seem bleak, indeed, but we get the sense that they can go on and will go on. Like Beckett's Gogo and Didi, they will carve out some kind of life together from the wreckage, moment by moment. No one would mistake this play's conclusion for optimism, but this act of gaiety does represent a kind of resolute cheerfulness in which the characters and the audience can take pleasure.

This dark comedy brings to conceptual crisis contradictions of queer kinships and national belonging as it begs further conversation about the incommensurability of lesbian sexuality and fully enfranchised citizenship. The play asks: what sacrifices does acceptance into the mainstream entail? What types of concession does allegiance to the nation-state demand? *Oedipus at Palm Springs* questions marriage and domesticity as indices of political and social advancement. Rather than benchmarks for human liberty and freedom, these phenomena are cast as antithetical to a transformational polity. The demonization of Prin lays bare the false equivalencies of homoliberalism and LGBT equality while marking the constitutive limits of the contemporary queer agenda. Fran's rejection of Prin, and her retreat into a puritanical attack on sexual pleasure shows that morality is not a discourse articulately solely by a reactionary religious right mobilized around the promotion of heteronormativity and proclaimed from a pulpit by fathers of the church. In recent years, the LGBT movement has produced a congregation of converts and a choir of moralizing queers who are all too happy to assume the task of condemning and excommunicating the sinners among us. Fran's turning against her friend in this manner embodies a fundamental tenet of neoliberalism: accumulation by dispossession. This lesbian mother gains and secures access to social respectability by depriving a dyke who gave her child up for adoption of her humanity. This devastating scene underscores the ways in which homoliberalism reconciles desires and feelings to the exacting demands of rational subject formation through a logic of normalization that depicts assimilationists as "good" while castigating those with deviant histories and aberrant inclinations as a "bad" and therefore undeserving of rights and recognition. The profoundly antidemocratic tendencies of homoliberalism are made explicit through Fran's authoritarian, hierarchical, and moralizing means of maintaining the status quo.

Gayle Rubin predicted in the early 1980s, around the time of the WOW Café's founding and just a few years before the Brothers formed their fraternity, that when homosexuals enter the "charmed circle" of legitimate sexuality, gender conforming queers in normative kinship structures will become the standard by which all other lesbians and gays are judged. Those who fail to comply with or who dissent from this mold will be ostracized and penalized.[78] Like Joni's prophecy, Rubin's alarming prognostication has come true. The reality for those left behind or cast outside the borders of the newly queered nation—a vast multitude of apparently dispensable people bereft of sustaining networks and social safety nets—is that there is little to be gained from progress except alienation, humiliation, and despair. Obliged to live among the abject underclass of a nation made a more perfect union by its tacit tolerance of respectable homosexuals, Prin's hopes for life, liberty, and the pursuit of happiness evaporate before the violent logic and shallow rhetoric of homoliberalism.

Rubin illustrates how "playing with" dominant categories of sexuality and sexual identity by members of the "outer limits" can disrupt the very premises on which these rubrics rely for their legitimization. In its playing with and denaturalizing of lesbian maternity, *Oedipus at Palm Springs* dramatizes what might be gained politically by troubling the nuclear family romance on which this plot hinges. By reconceptualizing intimate relationships not in terms of filiation and genetics, but rather in terms of perverse affiliations and social contingency, the New York Theatre Workshop production emerges as a critical site contesting homonormative family and kinship structures. The final scene between Prin and Joni recasts domestic and political communities so that they are based not on blood ties and biological reproduction but on adoptive relationality and the assumption of a contested set of social practices and ethical commitments. While the Brothers' decision to play it "straight" with *Oedipus at Palm Springs* has disappointed many fans and critics, I see the troupe's use of dramatic realism as an ideal and ingenious vehicle for a cynical tendentious joke about how, in our quest for legitimacy, we lesbians have come to take ourselves too seriously.

Afterword

Acts of Gaiety attests to the salubrious social and political transformations that have taken place over the past five decades and to ever-expanding definitions of what it means to be a sexual subject. This progress, and the progressive visibility of LGBT life, reflects the incredible successes of queer uprisings, insurrections, liberation movements, and critical theories that have made homosexuality and same-sex desire historical possibilities. As we revel in our place of pride in the public sphere and celebrate landmark legal victories, it behooves us to note that these advances are not simply the result of radical interventions into American polity. Conservative cultural currents and socio-economic policies have underwritten the assimilation of sexual minorities into the mainstream. Many activists and scholars have cited specific juridical reforms (e.g., the decriminalization of sodomy in the Supreme Court case *Lawrence v. Texas* and the end of the U.S. military's ban on gay soldiers) not as indices of sexual freedom but as reactionary responses linked directly to the privatizing imperatives of a powerful, ascendant brand of neoliberal politics that gained traction in the 1970s and coalesced in the 1990s.

In this book I deploy the term *homoliberalism* to describe a set of sexual and fiscal practices advancing the notion that equality for LGBT subjects can best be secured by liberating individual entrepreneurial desires for wealth and status accumulation within a national framework characterized by rights (to marriage, government service, and private property) secured through the monetizing precepts of unfettered access to free markets and the unregulated flow of free trade. The role of the sexual minority in this speculative form of citizenship is to support and defend the socioeconomic structures that enable and maintain these degraded notions of rights, dignities, and freedoms, while the state, in turn, guarantees homosexuals and transexuals the defenses and protections necessary for the pursuit of these liberties. The false promises of homoliberalism function as a mask for protocols that serve, above all else, to maintain, reconstitute, and restore the discriminatory operations of the nation-state. The degree to which homoliberalism has become embedded in the theory and practice of contemporary sexual politics has created imbalances and exacerbated inequalities to such an extent that we are facing a conceptual and political crisis. The widening gap between rhetoric (that queer is a potent alternative to the mainstreaming of the LGBT movement) and the realization (that queer aids and abets the workings of neoliberalism) is now all too visible. The more that queer nationality is recognized as a compromised utopian ideal facilitating the assimilation of gays and lesbians into the restrictive confines of civic society, the more the foundation is laid for forging political alternatives that promote social and economic justice for all.

How will this crisis play out? Can we forestall the instrumentalizing and monetizing course of sexual politics? How might we counter such a narrow entrepreneurial conception of sexual agency and thwart the homoliberal debasement of sexual freedom into a synonym for free enterprise? Is a yet-to-be articulated cutting-edge discourse the best hope we have for doing so, or does some revitalized notion of lesbian feminist theory hold greater political promise? *Acts of Gaiety* does not provide answers to these questions, which defy easy or obvious solutions. It does recognize that in the struggle to articulate possibilities for being with each other and being in the world internecine struggles will be not only inevitable but desirable, as they generate ideas, debates, and options. While we need to foster communication, build coalitions, and practice the art of compromise, we also need to promote dialogue, disagreement, and dissent. What we don't need is a moratorium on discord or the silencing of oppositional views, nor do we need paranoid proclamations that indict anyone and everyone who isn't an anarchist or political extremist as an enemy of the people.

The current state of affairs is definitely depression inducing, and it is no wonder that the anti-social thesis has gained such traction in queer theory in recent years. I acknowledge that progressive attempts to exhibit lateral agency and locate in-between spaces that eschew the hitches of hegemony and the shallow satisfactions of consumer citizenship entail traversing, if not dwelling in, critical realms of rejection, negation, and refusal. However,

I resist the notion that we should take up permanent residence in the shadowy depths of these murky milieus. My relationships to feminism and LGBT politics have never felt anti-social or anti-relational, not even at this critical junction in history. My attraction to these world-making projects has never been limited to feelings of shame, melancholy, pain, or rage, though these emotions have, most certainly, catalyzed my activism, imbuing it with both a vibrant intensity and sense of urgency. My participation in transformative social movements has felt like something more creative, constructive, and life-affirming. Insouciant acts of gaiety are what attracted me to politics, what gave me the capacity and courage to call myself a lesbian, a feminist, a queer, and what makes me enjoy the continued fight for programs and projects that will probably never come to fruition in my lifetime. Gaiety enacts the promise of transformation, and while it can't promise us a better tomorrow, it can certainly help balm our wounds, soothe our suffering, and bolster our spirits.

This book takes as axiomatic the notion that politics, like theater, is a sphere of active emotions, and it argues that the ways categories of feelings have become differentiated and delineated over the past several decades determines, to a great extent, how sexual politics have come to matter, how certain emotions have come to be valued (or devalued), and how specific sentiments have come to have social and political import. Seeking to understand how affects come to mean and make a difference in the public sphere, I have offered a critical history of emotions commonly associated with LGBT art and activism and an assessment of contemporary studies of queer feelings. What might "thinking feelings" tell us about the ethics and efficacy of feminist and queer studies? Which emotions are likely to marshal and mobilize subjects into collectives and communities? What can a renewed interest in gaiety contribute to our understanding of performance and politics? These questions that highlight affect, emotion, and feeling in relation to public displays and their activist potentials are among those that animate this scholarly inquiry.

The turn to affect in theater and performance studies, increasingly evident in conferences, course offerings, journal issues, and books, is indicative of a more far-reaching shift in the humanities and social sciences toward non-representational theory. The affective turn signals a renewed interest in corporeality and the sensate body; live art, and in particular time-based performing arts, are particularly relevant here as they enact the emotional labor of giving form and expression to human experiences, wishes, and desires through embodied spectacles and the seduction of spectatorship. In contrast to the linguistic turn and the cultural turn that precede it, the affective turn indexes the need to consider the vagaries of ontology as lived in and through an array of cultural forms within systems of knowledge and power. This paradigm shift represents the desire to eke out some conceptual space for facets of human behavior and motivation that are not harnessed to consciousness, cognition, and rationality, to acknowledge somatic and social dynamics that are labile and inchoate, and to explore impulses and responses that conventions contour but do not circumscribe. Attention to affects bring us closer to those dimensions of conduct and culture that cannot be broached by semiotic analysis or a constructivist lens, privileging those unruly and capricious forces that cannot be fully determined and, as a result, may be less prone to discipline, regulation, and control.

Gaiety is a form of embodied thought, a ludic rejoinder to historical injury; acts of gaiety are performances of redress that transform the vicious banality of homophobia and misogyny into something fantastic and fabulous. Emotional responses reflect the capacity of bodies to affect and be affected by others. As such, they entail a recalibration of one's corporeal relation to social and cultural norms. Whereas fear and hatred can distort bodies in anticipation of harm, gaiety expands our physical form in the expectation of pleasurable communion. A gesture of radical openness, gaiety shows us that what hurts, what causes us shame, and what we feel is wrong with the world is not necessary or inevitable, and it gives us license to unmake and remake it in other guises. Tacking with the affective turn, this book attempts to capture what it *feels* like to be gay, not what it *means* to be gay. Theories of identity, ideology, representation, and signification are not sufficient to address the complexities and contradictions of contemporary sexual politics, and these discourses can't retard or remediate the neoliberalization of the LGBT movement.

The case studies I survey here bring gaiety into focus as a research object, a methodology, and a pedagogical project. The exploits of the humorous homosexuals, droll dykes, and laughing lesbians that populate this book could be categorized as a "silly archive," Lauren Berlant's term for repertoires of "dangerous subrationality, superficiality, or hysteria" that are integral to the creation of queer counterpublics.[1] Silliness is typically associated with child's play, and with girl culture in particular; the disavowal of silliness by members of the male-dominated left reflects, according to Lisa Duggan, a rejection of the feminine.[2] She links the privileging of seriousness, rigor, difficulty, mastery, disciplinarity, and hard-reasoning to a virulent variety of masculinism. Judith Halberstam contributes to the silly archive in her recent book, *The Queer Art of Failure* in order to stress the importance of seeking knowledge in all the wrong places: television, children's animation, horror films, and other low-cultural sites. Gaiety, as I have shown, is a type of imaginative playfulness typically associated with silly subjects, and with gay males in particular. In constructing an archive of lesbian gaiety, I am driven by the desire to revivify subjugated knowledges and ecstatic practices that have been cast aside in the rush to inaugurate queer theory as a novel praxis. Lesbian gaiety has been disavowed by self-described radical members of the queer nation and by more conservative factions as well, who see it as antithetical to their quest for social respectability.

I realize that in promoting lesbian gaiety and indulging in instances of it, I run the risk of not being taken seriously. In some ways, this is my aim. I lament the fact that in the quest for legitimization, lesbians and gays have lost their sense of humor and abdicated their investments in fun, frivolity, mirth, and merriment. Being taken seriously means renouncing play and promiscuity, growing up and growing old, and sublimating those penchants and proclivities that divert us from appropriate aims and aspirations. The desire to be seen in a proper and dignified light is precisely what compels people to consent to the disciplining of their desires and the commodification of their emotions. In an era of homoliberalism, a call to acts of gaiety serves as a heuristic devise to explore what a more euphoric and ecstatic world might feel like. In our sober age of compulsory assimilation, a return to gaiety is urgent. Attention to carnal delights, lavender menacement, and consuming passions figure here as a modest attempt to realign sexual politics within an affective economy of pleasure. With this book, I want to interject some comic relief into the toxic tempest of contemporary sexual politics and hope that others might join me in staging acts of gaiety.

Notes

Preface

1. Karla Jay, *Tales of a Lavender Menace: A Memoir of Liberation* (New York: Basic Books, 2000), 143.

2. Ibid.

3. Ibid.

4. Ibid., 144.

5. Betty Friedan, "Up from the Kitchen Floor," *New York Times Magazine,* March 4, 1973, 33–34.

6. Ibid.

7. Lisa Duggan, "The New Homonormativity: The Sexual Politics of Neoliberalism," in *Materializing Democracy: Toward a Revitalized Cultural Politics,* ed. Russ Castronovo and Dana D. Nelson (Durham: Duke University Press, 2002), 179. For an excellent primer on neoliberalism, see David Harvey, *A Brief History of Neoliberalism* (Oxford: Oxford University Press, 2005).

8. The central tenet of the antirelational thesis is that homosexual male desire is inherently anti-identitarian and antisocial. See Leo Bersani, *Homos* (Cambridge, MA: Harvard University Press, 1995). See also Lee Edelman, *No Future: Queer Theory and the Death Drive* (Durham: Duke University Press, 2004); Tim Dean, *Unlimited Intimacy: Reflections on the Subculture of Barebacking* (Chicago: University of Chicago Press, 2009); and Robert L. Caserio, Tim Dean, Lee Edelman, Judith Halberstam, and José Esteban Muñoz, "Forum: Conference Debates—the Antisocial Thesis in Queer Theory," *PMLA* 121, no. 3 (May 2006): 819–36.

9. José Esteban Muñoz, *Cruising Utopia: The Then and There of Queer Futurity* (New York: New York University Press, 2009), 10–11.

10. Elizabeth Grosz, "Histories of a Feminist Future," *Signs* 25, no. 4 (Summer 2000): 1019.

11. Muñoz, *Cruising Utopia,* 12.

12. Dana Luciano, *Arranging Grief: Sacred Time and the Body in Nineteenth-Century America* (New York: New York University Press, 2007).

13. Alina Troyano [Carmelita Tropicana], *I, Carmelita Tropicana: Performing between Cultures* (Boston: Beacon Press, 2000), xiv.

14. Valerie Solanas, *SCUM Manifesto* (New York: SCUM Book, 1977), 2. This citation refers to Solanas's 1977 edition of *SCUM Manifesto,* published after she was re-

leased from prison and intended to correct errors in the Olympia Press edition of 1968. In Solanas's original self-published 1967 edition of the document, this line reads, "In actual fact, the female function is to relate, groove, love and be herself, irreplaceable by anyone else" (6).

15. Eve Kosofsky Sedgwick, *Touching Feeling: Affect, Pedagogy, Performativity* (Durham: Duke University Press, 2003).

16. The chief authors of the "Woman-Identified Woman" manifesto were Rita Mae Brown, Lois Hart, Cynthia Funk, Barbara Love, Artemis March, and Elen Shumsky. The document was created for and distributed at the Second Congress to Unite Women by members of the Lavender Menace zap, but it was published under the name Radicalesbians (Radicalesbians, "The Woman-Identified-Woman," in *Radical Feminism,* eds. Anne Koedt, Ellen Levine, and Anita Rapone [New York: Quadrangle Books, (1970) 1973], 240–45). Though enormously influential in the 1970s, "The Woman-Identified Woman" came under fire by subsequent generations of feminists for its perceived essentialism and asexual portrait of lesbianism. The Radicalesbians' decision to privilege affect rather than sex as the marker of lesbian identity seemed positively puritanical to pro-sex feminists in the 1980s and 1990s, many of whom singled out "The Woman-Identified Woman" as the spark that ignited the sex wars. See Ann Snitow, Christine Stansell, and Sharon Thompson, "Introduction," in *Powers of Desire: The Politics of Sexuality,* eds. Ann Snitow, Christine Stansell, and Sharon Thompson (New York: Monthly Review Press, 1983), 9–50; Alice Echols, *Daring to Be Bad: Radical Feminism in America, 1967–1975* (Minneapolis: University of Minnesota Press, 1989); Biddy Martin, "Sexualities without Genders and Other Queer Utopias," in *Femininity Played Straight: The Significance of Being Lesbian* (New York: Routledge, 1996), 71–96; Amber Hollibaugh, *My Dangerous Desires: A Queer Girl Dreaming Her Way Home* (Durham: Duke University Press, 2000); and Joan Nestle, "Flamboyance and Fortitude," in *The Persistent Desire: A Femme-Butch Reader,* ed. Joan Nestle (New York: Alyson Books, 1992), 13–22.

17. The first women's dance was held on April 3, 1970, at Alternate University. It was organized by a radical lesbian contingent of the Gay Liberation Front (GLF). Many members of the dance committee were involved in the Lavender Menace zap.

18. The effects of the protest were wide-ranging. At the next national conference of NOW, held September 1971, delegates adopted a resolution recognizing lesbianism as a legitimate concern for feminism, despite continued objections by Friedan.

19. Kate Millett, "How Many Lives Are Here," in *The Feminist Memoir Project: Voices from Women's Liberation,* ed. Rachel Blau DuPlessis and Ann Snitow (New Brunswick: Rutgers University Press, 2007), 494.

20. Quoted in Echols, *Daring to Be Bad,* 219.

21. Anselma Dell'Olio, "Home before Sundown," in *The Feminist Memoir Project: Voices From Women's Liberation,* ed. Rachel Blau DuPlessis and Ann Snitow (New Brunswick: Rutgers University Press, 2007), 161.

22. Jay, *Tales of a Lavender Menace,* 137.

23. Kate Davy, *Lady Dicks and Lesbian Brothers: Staging the Unimaginable at the WOW Café Theatre* (Ann Arbor: University of Michigan Press, 2010), 2, 19.

24. Sue-Ellen Case, "Toward a Butch-Feminist Retro-Future," in *Feminist and Queer Performance: Critical Strategies* (New York: Palgrave Macmillan, 2009), 54.

25. Jill Dolan, *Geographies of Learning: Theory and Practice, Activism and Performance* (Middletown, Conn.: Wesleyan University Press, 2001), 107.

26. Davy, *Lady Dicks and Lesbian Brothers,* 98.

27. Dolan, *Geographies of Learning,* 99.

28. Ibid.

29. Ann Cvetkovich, *An Archive of Feelings: Trauma, Sexuality, and Lesbian Public Cultures* (Durham: Duke University Press, 2003).

30. Kenyon Farrow, "Gay Marriage in New York: Progressive Victory or GOP Road-map?," June 27, 2011, Alternet.org, http://www.alternet.org/story/151444/gay_marriage _in_new_york%3A_progressive_victory_or_gop_roadmap/ (accessed July 2011).

31. Lauren Berlant, *The Queen of America Goes to Washington City: Essays on Sex and Citizenship* (Durham: Duke University Press, 1997), 1.

32. Jack Smith, J. Hoberman, and Edward Leffingwell, *Wait for Me at the Bottom of the Pool: The Writings of Jack Smith* (New York: Serpent's Tail, 1997), 11.

Introduction

The epigraph is from Bertha Harris, introduction to *Lover* (New York: New York University Press, 1976), xxix.

1. Teresa de Lauretis, "Habit Changes," *differences: A Journal of Feminist Cultural Studies* 6, nos. 2–3 (1994): 297. De Lauretis coined the term *queer theory* in 1990 at a conference on gay and lesbian sexualities at the University of California, Santa Cruz. That same year, activists associated with ACT-UP in New York City formed Queer Nation, a direct-action organization aimed at eliminating homophobia and increasing gay, lesbian, and bisexual visibility through guerrilla tactics and media manipulation. The year 1990 also saw the publication of Eve Kosofsky Sedgwick's *Epistemology of the Closet* (Los Angeles: University of California Press, 1990) and Judith Butler's *Gender Trouble: Feminism and the Subversion of Identity* (New York: Routledge, 1990). While neither of these texts uses the word *queer,* both are considered foundational texts of queer theory.

2. Jasbir Puar, *Terrorist Assemblages: Homonationalism in Queer Times* (Durham: Duke University Press, 2007), xiii.

3. Judith Butler, "Critically Queer," *GLQ: A Journal of Lesbian and Gay Studies* 1, no. 1 (1993): 17.

4. The occasion for the conference was the twenty-fifth anniversary of the publication of Gayle Rubin's 1984 essay "Thinking Sex," which many credit, along with "The Traffic in Women" (1975), with inaugurating the field of sexuality studies in its call for the recognition of the political dimensions of erotic life. See Gayle Rubin, "The Traffic in Women: Notes on the 'Political Economy' of Sex," in *Toward an Anthropology of Women,* ed. Rayna Reiter (New York: Monthly View Press, 1975), 157–210, and "Thinking Sex: Notes for a Radical Theory of the Politics of Sexuality," in *Pleasure and Danger: Exploring Female Sexuality,* ed. Carole Vance (New York: Routledge and Kegan Paul, 1984), 267–319. See Heather Love, ed. "Rethinking Sex," *GLQ: A Journal of Lesbian and Gay Studies* 17, no. 1 (2011).

5. Carolyn Dinshaw et al., "Theorizing Queer Temporalities: A Roundtable Discussion," *GLQ: A Journal of Lesbian and Gay Studies* 13, nos. 2–3 (2007): 13. The roundtable took place via e-mail in March, April, and May of 2006 and included Dinshaw, Lee Edelman, Roderick A. Ferguson, Carla Freccero, Elizabeth Freeman, Judith Halberstam, Annamarie Jagose, Christopher S. Nealon, and Tan Hoang Nguyen.

6. Ann Pellegrini, "Touching the Past, or, Hanging Chad, 'History's Queer Touch: Responses to Carolyn Dinshaw's *Getting Medieval: Sexualities and Communities, Pre- and Postmodern,*'" *Journal of the History of Sexuality* 10, no. 2 (April 2001): 192.

7. Patricia Ticineto Clough and Jean O'Malley Halley, eds., *The Affective Turn: Theorizing the Social* (Durham: Duke University Press, 2007), 1.

8. Judith Butler, *Bodies that Matter: On the Discursive Limits of "Sex"* (New York: Routledge, 1993), 223.

9. Ibid.

10. Sianne Ngai, *Ugly Feelings* (Cambridge, Mass.: Harvard University Press, 2005).

11. Charlotte Bunch, *Passionate Politics: Feminist Theory in Action* (New York: St. Martin's Press, 1987).

12. Raymond Williams, "Structures of Feeling," in *Marxism and Literature* (Oxford: Oxford University Press, 1977), 128–35.

13. Ibid., 132.

14. For example, someone, possibly Rita Mae Brown, destroyed the video recording of the Lavender Menace zap out of fear that it would fall into the wrong hands.

15. Joan Nestle, *A Restricted Country* (Ithaca, NY: Firebrand Books, 1987), 9.

16. *Rhizomatic* and *filiative* are key terms in *Capitalism and Schizophrenia,* published in two volumes as *Anti-Oedipus* and, eight years later, *A Thousand Plateaus.* See Gilles Deleuze and Félix Guattari, *Anti-Oedipus,* trans. Robert Hurley, Mark Seem, and Helen R. Lane (New York: Continuum, [1972] 2004); and *A Thousand Plateaus: Capitalism and Schizophrenia,* trans. Brian Massumi (Minneapolis: University of Minnesota Press, [1980] 1987).

17. Ibid.

18. David Román and Holly Hughes, "*O Solo Homo:* An Introductory Conversation," in *O Solo Homo: The New Queer Performance,* eds. Holly Hughes and David Román (New York: Grove Press, 1988), 6–7.

19. On the relationship between actresses and sex workers, see Kirsten Pullen, *Actresses and Whores: On Stage and in Society* (Cambridge: Cambridge University Press, 2005). See also Tracy Davis, *Actresses as Working Women: Their Social Identity in Victorian Culture* (New York: Routledge, 2002).

20. Jill Dolan, *Utopia in Performance: Finding Hope at the Theater* (Ann Arbor: University of Michigan Press, 2005), 1, 33.

21. Judith Butler, *Gender Trouble: Feminism and the Subversion of Identity* (New York: Routledge, 1990), 33.

22. See Robin Bernstein, ed. *Cast Out: Queer Lives in Theater* (Ann Arbor: University of Michigan Press, 2006).

23. Mart Crowley, *The Boys in the Band,* in *Forbidden Acts: Pioneering Gay and Lesbian Plays of the Twentieth Century,* ed. Benjamin A. Hodges (New York: Applause Books, 2003), 490. *The Boys in the Band* ran for 1,001 performances off-Broadway (at Theater Four), was made into a successful film by director William Friedkin in 1970, and enjoys a healthy afterlife in regional theaters.

24. Ibid., 516.

25. Sara Ahmed, *The Promise of Happiness* (Durham: Duke University Press, 2010).

26. See Matthew Kaiser, "A History of 'Ludicrous,'" *English Literary History 71,* no. 3 (Fall 2004): 631–60. We typically think of theatricality in terms of *theatrum mundi,* the world as a stage, which is related to but not the same as the concept of *mundus ludibundus.* See Tracy C. Davis and Thomas Postlewait, eds., *Theatricality* (Cambridge: Cambridge University Press, 2003). Scholars of theater and performance have a vested interest in play. As with the case of ritual, much of our foundational literature on the subject comes from anthropology and sociology. Key texts on play include Johan Huizinga, *Homo Ludens: A Study of the Play Element in Culture* (New York: Taylor and Francis, [1944] 2003); Brian Sutton-Smith, *The Ambiguity of Play* (Cambridge, Mass.: Harvard University Press, 2001); Clifford Geertz, *The Interpretation of Cultures* (New York: Basic Books, 1973); Richard Schechner, *Performance Studies: An Introduction* (New York: Routledge, 2006); Roger Caillois, *Man, Play, and Games,* trans. Meyer Barash (Chicago: University of Illinois Press, 2001); and Baz Kershaw, *The Politics of Performance: Radical Theatre as Cultural Intervention* (London: Routledge, 1992).

27. Susan Sontag, "Notes on 'Camp,'" in *Against Interpretation and Other Essays* (New York: Dell, 1966), 290.

28. Debates about the relevance, efficacy, and ethics of camp as a mode of lesbian performance took place in the 1980s and 1990s. Conversation has waned in recent

decades, however, as camp has been commodified by the mainstream and no longer offers the pointed social critique it did at earlier moments in the LGBT movement. In the pro-camp corner are critics like Sue-Ellen Case, who championed Split Britches' butch/femme role-playing, and Judith Halberstam, who chronicled the rise of the drag king movement. See Sue-Ellen Case, "Toward a Butch/Femme Aesthetic," in *Feminist and Queer Performance: Critical Strategies* (New York: Palgrave, 2009), 31–48; and Judith Halberstam and Del LaGrace Volcano, *The Drag King Handbook* (New York: Serpent's Tail, 1999). Kate Davy took the opposite position, arguing that camp cannot work for women because it reinscribes the technologies of sex and gender that it deploys in its farcical and parodic performances. See Kate Davy, "Fe/Male Impersonation: The Discourse of Camp," in *Critical Theory and Performance*, eds. Janelle Reinelt and Joseph R. Roach (Ann Arbor: University of Michigan Press, 2010), 355–71. Alisa Solomon critiques the misogynist component in gay male drag, noting that it is akin to the racism in minstrel shows. See her *Re-dressing the Canon: Essays on Theatre and Gender* (New York: Routledge, 1997). Susan Sontag is mum on the subject, and Esther Newton neither confirms nor denies the possibility of lesbian camp, but she does claim that drag queens are its natural exponent. See her *Mother Camp: Female Impersonators in America* (Chicago: University of Chicago Press, 1979). Lauren Berlant and Elizabeth Freeman are among the theorists who believe that camp was not possible for dyke performers prior to the advent of queer theory. See their "Queer Nationality," in *The Queen of America Goes to Washington City: Essays on Sex and Citizenship* (Durham: Duke University Press, 1997), 145–74.

29. Quoted in Davy, *Lady Dicks and Lesbian Brothers*, 358.

30. Busch's *Vampire Lesbians of Sodom*, which was first performed at the Limbo Lounge in New York City's East Village in 1984, became so popular that it was moved to off-Broadway in June 1985. It ran for five years at the Provincetown Playhouse and has enjoyed a healthy run at regional and independent theaters across the country.

31. Roberta Sklar made this statement during a "Women's Theater in the 1970s" panel with Sondra Segal, Clare Coss, Sue Perlgut, and Muriel Miguel, hosted by Jill Dolan. It took place at the CLAGS conference "In Amerika They Call Us Dykes: Lesbian Lives in the '70s," October 8–10, 2010, at the Graduate Center, City University of New York.

32. There were lesbians who both frequented and worked at Caffe Cino, including director Roberta Sklar, but it was primarily a venue for gay male playmakers and is best known for launching the careers of Robert Patrick, Doric Wilson, and Lanford Wilson.

33. Davy, *Lady Dicks and Lesbian Brothers*, 42.

34. *Oxford English Dictionary*, http://www.oed.com (accessed January 2010).

35. John Leech, "The Great Social Evil," *Punch* 33 (January 10, 1857), 114.

36. Eric Marcus, *Making Gay History: The Half Century Fight for Lesbian and Gay Equal Rights* (New York: Harper, 2002), 57.

37. *Tiny and Ruby: Hell Divin' Women*, dir. Greta Schiller and Andrea Weiss, 1986, Channel 4, London, DVD.

38. For more on Davis and her bands, see Marilyn Nelson, *Sweethearts of Rhythm: The Story of the Greatest All-Girl Swing Band in the World* (New York: Dial Books, 2009); and D. Antoinette Handy, *The International Sweethearts of Rhythm: The Ladies Jazz Band from Piney Woods Country Life School* (Lanham, MD: Scarecrow Press, 1998).

39. "Harry Hay: Founding the Mattachine," Outhistory.org., http://www.outhistory.org/wiki/Harry_Hay:_Founding_the_Mattachine,_part_2 (accessed January 2009).

40. The Daughters of Bilitis is named after a contemporary of Sappho identified in a book of poetry by Pierre Louÿs, *The Songs of Bilitis*, trans. Alvah C. Bessie (New York: Dover, 1988).

41. *The Ladder* was published from 1956 to 1972, and Lisa Ben was a frequent

contributor. The Mattachine Society published its own journal, the *Mattachine Review,* beginning in 1955. Arguably the most important homophile publications was *One,* which was launched in 1953. Though produced independently of the Mattachine Society, many of its contributors, including editor Dale Jennings, were members.

42. Lillian Faderman, *Odd Girls and Twilight Lovers: A History of Lesbian Life in Twentieth Century America* (New York: Penguin, 1999), 190–91.

43. See Marcia Gallo, *Different Daughters: A History of the Daughters of Bilitis and the Birth of the Lesbian Rights Movement* (New York: Carroll and Graf, 2006).

44. Flavia Rondo, "Between Bohemia and Revolution," in *Smash the Church, Smash the State,* ed. Tommi Avicolli Mecca (San Francisco: City Lights, 2009), 163–67.

45. Phyllis Lyon and Del Martin, *Lesbian/Woman* (Ann Arbor: University of Michigan Press, 1997), 273.

46. Doric Wilson, "Stonewall + 40," May 20, 2009, http://doricwilson.blogspot.com/2009/05/stonewall-40_20.html (accessed December 2009).

47. Quoted in John D'Emilio, *Sexual Politics, Sexual Communities: The Making of a Homosexual Minority in the United States, 1940–1970* (Chicago: University of Chicago Press, 1983), 234. The GLF's statement of purpose was originally published in *RAT: Subterranean News* on August 12, 1969.

48. Allen Young, "Out of the Closets, into the Streets," in *Out of the Closets: Voices of Gay Liberation,* eds. Karla Jay and Allen Young (New York: New York University Press, 1992), 7–10.

49. Shelley does not recall this being her suggestion but rather the consensus of the collective. See Shelley Anderson, "Interview with Martha Shelley," which is part of the Voices of Feminism Oral History Project located at Smith College. The interview took place on October 12, 2003.

50. The phrase "gay is good" was first used by Frank Kameny, founder of the Washington, DC, branch of the Mattachine Society, in a resolution adopted by NACHO, the North American Conference of Homophile Organizations, in 1951. See Donn Teal, *The Gay Militants* (New York: St. Martin's Press, 1971), 59.

51. Donald Webster Cory, *The Homosexual in America: A Subjective Approach* (New York: Greenberg, 1951), 108. This book, which Cory, the pseudonym of Edward Sagarin, would later recant, charts the etymology of the term *gay,* and it argues that homosexuals constitute an oppressed minority and should organize under this rubric to achieve social justice and end the conspiracy of silence surrounding same-sex attraction.

52. Young, "Out of the Closets," 28.

53. Ibid., 28–29.

54. Martha Shelley, "Our Passion Shook the World," in *Smash the Church, Smash the State,* ed. Tommi Avicolli Mecca (San Francisco: City Lights, 2009), 96.

55. Ibid., 93.

56. Quoted in Teal, *The Gay Militants,* 87.

57. The mission statement of the conference is archived at http://www.umich.edu/~lgqri/gayshame.html (accessed January 2009). Conference papers were published in David Halperin and Valerie Traub, eds., *Gay Shame* (Chicago: University of Chicago Press, 2009). For the controversy the conference generated with respect to racial politics, see Hiram Perez and Judith Halberstam's contributions to David Eng, Judith Halberstam, and José Esteban Muñoz, eds., *What's Queer about Queer Studies Now? Social Text,* nos. 84–85 (Winter 2005).

For an analysis of the tensions between academics and activists, see Matilda Bernstein Sycamore, "Gay Shame: From Queer Autonomous Space to Direct Action Extravaganza," in *That's Revolting: Queer Strategies for Resisting Assimilation* (Brooklyn: Soft Scull Press, [2004] 2008), 268–95.

58. WOW Café was located at 330 East 11th Street in New York from 1982 to 1984, when the collective moved to its current site, 59–61 East 4th Street. For more on the history and criticism of WOW, see Sue-Ellen Case, *Split Britches: Lesbian Practice/Feminist Performance* (New York: Routledge, 1996); Jill Dolan, *The Feminist Spectator as Critic* (Ann Arbor: University of Michigan Press, 1991); Kate Davy, *Lady Dicks and Lesbian Brothers: Staging the Unimaginable at the WOW Café Theatre* (Ann Arbor: University of Michigan Press, 2010); and Alisa Solomon, "The WOW Café," in *A Sourcebook of Feminist Theatre and Performance: On and Beyond the Stage,* ed. Carol Martin (New York: Routledge, 1996), 42–52.

59. Hughes became one of the artists known as the NEA Four (along with Tim Miller, John Fleck and Karen Finley) who sued the National Endowment for the Humanities to have their grants reinstated after the NEA rescinded them.

60. The most comprehensive book of AIDS performance and protest is David Román's *Acts of Intervention: Performance, Gay Culture, and AIDS* (Bloomington: Indiana University Press, 1998).

61. Larry Kramer, *The Normal Heart and The Destiny of Me: Two Plays* (New York: Grove, 2000), 78.

62. Michael Warner, *The Trouble with Normal: Sex, Politics, and the Ethics of Queer Life* (New York: Free Press, 1999).

63. Carolyn Dinshaw, *Getting Medieval: Sexualities and Communities, Pre- and Postmodern* (Durham: Duke University Press, 1999).

64. Heather Love, *Feeling Backward: Loss and the Politics of Queer History* (Cambridge, Mass.: Harvard University Press, 2007).

65. Ibid., 4.

66. Elizabeth Freeman, *Time Binds: Queer Temporalities, Queer Histories* (Durham: Duke University Press, 2010), 62.

Chapter 1

The epigraph is from Valerie Solanas, letter to the editor of *The Diamondback,* the school newspaper of the University of Maryland, December 5, 1957, 4.

1. Paul Krassner, "Wonder Waif Meets Super Neuter," in *S.C.U.M. Manifesto,* by Valerie Solanas (New York: Olympia Press, 1968), 88.

2. Valerie Solanas, *Up Your Ass, or From the Cradle to the Boat, or The Big Suck, or Up from the Slime and "A Young Girl's Primer on How to Attain the Leisure Class, a Non-fictional Article Reprinted from Cavalier"* (NY: SCUM Book, 1967), 28. All citations from the play are taken from the copy of this book in the Avant-Garde Literature Collection at the Hofstra University Library.

3. I have consulted the following sources for biographical, historical, and critical information: Judy Michaelson, "Valerie: The Trouble Was Men," *New York Post,* June 5, 1968, 57; Marylin Bender, "Valeria Solanis [*sic*] a Heroine to Feminists," *New York Times,* June 14, 1968, 52; Diane Dorr-Dorynek, "Lonesome Cowboy—Reel 606," *East Village Other* 3, no. 26 (June 15, 1968): n.p.; Raphael Lennox, "The Martyrization of Valerie Solanas," *East Village Other* 3, no. 30 (June 28, 1968): 3, 20; Howard Smith and Brian Van der Horst, "Valerie Solanas Interview," *Village Voice,* July 25, 1977, 32; B. Ruby Rich, "Manifesto Destiny: Drawing a Bead on Valerie Solanas," *Village Voice Literary Supplement,* October 12, 1993, 18–19; Donny Smith, "Solanas," *Supplement to Dwan,* March 1994; Mary Harron, "Introduction: On Valerie Solanas," in *I Shot Andy Warhol,* by Mary Harron and Daniel Minahan (New York: Grove Press, 1995); Freddie Baer, "About Valerie Solanas," in *SCUM Manifesto,* by Valerie Solanas (San Francisco: AK Press, 1996), 51–60; Melissa Deem, "From Bobbitt to SCUM: Re-memberment,

Scatological Rhetorics, and Feminist Strategies in the Contemporary United States," *Public Culture* 8, no. 3 (1996): 511–37; Liz Jobey, "Solanas and Son," *Guardian Weekend*, August 24, 1996, T10; Donny Smith, *Solanas Supplement to Dwan Number 2*, May 1997; Donny Smith, "To Live with a Man is to Hate a Man (or Vice Versa)," *Holy Titclamps*, January 16, 1998; Judith Coburn, "Valerie's Gang," *East Bay Express*, November 19, 1999, 1, 8–9, 11, 13, 16; Laura Winkiel, "The 'Sweet Assassin' and the Performative Politics of *SCUM Manifesto*," in *The Queer Sixties*, ed. Patricia Juliana Smith (New York: Routledge, 1999), 62–86; Judith Coburn, "Solanes Lost and Found," *Village Voice*, January 12, 2000; Donny Smith, *The Third Solanas Supplement to Dwan*, n.d.; Dana Heller, "Shooting Solanas," *Feminist Studies* 27, no. 1 (2001): 167–89; James Harding, "The Simplest Surrealist Act: Valerie Solanas and the (Re)Assertion of Avant-garde Priorities," *TDR* 45, no. 4 (Winter 2001): 142–62; Steven Watson, *Factory Made: Warhol and the Sixties* (New York: Pantheon, 2003); Isabelle Collin Dufresne [Ultra Violet], *Famous for 15 Minutes: My Years with Andy Warhol* (New York: Harcourt Brace Jovanovich, 1988); Amanda Third, "'Shooting from the Hip': Valerie Solanas, the *SCUM Manifesto*, and the Apocalyptic Politics of Radical Feminism," *Hecate* 32, no. 2 (2006): 104–32; Breanne Fahs, "The Radical Possibilities of Valerie Solanas," *Feminist Studies* 34, no. 3 (Fall 2008): 591–621; Catherine Lord, "Wonder Waif Meets Super Neuter," *October* 132 (Spring 2010): 135–63; and Breanne Fahs, "Ti-Grace Atkinson and the Legacy of Radical Feminism," *Feminist Studies* 37, no. 3 (Fall 2011): 561–90.

4. E-mail correspondence with Judith Martinez, January 22, 2011.

5. Jon McKenzie, *Perform or Else: From Discipline to Performance* (New York: Routledge, 2001).

6. Watson, *Factory Made*, 36. The pregnancy to which Judith Martinez refers here was actually Solanas's second. The first occurred when she was fourteen.

7. In a letter to filmmaker Mary Harron complaining about her representation of the facts in *I Shot Andy Warhol*, Solanas's son, David Blackwell, states that the sailor who impregnated Valerie was married with three children, which is why the Blackwells took her and the baby in. The letter was sent care of the Andy Warhol Museum and is housed in its archives.

8. Watson, *Factory Made*, 36.

9. Ibid.

10. Valerie Solanas, *SCUM Manifesto* (New York: SCUM Book, 1967), 9. Unless otherwise noted, all citations are from this edition of the text, which Solanas self-published prior to the Olympia Press edition of 1968. This document is widely available in a number of libraries, including the Judson Memorial Church Archives at New York University's Fales Library.

11. The editors changed the title of Solanas's article from "A Young Girl's Primer on How to Attain the Leisure Class" to "For 2¢: Pain, the Survival Game Gets Pretty Ugly," ostensibly because they wanted to play on Harry Golden's popular 1959 memoir of Depression era New York, *For 2¢ Plain*. During the 1930s, one could get an egg cream for twenty-five cents, a chocolate milk for a dime, a chocolate soda for a nickel, or seltzer water, as the saying went, for "two cents plain." See Harry Golden, *For 2¢ Plain* (New York: World Publishing: 1958).

12. Valerie Solanas, "For 2¢: Pain, the Survival Game Gets Pretty Ugly," *Cavalier*, July 1966, 38.

13. Ibid., 40.

14. Solanas, *Up Your Ass*, n.p.

15. Ibid., 1.

16. Ibid.

17. Ibid.

18. Judith Halberstam, *Female Masculinity* (Durham: Duke University Press, 1998).
19. Solanas, *Up Your Ass*, 3.
20. Ibid., 5.
21. Ibid.
22. Ibid., 6.
23. Ibid., 5.
24. Ibid., 7.
25. Ibid., 7–8.
26. Ibid., 8.
27. Ibid.
28. Ibid., 8–9.
29. Ibid., 19.
30. Ibid., 10.
31. Solanas, *SCUM Manifesto*, 23.
32. Solanas, *Up Your Ass*, 10.
33. Ibid.
34. Ibid., 11.
35. Ibid., 13.
36. Ibid., 11.
37. Ibid., 12.
38. Ibid., 13.
39. Ibid., 14.
40. Ibid., 15.
41. Ibid.
42. Ibid.
43. Ibid., 16.
44. Ibid., 17.
45. Ibid.
46. Ibid.
47. Ibid.
48. Solanas, *SCUM Manifesto*, 1.
49. Ibid.
50. Solanas, *Up Your Ass*, 18.
51. Ibid., 23.
52. Ibid., 18.
53. Solanas, *SCUM Manifesto*, 1–2.
54. Solanas, *Up Your Ass*, 19.
55. When word got out that Oscar Wilde was to play *Salome* in drag, the play was banned by Lord Chamberlain's licensor of plays. Doric Wilson staged an adaptation of this play, titled *Now She Dances!*, at Caffe Cino in 1961.
56. Solanas, *Up Your Ass*, 21.
57. Ibid., 22.
58. Ibid., 23.
59. Ibid.
60. Ibid.
61. Ibid.
62. Ibid., 24.
63. Ibid., 24.
64. Ibid., 25.
65. Ibid.
66. Ibid.

67. Ibid.
68. Ibid., 26.
69. Ibid.
70. Ibid.
71. Ibid., 27.
72. Ibid.
73. Ibid.
74. Ibid., 28.
75. Ibid.
76. Ibid.
77. Ibid.
78. Ibid.
79. Ibid.
80. Ibid.
81. Ibid.
82. "We have passed beyond the absurd: our position is absolutely preposterous." This is the one-line manifesto of the Theatre of the Ridiculous. Ron Tavel hit on the term *ridiculous* while studying the Theatre of the Absurd in college. His collaborator, John Vaccaro, said the name was inspired by the actress Yvette Hawkins, who used *ridiculous* to describe the group's rehearsal process. See Bonnie Marranca, Gautam Dasgupta, and Jack Smith, eds., *Theatre of the Ridiculous* (Baltimore: Johns Hopkins University Press, 1998); David Kaufman, *Ridiculous! The Theatrical Life and Times of Charles Ludlam* (New York: Applause Books, 2002); Stephen J. Bottoms, *Playing Underground: A Critical History of the 1960s Off-Off-Broadway Movement* (Ann Arbor: University of Michigan Press, 2004); and Rick Roemer, *Charles Ludlam and the Ridiculous Theatrical Company: Critical Analyses of 29 Plays* (Jefferson, NC: McFarland, 2010).
83. The inaugural evening of the Theatre of the Ridiculous consisted of a double bill at Manhattan's Coda Gallery on July 29, 1965, featuring *Shower* and *The Life of Juanita Castro,* both of which were originally film scenarios Ron Tavel had written for Andy Warhol's Factory. Soon after, Vaccaro and Tavel founded The Play-House of the Ridiculous, which featured a number of Factory superstars. A conflict over *Conquest of the Universe* (aka *When Queens Collide*) led actor and playwright Charles Ludlam to form his own troupe, the Ridiculous Theatrical Company, in 1967.
84. Lola Pashalinski plays a psychiatrist who analyzes Solanas after the shooting in the film *I Shot Andy Warhol.*
85. E-mail correspondence with Judith Martinez, January 19, 2011.
86. The Village Plaza hotel is the return address listed on Solanas's 1965 copyright application for the play.
87. *The Realist* debuted in the spring of 1958 and was published out of the offices of *Mad* magazine. Famous for its parodies and political cartoons, the periodical also provided a forum for a number of conspiracy theories.
88. E-mail correspondence with Paul Krassner, November 8, 2010.
89. Krassner, "Wonder Waif Meets Super Neuter," 88.
90. Ibid., 89.
91. Launched in 1952 by Fawcett Publications, *Cavalier* originally featured short stories and serial novels by the press's Gold Medal authors, including Richard Prather and Mickey Spillane. Purchased in the 1960s by the DuGent Publishing Corporation, *Cavalier* evolved into an erotica magazine. It continues today as an online porn site.
92. The Supreme Court upheld the decision in *Ginzburg v. United States,* 383 U.S. 463 (March 21, 1966), and the publisher served eight months in a federal prison on obscenity charges.

93. Krassner, "Wonder Waif Meets Super Neuter," 88.

94. Nat Finkelstein, a Factory photographer from 1964 to 1966, claims he introduced Solanas to Warhol at the behest of an ex-girlfriend named Ellen Marcus, who met Richie Berlin, sister of Factory superstar Brigid Polk, and Solanas in a mental institution. After a falling out with Warhol, Nat gave Valerie his private phone number. While Solanas did have Warhol's private phone number and address, I can find no confirmation that she was institutionalized prior to the assassination attempt in 1968. See Nat Finkelstein, "The Nat Finkelstein Interview," Planet Group Entertainment, 2009, http://planetgroupentertainment.squarespace.com/the-nat-finkelstein-interview/ (accessed January 2010).

95. Robert Heide's *The Bed* premiered at the Sullivan Street Theater in March 1965 before moving to Caffe Cino on July 7, 1965, where it ran for 150 performances. Warhol filmed the play in the fall of 1965. According to Heide, "[T]here followed a quarrel with FuFu Smith, the producer, about who owned the film. Andy put *The Bed* into his secret vault though he later spliced portions of it into *Chelsea Girls*" (Robert Heide, "Village '65 Revisited," letter to the editor, *Village Voice,* July 27, 1982). The film version of *The Bed* opened on April 26, 1966, at Jonas Mekas's Filmmakers Cinematheque on 41st Street.

96. Andy Warhol and Pat Hackett, *Popism: The Warhol Sixties* (New York: Mariner Books, 1990), 190.

97. Ibid.

98. This letter is in the Valerie Solanas collection at the Warhol Museum archives. Solanas mailed it to Andy at his home address, 1342 Lexington Avenue, as she did on every known occasion she wrote to him. Her return address is listed as the Village Plaza hotel.

99. Gretchen Berg, "Andy Warhol: My True Story," in *I'll Be Your Mirror: The Selected Andy Warhol Interviews, 1962–1987,* eds. Goldsmith, Wolf, and Koestenbaum, (New York: Da Capo Press, 2004), 91–92. This interview, considered by many to be "the most important that Andy Warhol gave in the '60s," was first published November 1, 1966, in *East Village Other.*

100. Krassner, "Wonder Waif Meets Super Neuter," 87.

101. Goldsmith, Wolf, and Koestenbaum, *I'll Be Your Mirror,* 92. Some of the dialogue attributed to Warhol in this interview is actually the reporter's questions and comments converted into responses. For example, "I guess she thought that was the perfect thing for Andy Warhol" is something Gretchen Berg said to Andy during their conversation. I realized this when I saw a rerun of Ric Burns's *Andy Warhol: A Documentary Film* (PBS, 2006), which incorporates part of the audiotape of the Berg-Warhol interview. Anyone who has participated in or viewed an interview with Warhol knows that he actively tried to seduce his interlocutor into the position of speaking for him.

102. Mary Harron suggests that Warhol saw in Solanas a kindred spirit. She writes, "When Andy Warhol looked into the eyes of Valerie Solanas, he would have seen much more of himself than when he looked into the eyes of a beautiful debutante like Edie Sedgewick [sic] or one of the gorgeous male hustlers who decorated the Factory. Warhol and Valerie had much in common: both were Catholic, born into blue-collar families; had spent their childhood in poverty; were intellectually precocious; and had experienced being tormented at school. Perhaps, most importantly, both claimed to have rejected sex, although for different reasons: Valerie had too much sex; Warhol, too little" (Harron, "Introduction," xix).

103. After it became clear that Warhol had lost Edie Sedgwick to Bob Dylan, he said to Robert Heide, on the sidewalk at the site where dancer Fred Herko had jumped to his death from his apartment window, "I wonder if Edie will commit suicide. I hope

she lets me know so I can film it." Victor Bockris, *The Life and Death of Andy Warhol* (London: Fourth Estate, 1998), 236.

104. Catherine Lord cites this ad in the version of "Wonder Waif Meets Super Neuter" published in *The Art of Queering in Art*, ed. Gavin Butts (Birmingham, UK: Article Press, 2007). She was also the first person to cite Solanas's letter asking Warhol to return the script. The *Village Voice* ad offering "photo offset copies" of the play might explain the existence of a partial script (starting with page 30) in the hands of a New York art dealer named Margo Feiden, who claims Solanas gave her the play on the morning of the shooting. Glenn O'Brien, who viewed the document in Feiden's possession, wrote, "It seems to be the original typescript. It's not a carbon copy." Feiden declined my request to examine the script. See Glenn O'Brien, "History ReWrite," *Interview*, April 24, 2009, http://www.interviewmagazine.com/culture/history-rewrite/ (accessed January 2010).

105. This ad appeared in the *Village Voice*, February 2, 1967, 5.

106. That Solanas was a terrible typist is corroborated by the fact that the New York NOW chapter's president, Ti-Grace Atkinson, had *SCUM Manifesto* retyped before she issued it in a press release after Solanas's arrest. See the transcript of Ti-Grace Atkinson's press release, delivered June 13, 1968, at the New York Criminal Court, in the Florynce Kennedy Papers at Harvard's Schlesinger Library. Solanas clearly had a deep-seated aversion to secretarial labor of any kind. Her prison records indicate that she refused to take clerical courses as part of her rehabilitation training, opting instead to study cosmetology and work in the kitchen.

107. Phone conversation with Mary Harron, March 24, 2011.

108. *Up Your Ass* opened for previews in November 1999 at George Coates's Performance Works Theater on McAllister Street in San Francisco's Tenderloin district. Coates learned about the play from his assistant director, Eddy Falconer, who after seeing Harron's film suggested that they stage *Up Your Ass*. Coates was less interested in exploring the play's relevance to feminist and queer history than he was in using *Up Your Ass* as a vehicle through which to talk about censorship in the wake of the National Endowment for the Arts' recently instituted decency clause. He staged the play on a double bill with *The Archbishop's Ceiling* by Arthur Miller, whom Solanas had met in the lobby of the Chelsea Hotel in the 1960s. Because *Up Your Ass* was ineligible for funding, based on the new NEA guidelines, Coates produced it on a shoestring budget, double and in some cases triple casting many of the roles, which he filled by capitalizing on the abundance of talent in the Bay Area's underground (i.e., "amateur") performance community. Worried that he would have trouble pitching the play as a comedy, not just because of its subject matter but because of the author's reputation as a humorless, homicidal dyke, Coates staged *Up Your Ass* as a musical, setting it on a sidewalk in front of a karaoke bar. To increase the camp factor, Coates went with an all-female cast featuring many members of the drag king community. The show ran at Coates's theater in San Francisco January 12–April 8, 2000, and again January 18–21, 2001, traveling between these dates to PS122 in New York, where it played February 7–25, 2001. Conversation with Eddy Falconer, May 26, 2004.

109. The copy of the script Billy Name found in his lighting trunk, which is now housed in the Warhol Museum, is missing both the front and back covers as well as the final pages of the book, which consists primarily of the conclusion of the *Cavalier* article. In addition, the Name/Warhol copy includes corrections, in Solanas's handwriting, on the bottom of page 4, another on the top of page 8, and it also shows the phone number of the Chelsea Hotel scribbled on the front. None of these edits appear in the Hofstra script, which is otherwise full and complete and includes the covers and manuscript pages the Name/Warhol copy are missing. In a 1996 article by Paul Morrissey in

Vogue magazine, he confirms that the 1967 version of the play circulating at the Factory had, at one time, a cover. See Paul Morrissey, "Pop Shots" *Vogue*, May 1996, 152.

110. Harron, "Introduction," xviii. In 1996, Harron stated that she would not be surprised if other copies of the (1967) script existed. See Donny Smith, "Valerie Is Good and Bad . . . Crazy and Sane: An Interview with Mary Harron," in *Solanas Supplement to Dwan*, Number 2, May 1997.

111. Martin Puchner, *Poetry of the Revolution: Marx, Manifestos, and the Avant-Gardes* (Princeton: Princeton University Press, 2006), 215–16.

112. Harding, "The Simplest Surrealist Act," 143.

113. Ibid., 158, 151.

114. Ibid., 154.

115. Ibid.

116. Harding cites Freddie Baer's essay "About Valerie Solanas" in the 1996 AK Press edition of *SCUM Manifesto* as evidence that there are two different plots of *Up Your Ass*. Baer's source is Donny Smith's *Solanas Supplement to Dwan*, a queer poetry zine (March 1994). Smith's account is drawn from Ultra Violet's fictionalized memoir, *Famous for Fifteen Minutes: My Years with Andy Warhol* (1988). Ultra Violet's "evidence" is an ambiguously worded paragraph in a *New York Post* story by Judy Michaelson, "Valerie: The Trouble Was Men," which ran just two days after the shooting. The article states that Solanas "wrote a play with an unprintable title whose hero or heroine was a man-hating hustler and panhandler named Bongi. It ends with a mother strangling her son—woman killing man" (57). It is clear from this sentence that Michaelson had neither read nor seen the play, as she does not know Bongi's gender.

117. As part of their routine maintenance, archivists at the Library of Congress purged the script of *Up Your Ass* that Solanas submitted as part of her 1967 copyright application. Because the library retains unpublished manuscripts for a longer period of time than it does published ones, the 1965 script is still on file.

118. See Pati Hertling's interview with Bettina Köster, a former student of Bob Brady's, in *Girls Like Us,* no. 2 (Spring 2006).

119. E-mail correspondence with Norman Marshal, November 16, 2010.

120. This ad appeared in the *Village Voice* on February 2, 1967, 22.

121. Carolee Schneemann, "Solanas in a Sea of Men," in *Imagining Her Erotics: Essays, Interviews, Projects* (Cambridge, MA.: MIT Press, 2003), 90–94.

122. The ad appeared in the *Village Voice* on February 9, 1967, 24. Tony Scherman and David Dalton cite this ad in *Pop: The Genius of Andy Warhol*, but they make no reference to Solanas's other ad in the same issue (in the book section), nor do they mention the notices she placed on February 2, February 16, and February 23. See their *Pop: The Genius of Andy Warhol* (New York: Harper, 2009), 374. The February 2 ad suggests that the staged reading was originally scheduled as a single evening's performance but was extended. The February 9 notice states that the show would "Beg. Feb. 15." The fourth and final *Village Voice* ad for the script appeared on February 23 in the Bulletin Board section, on page 2.

123. The February 9 ad also mentions the Randy Wicker radio show, but it does not include the cast list. Unfortunately, Wicker cannot remember the date on which the interview with Solanas took place, and I have been unable to locate a tape or transcript of her appearance on the show. Phone conversation with Randy Wicker, February 7, 2011. From 1967 to 1971, Wicker operated Underground Uplift Unlimited, a head shop that sold slogan buttons, posters, and books. This is one of the shops Solanas lists as locations selling her play in a companion ad in the book section, which I cited earlier.

124. This ad appeared in the *Village Voice* on February 16, 1967, 22. An ad for the script appears on page 2.

125. Albert Williams, "The Quintessential Image/In Her Own Words," *Chicago Reader,* January 18, 1990, http://m.chicagoreader.com/chicago/the-quintessential-im agein-her-own-words/Content?oid=875070 (accessed January 2010).

126. Gary Tucker is best known for his personal and professional association with Tennessee Williams. He directed Williams's *A House Not Meant to Stand* at the Goodman Theater in Chicago, and he also worked with the playwright at the Alliance Theater in Atlanta. Tucker died of AIDS in 1989. See Kaufman, *Ridiculous!,* esp. 134–41.

127. See Ellen Stern, "Best Bets," *New York,* April 10, 1978, 62.

128. Actress Phyllis Raphael recalls auditioning for Solanas's *Up Your Ass.* She told me, "I'm pretty sure it was for La MaMa as I had done some work there before and I suspect that's how I knew about the audition. I recall the audition being held in a large space somewhere in the East Village . . . not an orthodox theater." E-mail correspondence with Phyllis Raphael November 14, 2010. From Raphael's description, the location sounds as if it could have been the Directors' Theater. Raphael admits her memory is cloudy: "It wasn't exactly a highlight of my acting career and my best sense of it was that the material wasn't of very much dramatic value or importance nor did the audition appear to me to be on the up and up. I can tell you that she came on to me and called the next day to offer me a part but I wasn't interested. The experience slipped completely from my memory until three or four years later when I read about the Warhol shooting and recognized the shooter as the woman I'd auditioned for." E-mail correspondence with Phyllis Raphael, November 12, 2010. See also her book, *Off the Kings Road: Lost and Found in London* (London: Other Press, 2006). It seems likely that Solanas would have pitched her play to Ellen Stewart at La MaMa, but I have not been able to find any evidence of this.

129. Paul Krassner, *Confessions of a Raving, Unconfined Nut: Misadventures in the Counter-Culture* (New York: Simon and Schuster, 1993), 122.

130. The Evergreen Theatre, located at 53 E. 11th Street, served as the home of Charles Ludlam's Ridiculous Theatrical Company in the mid-1970s. Strapped for cash, Evergreen's owner, Barney Rosset sold the building to the Baha'i Foundation, prompting the troupe to move to One Sheridan Square. For an analysis of Solanas's turn in *I, a Man,* see Jennifer Doyle, *Sex Objects: Art and the Dialectics of Desire* (Minneapolis: University of Minnesota Press, 2006).

131. Letter from Geoffrey LeGear to Andy Warhol, December 3, 1968, Warhol Museum archives.

132. Maurice Girodias, Publisher's preface to *S.C.U.M. Manifesto,* by Valerie Solanas (New York: Grove Press, 1968), vii–viii.

133. Solanas took issue with changes Girodias made to her text, including the title, which he printed as *S.C.U.M. Manifesto.* Solanas issued a corrected edition in 1977, after she was released from prison.

134. Scherman and Dalton, *Pop,* 420. Feist does not give the date Solanas came to the Roundabout. Scherman and Dalton state that the encounter took place in "mid-1967" (419).

135. Robert Patrick, "Caffe Cino Pictures," Caffe Cino blog, http://caffecino.word press.com/1915/01/01/issues/img_0004_2-2/ (accessed January 2010).

136. E-mail correspondence with Robert Patrick, November 10, 2010.

137. Ibid.

138. Patrick, a self-described "temple slave," his term for Cino devotees, played a primary role in the Caffe's scheduled productions and the improvisational performances that took place behind the scenes. His semiautobiographical novel about a fictitious Greenwich Village coffeehouse describes in salacious detail the hedonistic pursuits and homoerotic activities of the inner circle, including rampant drug use and casual group sex. See Robert Patrick, *Temple Slave* (New York: Masquerade Books, 1994).

139. Magie Dominic, *The Queen of Peace Room* (Waterloo, ON: Wilfrid Laurier University Press, 2002), 56.

140. Ibid.

141. Ibid.

142. Ibid.

143. Ibid.

144. Ibid.

145. Ibid. Dominic writes, "There were no Xerox machines in the '60s and she'd trusted him with the only copy of her manuscript" (60). As I have shown, Solanas had multiple copies of both editions of her play.

146. Koutoukas's *Medea* premiered at La MaMa (October 13–17, 1965) before moving to Cino (October 19–31). See Wendell C. Stone, *Caffe Cino: The Birthplace of Off-Off-Broadway* (Carbondale, IL: Southern Illinois University Press, 2005), 89.

147. E-mail correspondence with Robert Patrick, November 10, 2010.

148. Unsuited for the management position in which he had been cast, and caught in a spiral of drug addiction, Charles Stanley almost ran Caffe Cino into the ground. Were it not for Michael Smith and Wolfgang Zimmerman's assumption of the financial and clerical responsibilities, the Caffe would not have survived into 1968.

149. In an interview with *Village Voice* reporter Howard Smith, conducted after Solanas was released from prison, she says about the Society for Cutting Up Men, "It's hypothetical. No, hypothetical is the wrong word. It's just a literary device. There's no organization called SCUM—there never was, and there never will be." Pressing Solanas on her statement, Smith interjects, "It's just you." To which Solanas replies, "It's not even me. There's no organization. It's either nothing or it's just me, depending on how you define it. I mean, I thought of it as a state of mind. In other words, women who think a certain way are in SCUM. Men who think a certain way are in the men's auxiliary of SCUM." See Smith and Van der Horst, "Valerie Solanas Interview," 32.

150. This ad appears in the *Village Voice's* Bulletin Board on page 2. The Farband House served as the international headquarters of the Farband Labor Zionist Order. It housed many groups, including the Jewish National Workers Alliance of America. The building consisted of meeting rooms and an auditorium/theater space.

151. "Valerie Solanis [*sic*] Interviews Andy," an undated transcript of an undated audio file in the Warhol Museum archives. The events discussed, including Solanas's ejection from the Chelsea Hotel and the production of Tavel's *Vinyl* at Caffe Cino (which opened October 31, 1967), suggest that the audiotape was made in early November. The title of the document and the artificially structured way in which Solanas begins asking Warhol questions about *SCUM* suggest that the interview may have been an assignment Andy paid Valerie to do or that it was a story she was preparing in the hopes of selling it to a newspaper or magazine. Any "formal" interview Solanas may have been conducting was interrupted by the arrival of several superstars, including Viva, Brigid Polk, and Lou Reed, all of whom, interestingly enough, were arguing with Warhol about money.

152. This ad appeared in the *Village Voice,* May 18, 1967, 2.

153. "Valerie Solanis Interviews Andy." A copy of this edition of *SCUM Manifesto* is housed in the Warhol Museum archives.

154. This letter to Andy Warhol, dated August 1, 1967, is housed in the Warhol Museum archives. Solanas began selling the complete edition of the *Manifesto* in the *Village Voice* on October 19, 1967. *I, a Man* was shot in July and opened at the Hudson Theatre near Times Square on August 24.

155. "Valerie Solanis Interviews Andy."

156. E-mail correspondence with Judith Martinez, January 22, 2011.

157. The copy of *SCUM Manifesto* in the Judson Memorial Church Archives in New

York University's Fales Library is housed with all of the scripts that were sent to the theater for consideration.

158. Bob Spitz, *Dylan: A Biography* (New York: W. W. Norton, 1991), 115.

159. Candy Cane, aka Candy Darling (né James Lawrence Slattery), was a theater actress who met Warhol in 1967. She starred in several Factory films, including *Women in Revolt* (1971), a satire of Solanas's *SCUM Manifesto,* in which she plays a Long Island socialite drawn into a woman's liberation group called PIGS (Politically Involved Girls). According to Mary Harron, Solanas knew Candy from the Hotel Earle, an SRO that served as "a kind of terminus for deviants, with separate wings for lesbians and drag queens" (Harron, "Introduction," xv).

160. "Valerie Solanis Interviews Andy."

161. This original "Silver" Factory (1962–68) was located on the fifth floor of 231 East 47th Street. The building no longer exists.

162. "Long involved story" is the phrase Solanas used to describe her relationship with Andy Warhol during her intake interview at Westfield State Farm, New York State Department of Corrections, in Bedford Hills on June 13, 1969. I received a copy of this intake interview through the New York State Freedom of Information Law (FOIL).

163. Girodias, Publisher's preface to *S.C.U.M. Manifesto,* 17.

164. Roxanne Dunbar-Ortiz, *Outlaw Woman: A Memoir of the War Years, 1960–1975* (San Francisco: City Lights, 2001), 119.

165. Ibid., 120. Dunbar-Ortiz flew from Mexico to Boston, the site of early-nineteenth-century feminist and abolitionist activism. She met a woman named Dana Densmore at a Draft Resistance meeting, and together they placed an ad announcing the formation of "the FEMALE LIBERATION FRONT FOR HUMAN LIBERATION." At the meeting, the group "read the 'SCUM Manifesto' as a sacred text while laughing hilariously at Valerie's wicked satire," and they emulated Valerie by writing and selling their propaganda on the street, charging men more than women (128). Dunbar-Ortiz and Densmore founded Cell 16 and the journal *No More Fun and Games.*

166. Bender, "Valeria Solanis a Heroine to Feminists," 52; Lennox, "The Martyrization of Valerie Solanas," 20.

167. Ti-Grace Atkinson, *Amazon Odyssey: The First Collection of Writings by the Political Pioneer of the Women's Movement* (New York: Link Books, 1974), 14. In fall of 1967, Shulamith Firestone and Pam Allen founded New York Radical Women. Early members included Ros Baxandall, Carol Hanisch, Pat Mainardi, Robin Morgan, Irene Peslikis, Kathie Sarachild, and Ellen Willis. In *Daring to Be Bad: Radical Feminism in America, 1967–1975* (Minneapolis: University of Minnesota Press, 1989), Alice Echols notes, "Radical feminists in NYRW knew next to nothing about Solanas until she shot and nearly killed Pop artist Andy Warhol in June 1968" (105).

168. Lennox, "The Martyrization of Valerie Solanas," 9.

169. Dunbar-Ortiz, *Outlaw Woman,* 123.

170. Ibid., 138.

171. Roxanne Dunbar-Ortiz, "From the Cradle to the Boat: On the Occasion of the World Premiere of *Up Your Ass,* a Feminist Historian Remembers Valerie Solanas," *San Francisco Bay Guardian Online,* January 5, 2000, http://sfbg.com (accessed January 2010). Dunbar-Ortiz states in this article, which she published after seeing the George Coates production of *Up Your Ass* in San Francisco, that Solanas charged her and Dana Densmore with "a big task—to get a copy of Valerie's play, *Up Your Ass,* for her. That's the only regret she seems to have about shooting Warhol, that she didn't get her play back. He had the only copy of the play for two years and kept putting Valerie off, then he either lost or stole it. . . . the document itself is important to her, her own type-written copy." E-mail correspondence with Roxanne Dunbar-Ortiz, November 15–16,

2010. As I have demonstrated, Solanas appears to have always been in possession of a copy of the script. If Warhol lost her original or a mimeograph, it was not her *only* copy of the play.

Chapter 2

1. Ti-Grace Atkinson, *Amazon Odyssey: The First Collection of Writings by the Political Pioneer of the Women's Movement* (New York: Link Books, 1974), 9. The Feminists (1968–73) included Sheila Michaels, Barbara Mehrhof, Pamela Kearon, Sheila Cronan, and Anne Koedt (author of the influential "Myth of the Vaginal Orgasm," who left the group in 1969 to cofound New York Radical Feminists). Atkinson parted with The Feminists in 1971.

2. Ibid., 41.

3. Ibid., 132.

4. Ibid., 134.

5. Ibid., 99.

6. Alice Echols, *Daring to Be Bad: Radical Feminism in America, 1967–1975* (Minneapolis: University of Minnesota Press, 1989), 178.

7. The Feminists, "Women: Do You Know the Facts about Marriage?," in *Sisterhood Is Powerful: An Anthology of Writings from the Women's Liberation Movement,* ed. Robin Morgan (New York: Vintage Books, 1970), 601.

8. Ibid., 602.

9. See Sara Davidson, "An 'Oppressed Majority' Demands Its Rights: The Cause of Women's Equality Draws a Growing Number of Active—and Angry—Female Militants," *Life,* December 12, 1969, 66–78.

10. The Feminists, "Women," 603.

11. Sheila Cronan, "Marriage," in *Radical Feminism,* eds. Anne Koedt, Ellen Levine, and Anita Rapone (New York: Harper Collins, 1973), 219.

12. Adrienne Rich, "Compulsory Heterosexuality and Lesbian Existence," *Signs: Journal of Women in Culture and Society* 5, no. 4 (Summer 1980). A critique of marriage was integral to first-wave feminism. Although suffrage was the primary goal of this movement, marriage reform was of central concern, as is evidenced by one of the founding documents, the *Declaration of Rights and Sentiments,* delivered at the first women's rights convention in Seneca Falls, New York, in 1848 and signed by sixty-eight women and thirty-two men. See "Report of the Women's Rights Convention," http://www.nps.gov/wori/historyculture/report-of-the-womans-rights-convention.htm (accessed January 2009).

13. Barbara Smith, Preface to *Home Girls: A Black Feminist Anthology,* ed. Barbara Smith (New Brunswick, NJ: Rutgers University Press, 2000), xiv.

14. Pat Parker, "Revolution: It's Not Neat or Pretty or Quick," in *This Bridge Called My Back: Writings by Radical Women of Color,* ed. Cherríe Moraga and Gloria Anzaldúa (San Francisco: Kitchen Table Women of Color Press, 1983), 241. Parker's poem "Womanslaughter" (1978) chronicles her sister's death at the hands of her estranged husband, who was convicted not of murder but of manslaughter. Outraged by this travesty of justice, Parker went to Brussels in 1976 to file a complaint with the International Tribunal on Crimes against Women.

15. Beverly Smith, "The Wedding," in *Home Girls: A Black Feminist Anthology,* ed. Barbara Smith (New Brunswick, NJ: Rutgers University Press, 2000), 166–67.

16. Gloria Anzaldúa, *Borderlands/LaFrontera: The New Mestiza* (San Francisco: Spinsters and Aunt Lute, 1987), 22.

17. Marianne Moore, "Marriage," in *Complete Poems* (New York: Penguin, 1994), 69, 68.

18. Carolyn Dinshaw, *Getting Medieval: Sexualities and Communities, Pre- and Postmodern* (Durham: Duke University Press, 1999), 1.

19. The very first WITCH zap took place on Halloween 1968 when a group of protesters hexed Wall Street. In covens across the country, protesters targeted sexist, racist, and imperialist corporations such as the United Fruit Company, AT&T, and Traveler's Insurance Company. One of the cells showered the Sociology Department at the University of Chicago with hair and nail trimmings after it denied tenure to a feminist professor.

20. WITCH, "WITCH Documents," in *Sisterhood Is Powerful: An Anthology of Writings from the Women's Liberation Movement,* ed. Robin Morgan (New York: Vintage Books, 1970), 610.

21. Ibid., 610, 613.

22. Ibid., 613.

23. Ibid.

24. *Oxford English Dictionary,* www.oed.com (accessed January 2010).

25. See, for example, *The Zap Gun,* a 1967 science fiction novel by Phillip K. Dick.

26. Tom Dalzell, ed., *The Routledge Dictionary of Modern American Slang and Unconventional English* (New York: Routledge, 2005), 1075.

27. Tom Hayden, *Port Huron Statement: The Visionary Call of the 1960s Revolution* (New York: Thunder's Mouth Press, 2005), 53.

28. Ibid.

29. Zaps share many features of *actos,* Luis Valdez's term for the short, comical skits created by Teatro Campesino, which blend Brechtian tactics with elements of the commedia dell'arte, folk plays, and agitprop that were staged, from 1965 on, in union halls, churches, and on flatbed trucks in fields in order to educate farmworkers about their rights and inspire action, specifically to strike against the growers. See Jorge Huerta, *Chicano Theater: Themes and Forms* (Bloomington: Indiana University Press, 1982). See also Yolanda Broyles-González, *El Teatro Campesino: Theater in the Chicano Movement* (Austin: University of Texas Press, 1994). *Actos* may have directly or indirectly influenced the Yippies' zap actions as Teatro Campesino and the Diggers both have roots in the San Francisco Mime Troupe.

30. Charlotte Canning, *Feminist Theaters in the U.S.A.: Staging Women's Experience* (New York: Routledge, 1996), 42.

31. Abbie Hoffman, *Revolution for the Hell of It* (New York: Dial Press, 1968), 59. See also Jerry Rubin, *Do IT! Scenarios of Revolution* (New York: Simon and Schuster, 1970).

32. Hoffman, *Revolution for the Hell of It,* 81.

33. Other Yippies who participated in WITCH were Nancy Kurshan, Sharon Krebs, and Judy Gumbo. Noteworthy members who were not Yippies but were active in the New Left include Jo Freeman, Florika, Peggy Dobbins, and Naomi Jaffe.

34. Organized by New York Radical Women (NYRW), the 1968 Miss America zap protested women's enslavement to beauty standards. Hundreds of demonstrators picketed the pageant, tossed implements of patriarchal oppression and female torture (including bras, high heels, *Playboy,* and *Ladies Home Journal*) into a Freedom Trash can, and called for a boycott of all commercial products supporting the beauty industry. Activists took turns parading a live sheep up and down the boardwalk before crowning it queen in a mock ceremony. A handful of radicals posing as pageant viewers infiltrated the convention hall, smuggling in banners, which they unfurled from the balcony the moment the beauty queen was announced, shouting, "No More Miss America!," "Freedom for Women!," and "Women's Liberation." As riot police descended on the demonstrators, camera operators panned from the stage to the commotion, giving

viewers across the country their first glimpse of the women's liberation movement, live on network television. The Redstockings' online archive contains photographs, press releases, and newspaper reports from the 1968 and 1969 demonstrations (http://www.redstockings.org), as does Jo Freeman's web archive (http://www.jofreeman.com/photos/MissAm1969.html). See also Carol Hanisch, "What Can Be Learned: A Critique of the Miss America Protest," originally published in *Notes from the Second Year*, archived on her website (http://www.carolhanisch.org/CHwritings/MissACritique.html).

35. Robin Morgan, ed., *Sisterhood Is Powerful: An Anthology of Writings from the Women's Liberation Movement* (New York: Vintage Books, 1970), 603.

36. Ibid., 605.

37. Ibid., 604.

38. Robin Morgan, *Going Too Far: The Personal Chronicle of a Feminist* (New York: Random House, 1977), 64.

39. Judy Klemesrud, "It Was a Special Show—and the Audience Was Special Too," *New York Times*, February 17, 1969, 39.

40. Ibid.

41. Morgan was married from 1962 to 1983 to Kenneth Pitchford, who would go on to become one of the founding members of the Gay Liberation Front and the Effeminists.

42. Morgan, *Going Too Far*, 78.

43. Ibid., 79.

44. Ibid., 72, emphasis original.

45. Morgan and her fellow WITCHes identified as "self-styled politicos" rather than "radical feminists," the term used by the Redstockings and groups that privileged consciousness-raising and the development of theoretical tracts over direct action. Despite Morgan's efforts to separate WITCH from the Redstockings, both groups shared a common origin, the NYRW, and both aimed to make visible the relationship between the personal and the political. See Morgan's "Three Articles on WITCH" in *Going Too Far*, 71–81.

46. Canning, *Feminist Theaters in the U.S.A.*, 43. For additional accounts of the WITCH Bridal Fair protest, see Echols, *Daring to Be Bad*; Karla Jay, *A Dyke Life: From Growing Up to Growing Old, A Celebration of Lesbian Experience* (New York: Basic Books, 1995); and Susan Brownmiller, in *Our Time: Memoir of a Revolution* (New York: Dell, 1999).

47. Morgan, *Going Too Far*, 122.

48. Ibid., 81.

49. Ibid., 122.

50. Ibid., 123.

51. Ibid., 10, 72.

52. Ibid., 127.

53. Ibid., 126, emphasis original.

54. For more on *How to Make a Woman*, see Helen Krich Chinoy and Linda Walsh Jenkins, *Women in American Theatre*, 3rd ed. (New York: Theatre Communications Group, 2006), 275–77; and Canning, *Feminist Theaters in the U.S.A.*, 160–61.

55. Simone de Beauvoir, *The Second Sex*, trans. and ed. H. M. Parshley (New York: Vintage Books, [1952] 1989), 267.

56. See, for example, David Eisenbach, *Gay Power: An American Revolution* (New York: Carroll and Graf Publishers, 2006); Vern L. Bullough, *Before Stonewall: Activists for Gay and Lesbian Rights in Historical Context* (Binghamton, NY: Harrington Park Press, 2002); and Steve Capsuto, *Alternate Channels: The Uncensored Story of Gay and Lesbian Images on Radio and Television* (New York: Ballantine Books, 2000).

57. Early GAA members included Arthur Evans, Arthur Bell, Jim Owles (the first president), Marty Robinson, Kay Lahusen, Sylvia Rivera, Marsha P. Johnson, Brenda Howard, Vito Russo, and Morty Manford. The group was most active from 1970 to 1974, when its headquarters (the Firehouse on Wooster Street in Soho, an important LGBT community center) was set ablaze by arsonists. The collective published the *Gay Activist* newspaper until 1980.

58. For accounts of GAA from founding and early members, see Donn Teal, *The Gay Militants* (New York: St. Martin's Press, 1971) and Arthur Bell, *Dancing the Gay Lib Blues: A Year in the Homosexual Liberation Movement* (New York: Simon and Schuster, 1971). For a less celebratory, more critical history, see Toby Marotta, *The Politics of Homosexuality: How Lesbians and Gay Men Have Made Themselves a Political and Social Force in Modern America* (Boston: Houghton Mifflin, 1981), 71–195.

59. Larry P. Gross, *Up from Invisibility: Lesbians, Gay Men, and the Media in America* (New York: Columbia University Press, 2001), 46.

60. GAA zapped conferences by the Association for the Advancement of Behavior Therapy and the American Psychological Association where motions to change the classification of homosexuality as a psychopathology were hotly debated.

61. Michael Durham, "Homosexuals in Revolt: The Year One Liberation Movement Turned Militant," *Life,* December 31, 1971, 65.

62. Quoted in Gross, *Up from Invisibility,* 46.

63. Eisenbach, *Gay Power,* 157, emphasis mine.

64. Eric Marcus, *Making Gay History: The Half Century Fight for Lesbian and Gay Equal Rights* (New York: Harper, 2002), 154.

65. Randy Wicker filmed the zap and the GAA meeting at the Firehouse in which activists plotted precisely how they would execute the protest, including who would serve as spokesmen for the event and what they would say. Whereas many political organizations in the 1960s and 1970s avoided archiving their material, for fear it would fall into the hands of government agencies, GAA recorded most of its protests. It used these tapes to rehearse for future events but also as recruiting tools. Members often played footage of zaps during community meetings, conferences, and dances at the Firehouse.

66. Father Clement founded The Church of the Beloved Disciple (1968–1986), the first major urban apostolic and sacramental house of worship serving the LGBT community in New York. He performed "Holy Unions" for couples, and took part in this ceremony himself. In 1970, he was joined with his partner John Noble by the Revered Troy Perry of the Metropolitan Community Church in a service at the Performing Garage Theatre.

67. During the planning meeting, GAA members agreed that it was best to avoid the topic of *gay marriage* and to focus instead on the issue of *gay rights*, specifically the right of gays to their own relationships. Thus the decision to call the action an "engagement party." Once the zap began, however, both the activists and the employees at the Marriage Licensing Bureau referred to the event as a "wedding reception."

68. David Eng, *The Feeling of Kinship: Queer Liberalism and the Racialization of Intimacy* (Durham: Duke University Press, 2010).

69. Bruce Voeller, the third president of GAA, was a biology professor and a divorced father of three. He used his charisma and movie star good looks to achieve important legal and social reforms such as child custody rights and encouraging health officials and politicians to use the name AIDS instead of the more stigma-inducing GRID (Gay-Related Immune Deficiency). Voeller disapproved of more militant gay activists, whom he often disparagingly referred to as "trolls" (Eisenbach, *Gay Power,* 243).

70. Diana Cage, "Up Close with the Iconic Holly Hughes: Video Interview," *SheWired,* October 15, 2010, http://www.shewired.com/box-office/close-iconic-holly-

hughes-video-interview (accessed January 2011). I saw Holly Hughes's *Let Them Eat Cake* at Dixon Place on December 4, 2010.

71. While I did not have the opportunity to see *State of Marriage,* I have enjoyed many conversations with Joan Lipkin about its creation and staging. Performance artist Tim Miller also toured a show with a pro-marriage platform in 2010. Like *Let Them Eat Cake* and *State of Marriage, Lay of the Land* was inspired by Proposition 8, though Miller, whose partner is a foreign national, has long supported the cause of gay marriage. I saw *Lay of the Land* when it played at the Kitchen Theater in my hometown of Ithaca, NY.

72. The State Supreme Court of California ruled four to three that denying same-sex marriage violated the equal protection clause of the US Constitution. This case was prompted by the city of San Francisco's decision to issue marriage licenses to gay couples in 2004.

73. While many African Americans supported Proposition 8 on the grounds that same-sex marriage does not constitute a civil rights issue, this response is complicated by the complex relationship many African Americas have with the institution of marriage, which was outlawed during slavery. Even after it was legalized, racist miscegenation laws dictated who blacks could and could not wed. See Frances Foster, *Love and Marriage in Early African America* (Boston: Northeastern University Press, 2007).

74. Dan Savage, "Black Homophobia," *Slog,* November 5, 2008, http://slog.the stranger.com/2008/11/black_homophobia (accessed January 2011).

75. Urvashi Vaid, "Beyond the Wedding Ring: LGBT Issues in the Age of Obama," Texts and Speeches, August 16, 2010, http://urvashivaid.net/wp/?p=344 (accessed January 2010).

76. Ibid. See also Vaid's essay, "What Can Brown Do For You: Race, Sexuality, and the Future of LGBT Politics," Texts and Speeches, November 24, 2010, http://urvashivaid.net/wp/?p=709 (accessed January 2010).

77. Many members of ACT-UP and Queer Nation were opposed to same-sex marriage, including Michael Warner, who engaged in heated public debates on the matter with both Larry Kramer and Andrew Sullivan. See Michael Warner, *The Trouble with Normal: Sex, Politics, and the Ethics of Queer Life* (New York: Free Press, 1999). National debate about the legal status of LGBT partners began prior to the AIDS epidemic, of course, and lesbians have been the subject of a number of important court cases, including *In re Guardianship of Kowalski,* in which Karen Tompson filed a successful lawsuit for the right to care for her partner, Sharon Kowalski, who suffered a brain injury in a fatal car crash with a drunk driver in 1983. See Casey Charles, *The Sharon Kowalski Case: Lesbian and Gay Rights on Trial* (Topeka: University of Kansas Press, 2003). See also Nan D. Hunter, "Sexual Dissent and the Family: The Sharon Kowalski Case," in *Sex Wars: Sexual Dissent and Political Culture,* eds. Lisa Duggan and Nan Hunter (New York: Routledge, 2006), 99–104. There have also been a number of lawsuits filed by lesbian mothers over custody of their children since the 1970s.

78. Founding members of the Lesbian Avengers include Ana Maria Simo, of Medusa's Revenge, playwright and novelist Sarah Schulman, Maxine Wolfe, Anne-Christine D'Adesky, Marie Honan, and Anne Maguire. The group, which began in Manhattan, soon sprouted cells across the United States. See Sarah Schulman, *My American History: Lesbian and Gay Life during the Reagan/Bush Years* (New York: Routledge, 1994).

79. In 2008 and 2009, small bands of women in California and Texas marched in support of same-sex marriage under the banner of the Lesbian Avengers. This position is antithetical to the groups' foundational principles.

80. Lisa Duggan, "The New Homonormativity: The Sexual Politics of Neoliberalism," in *Materializing Democracy: Toward a Revitalized Cultural Politics,* eds. Russ Castronovo and Dana D. Nelson (Durham: Duke University Press, 2002), 25.

81. Jesse McKinley, "Theater Director Resigns amid Gay-Rights Ire," *New York Times,* November 12, 2008, http://www.nytimes.com/2008/11/13/arts/13iht-13thea.17797780.html (accessed January 2011).

82. Dave Itzkoff, "Marc Shaiman on *Prop 8—The Musical,*" *New York Times Art Beat,* December 4, 2008, http://artsbeat.blogs.nytimes.com/2008/12/04/marc-shaiman-on-prop-8-the-musical/ (accessed January 2010).

83. Many out lesbians openly support same-sex marriage, including Ellen DeGeneres and Rosie O'Donnell, both of whom have been married twice, and Jane Lynch and Wanda Sykes, both of whom recently tied the knot.

84. The ensemble is comprised of Jordan Ballard, Margaret Cho, Barrett Foa, J. B. Ghuman Jr., John Hill, Andy Richter, Maya Rudolph, Rashad Naylor, and Nicole Parker.

85. Jenifer Lewis stars as Riffing Prop 8'er; Craig Robinson plays A Preacher; and Rashida Jones, Lake Bell, and Sarah Chalke form a chorus called Scary Catholic School Girls from Hell.

86. Justin Ewers, "Same-sex Marriage Is Expected to Add Millions to California Coffers," *US News and World Report,* June 11, 2008, http://www.usnews.com/news/national/articles/2008/06/11/an-economic-boost-from-gay-marriage (accessed January 2011). The study's authors, Brad Sears, an adjunct professor of law at UCLA, and Lee Badgett, an economics professor at the University of Massachusetts-Amherst, based their calculations on the assumption that half of the 103,000 same-sex couples living in the state would marry by 2011 along with 70,000 same-sex couples from other states.

87. Ibid.

88. Vaid, "Beyond the Wedding Ring."

89. Adam Bouska and Jeff Parshley, NOH8 Campaign, http://noh8campaign.com (accessed January 2010).

90. Only a few photographs deviate from this formula. Lieutenant Dan Choi, who was instrumental in the repeal of the military's "Don't Ask, Don't Tell" (DADT) policy, is featured in camouflage (with fist raised in a defiant salute), and celebrity attorney Gloria Allred is shot all in red, her signature color.

91. For Cindy McCain's photo, see http://www.noh8campaign.com/photo-gallery/familiar-faces/photo/5722; for Meghan McCain's photos, see http://www.noh8campaign.com/photo-gallery/familiar-faces/photo/5566. Meghan posed for several shots, including one with her mother and one in which she holds her fingers, tips painted black, to her lips in a gesture of silence.

92. Republicans were responsible for New York's marriage equality victory, which was financed by an elite group of gay, white, male billionaires. See Kenyon Farrow, "Gay Marriage in New York: Progressive Victory or GOP Roadmap?," Alternet.org, June 27, 2011, http://www.alternet.org/story/151444/gay_marriage_in_new_york%3A_progressive_victory_or_gop_roadmap/ (accessed July 2011). See also Michael Barbaro, "Behind N.Y. Gay Marriage, an Unlikely Mix of Forces," *New York Times,* June 25, 2011.

93. The plaintiffs in *Perry v. Schwarzenegger* were Kris Perry and Sandy Stier, a lesbian couple from Berkeley who have been together for ten years and are raising four boys, and male partners from Burbank, Paul Katami and Jeff Zarrillo, who have cohabitated for nine years. The case was financed by the American Foundation for Equal Rights (AFER), which was created by political consultant and Washington insider Chad Griffin, the youngest member of President Bill Clinton's White House communications team, on May 26, 2008, the day after the Supreme Court verdict upholding Proposition 8. Griffin's official bio boasts that his "experience and expertise have made him a go-to resource for reporters on the intersection of Hollywood and politics" (http://www.griffinschake.com/chadGriffinBio.html). The case, now *Perry v. Brown,* and the appeals it will undoubtedly generate, continue as this book goes to press.

94. Theodore Olson, "The Conservative Case for Gay Marriage: Why Same-Sex Marriage Is an American Value," *Newsweek,* January 8, 2010, reposted on the *Daily Beast,* http://www.thedailybeast.com/newsweek/2010/01/08/the-conservative-case-for-gay-marriage.html (accessed January 2011).

95. Ibid.

96. Carl Wittman, "A Gay Manifesto," in *Out of the Closets: Voices of Gay Liberation,* eds. Karla Jay and Allen Young, twentieth anniversary ed. (New York: New York University Press, 1992), 333.

97. Ibid., 334.

98. Duggan, "The New Homonormativity," 8–9.

99. Urvashi Vaid, *Virtual Equality: The Mainstreaming of Gay and Lesbian Liberation* (New York: Anchor Books, 1996).

100. In 1984, Berkeley, California, became the first city to offer a "domestic partnership" to same-sex and opposite-sex couples. Other cities and counties soon followed suit.

101. Andrew Parker and Eve Kosofsky Sedgwick, Introduction to *Performativity and Performance,* eds. Andrew Parker and Eve Kosofsky Sedgwick (New York: Routledge, 1995), 10. Marriage, the authors remind us, is J. L. Austin's primary illustration of the speech act he calls explicit performatives in *How To Do Things With Words* (Cambridge, MA: Harvard University Press, 1979). Antimarriage zaps fall under the category of "negative performatives" in Austen's schema. As Parker and Sedgwick note, "The fascinating and powerful class of negative performatives—disavowal, renunciation, repudiation, 'count me out'—is marked, in almost every instance, by the asymmetrical property of being much less prone to becoming conventional than the positive performatives" (9). My aim in this chapter has been, in part, to show that promarriage zaps are indeed the most prone to becoming conventional. On the "weird centrality of the marriage example for performativity," see chapter 2 of Eve Kosofsky Sedgwick's *Touching Feeling: Affect, Pedagogy, Performativity* (Durham: Duke University Press, 2003), which was originally published as "Queer Performativity: Henry James's *The Art of the Novel*" GLQ 1 (1993): 1–16.

Chapter 3

The epigraphs are from Jill Johnston, *Mother Bound: Autobiography in Search of a Father* (New York: Knopf, 1983), 132; and Jill Johnston, "Writing into the Sunset," *Village Voice,* September 27, 1972, 44.

1. Andy Warhol's *Ethel Scull 36 Times* (1963) is considered one of his finest portraits.

2. Jill Johnston, *Admission Accomplished: The Lesbian Nation Years, 1970–75* (London: Serpent's Tail, 1998), x.

3. Jill Johnston, *Lesbian Nation: The Feminist Solution* (New York: Simon and Schuster, 1973), 118.

4. Alisa Solomon, "Our Hearts Were Young and Gay: The 'Voice' Reports the Queer Revolution," *Village Voice,* October 18, 2005, http://www.villagevoice.com/2005-10-18/specials/our-hearts-were-young-and-gay/ (accessed October 2009). Years later, Johnston claimed to have publicly come out in the winter of 1969, prior to the Stonewall uprising. See "Writing into the Sunset," 44. To put Johnston's coming out in perspective, we need only remember the waves Ellen DeGeneres made when she did the same in 1997. Prior to the 1990s, the only time lesbians graced the covers of national publications was when they felt the need to publicly denounce rumors that they were gay, as Martina Navratilova did in 1982. See Martha Gever, *Entertaining Lesbians: Celebrity, Sexuality, and Self-Invention* (New York: Routledge, 2003).

5. Johnston, *Lesbian Nation,* 120.

6. Ibid., 121.

7. Ibid., 123.

8. Ibid.

9. Ibid., 19.

10. Charlotte Curtis, "Women's Liberation Gets into the Long Island Swim," *New York Times,* August 10, 1970, 32.

11. Johnston, *Lesbian Nation,* 16.

12. Ibid., 17.

13. Ibid., 39.

14. Lauren Berlant, *The Queen of America Goes to Washington City: Essays on Sex and Citizenship* (Durham: Duke University Press, 1997), 11. One of Berlant's primary interlocutors here is Wendy Brown's *States of Injury: Power and Freedom in Late Modernity* (Princeton: Princeton University Press, 1995).

15. Ibid., 264, 11.

16. Lauren Berlant, "The Subject of True Feeling: Pain, Privacy, and Politics," in *Transformations: Thinking through Feminism,* eds. Sarah Ahmed and Jane Kilby (New York: Routledge, 2000), 34. See also Berlant's *The Female Complaint: The Unfinished Business of Sentimentality in American Culture* (Durham: Duke University Press, 2008); Linda Williams, *Playing the Race Card: Melodramas of Black and White from Uncle Tom to O. J. Simpson* (Princeton: Princeton University Press, 2002); and Jill Dolan, *Utopia in Performance: Finding Hope at the Theater* (Ann Arbor: University of Michigan Press, 2005).

17. Suzan-Lori Parks, "Elements of Style," in *The America Play and Other Works* (New York: Theatre Communications Group [TCG], 1995), 15.

18. Mady Schutzman, "Jok(er)ing: Joker Runs Wild," in *A Boal Companion: Dialogues on Theatre and Cultural Politics,* eds. Jan Cohen-Cruz and Mady Schutzman (New York: Routledge, 2006), 140. The joker occupies a pivotal role in Augusto Boal's dramaturgy, in both his Joker System and his Theatre of the Oppressed. Victor Turner employs the phrase "joker in the deck" to characterize the subjunctive mood of play. Comprised of elements of *paidia* (free play) and *ludus* (structured play, games), the joker is an animating and unpredictable force that "reveals to us the possibility of . . . restructuring . . . what our culture states to be reality." See Victor Turner, "Body, Brain and Culture," *Performing Arts Journal* 10, no. 2 (1986): 26–34. Illustrative of the animating force of the joker is a passage in Roland Barthes's *Leçon,* in which the author writes about wanting to convert his Chair of Literary Semiology into a wheelchair so as to be perpetually in motion, "the wildcard [joker] of contemporary knowledge." See Jonathan Culler, *Barthes: A Very Short Introduction* (Oxford: Oxford University Press, 2002), 58.

19. Johnston's mother, Olive Marjorie Crowe, had her only child out of wedlock, the result of an affair with a British bellfounder and clockmaker named Cyril F. Johnston. Rather than admit to her indiscretion, Crowe told everyone, including her daughter, that she was a widow. Johnston grew up believing that her father was dead.

20. Johnston, *Admission Accomplished,* v.

21. Johnston wrote for *Dance Observer* beginning in 1955 and for *Art News* from 1955 to 1966. From the mid-1980s until her death in 2010, she was a regular contributor to the *New York Times Book Review* and *Art in America.*

22. Jill Johnston, *Marmalade Me* (New York: E. P. Dutton, 1971), 194.

23. Johnston, *Lesbian Nation,* 40, 39, 58.

24. Ibid., 48.

25. Ibid., 80.

26. See Peggy Phelan, *Unmarked: The Politics of Performance* (New York: Routledge, 1993).

27. Johnston, *Lesbian Nation*, 54, 56.

28. Ibid., 70, 66, 75.

29. Ibid., 64.

30. Ibid., 70.

31. Ibid., 19.

32. Ibid., 44.

33. Lewis Hyde, *Trickster Makes This World: Mischief, Myth, and Art* (New York: Farrar, Straus and Giroux, 1998). See, in particular, chapter 11.

34. Schutzman, "Jok(er)ing," 143.

35. Friedrich Wilhelm Nietzsche, *The Gay Science: With a Prelude in Rhymes and an Appendix of Songs,* trans. Walter Kaufmann (New York: Random House, 1974), 32.

36. Ibid.

37. Johnston, *Lesbian Nation*, 79.

38. Ibid.

39. Ibid., 117.

40. Of *Music Walk with Dancer,* Johnston writes, "I managed to present together my three female travesties: the hoyden, the dancer, and the wife-and-mother. Wearing my loud red dress and my stockings, I executed a number of household chores—cleaning a baby bottle, vacuuming, frying bacon, pulling a vehicular toy dog on a string, and so on—stopping long enough downstage to perform a slinky sort of dance plastique" (*Mother Bound,* 141). In *Inside Originale,* Johnston played the part of a free agent trickster. She recalls, "Five nights in a row, I appeared quite drunk in outlandish female accoutrements and hung upside down from a scaffolding and did my best to disrupt the performances of the other artists involved. Several sensitive artists were offended or outraged" (142).

41. Sally Banes, *Writing Dance in the Age of Postmodernism* (Middletown, CT: Wesleyan University Press, 1994), 7.

42. Johnston, *Admission Accomplished,* vi.

43. Michel Foucault, "What Is Enlightenment?," in *Ethics: Subjectivity, and Truth,* trans. Robert Hurley (New York: New Press, 1997), 311.

44. Ibid., 310.

45. Johnston, *Admission Accomplished,* 201.

46. Johnston, *Lesbian Nation,* 79.

47. Johnston, *Marmalade Me,* 83; Johnston, *Admission Accomplished,* vi.

48. Melissa Deem, "Disrupting the Nuptials at the Town Hall Debate: Feminism and the Politics of Cultural Memory in the USA," *Cultural Studies* 17, no. 5 (2003): 621.

49. Johnston appears as a marginal figure in Mike Sell's *Avant-Garde Performance and the Limits of Criticism: Approaching the Living Theatre, Happenings/Fluxus, and the Black Arts Movement* (Ann Arbor: University of Michigan Press, 2008). She receives only scant attention in both Alice Echols's *Daring to be Bad: Radical Feminism in America, 1967–1975* (Minneapolis: University of Minnesota Press, 1989); and Lillian Faderman's *Odd Girls and Twilight Lovers: A History of Lesbian Life in Twentieth Century America* (New York: Penguin, 1999), where she haunts the chapter titled "Lesbian Nation," but is discussed only in relation to mainstream publishers poaching texts from lesbian-feminist presses and anxiety about bisexuality. Johnston does not appear at all in Sarah Evans's *Personal Politics* (New York: Vintage Books, 1979); or Ginette Castro's *American Feminism, a Contemporary History,* trans. Elizabeth Loverde-Bagwell (New York: New York University Press, 1990). The only anthology that includes Johnston's work is the

one she coedited. See Phyllis Birkby, Bertha Harris, Jill Johnston, Esther Newton, and Jane O'Wyatt, eds., *Amazon Expedition: A Lesbian Feminist Anthology* (New York: Times Change Press, 1973).

50. Elizabeth Freeman, "Packing History, Count(er)ing Generations," *New Literary History* 31, no. 4 (Autumn 2000): 728.

51. Johnston, *Admission Accomplished,* 145.

52. Johnston, *Lesbian Nation,* 79, 119.

53. Jill Johnston, "Of This Pure but Irregular Passion," *Village Voice,* July 2, 1970, 29–30, 38–39, 55.

54. Johnston, *Lesbian Nation,* 79.

55. Johnston, "Of this Pure but Irregular Passion," 29.

56. Ibid., 29–30.

57. Ibid., 38.

58. Ibid.

59. Johnston, *Lesbian Nation,* 119.

60. Ibid., 118.

61. Ibid.

62. Ibid., 183.

63. Ibid., 267.

64. Banes, *Writing Dance in the Age of Postmodernism,* 8.

65. Edward Alwood, *Straight News: Gays, Lesbians, and the News Media* (New York: Columbia University Press, 1998), 114. Johnston's coming-out column was reprinted in *The Ladder.*

66. María Irene Fornés, Bertha Harris, Jill Johnston, Lisa Kennedy, and Barbara Smith, "On the Beginnings of Lesbian Literature," in *Queer Representations: Reading Lives, Reading Cultures, a Center for Lesbian and Gay Studies Book,* ed. Martin B. Duberman (New York: New York University Press, 1997), 349. These comments were made on a CLAGS panel in 1993, which was structured as a moderated conversation among María Irene Fornés, Bertha Harris, Jill Johnston, Barbara Smith, and Lisa Smith.

67. Johnston, *Lesbian Nation,* 39.

68. Ibid., 19.

69. Ibid., 314.

70. Ibid., 25.

71. Ibid., 26.

72. Ibid., 25.

73. Ibid., 24.

74. Ibid., 25.

75. There were a number of feminists and lesbians in the audience, including Betty Friedan, Susan Sontag, and Cynthia Ozick, who asked questions of the panelists during the Q&A session.

76. Steinem came to be a political ally of Mailer's. She encouraged and endorsed his candidacy for mayor of New York City in 1973.

77. Germaine Greer, "My Mailer Problem," *Esquire* 76, no. 3 (1971): 92–93, 214–16.

78. Johnston, *Lesbian Nation,* 40; Solanas, *SCUM Manifesto* (New York: SCUM Book, 1967), 19. According to Johnston, Valerie harassed her and sent her death threats for misspelling her name in *Lesbian Nation* as Solanis (a common error that stems from Warhol listing her as Valeria Solanis in the credits of *I, a Man,* which is, incidentally, how the press referred to her after the shooting). See Deem, "Disrupting the Nuptials at the Town Hall Debate," 643, n. 30.

79. Johnston, *Lesbian Nation,* 17.

80. Ibid., 22.

81. Johnston claimed that had she actually read "The Prisoner of Sex" before she agreed to participate in the debate, she might have approached the event "with more righteous indignation and intent to murder if not simply destroy" (ibid., 26).

82. Clifford Geertz, *The Interpretation of Cultures* (New York: Basic Books, 1977), 412–54.

83. Johnston, "Writing Into the Sunset," 44.

84. One month after Town Hall, Germaine Greer would grace the cover of *Life* magazine (May 1971) alongside a caption proclaiming her a "saucy feminist that even men like."

85. Johnston, *Lesbian Nation*, 266.

86. Ibid.

87. *Town Bloody Hall*, dir. Chris Hegedus and D. A. Pennebaker, 1979, Pennebaker Hegedus Films, New York, DVD. All quotes from the debate not attributed elsewhere are taken from this film.

88. Johnston identifies her costars as Robyn and SK (*Lesbian Nation*, 36).

89. Victor Turner coined the term *liminoid* to denote cultural performances and leisure activities that have characteristics of liminal rites but are optional and don't involve the resolution of a crisis. Play is integral to these post-industrial, secular phenomena, which fracture social relations, expectations and mores and "ludicly" recombine them. "One *works* at the liminal, one *plays at* the limonoid." Victor Turner, *From Ritual to Theatre: The Human Seriousness of Play* (New York: PAJ, 1982), 27, 55.

90. Johnston, *Lesbian Nation*, 165.

91. Ibid., 26.

92. Johnston, *Lesbian Nation*, 15.

93. Ibid., 36.

94. Johnston writes that Town Hall "was accorded the kind of front page attention you might expect to see for a new episode of alice crimmins or the sinking of the queen mary" (ibid., 23).

95. See Rita Mae Brown, "Leadership v Stardom," *Furies* 1, no. 2 (February 1972).

96. Joseph Roach, *It* (Ann Arbor: University of Michigan Press, 2007), 1.

97. Johnston, *Lesbian Nation*, 171.

98. Ibid., 96.

99. Ibid., 156, 277.

100. Lauren Berlant and Elizabeth Freeman, "Queer Nationality," in *The Queen of America Goes to Washington City: Essays on Sex and Citizenship,* by Lauren Berlant (Durham: Duke University Press, 1997), 168.

101. Johnston, *Lesbian Nation*, 122.

102. Becki Ross, *The House That Jill Built: A Lesbian Nation in Formation* (Toronto: University of Toronto Press, 1995). Aside from the title, Ross does not discuss Johnston in this text.

103. A few examples of the many separatist collectives that existed at the time Johnston compiled *Lesbian Nation* include the Revolutionary Lesbians, the Gutter Dyke Collective (Berkeley), CLIT (the Collective Lesbian International Terrors in New York City), the Radicalesbians (New York), the Gorgons (Seattle), the Flippies (Feminist Lesbian Intergalactic Party in Chicago), and the Furies (Washington, DC).

104. Johnston, *Lesbian Nation*, 210–11.

105. Ibid., 224.

106. Ibid.

107. Ibid., 235.

108. See Grace Lichtenstein, "Women's Lib Wooed by Publishers," *New York Times,* August 17, 1970, 32. See also Faderman, *Odd Girls and Twilight Lovers,* chapter 9.

109. Jill Johnston, "Write First, Then Live," in *Queer Representations: Reading Lives, Reading Cultures, a Center for Lesbian and Gay Studies Book*, ed. Martin B. Duberman (New York: New York University Press, 1997), 350.

110. Ibid.

111. Many lesbian feminists saw working with the mainstream as a form of selling out and chose only to publish with women's press collectives or to self-publish. Others, like Morgan and Johnston, saw this as a way to reach a wider audience.

112. Jill Johnston, "Was Lesbian Separatism Inevitable?," *Gay and Lesbian Review* 13, no. 2, (March–April 2006), http://www.glreview.com/issues/13.2/13.2-johnston .php (accessed August 2009).

113. Johnston, "Write First, Then Live," 350.

114. Johnston, *Lesbian Nation*, 11.

115. *Lesbian Nation* is comprised of selected reviews published in the *Village Voice* from 1970 to 1972 along with excerpts from the author's diary and other writings.

116. Johnston, "Was Lesbian Separatism Inevitable?"

117. Johnston, *Lesbian Nation*, 76.

118. Ibid., 76.

119. Ibid., 271.

120. Erving Goffman, *The Presentation of Self in Everyday Life* (New York: Doubleday, 1959), 252–53.

121. Benedict Anderson, *Imagined Communities: Reflections on the Origin and Spread of Nationalism* (New York: Verso, 1983), 6.

122. Erin Hurley, *National Performance: Representing Quebec from Expo 67 to Celine Dion* (Toronto: University of Toronto Press, 2010), 24.

123. Ross, *The House That Jill Built*, 16.

124. José Esteban Muñoz, *Cruising Utopia: The Then and There of Queer Futurity* (New York: New York University Press, 2009), 18.

125. Johnston, *Lesbian Nation*, 158.

126. Deem, "Disrupting the Nuptials at the Town Hall Debate," 641, n. 10.

127. Temporal drag is inherent in all weddings. Part of what makes this event a tradition is "restored" or "twice-behaved behavior," its connection to and replaying of the past. See Richard Schechner, *Between Theatre and Anthropology* (Pittsburgh: University of Pennsylvania Press, 1985), 36.

128. Geoffrey Hendricks has been associated with Fluxus since the mid-1960s. Known as "cloudsmith" for his extensive exploration of sky imagery in his art, Hendricks taught at Rutgers University, my alma mater, from 1956 to 2003, where he worked closely with his colleagues Allan Kaprow, Roy Lichtenstein, and Lucas Samaras. See Geoffrey Hendricks, *Critical Mass: Happenings, Fluxus, Performance, Intermedia, and Rutgers University, 1958–1972* (New Brunswick, NJ: Rutgers University Press, 2003). See also Dick Higgins, *Horizons: The Poetics and Theory of Intermedia* (Carbondale: Southern Illinois University Press, 1984).

129. Jill Johnston, "Wedding in Denmark," *Art in America* 82, no. 6 (June 1994): 76.

130. Ibid.

131. Ibid.

132. Ibid.

133. In 1978 Hendricks performed his first Fluxwedding. George Maciunas, dying of liver cancer, asked Geoff to serve as Fluxminister at his marriage to Billie Hutching. The event took place at the Grommet Art Theater (now the Emily Harvey Gallery). Maciunas died three months later, and Hendricks served as Fluxminister at his Fluxfuneral.

134. "Call me a Fluxus artist," wrote Johnston, who considered herself not simply

a critic but a partner in performance. See "George Brecht, the Philosopher of Fluxus," *Art in America* 94, no. 4 (April 2006): 112–18.

135. Estera Milman, "Introduction: Fluxus: A Conceptual Country," *Visible Language* 26, nos. 1/2 (Winter/Spring 1992): 13. Milman acknowledges that her description of Fluxus as a conceptual country was influenced by Ken Friedman and George Maciunas's *Visa TouRistE: Passport to the State of Flux,* a work first proposed by Friedman in 1966 and realized by Maciunas in 1977.

136. In addition to Johnston, Fluxus women include Yoko Ono, Yayoi Kusama, Alison Knowles, Carolee Schneemann, and Sara Seagull. The queer dimensions of Fluxus go back to John Cage and his coterie. In addition to being popularized by Eastern Europeans, in both Europe and the United States, Fluxus found a home in Asia, especially in Japan. See Midori Yoshimoto, "An Evening with Fluxus Women: A Roundtable Discussion," *Women and Performance: A Journal of Feminist Theory* 19, no. 3 (November 2009): 369–89.

137. Johnston, "Wedding in Denmark," 75.

138. Ibid., 76.

139. Mary T. Conway, "A Becoming Queer Aesthetic," *Discourse* 26, no. 3 (2004): 178.

140. Michael Rush, *New Media in Art* (London: Thames and Hudson, 2005), 24.

141. Kristine Stiles, "Between Water and Stone: Fluxus Performance: A Metaphysics of Acts," in *In the Spirit of Fluxus,* ed. Janet Jenkins (Minneapolis: Walker Art Center, 1993), 77.

142. Johnston, "Wedding in Denmark," 75.

143. Ibid., 76.

144. Johnston, *Admission Accomplished,* viii.

145. Ibid.

146. Robert, Pincus-Witten, "Fluxus and the Silvermans: An Introduction," in *Fluxus Codex,* ed. Jon Hendricks (New York: Harry N. Abrams, 1988), 26.

Chapter 4

The epigraph is from John Waters's gay rant on "I Advocate," episode 103-I, *The Advocate On-Air,* http://www.advocate.com/Video/?pid=XO5uBRfc6aOX1A4aScdU5K1z4qR UjKri (accessed January 2011).

1. Diane DiMassa, *Hothead Paisan: Homicidal Lesbian Terrorist,* http://hotheadpaisan.com (accessed June 2008). Ariel Levy, "Lesbian Nation: When Gay Women Took to the Road," *New Yorker,* March 2, 2009, http://www.newyorker.com/reporting/2009/03/02/090302fa_fact_levy (accessed March 2012). See also Jill Dolan, "Feeling Women's Culture: Women's Music, Lesbian Feminism, and the Impact of Emotional Memory," in *The Journal of Dramatic Theory and Criticism* 26, no. 2 (Spring 2012): 205–19.

2. Jasbir Puar, *Terrorist Assemblages: Homonationalism in Queer Times* (Durham: Duke University Press, 2007), xi.

3. Ibid., xiv.

4. K. Martin and G. Moon, "Hothead Goes Musical: Agitate, Agitate, Agitate," *Velvet Park,* no. 8 (Winter 2005): 15.

5. Ibid.

6. Ibid.

7. Monique Wittig, *Les Guérillères,* trans. David Le Vay (Boston: Beacon, 1985).

8. Kate Bornstein, *Gender Outlaw: On Men, Women, and the Rest of Us* (New York: Vintage Books, 1994), 71–72.

9. Lynda Hart, *Fatal Women: Lesbian Sexuality and the Mark of Aggression* (Princeton: Princeton University Press, 1994), x.

10. *Born in Flames,* dir. Lizzie Borden, 1983, New York, First Run Features, VHS; Five Lesbian Brothers, *The Secretaries,* in *Five Lesbian Brothers: Four Plays* (New York: Theatre Communications Group, 2000), 117–91; Split Britches, *Lesbians Who Kill,* in *Split Britches: Lesbian Practice/Feminist Performance,* ed. Sue-Ellen Case (New York: Routledge, 1996), 185–224; *Set it Off,* dir. Gary F. Gray, 1996, New Line Cinema, Los Angeles, DVD; Staceyann Chin, "Dykepoem," in *Wildcat Woman: Poetry* (N.p., Staceyann Chin, 1998). For a history of the Lesbian Avengers, see Sarah Schulman, *My American History: Lesbian and Gay Life during the Reagan//Bush Years* (New York: Routledge, 1994), 283–319. One might be tempted to ally the bicurious heroines of Ridley Scott's 1991 film *Thelma and Louise* with homicidal lesbian terrorists, but this narrative is a (failed) revenge fantasy that ends with the women committing suicide by driving off a cliff rather than facing a showdown with the authorities.

11. Diane DiMassa, *The Complete Hothead Paisan: Homicidal Lesbian Terrorist* (San Francisco: Cleis Press, 1999), 11. Cleiss Press reassembled early issues of the zine, and DiMassa added additional content to produce a more coherent narrative for the anthologies.

12. Ibid., 16.

13. *Terrorist drag* is the term José Muñoz uses to describe the disidentificatory performance style of Vagina Crème Davis. See José Esteban Muñoz, *Disidentifications: Queers of Color and the Performance of Politics* (Minneapolis: University of Minnesota Press, 1999), 97.

14. The labrys is a double-headed ax associated with Amazon warriors and resurrected as a symbol of lesbian feminism in the 1970s. It serves as the cover for Mary Daly's *Gyn/ecology: The Metaethics of Radical Feminism* (Boston: Beacon Press, 1978).

15. Dana Heller makes this point in "Hothead Paisan: Clearing a Space for Lesbian Feminist Folklore," *New York Folklore* 19, nos. 1–2 (1993): 157–83.

16. Stephen Duncombe, *Notes from Underground: Zines and the Politics of Alternative Culture* (New York: Verso, 1997), 2.

17. Ibid.

18. Ibid.

19. *Dykes to Watch Out For* began in 1983 and ran until 2008, when Alison Bechdel put the strip on hiatus to complete her award-winning graphic novel *Fun Home.* That year, in celebration of the twenty-fifth anniversary of the comic, she published *The Essential Dykes to Watch Out For* (New York: Houghton Mifflin Harcourt, 2008).

20. Cleis Press, founded in 1980 by Felice Newman and Frédérique Delacoste, is the largest independent queer publishing company in the United States and the only organization of its kind still run by its founders. The first anthology, *Hothead Paisan: Homicidal Lesbian Terrorist* (1993), consists of the first nine issues along with twenty pages of new material. The second, *The Revenge of Hothead Paisan: Homicidal Lesbian Terrorist* (1995), contains issues ten through eighteen with thirty new pages, and the final volume, The *Complete Hothead Paisan: Homicidal Lesbian Terrorist* (1999), includes all twenty-one issues with a ten-page introduction.

21. Kathleen Martindale, *Un/Popular Culture: Lesbian Writing after the Sex Wars* (New York: State University of New York Press, 1997), 59.

22. This issue originally appeared in the fourth quarterly publication of the zine, published in 1992. It is included in the Cleis anthologies of 1993 and 1999. See Heller, "Hothead Paisan."

23. Bruce Hoffman, *Inside Terrorism* (New York: Columbia University Press, 2006), 3.

24. The Robespierre of feminism is what Norman Mailer called Valerie Solanas after she shot Andy Warhol. See Dana Heller, "Shooting Solanas," *Feminist Studies* 27, no. 1 (2001): 167–89. Robespierre defined terror as "nothing but justice, prompt, severe, and inflexible." If the basis of a popular government in peacetime is virtue, he reasoned, then its basis in a time of revolution is virtue and terror—virtue, without which terror would be barbaric, and terror, without which virtue would be impotent (quoted in Hoffman, *Inside Terrorism*, 3). Of course, terrorism as a political program existed long before Robespierre gave it a proper name.

25. During the Reign of Terror (1793–1794; sometimes called simply The Terror), an estimated 300,000 people were arrested and 17,000–40,000 were guillotined, a fate Robespierre himself would eventually suffer.

26. Walter Laqueur, *No End to War: Terrorism in the Twenty-First Century* (New York: Continuum International, 2004), 4. See also Walter Reich, *Origins of Terrorism: Psychologies, Ideologies, Theologies, States of Mind* (Princeton: Woodrow Wilson Press Center, 1998); Gérard Chaliand and Arnaud Blin, eds., *The History of Terrorism: From Antiquity to al Qaeda* (Los Angeles: University of California Press, 2007); Martha Crenshaw, ed., *Terrorism in Context* (Pittsburgh: University of Pennsylvania Press, 1995); and Mark Juergensmeyer, *Terror in the Mind of God: The Global Rise of Religion's Violence* (Los Angeles: University of California Press, 2000).

27. Jean Baudrillard, "Our Theatre of Cruelty," trans. John Johnston, *Semiotext(e)* 4 (1982): 108. See also Herb Blau, *Blooded Thought: Occasions of Theatre* (New York: Performing Arts Journal, 1982); and *Take Up the Bodies: Theater at the Vanishing Point* (Chicago: University of Illinois Press, 1982).

28. Jean-François Lyotard, *The Postmodern Condition: A Report on Knowledge* (Minneapolis: University of Minnesota Press, 1984), 60–70.

29. Anthony Kubiak *Stages of Terror: Terror, Ideology, and Coercion as Theatre History* (Bloomington: Indiana University Press, 1991), 157.

30. DiMassa, *Hothead Paisan*, (1993), 9.

31. Ibid.

32. John Orr and Dragan Klaić, "Terrorism and Drama: Introduction," in *Terrorism and Modern Drama*, eds. John Orr and Dragan Klaić (Edinburgh: Edinburgh University Press, 1990), 8.

33. The attacks by al-Qaeda included bombings of US embassies in Tanzania and Kenya in 1998 and the USS *Cole* in 2000; the thwarted shoe bombing of an American Airlines flight in 2001; and simultaneous attacks on the World Trade Center, Pentagon, and a third Washington location, most likely the White House or the Capitol. One could add to this list the 1993 car bombing of the World Trade Center.

34. Rebecca Schneider, *The Explicit Body in Performance* (New York: Routledge, 1997), 12.

35. Keely Savoie, "Hotheaded and Bothered: A Chat with Artist/Pen-Wielding Vigilante Diane DiMassa," *Bitch: Feminist Responses to Pop Culture*, no. 25 (Summer 2004): 36.

36. Lauren Berlant, "'68 or Something," *Critical Inquiry* 21, no. 1 (Autumn 1994): 128.

37. Ibid., 126.

38. Ibid., 130.

39. Ibid., 133, my emphasis.

40. Sally Munt, *Heroic Desire: Lesbian Identity and Cultural Space* (New York: New York University Press, 1998), 112.

41. DiMassa had very little to do with the musical aside from creating sets and props. Since retiring Hothead, she has put her energy into a number of artistic projects,

including painting. She has illustrated several books, including Kathy Acker's *Pussycat Fever*, Kate Bornstein's *My Gender Workbook*, and Anne-Fausto Sterling's *Sexing the Body*. DiMassa is coauthor of the graphic novel *Jokes and the Unconscious* with slam poet Daphne Gottlieb.

42. The founders of Bitch and Animal met at the Theatre School at DePaul University (formerly the Goodman School of Drama) in Chicago.

43. Judith Halberstam, *In a Queer Time and Place: Transgender Bodies, Subcultural Lives* (New York: New York University Press, 2005), 154.

44. Ibid., 172.

45. Folksinger and Michfest regular Ferron, along with Tribe 8's Lynn Breedlove, were scheduled to star in the musical but were unable to participate.

46. Stacy Wolf, *A Problem Like Maria: Gender and Sexuality in the American Musical* (Ann Arbor: University of Michigan Press, 2002), 17.

47. David Savran, *A Queer Sort of Materialism: Recontextualizing American Theater* (Ann Arbor: University of Michigan Press, 2003), 13.

48. For an interesting documentary film about Michfest, see *Radical Harmonies*, dir. Dee Mosbacher, 2002, San Francisco, Woman Vision, DVD.

49. Margaret Coble, "Hothead Does Michigan," *Advocate*, July 20, 2004, 56–57.

50. See Philip Gourevitch and Errol Morris Exposure, "The Woman behind the Camera at Abu Ghraib," *New Yorker*, March 24, 2008, http://www.newyorker.com/reporting/2008/03/24/080324fa_fact_gourevitch (accessed July 2009). Sabrina Harmon was charged with seven counts of mistreating detainees and convicted of six. She was sentenced to six months in prison. Harmon was one of eleven soldiers, most of whom were young, low-ranking service personnel, charged with dereliction of duty and other relatively minor offenses. Reservist and Gulf War veteran Charles Graner received one of the stiffer sentences: ten years in prison, demotion to private, dishonorable discharge, and forfeiture of pay and allowances. Both England and Ambuhl were romantically involved with him. England gave birth to Graner's child in 2004, and Ambuhl married him in 2005, while he was incarcerated. England's attempt to play the victim card is evidenced by her authorized biography, Gary S. Winkler, *Tortured: Lynndie England, Abu Ghraib, and the Photographs That Shocked the World* (Keyser, WV: Bad Apple, 2009).

51. *Viral Chaos: The Makings of an Animal Artist*, dir. Susan Powter, 2004, San Francisco, Animal's Farm, DVD.

52. Judith Butler, "Quotes," European Graduate School, http:www.egs.edu/faculty/judith-butler/quotes/ (accessed November 2011).

53. The subject of lesbian terrorism caused a stir at Michfest in 1994 when queercore band Tribe 8 performed "Frat Pig," a revenge fantasy song about gang castration. During the set, the band's lead singer, Lynn Breedlove, castrated the strap-on dildo she was sporting with a large knife. The incident prompted much discussion about sexual abuse, as some of the festival attendees objected on the grounds that it caused and/or enflamed past trauma. Ann Cvetkovich discusses this episode in *An Archive of Feeling: Trauma, Sexuality, and Lesbian Public Cultures* (Durham: Duke University Press, 2003), in the chapter titled "Sexual Trauma/Queer Memory: Incest, Lesbianism, and Therapeutic Culture," 83–117.

54. Sarah Pebworth, "Interview with Animal Prufrock," *Lavenderlips*, March 2004, http://www.lavenderlips.com/articles/animal.html (accessed May 2009).

55. "Letter from Diana DiMassa," July 2004, http://eminism.org/michigan/20040700-dimassa.txt (accessed July 2009). Michigan Women's Music Festival excludes MTF's, male-to-female transexuals but it allows pre-operative FTM's, female-to-male transexuals.

56. DiMassa, *The Complete Hothead Paisan,* 34.

57. Martin and Moon, Hothead Goes Musical, 16.

58. Alisa Solomon and Framji Minwalla, eds., *The Queerest Art: Essays on Lesbian and Gay Theater* (New York: New York University Press, 1992).

59. Judith Halberstam, *The Queer Art of Failure* (Durham: Duke University Press, 2011), 3.

Chapter 5

1. Holly Hughes, "Preface," in *Five Lesbian Brothers: Four Plays,* by Five Lesbian Brothers (New York: Theatre Communications Group, 2000), xi.

2. Five Lesbian Brothers, playbill, *The Secretaries,* New York Theatre Workshop, 1994, n.p.

3. Five Lesbian Brothers, *Five Lesbian Brothers: Four Plays* (New York: TCG, 2000), 3.

4. Mark Blankenship, "'Oedipus' Gets Complex in Updated Classic," *Variety,* August 4, 2005, http://www.variety.com/review/VE1117927829?refCatId=33 (accessed September 2005).

5. Christopher Isherwood, "When Sappho Meets Sophocles in a California Hot Tub," *New York Times Art Beat,* August 5, 2005, http://www.nytimes.com (accessed September 2005).

6. Jill Dolan, "The Return of the Five Lesbian Brothers," *The Feminist Spectator,* August 26, 2005, http://feministspectator.blogspot.com/2005/08/return-of-five-lesbi an-brothers.html (accessed December 2005).

7. Hilton Als, "A New Age Oedipus: The Five Lesbian Brothers Update a Myth," *New Yorker,* August 25, 2005, http://www.newyorker.com/archive/2005/08/22/050822crth_ theatre (accessed December 2005).

8. Ibid.

9. Ibid.

10. All of the Brothers' collaborations, save *Brides of the Moon,* incorporate Brechtian-style musical interludes into the dramatic action. So integral is song to their work that the Brothers published the lyrics and music in the anthology of their collected plays. With no music in *Oedipus,* the Brothers have fewer alienation effects in their arsenal and fewer tools with which to promote critical thinking and thwart audience absorption in the theatrical spectacle.

11. Five Lesbian Brothers, *Five Lesbian Brothers,* 2.

12. Ibid.

13. Ibid., 14.

14. Ibid., 9, 17. The troupe's members had heated discussions about Brad—whether or not to have him appear onstage, but also how to dispose of him, by leaving him at the altar or killing him. As Brother Healey notes, "Interesting, with five lesbians on stage and Brad nowhere to be seen, merely a name on our lips, he some how managed to get into the reviews" (3).

15. Peggy Phelan, "The Serious Comedy of Hope: Introducing the Five Lesbian Brothers," in *Five Lesbian Brothers: Four Plays,* by Five Lesbian Brothers (New York: Theatre Communications Group, 2000), xvii.

16. See Sara Warner, "Rage Slaves: The Commodification of Affect in the Five Lesbian Brothers' *The Secretaries,*" *Journal of Dramatic Theory and Criticism* 23, no. 1 (Fall 2008): 21–45.

17. Lisa Kron, "Work with the Five Lesbian Brothers," http://www.lisakron.com (accessed June 2009).

18. Alisa Solomon, "Five Lesbian Brothers: No Whining!" *American Theatre* 15, no. 7 (September 1998): 62.

19. Five Lesbian Brothers, *Five Lesbian Brothers*, 44.

20. Phelan, "The Serious Comedy of Hope," xvii.

21. Five Lesbian Brothers, *Five Lesbian Brothers*, 46.

22. Holly Hughes, a WOW Café veteran, was one of the famed NEA Four artists (along with Karen Finley, Tim Miller, and John Fleck) whose grants were rescinded in 1990 due to the controversial and objectionable content of their work. See Richard Meyer, "Have You Heard the One about the Lesbian Who Goes to the Supreme Court? Holly Hughes and the Case against Censorship," *Theatre Journal* 52, no. 4 (2000): 543–52; Peggy Phelan, "Serrano, Mapplethorpe, the NEA, and You: 'Money Talks,'" *Drama Review* 34, no. 1 (1990): 4–15; and Jill Dolan, *Geographies of Learning: Theory and Practice, Activism and Performance* (Middletown, CT: Wesleyan University Press, 2001), 47–64.

23. Kate Davy, *Lady Dicks and Lesbian Brothers: Staging the Unimaginable at the WOW Café Theatre* (Ann Arbor: University of Michigan Press, 2010), 9.

24. *Preaching to the Perverted* is the title of Holly Hughes's solo performance piece about her NEA ordeal. See also Tim Miller and David Román, "Preaching to the Converted," *Theatre Journal* 47, no. 2 (May 1995): 169–88.

25. Diana Taylor, *The Archive and the Repertoire: Performing Cultural Memory in the Americas* (Durham: Duke University Press, 2003), 2.

26. Dolan, "The Return of the Five Lesbian Brothers."

27. E-mail correspondence with Kate Davy, December 12, 2007.

28. Five Lesbian Brothers, *Five Lesbian Brothers*, 197.

29. During the run of *Brides*, Molly Smith was named artistic director of Arena Stage.

30. Peter Marks, "Encounters of the Sexual Kind," *New York Times*, December 11, 1997, http://www.nytimes.com/1997/12/11/movies/theater-review-encounters-of-the-sexual-kind.html (accessed June 2008).

31. Some members of the Brothers had experience in television. They wrote three short films for HBO, and they were invited to host, along with Kiki and Herb, episodes of Showtime's "Late Night Out," which never aired.

32. Lisa Kron, *Well* (New York: Theatre Communications Group, 2006), 16.

33. After twenty-three previews, Kron's *Well* opened at the Longacre Theatre on Broadway, where it ran from March 3, 2006, to May 14, 2006 (for a total of fifty-two performances). Lisa Kron was nominated for a Tony for best leading actress (she lost to Cynthia Nixon in *Rabbit Hole*), and Jayne Houdyshell was nominated for a Tony for best featured actress (she lost to Frances de la Tour in *The History Boys*). For more on *Well*, see Davy, *Lady Dicks and Lesbian Brothers*, especially chapter 1.

34. *Love! Valor! Compassion!*, directed by Joe Mantello, opened at the Manhattan Theatre Club on October 11, 1994, and ran for 72 performances. It reopened at the Walter Kerr Theatre on Valentine's Day the following year, after 28 previews, and ran for an additional 248 performances. The play was nominated for a total of five Tony awards. It won numerous other accolades, including a pair of Drama Desk awards (out of the six nominations it received), a pair of Obies, and the Evening Standard award for best play.

35. *Oedipus at Palm Springs* was cowritten by all members of the troupe with the exception of Babs Davy, who did not participate in the retreat.

36. Charlotte Stoudt, "Oedipus Resexed: The Five Lesbian Brothers Reveal Why They've Gone Greek," *Village Voice*, July 26, 2005, http://www.villagevoice.com/2005-7-26/theater/oedipus-resexed (accessed June 2008).

37. Ibid.

38. Ibid.

39. Five Lesbian Brothers, *Oedipus at Palm Springs* (New York: Samuel French, 2010), 7.

40. Ibid., 8.

41. Ibid., 23.

42. Ibid., 87.

43. Ibid., 88.

44. Ibid.

45. Dolan, "The Return of the Five Lesbian Brothers."

46. Samuel Beckett, *Endgame and Act without Words* (New York: Grove, 1958), 18.

47. Five Lesbian Brothers, *Oedipus at Palm Springs*, 88.

48. Ibid.

49. Stoudt, "Oedipus Resexed."

50. Ibid.

51. Sigmund Freud, *Jokes and Their Relation to the Unconscious*, trans. Peter Gay (New York: W. W. Norton, [1905] 1969), 133.

52. Ibid., 131. When Freud said "the wishes and desires of men," he meant males (not humans), as he believed women were fulfilled, sexually and emotionally, by marriage and childbirth.

53. Kate Clinton, *What the L?* (New York: Carroll and Graf, 2005), 241.

54. Ibid.

55. The Five Lesbian Brothers, *Oedipus at Palm Springs*, 43.

56. Ibid.

57. Ibid.

58. Ibid., 66.

59. Ibid.

60. Ibid.

61. Ibid., 49.

62. Ibid., 48.

63. Ibid.

64. Ibid., 47–48.

65. Sue-Ellen Case, "Toward a Butch-Femme Aesthetic," in *Feminist and Queer Performance: Critical Strategies* (New York: Palgrave Macmillan, 2009), 32.

66. The Five Lesbian Brothers, *Oedipus at Palm Springs*, 77.

67. Ibid., 87.

68. Diana Taylor, *Disappearing Acts: Spectacles of Gender and Nationalism in Argentina's "Dirty War"* (Durham: Duke University Press, 1997), 123.

69. Ibid., 123–24.

70. André Breton, *Anthology of Black Humor*, trans. Mark Polizzotti (San Francisco: City Lights, 1997), xiv.

71. Louise Kennedy, "'Oedipus' Deftly Mixes Comedy, Tragedy," *Boston Globe*, October 27, 2007, http://articles.boston.com/2007-10-27/ae/29226516_1_oedipus-palm-springs-comedy (accessed June 2009).

72. Breton, *Anthology of Black Humor*, 212, xvi.

73. Ibid., xix, xiv.

74. Samuel Beckett, *Watt* (New York: Grove, 1994), 48.

75. See Mary Whitlock Blundell, "Ethos and Dianoia Reconsidered," in *Essays on Aristotle's Poetics*, ed. Amélie Rorty (Princeton: Princeton University Press, 1992), 155–76.

76. Five Lesbian Brothers, *Oedipus at Palm Springs*, 87.

77. Breton, *Anthology of Black Humor*, xviii.

78. Gayle Rubin, "Thinking Sex: Notes for a Radical Theory of the Politics of Sexuality," in *Pleasure and Danger: Exploring Female Sexuality*, ed. Carole Vance (New York: routledge & Kegan, 1984), 13.

Afterword

1. Lauren Berlant, *The Queen of America Goes to Washington City: Essays on Sex and Citizenship* (Durham: Duke University Press, 1997), 180.

2. Lisa Duggan, "On Queer Failure," Bully Bloggers on the Failure and the Future of Queer Studies, *Bully Bloggers,* April 2, 2012, http://bullybloggers.woodpress.com/2012/04/02/bullybloggers-on-failure-and-the-future-of-queer-studies/ (accessed April 2012).

Bibliography

Ahmed, Sara. *The Promise of Happiness*. Durham: Duke University Press, 2010.

Andy Warhol: A Documentary Film. Dir. Ric Burns. 2006. PBS.

Altman, Alex. "That Viral Thing: Prop. 8, the Musical." *Time,* December 8, 2008. http://www.time.com/time/arts/article/0,8599,1864797,00.html (accessed January 2010).

Alwood, Edward. *Straight News: Gays, Lesbians, and the News Media*. New York: Columbia University Press, 1998.

Als, Hilton. "A New Age Oedipus: The Five Lesbian Brothers Update a Myth." *New Yorker,* August 22, 2005. http://www.newyorker.com/archive/2005/08/22/050822crth_theatre (accessed December 2005).

Anderson, Benedict. *Imagined Communities: Reflections on the Origin and Spread of Nationalism*. New York: Verso, 1983.

Anzaldúa, Gloria. *Borderlands/La Frontera: The New Mestiza*. San Francisco: Spinsters and Aunt Lute, 1987.

Anzaldúa, Gloria, and Cherríe Moraga, eds. *This Bridge Called My Back: Writings by Radical Women of Color*. New York: Kitchen Table Women of Color Press, 1981.

Armstrong, Elizabeth, Joan Rothfuss, and Janet Jenkins, eds. *In the Spirit of Fluxus*. Minneapolis: Walker Art Center, 1993.

Atkinson, Ti-Grace. *Amazon Odyssey: The First Collection of Writings by the Political Pioneer of the Women's Movement*. New York: Link Books, 1974.

Austin, J. L. *How to Do Things With Words*. Cambridge, MA: Harvard University Press, 1975.

Avrich, Paul. *Anarchist Voices: An Oral History of Anarchism in America*. San Francisco: AK Press, 2006.

Baer, Freddie. "About Valerie Solanas." In *SCUM Manifesto,* by Valerie Solanas, 51–60. Edinburgh and San Francisco: AK Press, 1996.

Banes, Sally. *Writing Dance in the Age of Postmodernism*. Middletown, CT: Wesleyan University Press, 1994.

Barbaro, Michael. "Behind N.Y. Gay Marriage, an Unlikely Mix of Forces." *New York Times,* June 25, 2011.

Bateman, Geoffrey W. "Gay Liberation Front." In *GLBTQ: An Encyclopedia of Gay, Lesbian, Bisexual, Transgender, and Queer Culture,* edited by Claude J. Summers. Chicago: GLBTQ, 2004. http://www.glbtq.com/social_sciences/gay_liberation_front.html (accessed January 2010).

Baudrillard, Jean. "Our Theatre of Cruelty," translated by John Johnston. *Semiotext(e)* 4 (1982): 108–9.

Bechdel, Alison. *The Essential Dykes to Watch Out For.* New York: Houghton Mifflin Harcourt, 2008.

Beckett, Samuel. *Endgame and Act without Words.* New York: Grove Press, 1958.

Beckett, Samuel. *Watt.* New York: Grove Press, 1994.

Bell, Arthur. *Dancing the Gay Lib Blues: A Year in the Homosexual Liberation Movement.* New York: Simon and Schuster, 1971.

Bender, Marylin. "Valeria Solanis [sic] a Heroine to Feminists." *New York Times,* June 14, 1968, 52.

Berg, Gretchen. "Andy Warhol: My True Story." In *I'll Be Your Mirror: The Selected Andy Warhol Interviews: 1962–1987,* edited by Kenneth Goldsmith, Reva Wolf, and Wayne Koestenbaum, 85–96. New York: Da Capo Press, 2004.

Berlant, Lauren. *The Female Complaint: The Unfinished Business of Sentimentality in American Culture.* Durham: Duke University Press, 2008.

Berlant, Lauren, ed. *Intimacy.* Chicago: University of Chicago Press Journals, 2000.

Berlant, Lauren. "Live Sex Acts." *Feminist Studies* 21, no. 2 (1995): 379–404.

Berlant, Lauren. *The Queen of America Goes to Washington City: Essays on Sex and Citizenship.* Durham: Duke University Press, 1997.

Berlant, Lauren. "'68 or Something." *Critical Inquiry* 21, no. 1 (Autumn 1994): 124–55.

Berlant, Lauren. "The Subject of True Feeling: Pain, Privacy, and Politics." In *Transformations: Thinking through Feminism,* edited by Sara Ahmed and Jane Kilby, 33–47. New York: Routledge, 2000.

Berlant, Lauren, and Elizabeth Freeman. "Queer Nationality." In *The Queen of America Goes to Washington City: Essays on Sex and Citizenship,* by Lauren Berlant, 146–74. Durham: Duke University Press, 1997.

Berlant, Lauren, and Michael Warner. "Sex in Public." In *Intimacy,* by Lauren Berlant, 311–30. Chicago: University of Chicago Press Journals, 2000.

Bernstein, Robin, ed. *Cast Out: Queer Lives in Theater.* Ann Arbor: University of Michigan Press, 2006.

Bersani, Leo. *Homos.* Cambridge, MA: Harvard University Press, 1995.

Birimisa, George, and Steve Susoyev. *Return to the Caffe Cino: A Collection of Plays and Memoirs.* San Francisco: Moving Finger Press, 2007.

Birkby, Phyllis, Bertha Harris, Jill Johnston, Esther Newton, and Jane O'Wyatt, eds. *Amazon Expedition: A Lesbian Feminist Anthology.* New York: Times Change Press, 1973.

Blankenship, Mark. "'Oedipus' Gets Complex in Updated Classic." *Variety,* August 4, 2005. http://www.variety.com/review/VE1117927829?refCatId=33 (accessed September 2005).

Blau, Herbert. *Blooded Thought: Occasions of Theatre.* New York: Performing Arts Journal, 1982.

Blau, Herbert. *Take Up the Bodies: Theater at the Vanishing Point.* Chicago: University of Illinois Press, 1982.

Blundell, Mary Whitlock. "Ethos and Dianoia Reconsidered." In *Essays on Aristotle's Poetics,* edited by Amélie Rorty, 155–76. Princeton: Princeton University Press, 1992.

Boal, Augusto. *Theatre of the Oppressed.* New York: Theatre Communications Group, 1979.

Bockris, Victor. *The Life and Death of Andy Warhol.* London: Fourth Estate, 1998.

Born in Flames. Dir. Lizzie Borden. 1983. New York, First Run Features. VHS.

Bornstein, Kate. *Gender Outlaw: On Men, Women, and the Rest of Us.* New York: Vintage Books, 1994.

Bottoms, Stephen J. *Playing Underground: A Critical History of the 1960s Off-Off-Broadway Movement*. Ann Arbor: University of Michigan Press, 2004.

Breton, André. *Anthology of Black Humor*. Trans. Mark Polizzotti. San Francisco: City Lights, 1997.

Brown, Rita Mae. "Leadership v Stardom." *The Furies* 1, no. 2 (February 1972): 20–22.

Brown, Wendy. *States of Injury: Power and Freedom in Late Modernity*. Princeton: Princeton University Press, 1995.

Brownmiller, Susan. *In Our Time: Memoir of a Revolution*. New York: Dell, 1999.

Broyles-González, Yolanda. *El Teatro Campesino: Theater in the Chicano Movement*. Austin: University of Texas Press, 1994.

Bullough, Vern L. *Before Stonewall: Activists for Gay and Lesbian Rights in Historical Context*. Binghamton, NY: Harrington Park Press, 2002.

Bunch, Charlotte. "Lesbians in Revolt: Male Supremacy Shakes and Quivers." *The Furies* 1, no. 1 (January 1972): 8–9.

Bunch, Charlotte. *Passionate Politics: Feminist Theory in Action*. New York: St. Martin's Press, 1987.

Butler, Judith. *Bodies That Matter: On the Discursive Limits of "Sex."* New York: Routledge, 1993.

Butler, Judith. "Critically Queer." *GLQ: A Journal of Lesbian and Gay Studies* 1, no. 1 (1993): 17–32.

Butler, Judith. *Gender Trouble: Feminism and the Subversion of Identity*. New York: Routledge, 1990.

Butler, Judith. "Quotes." European Graduate School. http://www.egs.edu/faculty/judith_butler/quotes (accessed November 2011).

Cage, Diana. "Up Close with the Iconic Holly Hughes: Video Interview." SheWired, October 15, 2010. http://www.shewired.com/box-office/close-iconic-holly-hughes-video-interview (accessed January 2011).

Caillois, Roger. *Man, Play, and Games*. Translated by Meyer Barash. Chicago: University of Illinois Press, 2001.

Canning Charlotte. *Feminist Theaters in the U.S.A.: Staging Women's Experience*. New York: Routledge, 1996.

Capsuto, Steven. *Alternate Channels: The Uncensored Story of Gay and Lesbian Images on Radio and Television*. New York: Ballantine Books, 2000.

Carter, David. *Stonewall: The Riots That Sparked the Gay Revolution*. New York: Macmillan, 2005.

Case, Sue-Ellen. *Split Britches: Lesbian Practice/Feminist Performance*. New York: Routledge, 1996.

Case, Sue-Ellen. "Toward a Butch-Femme Aesthetic." In *Feminist and Queer Performance: Critical Strategies*, 31–48. New York: Palgrave Macmillan, 2009.

Case, Sue-Ellen. "Toward a Butch-Feminist Retro-Future." In *Feminist and Queer Performance: Critical Strategies*, 49–65. New York: Palgrave Macmillan, 2009.

Caserio, Robert L., Tim Dean, Lee Edelman, Judith Halberstam, and José Esteban Muñoz. "Forum: Conference Debates—the Antisocial Thesis in Queer Theory." *PMLA* 121, no. 3 (May 2006): 819–36.

Castro, Ginette. *American Feminism, a Contemporary History*. Translated by Elizabeth Loverde-Bagwell. New York: New York University Press, 1990.

Chaliand, Gérard, and Arnaud Blin, eds. *The History of Terrorism: From Antiquity to al Qaeda*. Los Angeles: University of California Press, 2007.

Charles, Casey. *The Sharon Kowalski Case: Lesbian and Gay Rights on Trial*. Topeka: University of Kansas Press, 2003.

Chauncey, George. *Gay New York: Gender, Urban Culture, and the Making of the Gay Male World, 1890–1940*. New York: Basic Books, 1995.

Chin, Staceyann. "Dykepoem." In *Wildcat Woman: Poetry.* N.p., Staceyann Chin, 1998.

Chinoy, Helen Krich, and Linda Walsh Jenkins. *Women in American Theatre.* 3rd ed. New York: Theatre Communications Group, 2006.

Clinton, Kate. *What the L?* New York: Carroll and Graf, 2005.

Clough, Patricia Ticineto, and Jean O'Malley Halley, eds. *The Affective Turn: Theorizing the Social.* Durham: Duke University Press, 2007.

Coble, Margaret. "Hothead Does Michigan." *Advocate,* July 20, 2004, 56–57.

Coburn, Judith. "Solanas Lost and Found." *Village Voice,* January 12, 2000. http://villa gevoice.com/2000_01_11/newssolanas_lost_and_found/ (accessed January 2010).

Coburn, Judith. "Valerie's Gang." *East Bay Express,* November 19, 1999, 1, 8, 9, 11, 13, 16.

Conway, Mary T. "A Becoming Queer Aesthetic." *Discourse* 26, no. 3 (2004): 166–89.

Cory, Donald Webster. *The Homosexual in America: A Subjective Approach.* New York: Greenberg, 1951.

Crenshaw, Martha, ed. *Terrorism in Context.* Pittsburgh: University of Pennsylvania Press, 1995.

Cronan, Sheila. "Marriage." In *Radical Feminism,* edited by Anne Koedt, Ellen Levine, and Anita Rapone, 213–21. New York: Harper Collins, 1973.

Crowley, Mart. *The Boys in the Band.* In *Forbidden Acts: Pioneering Gay and Lesbian Plays of the Twentieth Century,* edited by Benjamin A. Hodges, 443–518. New York: Applause Books, 2003.

Culler, Jonathan. *Barthes: A Very Short Introduction.* Oxford: Oxford University Press, 2002.

Curtis, Charlotte. "Women's Liberation Gets into the Long Island Swim." *New York Times,* August 10, 1970, 32.

Cvetkovich, Ann. *An Archive of Feelings: Trauma, Sexuality, and Lesbian Public Cultures.* Durham: Duke University Press, 2003.

Dalzell, Tom, ed. *The Routledge Dictionary of Modern American Slang and Unconventional English.* New York: Routledge, 2005.

Davidson, Sara. "An 'Oppressed Majority' Demands Its Rights: The Cause of Women's Equality Draws a Growing Number of Active—and Angry—Female Militants." *Life,* December 12, 1969, 66–78.

Davis, Tracy. *Actresses as Working Women: Their Social Identity in Victorian Culture.* New York: Routledge, 2002.

Davis, Tracy, and Thomas Postlewait, eds. *Theatricality.* Cambridge: Cambridge University Press, 2003.

Davy, Kate. "Fe/Male Impersonation: The Discourse of Camp." In *Critical Theory and Performance,* edited by Janelle Reinelt and Joseph R. Roach, 355–71. Ann Arbor: University of Michigan Press, 2010.

Davy, Kate. *Lady Dicks and Lesbian Brothers: Staging the Unimaginable at the WOW Café Theatre.* Ann Arbor: University of Michigan Press, 2010.

Dean, Tim. *Unlimited Intimacy: Reflections on the Subculture of Barebacking.* Chicago: University of Chicago Press, 2009.

de Beauvoir, Simone. *The Second Sex.* Translated and edited by H. M. Parshley. New York: Vintage Books, [1952] 1989.

de Lauretis, Teresa. "Habit Changes." *differences: A Journal of Feminist Cultural Studies* 6, nos. 2–3 (1994): 296–313.

Deem, Melissa. "From Bobbitt to SCUM: Re-memberment, Scatological Rhetorics, and Feminist Strategies in the Contemporary United States." *Public Culture* 8, no. 3 (1996): 511–37.

Deem, Melissa. "Disrupting the Nuptials at the Town Hall Debate: Feminism and the Politics of Cultural Memory in the USA." *Cultural Studies* 17, no. 5 (2003): 615–47.

Deleuze, Gilles, and Félix Guattari. *Anti-Oedipus: Capitalism and Schizophrenia*. Translated by Robert Hurley, Mark Seem, and Helen R. Lane. New York: Continuum, [1972] 2004.

Deleuze, Gilles, and Félix Guattari. *A Thousand Plateaus: Capitalism and Schizophrenia*. Translated by Brian Massumi. Minneapolis: University of Minnesota Press, 1987.

Dell'Olio, Anselma. "Home before Sundown." In *The Feminist Memoir Project: Voices from Women's Liberation*, edited by Rachel Blau DuPlessis and Ann Snitow, 149–70. New Brunswick, NJ: Rutgers University Press, 2007.

D'Emilio, John. *Sexual Politics, Sexual Communities: The Making of a Homosexual Minority in the United States, 1940–1970*. Chicago: University of Chicago Press, 1983.

DiMassa, Diane. *The Complete Hothead Paisan: Homicidal Lesbian Terrorist*. San Francisco: Cleis Press, 1999.

DiMassa, Diane. *Hothead Paisan: Homicidal Lesbian Terrorist*. San Francisco: Cleis Press, 1993.

DiMassa, Diane. *Hothead Paisan: Homicidal Lesbian Terrorist*. http://hotheadpaisan.com (accessed June 2009).

DiMassa, Diane. *The Revenge of Hothead Paisan: Homicidal Lesbian Terrorist*. San Francisco: Cleis Press, 1995.

Dinshaw, Carolyn. *Getting Medieval: Sexualities and Communities, Pre- and Postmodern*. Durham: Duke University Press, 1999.

Dinshaw, Carolyn, Lee Edelman, Roderick A. Ferguson, Carla Frecero, Elizabeth Freeman, Judith Halberstam, Annamarie Jagose, Christopher Nealon, and Nguyen Tan Hoang. "Theorizing Queer Temporalities: A Roundtable Discussion." *GLQ: A Journal of Lesbian and Gay Studies* 13, nos. 2–3 (2007): 177–95.

Dolan, Jill. "Feeling Women's Culture: Women's Music, Lesbian Feminism, and the Impact of Emotional Memory." *Journal of Dramatic Theory and Criticism* 26, no. 2 (Spring 2012): 205–19.

Dolan, Jill. *The Feminist Spectator as Critic*. Ann Arbor: University of Michigan Press, 1991.

Dolan, Jill. *Geographies of Learning: Theory and Practice, Activism and Performance*. Middletown, CT: Wesleyan University Press, 2001.

Dolan, Jill. "The Return of the Five Lesbian Brothers." *Feminist Spectator*, August 26, 2005. http://feministspectator.blogspot.com/2005/08/return-of-five-lesbian-brothers.html (accessed December 2005).

Dolan, Jill. *Utopia in Performance: Finding Hope at the Theater*. Ann Arbor: University of Michigan Press, 2005.

Dominic, Magie. *The Queen of Peace Room*. Waterloo, ON: Wilfrid Laurier University Press, 2002.

Dorr-Dorynek, Diane. "Lonesome Cowboy–Reel 606." *East Village Other* 3, no. 26, June 15, 1968. (unpaginated).

Doyle, Jennifer. *Sex Objects: Art and the Dialectics of Desire*. Minneapolis: University of Minnesota Press, 2006.

Drukman, Steven. "Doo-A-Diddly-Dit-Dit: An Interview with Suzan-Lori Parks and Liz Diamond." In *A Sourcebook of African-American Performance: Plays, People, Movements*, edited by Annemarie Bean, 284–306. New York: Routledge, 1999.

Duberman, Martin, ed. *Queer Representations: Reading Lives, Reading Cultures, a Center for Lesbian and Gay Studies Book*. New York: New York University Press, 1997.

Duberman, Martin. *Stonewall*. New York: Penguin Books, 1993.

Dufresne, Isabelle Collin [Ultra Violet]. *Famous for 15 Minutes: My Years with Andy Warhol*. New York: Harcourt Brace Jovanovich, 1988.

Duggan, Lisa. "On Queer Failure." In "Bully Bloggers on the Failure and Future of

Queer Studies." *Bully Bloggers*. http://bullybloggers.wordpress.com/2012/04/02/
bullybloggers_on_failure_and_the_future_of_queer_studies/   (accessed   April
2012).

Duggan, Lisa. "The New Homonormativity: The Sexual Politics of Neoliberalism." In
Materializing Democracy: Toward a Revitalized Cultural Politics, edited by Russ Castronovo and Dana D. Nelson, 175–94. Durham: Duke University Press, 2002.

Duggan, Lisa. *The Twilight of Equality: Neoliberalism, Cultural Politics, and the Attack on
Democracy.* Boston: Beacon Press, 2004.

Dunbar-Ortiz, Roxanne. "From the Cradle to the Boat: On the Occasion of the World
Premiere of *Up Your Ass,* a Feminist Historian Remembers Valerie Solanas." *San
Francisco Bay Guardian Online,* January 5, 2000. http://sfbg.com (accessed January
2010).

Dunbar-Ortiz, Roxanne. *Outlaw Woman: A Memoir of the War Years, 1960–1975.* San
Francisco: City Lights, 2001.

Duncombe, Stephen. *Notes from Underground: Zines and the Politics of Alternative Culture.* New York: Verso, 1997.

Duplessis, Rachel Blau, and Ann Snitow, eds. *The Feminist Memoir Project: Voices from
Women's Liberation.* New Brunswick, NJ: Rutgers University Press, 2007.

Durham, Michael. "Homosexuals in Revolt: The Year One Liberation Movement Turned
Militant." *Life,* December 31, 1971, 62–72.

Echols, Alice. *Daring to Be Bad: Radical Feminism in America, 1967–1975.* Minneapolis:
University of Minnesota Press, 1989.

Edelman, Lee. *No Future: Queer Theory and the Death Drive.* Durham: Duke University
Press, 2004.

Eisenbach, David. *Gay Power: An American Revolution.* New York: Carroll and Graf
Publishers, 2006.

Eng, David. *The Feelings of Queer Kinship: Queer Liberalism and the Racialization of
Intimacy.* Durham: Duke University Press, 2010.

Eng, David, Judith Halberstam, and José Esteban Muñoz, eds. *What's Queer about Queer
Studies Now? Social Text,* special issue, 23, nos. 3–4, 84–85 (Winter 2005).

Eugenios, Jillian. "Catching Up with Animal Prufrock." *Curve,* May 2011. http://www.
curvemag.com/Curve-Magazine/Web-Articles-2011/Catching-up-with-Animal-
Prufrock/ (accessed July 2011).

Evans, Sarah. *Personal Politics.* New York: Vintage Books, 1979.

Ewers, Justin. "Same-Sex Marriage Is Expected to Add Millions to California Coffers."
US News and World Report, June 11, 2008. http://www.usnews.com/news/nation
al/articles/2008/06/11/an-economic-boost-from-gay-marriage (accessed January
2011).

Faderman, Lillian. *Odd Girls and Twilight Lovers: A History of Lesbian Life in Twentieth
Century America.* New York: Penguin, 1999.

Fahs, Breanne. "The Radical Possibilities of Valerie Solanas." *Feminist Studies* 34, no. 3
(Fall 2008): 591–621.

Farrow, Kenyon. "Gay Marriage in New York: Progressive Victory or GOP Roadmap?"
Alternet.org, June 27, 2011. http://www.alternet.org/story/151444/gay_marriage_
in_new_york%3A_progressive_victory_or_gop_roadmap/ (accessed July 2011).

The Feminists. "Women: Do You Know the Facts about Marriage?" In *Sisterhood Is
Powerful: An Anthology of Writings from the Women's Liberation Movement,* edited by
Robin Morgan, 601–3. New York: Vintage Books, 1970.

Finkelstein, Nat. "The Nat Finkelstein Interview." Planet Group Entertainment, 2009.
http://planetgroupentertainment.squarespace.com/the-nat-finkelstein-interview/
(accessed January 2010).

Firestone, Shulamith. *Airless Spaces.* New York: Semiotext(e), 1998.

Five Lesbian Brothers. *Five Lesbian Brothers: Four Plays.* New York: Theatre Communication Group, 2000.

Five Lesbian Brothers. *Oedipus at Palm Springs.* New York: Samuel French, 2010.

Five Lesbian Brothers. Playbill for *The Secretaries.* New York Theatre Workshop, 1994.

Five Lesbian Brothers. *The Secretaries.* In *Five Lesbian Brothers: Four Plays,* 117–91. New York: Theatre Communications Group, 2000.

Fornés, María, Irene, Bertha Harris, Jill Johnston, Lisa Kennedy, and Barbara Smith. "On the Beginnings of Lesbian Literature in the United States." In *Queer Representations: Reading Lives, Reading Cultures, a Center for Lesbian and Gay Studies Book,* edited by Martin B. Duberman, 347–55. New York: New York University Press, 1995.

Foster, Frances. *Love and Marriage in Early African America.* Boston: Northeastern University Press, 2007.

Foucault, Michel. "What Is Enlightenment?" In *Ethics: Subjectivity and Truth.* Translated by Robert Hurley, 303–19. New York: New Press, 1997.

Freeman, Elizabeth. "Packing History, Count(er)ing Generations." *New Literary History* 31, no. 4 (Autumn 2000): 727–44.

Freeman, Elizabeth. *Time Binds: Queer Temporalities, Queer Histories.* Durham: Duke University Press, 2010.

Freeman, Jo. "WITCH." http://www.jofreeman.com/photos/witch.html (accessed January 2009).

Freud, Sigmund. *Jokes and Their Relation to the Unconscious.* Translated by Peter Gay. New York: W. W. Norton, [1905] 1969.

Friedan, Betty. "Up from the Kitchen Floor." *New York Times Magazine,* March 4, 1973, 8–9, 28–37.

Gaither, Rowan. "Andy Warhol's Feminist Nightmare." *New York,* January 14, 1991, 35.

Gallo, Marcia. *Different Daughters: A History of the Daughters of Bilitis and the Birth of the Lesbian Rights Movement.* New York: Carroll and Graf, 2006.

"Gay Liberation Front." Outhistory.org. http://outhistory.org/Wiki/Gay–Liberation-Front (accessed January 10, 2010).

Geertz, Clifford. *The Interpretation of Cultures.* New York: Basic Books, 1977.

Gever, Martha. *Entertaining Lesbians: Celebrity, Sexuality, and Self-Invention.* New York: Routledge, 2003.

Girodias, Maurice. Publisher's preface to *S.C.U.M. Manifesto,* by Valerie Solanas, vii–viii. New York: Grove Press, 1968.

Goffman, Erving. *The Presentation of Self in Everyday Life.* New York: Doubleday, 1959.

Golden, Harry. *For 2¢ Plain.* New York: World Publishing: 1958.

Goldsmith, Kenneth, Reva Wolf, and Wayne Koestenbaum. *I'll Be Your Mirror: The Selected Andy Warhol Interviews, 1962–1987.* New York: Da Capo Press, 2004.

Gourevitch, Philip, and Errol Morris Exposure. "The Woman behind the Camera at Abu Ghraib." *New Yorker,* March 24, 2008. http://www.newyorker.com/reporting/2008/03/24/080324fa_fact_gourevitch (accessed July 2009).

Grahn, Judy. *Another Mother Tongue: Gay Words, Gay Worlds.* Boston: Beacon Press, 2000.

Greer, Germaine. *The Female Eunuch.* London: MacGibbon and Kee, 1970.

Greer, Germaine. "My Mailer Problem." *Esquire* 76, no. 3 (1971): 92–93, 214–16.

Gross, Larry P. *Up from Invisibility: Lesbians, Gay Men, and the Media in America.* New York: Columbia University Press, 2001.

Grosz, Elizabeth. "Histories of a Feminist Future." *Signs* 25, no. 4 (Summer 2000): 1017–21.

Halberstam, Judith. "The Anti-social Turn in Queer Studies." *Graduate Journal of Social Science* 5, no. 2 (2008): 140–56.

Halberstam, Judith. *Female Masculinity*. Durham: Duke University Press, 1998.

Halberstam, Judith. *In a Queer Time and Place: Transgender Bodies, Subcultural Lives*. New York: New York University Press, 2005.

Halberstam, Judith. *The Queer Art of Failure*. Durham: Duke University Press, 2011.

Halberstam Judith, and Del LaGrace Volcano. *The Drag King Handbook*. New York: Serpent's Tail, 1999.

Halley, Janet, and Andrew Parker, eds. *After Sex? On Writing since Queer Theory*. Durham: Duke University Press, 2010.

Halley, Janet, and Andrew Parker, eds. "After Sex: On Writing since Queery Theory." *South Atlantic Quarterly*, special issue, 106, no. 3 (Summer 2007).

Halperin, David, and Valerie Traub, eds. *Gay Shame*. Chicago: University of Chicago Press, 2009.

Handy, D. Antoinette. *The International Sweethearts of Rhythm: The Ladies Jazz Band from Piney Woods Country Life School*. Lanham, MD: Scarecrow Press, 1998.

Hanisch, Carol. "The Personal Is Political." In *Notes from the Second Year: Women's Liberation in 1970—Major Writings of the Radical Feminists*, edited by Shulamith Firestone and Anne Koedt, 76–77. New York: New York Radical Women, 1970.

Hanisch, Carol. "What Can Be Learned: A Critique of the Miss America Protest" (1968). http://www.carolhanisch.org/CHwritings/MissACritique.html (accessed January 2009).

Harding, James. "The Simplest Surrealist Act: Valerie Solanas and the (Re)Assertion of Avant-garde Priorities." *TDR* 45, no. 4 (Winter 2001): 142–62.

Harris, Bertha. *Lover*. New York: New York University Press, 1976.

Harron, Mary. "Introduction: On Valerie Solanas." In *I Shot Andy Warhol*, by Mary Harron and Daniel Minahan, vii–xxxi. New York: Grove Press, 1995.

Harron, Mary, and Daniel Minahan. *I Shot Andy Warhol*. New York: Grove Press, 1995.

Harron, Mary, and Rose Troche. "Factory Outlet: Rose Troche talks with *I Shot Andy Warhol* director Mary Harron." *Filmmaker*, Spring 1996. http://www.filmmakermagazine.com/issues/spring1996/warhol.php (accessed January 2010).

"Harry Hay: Founding the Mattachine." Outhistory.org. http://www.outhistory.org/wiki/Harry_Hay:_Founding_the_Mattachine,_part_2 (accessed January 2009).

Hart, Lynda. *Fatal Women: Lesbian Sexuality and the Mark of Aggression*. Princeton: Princeton University Press, 1994.

Harvey, David. *A Brief History of Neoliberalism*. Oxford: Oxford University Press, 2005.

Hayden, Tom. *The Port Huron Statement: The Visionary Call of the 1960s Revolution*. New York: Thunder's Mouth Press, 2005.

Heide, Robert. "Village '65 Revisited." Letter to the editor, *Village Voice*, July 27, 1982.

Heller, Dana. "Hothead Paisan: Clearing a Space for Lesbian Feminist Folklore." *New York Folklore* 19, nos. 1–2 (1993): 157–83.

Heller, Dana. "Shooting Solanas." *Feminist Studies* 27, no. 1 (2001): 167–89.

Hendricks, Geoffrey. *Critical Mass: Happenings, Fluxus, Performance, Intermedia, and Rutgers University, 1958–1972*. New Brunswick, NJ: Rutgers University Press, 2003.

Hertling, Pati. "Bettina Köster." *GLU* Magazine 1, no. 2 (Spring 2006). http://www.glumagazine/vl/bettina_Koster (accessed January 2009).

Higgins, Dick. *Horizons: The Poetics and Theory of Intermedia*. Carbondale: Southern Illinois University Press, 1984.

Hildebrand, Lucas. "Retroactivism." *GLQ: A Journal of Lesbian and Gay Studies* 12, no. 2 (2006): 303–17.

Hoffman, Abbie. *Revolution for the Hell of It*. New York: Dial Press, 1968.

Hoffman, Bruce. *Inside Terrorism.* New York: Columbia University Press, 2006.

Hollibaugh, Amber. *My Dangerous Desires: A Queer Girl Dreaming Her Way Home.* Durham: Duke University Press, 2000.

Huerta, Jorge. *Chicano Theater: Themes and Forms.* Bloomington: Indiana University Press, 1982.

Hughes, Holly. *Clit Notes: A Sapphic Sampler.* New York: Grove Press, 1996.

Hughes, Holly. "Preface." In *Five Lesbian Brothers: Four Plays,* by Five Lesbian Brothers ix–xii. New York: Theatre Communication Group, 2000.

Hughes, Holly, and David Román, eds. *O Solo Homo: The New Queer Performance.* New York: Grove Press, 1988.

Hunter, Nan D. "Sexual Dissent and the Family: The Sharon Kowalski Case." In *Sex Wars: Sexual Dissent and Political Culture,* Tenth Anniversary Edition, edited by Lisa Duggan and Nan Hunter, 99–104. New York: Routledge, 2006.

Huizinga, Johan. *Homo Ludens: Study of the Play Element in Culture.* New York: Taylor and Francis, [1944] 2003.

Hurley, Erin. *National Performance: Representing Quebec from Expo 67 to Celine Dion.* Toronto: University of Toronto Press, 2010.

Hyde, Lewis. *Trickster Makes This World: Mischief, Myth, and Art.* New York: Farrar, Straus and Giroux, 1998.

Isherwood, Charles. "When Sappho Meets Sophocles in a California Hot Tub." *New York Times Art Beat,* August 5, 2005. http://www.nytimes.com (accessed September 2005).

Itzkoff, Dave. "Marc Shaiman on 'Prop 8—the Musical.'" *New York Times Art Beat* blog, December 4, 2008. http://artsbeat.blogs.nytimes.com/2008/12/04/marc-shaiman-on-prop-8-the-musical/ (accessed January 2010).

Jay, Karla. *Dyke Life: From Growing Up to Growing Old, A Celebration of the Lesbian Experience.* New York: Basic Books, 1995.

Jay, Karla. *Tales of a Lavender Menace: A Memoir of Liberation.* New York: Basic Books, 2000.

Jay, Karla, and Allen Young, eds. *Out of the Closets: Voices of Gay Liberation.* Twentieth Anniversary Edition. New York: New York University Press, 1992.

Jobey, Liz. "Solanas and Son." *Guardian Weekend,* August 24, 1996, T10.

Johnston, Jill. *Admission Accomplished: The Lesbian Nation Years (1970–75).* London: Serpent's Tail, 1998.

Johnston, Jill. "Biography." http://jilljohnston.com/Biography.aspx (accessed July 2009).

Johnston, Jill. "George Brecht, the Philosopher of Fluxus." *Art in America* 94, no. 4 (April 2006): 112–18.

Johnston, Jill. *Lesbian Nation: The Feminist Solution.* New York: Simon and Schuster, 1973.

Johnston, Jill. *Marmalade Me.* New York: E. P. Dutton, 1971.

Johnston, Jill. *Mother Bound: Autobiography in Search of a Father.* New York: Knopf, 1983.

Johnston, Jill. "Of This Pure but Irregular Passion." *Village Voice,* July 2, 1970, 29–30, 38–39, 55.

Johnston, Jill. "Was Lesbian Separatism Inevitable?" *Gay and Lesbian Review* 13, no. 2. (March–April 2006). http://www.glreview.com/issues/13.2/13.2-johnston.php (accessed August 2009).

Johnston, Jill. "Wedding in Denmark." *Art in America* 82, no. 6 (June 1994): 75–76.

Johnston, Jill. "Write First, Then Live." In *Queer Representations: Reading Lives, Reading Cultures, a Center for Lesbian and Gay Studies Book,* edited by Martin B. Duberman, 343–46. New York: New York University Press, 1997.

Johnston, Jill. "Writing into the Sunset." *Village Voice,* September 27, 1972, 41–44.
Juergensmeyer, Mark. *Terror in the Mind of God: The Global Rise of Religious Violence.* Los Angeles: University of California Press, 2000.
Kaiser, Matthew. "A History of 'Ludicrous.'" *English Literary History* 71, no. 3 (Fall 2004): 631–60.
Kaufman, David. *Ridiculous! The Theatrical Life and Times of Charles Ludlam.* New York: Applause Books, 2002.
Kennedy, Louise. "'Oedipus' Deftly Mixes Comedy, Tragedy." *Boston Globe,* October 27, 2007. http://articles.boston.com/2007-10-27/ae/29226516_1_oedipus-palm-springs-comedy (accessed June 2009).
Kershaw, Baz. *The Politics of Performance: Radical Theatre as Cultural Intervention.* London: Routledge, 1992.
Klemesrud, Judy. "It Was a Special Show—and the Audience Was Special Too." *New York Times,* February 17, 1969, 39.
Kramer, Larry. *The Normal Heart and The Destiny of Me: Two Plays.* New York: Grove Press, 2000.
Krassner, Paul. *Confessions of a Raving, Unconfined Nut: Misadventures in the Counter-Culture.* New York: Simon and Schuster, 1993.
Krassner, Paul. "Wonder Waif Meets Super Neuter." In *S.C.U.M. Manifesto,* by Valerie Solanas, 85–105. New York: Olympia Press, 1968.
Kron, Lisa. "About Lisa Kron." http://www.lisakron.com/ (accessed January 2010).
Kron, Lisa. *Well.* New York: Theatre Communications Group, 2006.
Kron, Lisa. "Work with the Five Lesbian Brothers." http://www.lisakron.com (accessed June 2009).
Kubiak, Anthony. *Stages of Terror: Terror, Ideology, and Coercion as Theatre History.* Bloomington: Indiana University Press, 1991.
Laqueur, Walter. *No End to War: Terrorism in the Twenty-First Century.* New York: Continuum International, 2003.
Lesbian Avengers. "An Incomplete History." 1992. http://www.lesbianavengers.com/ (accessed January 2010).
Leech, John. "The Great Social Evil." *Punch* 33 (January 10, 1857), 114.
Lennox, Raphael. "The Martyrization of Valerie Solanas." *East Village Other* 3, no. 30 (June 28, 1968): 3, 20.
Levy, Ariel. "Lesbian Nation: When Gay Women Took to the Road." *New Yorker,* March 2, 2009. http://newyorker.com/reporting/2009/03/02/090302fa_fact_levy (accessed March 2012).
Lichtenstein, Grace. "Women's Lib Wooed by Publishers." *New York Times,* August 17, 1970. 32.
Lord, Catherine. "Wonder Waif Meets Super Neuter." *October* 132 (Spring 2010): 135–63.
Lord, Catherine. "Wonder Waif Meets Super Neuter." In *The Art of Queering in Art,* edited by Gavin Butts, 55–84. Birmingham, UK: Article Press, 2007.
Lorde, Audre. "The Uses of the Erotic." In *Sister Outsider: Essays and Speeches.* Trumansburg, NY: The Crossing Press, 1984.
Louÿs, Pierre. *The Songs of Bilitis.* Translated by Alvah C. Bessie. New York: Dover, 1988.
Love, Heather. *Feeling Backward: Loss and the Politics of Queer History.* Cambridge, MA: Harvard University Press, 2007.
Love, Heather, ed. "Thinking Sex." *GLQ: A Journal of Lesbian and Gay Studies* 17, no. 1 (2011).

Luciano, Dana. *Arranging Grief: Sacred Time and the Body in Nineteenth-Century America*. New York: New York University Press, 2007.

Lyon, Phyllis, and Del Martin. *Lesbian/Woman*. Ann Arbor: University of Michigan Press, 1997.

Lyotard, Jean-François. *The Postmodern Condition: A Report on Knowledge*. Minneapolis: University of Minnesota Press, 1984.

Mailer, Norman. "The Prisoner of Sex." *Harpers*, March 1971, 41–92.

Marcus, Eric. *Making Gay History: The Half Century Fight for Lesbian and Gay Equal Rights*. New York: Harper, 2002.

Marks, Peter. "Encounters of the Sexual Kind." *New York Times*, December 11, 1997. http://www.nytimes.com/1997/12/11/movies/theater-review-encounters-of-the-sexual-kind.html (accessed June 2008).

Marmorstein, Robert. "Scum Goddess: A Winter Memory of Valerie Solanis [*sic*]." *Village Voice*, June 13, 1968, 9–11.

Marotta, Toby. *The Politics of Homosexuality: How Lesbians and Gay Men Have Made Themselves a Political and Social Force in Modern America*. Boston: Houghton Mifflin, 1981.

Marranca, Bonnie, Gautam Dasgupta, and Jack Smith, eds. *Theatre of the Ridiculous*. Baltimore: Johns Hopkins University Press, 1998.

Martin, Biddy. "Sexualities without Genders and Other Queer Utopias." In *Femininity Played Straight: The Significance of Being Lesbian*. New York: Routledge, 1996.

Martin, K., and G. Moon. "Hothead Goes Musical: Agitate, Agitate, Agitate." *Velvet Park*, no. 8 (Winter 2005): 14–16.

Martindale, Kathleen. *Un/Popular Culture: Lesbian Writing after the Sex Wars*. New York: State University of New York Press, 1997.

Mason, Susan Vaneta. "San Francisco Mime Troupe Legacy: Guerrilla Theater." In *Restaging the Sixties: Radical Theaters and Their Legacies*, edited by James M. Harding and Cindy Rosenthal, 196–212. Ann Arbor: University of Michigan Press, 2006.

McKenzie, Jon. *Perform or Else: From Discipline to Performance*. New York: Routledge, 2001.

McKinley, Jesse. "Theater Director Resigns amid Gay-Rights Ire." *New York Times*, November 12, 2008. http://www.nytimes.com/2008/11/13/arts/13iht13thea.17797780.html (accessed January 2011).

McNulty, Charles. "A Lesbian Reworking of Sophocles Turns a Classic into a Complex." *Village Voice*, August 2, 2005. http://www.villagevoice.com/2005-08-02/theater/a-lesbian-reworking-of-sophocles-turns-a-classic-into-a-complex/ (accessed June 2008).

Mecca, Tommi Avicolli, ed. *Smash the Church, Smash the State: The Early Years of Gay Liberation*. San Francisco: City Lights, 2009.

Meyer, Richard. "Have You Heard the One about the Lesbian Who Goes to the Supreme Court? Holly Hughes and the Case against Censorship." *Theatre Journal* 52, no. 4 (2000): 543–52.

Michaelson, Judy. "Valerie: The Trouble Was Men." *New York Post*, June 5, 1968, 57.

Miller, Tim, and David Román. "Preaching to the Converted." *Theatre Journal* 47, no. 2 (May 1995): 169–88.

Millett, Kate. "How Many Lives Are Here." In *The Feminist Memoir Project: Voices from Women's Liberation*, edited by Rachel Blau DuPlessis and Ann Snitow, 493–95. New Brunswick, NJ: Rutgers University Press, 2007.

Milman, Estera. "Introduction: Fluxus: A Conceptual Country." *Visible Language* 26, no. 1–2 (Winter/Spring 1992): 11–16.

Milman, Estera. "Road Shows, Street Events, and Fluxus People: A Conversation with Alison Knowles." *Visible Language* 26, no. 1–2 (Winter/Spring 1992): 97–108.

Moore, Marianne. "Marriage." In *Complete Poems,* 62–70. New York: Penguin, 1994.

Morgan, Robin. *Going Too Far: The Personal Chronicle of a Feminist.* New York: Random House, 1977.

Morgan, Robin, ed. *Sisterhood Is Powerful: An Anthology of Writings from the Women's Liberation Movement.* New York: Random House, 1970.

Morrissey, Paul. "Pop Shots." *Vogue,* May 1996, 52.

Muñoz, José Esteban. *Cruising Utopia: The Then and There of Queer Futurity.* New York: New York University Press, 2009.

Muñoz, José Esteban. *Disidentifications: Queers of Color and the Performance of Politics.* Minneapolis: University of Minnesota Press, 1999.

Munt, Sally. *Heroic Desire: Lesbian Identity and Cultural Space.* New York: New York University Press, 1998.

Nelson, Marilyn. *Sweethearts of Rhythm: The Story of the Greatest All-Girl Swing Band in the World.* New York: Dial Books, 2009.

Nestle, Joan. "Flamboyance and Fortitude." In *The Persistent Desire: A Femme-Butch Reader,* edited by Joan Nestle, 13–22. New York: Alyson Books, 1992.

Nestle, Joan. *A Restricted Country.* Ithaca, NY: Firebrand Books, 1987.

Newton, Esther. *Mother Camp: Female Impersonators in America.* Chicago: University of Chicago Press, 1979.

Ngai, Sianne. *Ugly Feelings.* Cambridge, MA: Harvard University Press, 2005.

Nietzsche, Friedrich. *The Gay Science: With a Prelude in Rhymes and an Appendix of Songs.* Translated by Walter Kaufmann. New York: Vintage, 1974.

O'Brien, Glenn. "History ReWrite." *Interview,* April 24, 2009. http://www.interview magazine.com/culture/history-rewrite/ (accessed January 2010).

Oedipus at Palm Springs. By The Five Lesbian Brothers. Dir. Leigh Silverman. Perf. Maureen Angelos, Babs Davy, Dominique Dibbell, Peg Healey, and Lisa Kron. New York Theatre Workshop, New York. August 6, 2005. Performance.

Olson, Theodore. "The Conservative Case for Gay Marriage: Why Same-Sex Marriage Is an American Value." *Newsweek,* January 8, 2010. Reposted on the *Daily Beast.* http://www.thedailybeast.com/newsweek/2010/01/08/the-conservative-case-for-gay-marriage.html (accessed January 2011).

Orr, John, and Dragan Klaić. "Terrorism and Drama: Introduction." In *Terrorism and Modern Drama,* edited by John Orr and Dragan Klaić, 1–12. Edinburgh: Edinburgh University Press, 1990.

Parker, Andrew, and Eve Kosofsky Sedgwick. Introduction to *Performativity and Performance,* edited by Andrew Parker and Eve Kosofsky Sedgwick, 1–18. New York: Routledge, 1995.

Parker, Pat. "Revolution: It's Not Neat or Pretty or Quick." In *This Bridge Called My Back: Writings by Radical Women of Color,* edited by Cherríe Moraga and Gloria Anzaldúa, 238–42. San Francisco: Kitchen Table Women of Color Press, 1983.

Parks, Suzan-Lori. "Elements of Style." In *The America Play and Other Works,* 6–18. New York: Theatre Communications Group, 1995.

Patrick, Robert. "Caffe Cino Pictures." Caffe Cino Blog. http://caffecino.wordpress .com/1915/01/01/issues/img_0004_2-2/ (accessed January 2010).

Patrick, Robert. *Temple Slave.* New York: Masquerade Books, 1994.

Pebworth, Sarah. "Interview with Animal Prufrock." *Lavenderlips,* March 2004. http:// www.lavenderlips.com/articles/animal.html (accessed May 2009).

Pellegrini, Ann. "Touching the Past, or, Hanging Chad, 'History's Queer Touch: Responses to Carolyn Dinshaw's *Getting Medieval: Sexualities and Communities,*

Pre- and Postmodern.'" Journal of the History of Sexuality 10, no. 2 (April 2001): 185–94.

Phelan, Peggy. "Serious Comedy of Hope: Introducing the Five Lesbian Brothers." In *Five Lesbian Brothers: Four Plays,* by Five Lesbian Brothers, xiii–xix. New York: Theatre Communications Group, 2000..

Phelan, Peggy. "Serrano, Mapplethorpe, the NEA, and You: 'Money Talks.'" *Drama Review* 34, no. 1 (1990): 4–15.

Phelan, Peggy. *Unmarked: The Politics of Performance.* New York: Routledge, 1993.

Pincus-Witten, Robert. "Fluxus and the Silvermans: An Introduction." In *Fluxus Codex,* by Jon Hendricks, 15–18. Gilbert and Lila Silverman Fluxus Collection, New York: Harry N. Abrams, 1988.

Polikoff, Nancy. *Beyond (Straight and Gay) Marriage: Valuing All Families under the Law.* Boston: Beacon Press, 2008.

Prufrock, Animal. *Animal's Farm.* http://www.animalsfarm.net/ (accessed January 2010).

Puar, Jasbir. *Terrorist Assemblages: Homonationalism in Queer Times.* Durham: Duke University Press, 2007.

Puchner, Martin. *Poetry of the Revolution: Marx, Manifestos, and the Avant-Gardes.* Princeton: Princeton University Press, 2006.

Pullen, Kirsten. *Actresses and Whores: On Stage and in Society.* Cambridge: Cambridge University Press, 2005.

Radical Harmonies. Dir. Dee Mosbacher. 2002. San Francisco, Woman Vision. DVD.

Radicalesbians. "The Woman-Identified Woman." In *Radical Feminism,* edited by Anne Koedt, Ellen Levine, and Anita Rapone, 240–45. New York: Quadrangle Books, [1970] 1973.

Raphael, Phyllis. *Off the Kings Road: Lost and Found in London.* London: Other Press, 2006.

Raskin, Jonah. *For the Hell of It: The Life and Times of Abbie Hoffman.* Berkeley: University of California Press, 1998.

Reich, Walter. *Origins of Terrorism: Psychologies, Ideologies, Theologies, States of Mind.* Princeton: Woodrow Wilson Press Center, 1998.

"Report of the Women's Rights Convention." http://www.nps.gov/wori/historyculture/report-of-the-womans-rights-convention.htm (accessed January 2010).

Rich, Adrienne. "Compulsory Heterosexuality and Lesbian Existence." *Signs: Journal of Women in Culture and Society* 5, no. 4 (Summer 1980): 631–60.

Rich, B. Ruby. "Manifesto Destiny: Drawing a Bead on Valerie Solanas." *Village Voice Literary Supplement* 38, no. 41 (October 12, 1993): 18–19.

Roach, Joseph. *It.* Ann Arbor: University of Michigan Press, 2007.

Roemer, Rick. *Charles Ludlam and the Ridiculous Theatrical Company: Critical Analyses of 29 Plays.* Jefferson, NC: McFarland, 2010.

Román, David. *Acts of Intervention: Performance, Gay Culture, and AIDS.* Bloomington: Indiana University Press, 1998.

Román, David. *Performance in America: Contemporary U.S. Culture and the Performing Arts.* Durham: Duke University Press, 2005.

Román, David, and Holly Hughes. "*O Solo Homo:* An Introductory Conversation." In *O Solo Homo: The New Queer Performance,* edited by Holly Hughes and David Román, 1–16. New York: Grove Press, 1988.

Rondo, Flavia. "Between Bohemia and Revolution." In *Smash the Church, Smash the State,* edited by Tommi Avicolli Mecca, 163–67. San Francisco: City Lights, 2009.

Ross, Becki. *The House That Jill Built: A Lesbian Nation in Formation.* Toronto: University of Toronto Press, 1995.

Rubin, Gayle. "Thinking Sex: Notes for a Radical Theory of the Politics of Sexuality." In *Pleasure and Danger: Exploring Female Sexuality,* edited by Carole Vance, 267–319. New York: Routledge and Kegan Paul, 1984.

Rubin, Gayle. "The Traffic in Women: Notes on the 'Political Economy' of Sex." In *Toward an Anthropology of Women,* edited by Rayna Reiter, 157–210. New York: Monthly View Press, 1975.

Rubin, Jerry. *Do IT! Scenarios of Revolution.* New York: Simon and Schuster, 1970.

Rush, Michael. *New Media in Art.* London: Thames and Hudson, 2005.

Savage, Dan. "Black Homophobia." *Slog,* November 5, 2008. http://slog.thestranger.com/2008/11/black_homophobia (accessed January 2011).

Savoie, Keely. "Hotheaded and Bothered: A Chat with Artist/Pen-Wielding Vigilante Diane DiMassa." *Bitch: Feminist Responses to Pop Culture,* no. 25 (Summer 2004): 34–41.

Savran, David. *A Queer Sort of Materialism: Recontextualizing American Theater.* Ann Arbor: University of Michigan Press, 2003.

Scalettar, Liana. "Resistance, Representation, and the Subject of Violence." In *Queer Frontiers: Millennial Geographies, Genders, and Generations,* edited by Joseph Boone, Debra Silverman, Cindy Sarver, Karin Quimby, Martin Dupvis, Martin Mecker, and Rosemary Weatherston, 261–77. Madison: University of Wisconsin Press, 2000.

Schechner, Richard. *Between Theatre and Anthropology.* Philadelphia: University of Pennsylvania Press, 1985.

Schechner, Richard. *Performance Studies: An Introduction.* New York: Routledge, 2006.

Scherman, Tony, and David Dalton. *Pop: The Genius of Andy Warhol.* New York: Harper, 2009.

Schneemann, Carolee. "Solanas in a Sea of Men." In *Imagining Her Erotics: Essays, Interviews, Projects,* 90–94. Cambridge, MA: MIT Press, 2003.

Schneider, Rebecca. *The Explicit Body in Performance.* New York: Routledge, 1997.

Schulman, Sarah. *My American History: Lesbian and Gay Life during the Reagan/Bush Years.* New York: Routledge, 1994.

Schutzman, Mady. "Jok(er)ing: Joker Runs Wild." In *A Boal Companion: Dialogues on Theatre and Cultural Politics,* edited by Jan Cohen-Cruz and Mady Schutzman, 133–45. New York: Routledge, 2006.

Sedgwick, Eve Kosofsky. *Epistemology of the Closet.* Los Angeles: University of California Press, 1990.

Sedgwick, Eve Kosofsky. "Queer Performativity: Henry James's *The Art of the Novel.*" *GLQ: A Journal of Lesbian and Gay Studies* 1, no. 1 (November 1993): 1–16.

Sedgwick, Eve Kosofsky. *Touching Feeling: Affect, Pedagogy, Performativity.* Durham: Duke University Press, 2003.

Sell, Mike. *Avant-Garde Performance and the Limits of Criticism: Approaching the Living Theatre, Happenings/Fluxus, and the Black Arts Movement.* Ann Arbor: University of Michigan Press, 2008.

Set it Off. Dir. Gary F. Gray. 1996. Los Angeles, New Line Cinema. DVD.

Shaw, Helen. "Oedipus without the Complex." *New York Sun,* August 5, 2005. http://www.nysun.com/arts/oedipus-without-the-complex/18139/ (accessed June 2008).

Shelley, Martha. "Gay Is Good." In *Out of the Closets: Voices of Gay Liberation,* edited by Karla Jay and Allen Young, 31–34. New York: Douglas Book Corp., 1972.

Shelley, Martha. "Our Passion Shook the World." In *Smash the Church, Smash the State!: The Early Years of Gay Liberation,* edited by Tommi Avicolli Mecca, 93–96. San Francisco: City Lights, 2009.

Shewey, Don. *Out Front: Contemporary Gay and Lesbian Plays.* New York: Grove Press, 1988.

Smith, Barbara. Preface to The Rutgers University Press Edition of *Home Girls: A Black Feminist Anthology*, edited by Barbara Smith, xiii–xviii. New Brunswick, NJ: Rutgers University Press, 2000.

Smith, Beverly. "The Wedding." In *Home Girls: A Black Feminist Anthology*, edited by Barbara Smith, 164–69. New Brunswick, NJ: Rutgers University Press, 2000.

Smith, Donny. "To Live with a Man Is to Hate a Man (or Vice Versa)." *Holy Titclamps*, January 16, 1998.

Smith, Donny. *Solanas*. Supplement to *Dwan*, March 1994.

Smith, Donny. *Solanas*. Supplement to *Dwan*, Number 2, May 1997.

Smith, Donny. *The Third Solanas Supplement to Dwan*, n.d.

Smith, Donny. "Valerie Is Good and Bad . . . Crazy and Sane: An Interview with Mary Harron." In *Solanas, Supplement to Dwan*, Number 2, May 1997.

Smith, Howard, and Brian Van der Horst. "Valerie Solanas Interview." *Village Voice*, July 25, 1977, 32.

Smith, Jack, J. Hoberman, and Edward Leffingwell. *Wait for Me at the Bottom of the Pool: The Writings of Jack Smith*. New York: Serpent's Tail, 1997.

Snitow, Ann, Christine Stansell, and Sharon Thompson. "Introduction." In *Powers of Desire: The Politics of Sexuality*, edited by Ann Snitow, Christine Stansell, and Sharon Thompson, 9–50. New York: Monthly Review Press, 1983.

Solanas, Valerie. "For 2¢: Pain, the Survival Game Gets Pretty Ugly." *Cavalier*, July 1966, 38–40, 76–77.

Solanas, Valerie. *From the Cradle to the Boat, or Up from the Slime*. Unpublished manuscript, 1965.

Solanas, Valerie. Letter to the editor of *The Diamondback*, University of Maryland, December 5, 1957, 4.

Solanas, Valerie. *SCUM Manifesto*. New York: SCUM Book, 1967.

Solanas, Valerie. *S.C.U.M. Manifesto*. New York: Olympia Press, 1968.

Solanas, Valerie. *SCUM Manifesto*. New York: SCUM Book, 1977.

Solanas, Valerie. *SCUM Manifesto*. Edinburgh and New York: AK Press, 1996.

Solanas, Valerie. *Up Your Ass, or From the Cradle to the Boat, or The Big Suck, or Up from the Slime and "A Young Girl's Primer on How to Attain the Leisure Class, a Nonfictional Article Reprinted from Cavalier."* New York: SCUM Book, 1967.

Solomon, Alisa. "Five Lesbian Brothers: No Whining!" *American Theatre* 15, no. 7 (September 1998): 61–62.

Solomon, Alisa. "Our Hearts Were Young and Gay: The 'Voice' Reports the Queer Revolution." *Village Voice*, October 18, 2005. http://www.villagevoice.com/2005-10-18/specials/our-hearts-were-young-and-gay/ (accessed October 2009).

Solomon, Alisa. *Re-dressing the Canon: Essays on Theatre and Gender*. New York: Routledge, 1997.

Solomon, Alisa. "Whose Soiree Now?" *Village Voice*, February 21, 2001. http://www.villagevoice.com/2001-02-20/theater/whose-soiree-now/ (accessed January 2009).

Solomon, Alisa. "The WOW Café." In *A Sourcebook of Feminist Theatre and Performance: On and Beyond the Stage*, edited by Carol Martin, 42–52. New York: Routledge, 1996.

Solomon, Alisa, and Framji Minwalla, eds. *The Queerest Art: Essays on Lesbian and Gay Theater*. New York: New York University Press, 1992.

Sontag, Susan. "Notes on 'Camp.'" In *Against Interpretation and Other Essays*, 275–92. New York: Dell, 1966.

Spitz, Bob. *Dylan: A Biography*. New York: W. W. Norton, 1991.

Split Britches. *Lesbians Who Kill*. In *Split Britches: Lesbian Practice/Feminist Performance*, edited by Sue-Ellen Case, 185–224. New York: Routledge, 1996.

Stern, Ellen. "Best Bets." *New York,* April 10, 1978, 62.

Stiles, Kristine. "Between Water and Stone: Fluxus Performance: A Metaphysics of Acts." In *In the Spirit of Fluxus,* edited by Janet Jenkins, 62–99. Minneapolis: Walker Art Center, 1993.

Stone, Wendell. *Caffe Cino: The Birthplace of Off-Off Broadway.* Carbondale: Southern Illinois University Press, 2005.

Stoudt, Charlotte. "Oedipus Resexed: The Five Lesbian Brothers Reveal Why They've Gone Greek." *Village Voice,* July 26, 2005. http://www.villagevoice.com/2005-07-26/theater/oedipus-resexed (accessed June 2008).

Sullivan, Andrew. *Virtually Normal: An Argument about Homosexuality.* New York: Knopf, 1995.

Sutton-Smith, Brian. *The Ambiguity of Play.* Cambridge, MA: Harvard University Press, 2001.

Sycamore, Matilda Bernstein. "Gay Shame: From Queer Autonomous Space to Direct Action Extravaganza." In *That's Revolting: Queer Strategies for Resisting Assimilation,* 268–95. Brooklyn: Soft Scull Press, [2004] 2008.

Taylor, Diana. *The Archive and the Repertoire: Performing Cultural Memory in the Americas.* Durham: Duke University Press, 2003.

Taylor, Diana. *Disappearing Acts: Spectacles of Gender and Nationalism in Argentina's "Dirty War."* Durham: Duke University Press, 1997.

Teal, Donn. *The Gay Militants.* New York: St. Martin's Press, 1971.

Third, Amanda. "'Shooting from the Hip': Valerie Solanas, the *SCUM Manifesto,* and the Apocalyptic Politics of Radical Feminism." *Hecate* 32, no. 2 (2006): 104–32.

Tiny and Ruby: Hell Divin' Women. Dir. Greta Schiller and Andrea Weiss. 1986. Channel 4, London. DVD.

Town Bloody Hall. Dir. Chris Hegedus and D. A. Pennebaker. 1979. Pennebaker Hegedus Films, New York. DVD.

Tropiano, Stephen. *The Prime Time Closet: A History of Gays and Lesbians on TV.* New York: Applause Theatre and Cinema Books, 2002.

Troyano, Alina [Carmelita Tropicana]. *I, Carmelita Tropicana: Performing between Cultures.* Boston: Beacon Press, 2000.

Turner, Victor. "Body, Brain, and Culture." *Performing Arts Journal* 10, no. 2 (1986): 26–34.

Turner, Victor. *From Ritual to Theatre: The Seriousness of Human Play.* New York: PAJ, 1982.

Vaid, Urvashi. "Beyond the Wedding Ring: LGBT Issues in the Age of Obama." Texts and Speeches, August 16, 2010. http://urvashivaid.net/wp/?p=344 (accessed January 2010).

Vaid, Urvashi. "Defining the Boundaries of Lesbian Identity." Paper presented at the conference In Amerika They Call us Dykes: Lesbian Lives in the 1970's. Center for Lesbian and Gay Studies, City University of New York Graduate Center, 2010.

Vaid, Urvashi. *Virtual Equality: The Mainstreaming of Gay and Lesbian Liberation.* New York: Anchor Books, 1996.

Vaid, Urvashi. "What Can Brown Do for You: Race, Sexuality, and the Future of LGBT Politics." Kessler Lecture, Center for Lesbian and Gay Studies, City University of New York Graduate Center, November 18, 2010. http://urvashivaid.net/wp/?p=709 (accessed January 2010).

"Valerie Solanas Replies." *Village Voice,* August 1, 1977, 28.

Viral Chaos: The Makings of an Animal Artist. Dir. Susan Powter. 2004. San Francisco, Animal's Farm. DVD.

Vogel, Lisa. "Rebuttal: Michigan Womyn's Music Festival Sets the Record 'Straight,'"

2006. Indiana Transgender Rights. http://www.intraa.org/story/mwmfpolicyrebut tal (accessed April 1, 2007).

Warhol, Andy, and Pat Hackett. *Popism: The Warhol Sixties.* New York: Mariner Books, 1990.

Warner, Michael, ed. *Fear of a Queer Planet: Queer Politics and Social Theory.* Minneapolis: University of Minnesota Press, 1993.

Warner, Michael. *The Trouble with Normal: Sex, Politics, and the Ethics of Queer Life.* New York: Free Press, 1999.

Warner, Sara. "Rage Slaves: The Commodification of Affect in the Five Lesbian Brothers' *The Secretaries.*" *Journal of Dramatic Theory and Criticism* 23, no. 1 (Fall 2008): 21–45.

Waters, John. "I Advocate." Episode 103-I, *The Advocate On-Air,* http://www.advocate.com/Video/?pid=XO5uBRfc6aOX1A4aScdU5K1z4qRUjKri (accessed January 2011).

Watson, Steven. *Factory Made: Warhol and the Sixties.* New York: Pantheon, 2003.

Williams, Albert. "The Quintessential Image/In Her Own Words." *Chicago Reader,* January 18, 1990. http://m.chicagoreader.com/chicago/the-quintessential-imagein-her-own-words/Content?oid=875070 (accessed January 2010).

Williams, Linda. *Playing the Race Card: Melodramas of Black and White from Uncle Tom to O. J. Simpson.* Princeton: Princeton University Press, 2002.

Williams, Raymond. "Structures of Feeling." In *Marxism and Literature,* 128–35. Oxford: Oxford University Press, 1977.

Wilson, Doric. "Stonewall + 40." May 20, 2009. http://doricwilson.blogspot.com/2009/05/stonewall-40_20.html (accessed December 2009).

Winkiel, Laura. "The 'Sweet Assassin' and the Performative Politics of *SCUM Manifesto.*" In *The Queer Sixties,* edited by Patricia Juliana Smith, 62–86. New York: Routledge, 1999.

Winkler, Gary S. *Tortured: Lynndie England, Abu Ghraib, and the Photographs That Shocked the World.* Keyser, WV: Bad Apple, 2009.

WITCH. "WITCH Documents." In *Sisterhood Is Powerful: An Anthology of Writings from the Women's Liberation Movement,* edited by Robin Morgan, 538–53. New York: Vintage Books, 1970.

Wittig, Monique. *Les Guérillères.* Translated by David Le Vay. Boston: Beacon, 1985.

Wittman, Carl. "A Gay Manifesto." In *Out of the Closets: Voices of Gay Liberation,* edited by Karla Jay and Allen Young, 330–45. New York: New York University Press, 1992.

Wolf, Stacy. *A Problem Like Maria: Gender and Sexuality in the American Musical.* Ann Arbor: University of Michigan Press, 2002.

Yoshimoto, Midori. "An Evening with Fluxus Women: A Roundtable Discussion." *Women and Performance: A Journal of Feminist Theory* 19, no. 3 (November 2009): 369–89.

Young, Allen. "Out of the Closets, into the Streets." In *Out of the Closets: Voices of Gay Liberation,* edited by Karla Jay and Allen Young, 7–10. New York: New York University Press, 1992.

Index

Page references in italics indicate an illustration.